Giorgini suddenly shivered. The cold was not natural. And now he could feel a presence behind him. He instantly powered up his shield and turned to fight.

To be blasted off his feet the moment he moved.

Giorgini felt the presence come closer. A voice that was almost inhuman came to him in his pain.

"I came too late for other prey, so you will have to do."

Praise for
William R. Forstchen and Greg Morrison's

THE CRYSTAL WARRIORS

"Rousing action . . .
Some of the best
adventure writing in years."
Science Fiction Chronicle

"Forstchen and Morrison display
a remarkable diversity of skills . . .
The result is a story that admirably
lives up to its promotion."
Dragon

Other Avon Books by
William R. Forstchen and Greg Morrison

THE CRYSTAL WARRIORS

THE CRYSTAL SORCERERS

**William R. Forstchen
and Greg Morrison**

NANCY DUNNAN & JAY J. PACK

AVON BOOKS ◆ NEW YORK

AVON BOOKS
A division of
The Hearst Corporation
105 Madison Avenue
New York, New York 10016

Copyright © 1991 by William R. Forstchen and Greg Morrison
Cover art by Joseph DeVito
Published by arrangement with the authors
Library of Congress Catalog Card Number: 90-93421
ISBN: 0-380-76021-5

First Avon Books Printing: April 1991

This book is dedicated to
Kristin Ryan Morrison,
born October 21, 1988

Acknowledgments

Steve Bohn, Nate Breech, Lindsey Ebling, Lorella Huff, Mark and Terri Garlick, Lt. Col. Charles Ryan, William Scott who saved us when a disk crashed, our agent Eleanor Wood, Chris Miller our editor, and, of course, Patti

Prologue

The battlefield was deathly still. Overhead, the twin moons of Haven cast an eerie glow over the shattered remains of thousands who had struggled beneath the walls of Landra. The city was still ablaze, casting a flickering glow through the fog that seemed to rise ghostlike across the blood-soaked fields. The low cries of the wounded still echoed in the night air, whispering for help, water, or an end to their agonies. Like apparitions, numbed survivors searched the fields, looking for comrades, loved ones, hoping against hope.

The mist swirled and eddied, cloaking the fields before Landra where but hours before the armies of Sarnak had gone down to their ruin. Gradually it deepened, as if the earth wished to hide the brutal inhumanity of what had been accomplished, all for the vain-gloried dreams of a demigod who was now a hunted fugitive, his armies dead or scattered. In the drifting shroud of darkness, two forms clad in the livery of Allic, Prince and defender of Landra, appeared hovering in the air, looking furtively about, then floated on searching. More than one, still clinging to life, looked up to see the two sorcerers drift by. Yet the cries for help were futile, for the two were not searching for lost friends.

"There's one of Sarnak's sorcerers over there," Giorgini whispered.

"You check him out and I'll check out this one over here," commanded Younger.

Giorgini flew low, drifting in the mist to avoid detection. A cold shiver was running through him. Hours ago he had felt at least that he was part of a team, fighting alongside his old comrades. Granted, he felt his commander, Mark Phillips, was a fool for trusting the Japanese, but he had always despised officers who were always ordering him around—and Mark, who led by example, was nothing like that. Already Giorgini was wishing

1

he had not sided with Younger in the argument over command. If only he had kept his damn mouth shut he'd be back in the city now, a warm meal inside him and with a place to sleep. Instead he was skulking about like a thief, hoping to find and loot a set of crystals.

The damn crystals—he had never thought of that when he had quit Allic's service. He had not stopped to realize that he would be stripped of his offensive and defensive crystal weapons. Without them he was next to naked on this world.

Still not adapted to flying without the focusing of a crystal's power, he overshot the torn body of the sorcerer and fell to his knees. Cursing under his breath, Giorgini walked back to the corpse.

Jackpot! The woman had not been stripped of her weapons. Sitting down by her side, he quickly undid the bracelets around her arms and snapped them on to his own wrists, not looking at the horrible searing wound that had nearly torn her in half. He paused for a moment to look at her drawn, gray features which, strangely, had been untouched by the blast that had killed her. In life she must have been beautiful, Giorgini thought sadly. Her hair was barely scorched, her features quiet, as if death had taken her by surprise, not giving her time to feel pain. Who knows, he thought, perhaps he had even killed her in the mad confusion of battle. He could remember two kills of enemy sorcerers for sure, both of them pounces from above and behind. One of them had been a woman. He paused for a moment, lost in lonely contemplation. Yet he was alive and she was dead, that was the simple fact of it, he tried to tell himself, but the sickness of everything that had happened this day was impossible to shake.

A distant cry of pain echoed across the field, setting his hair on edge. A wounded demon. A moment later there was a muffled flash of light and the demon scream was cut off. As if by instinct, he snapped his defensive shield up.

"You stupid ass. Turn off that shield, someone might pick it up and come over here," snarled Younger from out of the shadows.

Giorgini clenched his teeth, biting back a sharp return, and turned the shield down to its lowest power. He glared back at Younger for a moment and then returned his attention to the body at his feet.

Why in the name of god did I leave the captain to desert with this jerk, he thought savagely. In frustration he ripped the crystals from the belt around the woman's body and began to examine them.

Younger landed beside him just as he was fitting the crystals into the empty slots on his belt.

"How did you make out, Sergeant?"

Giorgini kept his face impassive while he struggled for control. *What an asshole*, he thought. *The two of us haven't a friend in this whole world and he wants to play lieutenant.*

"Looks like I got a complete set except for a communications crystal," Giorgini replied coldly.

Giorgini was glancing around the body to see if the comm crystal had fallen nearby and failed to notice Younger stiffen slightly.

"Let's get one thing straight, Sergeant. Now that I'm in command you will address me as 'sir,' " Younger barked.

Giorgini struggled to control himself. An hour ago, Younger had been calling him "buddy," and now this old military crap again. Inwardly Giorgini knew the bastard was better than him in a one-on-one fight, at least with crystals. From the corner of his eye he saw that Younger had found a powerful looking offensive crystal, but his left wrist was still empty of a defensive shield. The tension coiled through him, but he forced it down. *So that's the game*, Giorgini thought, feeling stupid for not having guessed this would be how Younger acted once he had weapons again.

Apparently feeling that he had reestablished proper discipline, Lieutenant Younger continued:

"All right, Sergeant, the body I found had its defensive crystal destroyed, so give me the one you found until we locate another body. Then we can get the hell out of here."

Giorgini was so angry that he actually stammered as the first words came out of his mouth and had to stop and try again. His words were low but venomous, and there was no mistaking their meaning.

"Kiss my ass."

Younger made the mistake of trying to reestablish his authority.

"Come to attention this instant, Sergeant."

"Eat shit. Sir." Giorgini drawled the "sir" out as insultingly as possible, and continued, "You're a deserter yourself, Younger. Don't even try and pull that bullshit officer crap on me. In fact . . . " he paused as the decision he had been half mulling over crystallized in his mind, then went on, "I was an idiot to even come with you. Mark is not only a better leader, but a better man. I'm going back."

Younger's first reaction was to raise his offensive crystal. Instantly Giorgini's shield snapped on to full power and his offensive crystal was pointed at Younger's stomach.

"Lieutenant, that would be pretty stupid. How long do you expect to last without a shield?" Giorgini's voice conveyed vast amusement.

Younger carefully lowered his arm. "Come on," he whispered smoothly. "You can't go back. They'll send you to the mines as a deserter. Stick with me, buddy, it's safer."

"I'm not your goddamn buddy," Giorgini hissed. "You almost had me roped in. I let my hatred of the Japs blind me to what a bastard you are. But I'll take the Japs to you any day. You thought I'd be your little army and follow you around shouting yes sir, no sir, let me kiss your ass sir. I was an idiot to desert with you. I'm goin' back and take my chances."

Younger's anger overwhelmed him and he started to raise his crystal again . . . only to freeze as he stared at a sparkling offensive crystal pointed directly between his eyes from a distance of only five feet.

"Imagine what this could do at this range. Sir. Now why don't you crawl off to whatever cesspool you were going to in the first place."

Younger's face contorted. "I'll get you," he snarled. "You're as bad as the Japs, you little guinea. I'll get you some day."

"Come on Lieutenant," Giorgini laughed, "here and now."

Younger stood frozen for a moment, his features darkened with rage. Turning, he lifted into the air and disappeared into the fog.

He was almost across the field when he heard Giorgini's booming laugh. "Hey Lieutenant—while you're at it, why don't you take them gold bars of yours and stuff 'em up your ass!"

Giorgini stood on the crest of the hill smiling and chortling to himself. Ever since he had entered the Air Corps he had wanted to tell some chickenshit officer what he could do to himself. Extending his far-seeing skills, he tracked Younger as he disappeared eastward, toward where the shattered remnants of Sarnak's army had disappeared. Finally he was lost from view.

Turning back, Giorgini continued his train of thought. Hell, Mark would stick up for him if he handled it right. Christ, with all they had been through, a man could be excused a little battle fatigue. He'd be in the doghouse for a couple of months, but come the next fight they'd have to let him back in and he could prove himself in battle again. Even that Jap officer, Ikawa, had said he was a good fighter in a pinch. They'd *have* to let him back.

The only hairy part would be in surrendering. Without a communications crystal he couldn't call in and forewarn them. The best thing he could do was to wait until daylight and start walking. If he tried to go in now, they might pop him off, thinking he was a survivor of Sarnak's trying to escape, no questions asked. As long as he was wearing Allic's colors no one would shoot him on sight in the morning light, and once he got to another sorcerer with a way to connect him with Mark he was home free.

Giorgini was so deep in thought that he failed to notice the change in his surroundings.

The grass beneath his feet began to turn brown and brittle as if a sudden frost had overcome it. Not only the temperature, but the very feel of the air turned cold and crisp.

Giorgini suddenly shivered and, still deep in thought, half wondered at the change.

"Christ, feels like I'm standing in an icebox," he muttered to himself.

All at once he came to his senses and realized that this cold was not natural. That it had to be caused.

And now he could feel someone, a presence, behind him.

Knowing he was a dead man, he instantly powered up his shield and turned to fight.

To be blasted off his feet the moment he moved.

Giorgini laid there, barely conscious, and felt the presence come closer. The cold had become almost overwhelming, and he began to shiver uncontrollably.

A voice that was chilling, and almost inhuman in its lack of emotion, came to him through his pain:

"I came too late for other prey, so you will have to do."

Chapter 1

Captain Mark Phillips, formerly of the United States Army Air Corps and now one of the most highly regarded sorcerers of Prince Allic's realm, flew lazily through the morning air. The magical talents he had developed in this world were still a wonder to him, but the ability to fly had to be his favorite.

The land beneath him was as beautiful as ever, with small villages, well run farms, vineyards, and orchards. He could not recall ever being happier. Having powers that would have seemed godlike back on Earth, and being part of the ruling clique of gods and demigods, made his life far more rewarding than it had been flying B-29s with an average twenty mission life expectancy.

Extending his arms, Mark Phillips soared heavenward, up through the crystalline clouds that floated lazily with the morning breeze. Onward he climbed, the cool fresh air rippling past him. With a slight dip of his right arm he went into a roll, spinning through turn after turn as he punched through the opaque firmament of billowing clouds.

Reaching the top of the cloud, he skimmed along the surface until the edge suddenly dropped straight away to the ground more than a mile below. Laughing, Mark created a mental image and swept his hands slowly in front of him, drawing on the Essence and his still rough talent of creativity.

The cloud swirled up in response to his command to form a towering throne, complete to ornately carved lions' heads on the uprights. Gently, he lowered himself into his creation and, stretching out, he looked over the edge to survey the world beneath him.

The cloud marched onward with the breeze, its shadow rolling across the eastern marches of Landra. How different this all was. Less than a year before he had been flying across the flak-torn skies of China, drenched in fear-soaked sweat, listening to the pounding roar of the engines that kept his B-29 aloft. Always waiting, always fearing that inevitable slash of hot steel sent up to tear him and his comrades out of the sky.

And now he could fly like a god on the world of Haven. Flying as he had always dreamed to fly, by merely extending his arms and rising effortlessly into the heavens. There had been fighting as well, and death had still hovered by his shoulder. But for now the war on Haven was over, and there was the joy of soaring like an eagle without fear of attack.

And Allic had awarded them all small fiefdoms in return for their all-too-crucial services in the war with Sarnak. Only the day before, Mark had been enjoying a long promised rest at his manor, Homefree. As leaders of the outlanders, Mark and Captain Ikawa of the Japanese Army had received exceptionally beautiful estates of several hundred square miles along the river, in a region noted for its towering stands of eldar and derusa trees, and rocky cliffs that overlooked the river.

For two weeks Mark had known nothing but contented bliss. His lover Storm, Allic's sister, had flown in to spend the time with him. Eventually it had become a working vacation, as they tried to get the estate back in order after the recent conflict. They had visited all the villages in Mark's shire, and he had declared a feast day at his own expense for each visit. Not surprisingly, he had done very well in maintaining the good relationship that the people of Landra had traditionally had with their leaders. Ikawa and Allic's other sister, the demigod Leti, had exchanged regular visits with Mark and Storm, and the four companions had grown ever closer in their friendship.

Then the call to service had come from Allic. Ruefully, Mark turned back to his elaborate creation of cloud. Though he loved flying like this, at this moment he'd much rather be alone with Storm, watching the sleek ships sailing down the river on their way to the sea, or walking through a grove of red-hued trees in his garden.

"Aren't we getting a little godlike with the throne?"

Mark looked over his shoulder and smiled.

Allic, his liege lord, Prince of the province of Landra, hovered behind him.

"Have a seat, my lord," Mark said expansively, and with a wave of his hand he expanded the throne to accompany his ruler and friend.

Allic settled in alongside of Mark. Reaching into his tunic he pulled out a flask of brandy, took a long swallow, and then offered it to Mark.

After draining off a shot, Mark returned the gem-encrusted flask. Allic smiled and with a wink took another drink, then leaned back as if settling into the diaporous chair. Mark could see that Allic's scars of battle were almost healed, the healthy new skin gradually working its way out, replacing the darkened burns that had covered half of Allic's face. He still wore an eye patch to cover the left socket where the new eye was forming.

Of all the wonders of Haven—the flying by mere thought, the thousand year life span he now had, the magic which was a daily fact of life—this miracle of regeneration still awed him. Across three years of war back on Earth he had seen countless young bodies broken, torn apart, never to be healed. Yet here those who survived combat could again be made whole, at least in body, by the art of the sorcerer-healers.

Smiling, Allic winked at Mark and then leaned over the edge of the throne to look down. Mark still found it hard to understand this man, if he could be called such a thing. Allic was the son of god, imbued with powers that on Earth would seem divine. But then again, Mark realized, what would his own ability to fly like a bird, and fight with the power of magic crystals, seem like to his old comrades in the Air Corps?

Allic could at times come forth with a regal bearing and terrifying power; and yet at other times, he was like an old comrade, ready for a drink, a coarse joke, and a jovial smile.

There were hundreds of sorcerers, those mortals who could wield magic on this world, in Allic's service, but Mark noticed that it was the offworlders, the Japanese and American soldiers who had arrived here on Haven through the dimensional portal, whose company and friendship Allic preferred.

"Ah, here comes Ikawa," Allic announced, shaking his head and smiling as he pointed straight down.

Coming under the base of the cloud, Ikawa arched upward, his climb slow but steady, lacking the smooth precision of Mark, or the blinding swiftness of Allic. But then again, Allic was a demigod, the son of Jartan the Creator, and Mark had been a combat pilot, while Ikawa Yoshio had been an infantry officer in the Imperial Japanese Army, who still looked at flying with a bit of a jaundiced eye. Watching his friend fly up, Mark smiled over how strange this all was. A year ago he would have killed Ikawa without the slightest hesitation. Now he would lay down his life to protect the man he considered to be the closest friend he had ever had.

Ikawa pulled up before the two and shook his head with mock disdain.

"You and your damn games of darting all over the sky," Ikawa snapped. "And this throne on top of a cloud. Looks like your work, Mark: western European in style, and far too plain."

Ikawa waved his hands and the throne shifted in form, expanding outward with a wild assortment of swirls topped by a fanlike canopy. On both sides the clouds grew upward and turned into two giant samurailike guards who stood poised in watchful observance with blades drawn.

"Now I'm ready to sit," Ikawa announced with mock gravity, and swinging over, he settled down by Allic's side. Scooping up the proffered flask, Ikawa took a long drink and sighed.

The three friends sat in quiet contemplation of the beauty around them. To the east Mark could see the brooding heights of the Sarnastu, the barrier mountains that guarded the approach to what had once been the realm of Sarnak the Accursed. Their destination was just on the other side of those mountains. Though the war was over and Sarnak had fled in defeat, still there was a sense of foreboding to the place.

As he looked eastward at the Sarnastu he could not help but feel uneasy.

"My lord, would you mind sharing with us what this is all about?" Ikawa asked.

Allic looked at the two and smiled.

"I'd have told you earlier, but felt it best to wait till we were out here alone."

The two nodded. Ever since the war there had been some concern about a possible security leak in Allic's ranks. It wasn't so much that there was direct evidence, but rather just an uneasy feeling on Allic's part, backed up by Pina and Valdez, his two most trusted lieutenants, that somehow word was sifting out of the city regarding Allic's activities.

"Word came in yesterday that we've found Sarnak's secret office and command center."

"We've been tearing that palace apart for three months," Ikawa interjected. "I thought we'd never find his command center."

"One of his sorcerers had enough of hard labor and felt that his old master had sold them all out, so he decided to talk in return for a reduced sentence."

"Maybe now we can find out where that bastard Sarnak is hiding and finish off the job," Mark said grimly.

"My intentions exactly, and the sooner we get there the sooner we'll find out."

Leaping forward, Allic dived down the face of the cloud and rolled out eastward.

"Let's get going." Laughing, Mark gave Ikawa a friendly shove. His friend tumbled off the throne and with a curse plummeted down the side of the cloud. Mark focused his attention and did a magnificent spring upward, like a diver going off a board. He hovered for a moment above the throne and then jackknifed straight down. Snapping his shielding up to ease the buffeting of the wind on his face, he raced down the face of the cloud.

Ikawa had regained some semblance of stability, and as Mark raced past, the Japanese officer swung in alongside his comrade.

Below the base of the cloud the two leveled out and, riding the currents of air, swung in behind their lord, forming a protective cover to his rear. Though there was no war, they were still flying into a conquered territory and a moment of inattention could still result in tragedy.

The ground below was dotted with farmsteads and villages, but as the Eastern Marches drew closer the settled region finally gave way to wild tracks of forest. For three thousand years this had been the frontier between two rival powers, subject to raid and counterstrike, and only the border wardens and lords of the marches had stayed in this region, their settlements fortified positions set atop high peaked hills.

As the mountains rose below them, the three started to curve back skyward, passing again through the clouds which were billowing upward to form the first thunderheads of an afternoon storm.

The sight of the clouds made Mark think again of his lover. She was a demigod in her own right, the daughter of Jartan. Storm had in her powers the ability to create her own thunderstorms, the darkened sky her plaything for amusement or, as he had once witnessed, a terrifying power of war. It was, after all, in a storm cloud that he had first met her, and he smiled at the memory.

As they punched through the clouds, the towering peaks of the Sarnastu loomed ahead. Allic led the way through a narrow pass, the sheer rock walls of the mountains rising several thousand feet above them on either side. The air was cold and crisp, the sun illuminating the peaks with a golden light that rendered them in stark contrast against the mountain clouds.

Turning and weaving, the party continued on up into the mountain fastness.

"This is Red Leader to Gold Leader control," Mark announced through his communications crystal.

"Gold Leader to Red, go ahead please."

"Party of three approaching through sector five."

There was a pause on the other end.

"We have you in sight. Identification code please."

"Green, green, white," Mark announced.

One of the things Allic's people had picked up from Mark was the method of air control and identification codes he had learned in the Army Air Corps. He had designed the air approach systems into Allic's realm and Sarnak's territory, and if a flyer did not follow certain corridors, and have the right codes, it would trigger an instant scramble.

"You are cleared for approach through air corridor five," the controller responded, and the crystal fell silent.

Mark was pleased with the crispness of the operation, and Allic looked back at him approvingly. It had been difficult to convince Allic that he should never announce his presence or even speak via crystals when in the air, lest he tip some unwanted listener off. But since his injury in battle he had, at least for now, seemed a little more cautious.

Coming down out of the high pass, the ground dropped away to a broad plateau, broken occasionally by hills and river valleys. For a nation that had been at war there was little sign here that a conflict had ever been fought. But then, Mark reflected, there wouldn't be: Almost all the combat had taken place in Allic's realm.

The towns and cities were well ordered, in an almost military precision of squared fields and arrow-straight roads. If anything was lacking, it was the green lushness of Allic's kingdom, and that vague indefinable spirit that could instantly tell someone that the people were truly happy and contented with their life.

Swinging low for a closer look, Allic soared over his new territories.

Mark felt slightly nervous about this. In Allic's own realm the sight of their lord passing overhead would have been cause for jovial shouts and comments. Here his passage was met by stony silence. Mark kept a watchful eye for the slightest threatening sign.

"Can't expect them to like me yet," Allic said evenly, falling back to fly beside Mark.

They passed over a bevy of Sarnak's captured demons hard at work repairing a blown bridge that spanned a narrow chasm. Mark had already had several encounters with the ten-foot monsters and knew that they were fearsome opponents. Brought by Sarnak from their own worlds into this dimension, as guards and warriors they endured years of service to earn their freedom. Of course, these had been forced to sign allegiance to Allic, so they were theoretically harmless. Still, Mark noted that most of this group were winged, and he increased the strength of his shield slightly. The frightening creatures looked heavenward and glowered darkly, while their guards shouted a friendly greeting as Allic raced by.

Continuing across the plain, Mark could at last see their destination, the high mountains and river valley that marked Sarnak's castle and capital city.

"Red Leader, you are on final approach," a voice whispered through the communications crystal. "Do not deviate from your flight path unless ordered to do so."

Mark could see that Allic was tempted to announce his presence and wander about a bit, but decided against it. The wall crystal mounted atop the entry gate would have been brought instantly into play and a scramble of all sorcerers in the city would have come swarming out as a result. It was tight discipline, but Mark had suggested it be set up that way, until such time as every last corner of Sarnak's realm and hidden corridor of his castle had been explored and secured. Only the week before, half a dozen renegade demons had been flushed not five miles away from this spot. More than twenty soldiers had been killed, and a sorcerer injured, before they had been eliminated. Without the tight system of checks and controlled airspace it could have been a lot worse.

Rising again, they crested the city wall and headed for the twin towers of the main gate into the castle. Before them stood the hidden fortress of Sarnak. Half a hundred steel-grey towers encircled the keep, and in the center stood a single monolith of rock and iron.

Atop the tower fluttered the blue and white pennant of Allic, and the demigod smiled as the banner arched and snapped in the breeze.

Circling about the tower, the three swung in to alight on the arrival platform. From the shadows of the battlement wall a delegation came forward to meet the new arrivals. Allic was immediately surrounded by his sorcerers and servants, while Mark and Ikawa were the center of attention as their old comrades rushed out to greet them.

The outlanders split into two parties momentarily as the Japanese lined up to formally exchange bows with Ikawa, while the Americans simply crowded around Mark, exchanging handshakes and good-natured insults.

Mark easily entered into the clamor. Almost all his old friends and comrades were here. Only Kochanski was away, still up in the capital city, Asmara, working on a special assignment with the god Jartan.

Younger and Giorgini he simply did not think about anymore, and as for the others . . . *How few we are,* he thought sadly. He looked over at Ikawa and their gazes locked for a second. Too many of their original companions were already gone, and those who still lived seemed to cherish each other all the more.

Sergeant Saito broke away from Ikawa, and coming up to Mark, he saluted and smiled. He pulled a slender white cylinder from his pocket and offered it.

"A Lucky Strike." Mark laughed and accepted the treasured gift.

"Bucking for promotion, Saito?" Walker shot good-naturedly.

"It's just you are so decidedly poor at gambling," Saito replied. "Having won it from you, and not being addicted to the filthy habit, I thought the Captain would appreciate a smoke."

Mark concentrated for a moment, lighting the cigarette with sorcery, and inhaled luxuriously. Granted, it was really stale, but it still tasted wonderful, rekindling his old craving for tobacco which—tragically, in his mind—was not available on Haven.

Taking a couple of drags, he offered the butt to Walker, who then passed it around to the other men.

"If this little reunion is finished," Allic interrupted, his features now serious, "we've got some important business to attend to."

The group fell in behind their lord and followed him into the keep. Reaching the main staircase, they were met by several other sorcerers who had a hurried conference with their leader before leading him down the steps.

Level after level was passed. Mark still found this place to be unnerving. He had spent nearly a month here after the war, helping to secure the fortress and surrounding territory. The stark interior was such a chilling contrast to Allic's palace, and to his own estate, that the mere thought of coming back here had sent a chill through him. He felt as if somehow there was still an evil presence here, lurking, watching and waiting.

The party continued downward until at last an open platform was reached at what Mark assumed was near ground level. Half a dozen sorcerers, all wearing the sky blue livery of Allic's inner command, stood in a circle. In the middle of the group there was a lone sorcerer, wearing the brass collar of servitude, and the soiled remnants of Sarnak's deep burgundy uniform. His hair had gone to white, and grew now in only tattered batches on his balding skull. His grey eyes were deeply sunk into a skull-like visage that seemed to have already passed into the realm of the dead.

Though the old man had been stripped of all crystals, Mark sensed that he was not someone to be trifled with. Even crystal-less, he seemed to hold a power that deserved to be watched closely.

"So, Musta, the prospect of a hundred years in the mines started to wear thin, did it?" Allic said coldly.

"Your people promised me safe conduct out of here, if I agreed to cooperate with your search," Musta said sharply. "I want to at least die with the sun in my face rather than in one of your damned mines, all because I made the mistake of choosing the wrong side. Besides, Guild laws state that sorcerers who are prisoners of war can only be stripped of their crystals and must be set free after no more than two years of servitude."

"Quite correct regarding most of the other captured sorcer-ers," rejoined Allic in a mocking tone, "but you are also charged with a contract violation and theft of my crystals, and the law still applies even after seven hundred years."

Musta fell silent, eyeing Allic with open hatred.

"Let's get this done, shall we?" the demigod said evenly. "Show us into the offices, deactivate the traps, and then you're free to leave."

The two locked gazes until Musta finally turned away and started down the stairs.

Before long the party followed him, going ever deeper into the heart of Sarnak's citadel.

Reaching the bottom of the fortress at last, Musta started down the main corridor past the dungeons which now housed a few other sorcerers and demons who had been captured in the mop-up operations and who were off duty for various reasons.

The demons howled with fury at the sight of Allic, who hurled back a series of taunts in their own loathsome tongue, which set them to howling even louder. Mark covered his ears, half afraid he'd go deaf from the noise.

At the end of the main corridor Musta turned to the right and proceeded for another hundred yards before turning right again, and then yet again, till at last he came up against a blank wall.

"I've been here before," Ikawa commented. "We didn't notice a damn thing."

Musta looked over at Ikawa and smiled. Reaching down, he pushed a series of small stones set into the wall. Back and forth his hand danced, tapping out a rhythmic sequence.

Without a sound the wall before them parted.

"We could have spent a dozen lifetimes before finding this," one of Allic's sorcerers whispered.

"I probed this sector myself," another said openly. "Couldn't find a concealed passage anywhere."

"A lot of work went into this," Musta said proudly. "I helped in the building of it. There's a crystal set into the back of the wall, crafted to absorb any form of probing and return an image of impenetrable rock. A nice personal touch of mine."

"Enough boasting," Allic replied sharply. "Let's get on with this."

"After you, my lord." Musta bowed low.

A thin smile creased Allic's features, but he didn't move.

"It is hard at times to distinguish between caution and cowardice," Musta commented acidly. He turned and walked into the chamber.

Though Allic did not reply, all could see the rage that was building within him.

"My lord," Mark cautioned, "stay here, let some of us check it out first. Hell, this could be a trap, a way for that old sorcerer to get even."

"Damn it, I'm going in," Allic said impulsively. "It's nothing more than Sarnak's hidden office. You're acting like it's the gateway to hell."

Mark silently cursed and shouldered his way in directly behind Allic, Ikawa at his side. Though Allic had yet to do so, Mark snapped his shielding up, and the others in the group followed suit.

The narrow corridor took one final turn into a vast chamber, and at their approach the room snapped into blazing light from a dozen crystals mounted along the four walls.

Mark gave a gasp of amazement. The immense room was lined on all four walls with row after row of books—probably Sarnak's personal records. The information they contained could be invaluable. At the far end of the room was a raised dais surmounted by a desk a dozen feet across. It reminded Mark of the office of a corporate executive gone mad: If any underling came into this room he'd have to look almost straight up to see his master, seated in an overstuffed leather chair with a high back surmounted with demon heads. Mark shuddered at the realization that the heads were real, preserved and mounted for Sarnak's pleasure.

Musta paused, motioning for the party to stop, and reached down to brush his hand against the smooth stone floor. With a sudden snap, a row of razor-sharp spikes shot up across the length of the room.

"A little surprise for unwanted guests." Musta laughed at the uncomfortable exchange of stares among the others.

"Any other such toys?" Allic asked coldly.

Musta simply looked at him and smiled.

Mark realized there must be more dangers hidden in the room. He would have been a fool to think otherwise. He looked over at Allic, wishing he could get his lord out of the room until it was secured, but knew Allic, stubborn to the point of foolishness, would probably tell him to go to hell.

Allic looked over at Mark, and as if sensing his thoughts, gave him a look of disdain and strode up to the massive desk.

"Sarnak always did have a problem with wanting to impress others," he said contemptuously, glancing around the room.

Mark was tempted to comment that Allic did, too, when it came to a question of personally showing his courage when it wasn't necessary. The demigod strolled past a deep pile carpet covered with a frightening design of demons to ascend the platform and sit in Sarnak's chair.

Looking at the various drawers, Allic paused and then gingerly reached out, touching the lower right corner of one. There was the snick of metal on metal as a needle lashed out next to the drawer handle and then withdrew. Startled by the sound, Mark looked up, but Allic only shook his head and smiled.

"This desk was made by Berong, one of the best craftsmen who ever lived. I have one as well. The poison needle is the same—old Berong did lack imagination in that direction—but unless you know about it already, it usually gets you. Deadly stuff, kills in seconds.

"Anyhow, it's a good place to keep important paperwork."

Mark held his breath as Allic leaned over and pulled the drawer open. Nothing happened.

Allic gazed at Musta for a moment. "Thought you had me, you bastard, didn't you?"

Musta remained silent.

Allic reached in the open drawer, pulled out a sheaf of parchment, and began to thumb his way through.

"Most interesting," he murmured, shifting through the pile. "Some correspondence here with my dear cousin Patrice that might be worth researching."

For several minutes Allic sat back and read meditatively while the rest of the party started to edge nervously around the room. Mark, his eyes never leaving Musta, moved behind the sorcerer, while Ikawa came around to the side of the dais without letting his gaze move from where Allic sat.

After what seemed like an eternity Allic stood up, tossing the papers on the desk.

"Lousy bitch," he muttered. "I want this room swept from one end to the other," he commanded. "Once it's secure, you people can start in on the books. Maybe in them we can find out who his secret allies are and get some clue as to where he has fled—but these papers here are to be touched by no one but myself."

Grimly, Allic came out from behind the desk, stopped in the middle of the dais stairs to study a design on the far wall, then started to walk toward the door.

With a swiftness that was surprising coming from one of such age, Musta leaped forward, arms outstretched to push Allic from behind.

Shouting a warning, Mark sprang also, catching the sorcerer in the back. The two tumbled past Allic, who spun around like a cat. Twisting and writhing, the old sorcerer tried to grab Allic as he fell onto the carpet, Mark clinging desperately to the man's waist.

There was an explosion of light and instantly Mark's shield powered up to full strength as flames sprang up around him, roaring greedily. He tried to kick Musta away, but he felt as if his arms and legs had suddenly become bound.

The room seemed to disappear, replaced by a terror straight

out of hell. Mark found himself looking down into a fiery sea of flowing lava and a sky of darkest black, illuminated only by curtains of liquid flame. A howling filled his ears; then he heard guttural growls of delight as demons rose from the flaming pit, talons extended to render his flesh.

For the first time in years Mark Phillips shrieked with terror, unable to offer the slightest resistance.

Suddenly he felt as if he were falling upward, as if some distant thread was tugging at his doomed body. Musta still clung to him, but the enfeebled hands could not hold, and as a demon reached up and grabbed the aged sorcerer by the legs, the old man lost his grip on Mark and dropped into the nightmare of hell.

There was a violent jerk and Mark fell backward, tumbling back into the room. A cloak was thrown over him, smothering the flames that had started to lick at his clothing.

Where the carpet had been, a pentagram now stood revealed, the portal within ablaze with hellish light.

"You fell through when that damned Musta tried to push Allic in," Ikawa said, crouching over his friend, his face contorted with anxiety. "It took all of Allic's strength to pull you back through. If he hadn't grabbed you at the last second you'd have been lost."

One of the other sorcerers moaned and pointed at the floor. Apparently Mark had dragged his feet over the pentagram when he came back through, for all could see a break in the glowing lines.

A horrifying shriek filled the room and all looked up at the blazing portal.

Musta seemed to be rising out of a hole in the floor, writhing in pain, impaled through the chest by the talons of a demon who now stood before the party.

Still numbed by the horror he had seen, Mark scurried backward, while the other sorcerers snapped up their shields.

The towering demon struggled to push his way into the room even as Allic snapped out a cone of light around the pentagram, to which the rest of the sorcerers added their own energy.

The demon struggled against the wall of light for a moment longer; then his gaze fixed on Allic and a smile lit his twisted features.

"I had thought that Sarnak had sent through another tidbit for torment," he growled, "but I can see that you are now master here, Allic."

"Sarnak has been banished and this portal will be smashed forever," Allic snarled.

The demon barked out a howl of laughter that shook the room.

"My master will be pleased to hear that one of his old rivals still lives. Sarnak created this entrance into our realm for his secret torments, and for occasional help. But not even he really knew where it led."

The creature paused and the flames seemed to grow much stronger. "Ah, but do you not remember where we have met before? I am Kultha."

Even through his fear, Mark could see Allic start, and visibly pale.

"Yes, now you remember me," the demon screamed, "and the fields of Barquna. We have not forgotten."

"Gorgon," Allic whispered. "You were one of Gorgon's chieftains at the battle."

"Yes, I serve the lord Gorgon, you pale-skinned bastard," the demon roared. "He still lives and has not forgotten you or your father. Jartan would never have won without trickery, and he is a craven beast; Gorgon looks forward to the next encounter with him. And know this, Allic, son of Jartan the pig: I have reserved a place on my trophy rack for your head.

"Sarnak's treachery was only a shadow of what you shall face, though we helped to twist his thoughts, to feed his dreams."

"Why do you tell me this?" Allic whispered.

"Why not? You are powerless against those of us who dwell in hell, and we shall destroy you."

The demon roared out his laughter and raised his left hand, upon which Musta still writhed. From his right palm a bolt of flame shot out, but Allic and his companions were ready and it smashed ineffectively against their shields. Ikawa stood protectively over Mark, covering him with his own shielding as flame washed the room, igniting the books and desks into a raging inferno. Allic murmured the spell that would close the portal and the glowing lines began to shrink inward, growing smaller and smaller.

Kultha, still laughing, started to fall away, and as he did his gaze fixed on Mark. "Know this, tidbit: You are my prey, unjustly snatched from me. Soon you will be mine again, and I will bring you into eternal anguish by my own hands," the demon whispered.

The portal continued to close downward until all they could see was Musta, still twitching and shrieking on Kultha's talons; then sorcerer and demon were gone.

Allic rushed over to Mark, sweeping him into his arms and striding for the door.

"You've got to fight the terror," he said grimly, "or it will overwhelm you."

Mark tried to smile, but he wondered if ever again he could sleep, or wake in the night without the memory of that fear tormenting his soul.

Allic paused at the doorway and looked back into the burning room.

"The gods help us all," he said, his voice edged with fear, "if the demon lords are stirring again."

Chapter 2

Kochanski stood alone on the balcony of Jartan's private suite listening to the surf pounding, hundreds of feet below. The smells of the sea and the cries of the seabirds beneath him should have been relaxing, and several times he made a conscious effort to unwind, but he was still too tense.

He glanced over his shoulder at the ornate thronelike chair behind him. *Try the Godchair one more time and then call it a day*, a part of him urged. But he just didn't have the energy to make the attempt, so he returned to contemplating the coming sunset.

He had been out how many times today? Three? No, four. Each time he had sat in the Godchair and the chair's magic had taken his soul on a journey through this universe that they were marooned in, while his body stayed safely in the palace. And each time he had travelled to some Earthlike world among the stars. Some were so similar to the real thing that it had wrenched his heart to look upon them. As his mind's eye explored the surface of each planet he saw great wonders and beauty—but no Earth.

His skill in using the Godchair was growing stronger every day, and now he could make it respond to his slightest command. But the search for Earth seemed to be coming to a dead end. He had originally compared it to trying to find a needle in a haystack. But what if this particular universe was the wrong haystack? According to Jartan there were so many universes, or dimensions, that no one had ever bothered to count them all.

He felt a flow of the Essence surrounding him and turned to face a pillar of light forming behind him. An instant later there was a brightly glowing figure within the column: Jartan, one of the Creators and rulers of this universe.

"Try not to be too depressed, Kochanski," commented Jartan, as the pillar of light coalesced into a brilliant, luminous figure shining with an internal radiance. "This search of yours could take years. Allowing yourself to be disappointed this early is self-defeating."

Kochanski smiled and relaxed. "My lord, sometimes I do wonder why I even try. Hell, this world of yours is better than anything I ever dreamed of. I've got the powers of a sorcerer, a thousand year life span, and a whole universe to explore. This is the type of place I'd fantasize about when I was a kid growing up in Trenton."

"Trenton, is it a beautiful place?" Jartan asked.

Kochanski started to laugh so hard that tears came to his eyes.

"Did I say something funny?" Jartan inquired.

"Ah, my lord, if only you could experience Trenton on a hot summer night, and smell the Delaware River down by the sewer plant, you'd understand."

"May I look within?" he asked.

"Certainly, my lord," Kochanski replied, pleased that the god would ask permission before probing his private thoughts. Kochanski felt the gentle stirring within his mind and then the pulling away.

Jartan's features wrinkled in a grimace of disdain. "I see what you mean," he said, chuckling softly. "But there are loved ones there who can make even a place like that beautiful."

"My folks, my brothers and sisters, and my granny," Kochanski whispered. "I guess they would've gotten the telegram a long time ago."

"Telegram?"

"A message from my government. Since the war started back home everyone lives in dread of the messenger, bearing the statement 'On behalf of the President I regret to inform you that . . .'" He fell silent for a moment.

"I'll be reported missing in action, most likely. My family will hope against hope that after the war is over I'll show up. They'll carry that hope for years, always wondering, praying, never knowing. You see, it's all so strange. Here I've never been happier, yet at the same time there is that tug, that pull. If only I could spend one day back there, to tell them I'm safe, that I'm happy . . . Then I would return to your service."

"I guess that's what's tugging at most of us. For some there is family, several with wives and children. For others there's still the sense of duty to their country in time of war. Maybe one or two are just plain homesick. Yet I think most of us in the end would prefer to stay here, if only we could finish up our business back there first."

"It might not be possible that way," Jartan replied gently. "If, and I must emphasis the *if*, you do find a way, you might be able to cross back, but chances would be high that keeping a gate open to your world would be difficult. Because the Essence was drained from your world, your crystals would be useless for reforming a gate to return to Haven. Tracing and reopening a gate at a certain time later would be difficult. Chances are those of you who ventured through would be lost to us forever. It'll be a hard choice if that chance ever comes."

Kochanski looked away, unable to respond.

"Live your existence for what it is now," Jartan said in a fatherly tone. "All of you by rights should have died in that battle back on Earth. View what you have now as a gift of a new life, unexpected, and to be treasured as such. From what you have told me of the war on Earth, millions upon millions like you have died tragically without such a chance to live as you now have. You have also had the additional gift of finding former enemies, the Japanese, to be friends as well.

"I should add that your arrival here has been a gift to us. I fear to think what might have happened in the war between my son and Sarnak without you offworlders. Without all of you I probably would have lost him, and thousands more might have died as well. Know that I shall be forever grateful."

Kochanski looked into Jartan's eyes. The gaze held his, filling him with a sense of peace. Then, embarrassed, he chuckled softly.

"Ah, what the hell am I bitching about?"

Jartan patted Kochanski on the shoulder, then threw back his head and laughed, delighted with the pleasure of friendship with this mortal who did not grovel in the presence of a god.

"Good, very good. Anyhow, there's some business we need

to discuss, so why don't you call it a day as far as the practice goes? How about a drink first?"

Kochanski nodded, considering what kind of drink he felt like having today. Something stronger than beer . . . Rum and coke? No, too sweet. How about bourbon on the rocks? They hadn't tried that yet. And he concentrated on remembering the smell and taste of a tumbler of bourbon and ice as he sat with his dad on the back porch on a summer evening, listening to the radio broadcast a Phillies game. It had been the week before he was shipping out to Europe, his last night at home. The memory was sharp and poignant, standing out with crystal clarity: the taste of the bourbon, the clinking of the ice, and the warmth of that shared moment. He could sense Jartan's mind meshing with his, savoring the moment as well, feeling the warmth of the evening air, the sweet sadness of a time now lost to all but memory.

He could feel Jartan drifting out and away, and their eyes held again for a moment in understanding. A moment later, the god offered him an icy tumbler, the cubes clinking, the scent of fine aged bourbon tantalizing him.

Smiling, Kochanski took the tumbler and held it up.

"Your health, sire," he said formally before taking a sip. It was as good as the memory. Smiling, Jartan kept his hand extended. There was a flash of light and a second tumbler appeared. Jartan brought the drink to his lips and a smile crossed his features.

"Excellent. Now hold out your free hand."

Kochanski complied and there was another flash of light. A cry of delight escaped him: Between his fingers was a glowing cigarette. Taking a deep puff he exhaled luxuriantly.

"A Lucky Strike, no less!"

"Let's keep this one a secret," Jartan said in a conspiratorial whisper. "I don't approve of the habit—not good for your health and I dislike any addictions. But as you would say, 'what the hell.' I figured you'd enjoy it, but don't let the others know or they might start pestering me about it."

Kochanski smiled and nodded.

"Now to business," Jartan said smoothly, a smile still lighting his features.

"First, your progress with the Godchair has been remarkable. This search for your home world has served as excellent training for the development of your talents. However, you need to develop the skills of symbolic matching to a greater degree. I want you to try using actual models of landmarks or artifacts from your world, as opposed to just the world itself, and allow the Godchair to follow a solid image when you hunt."

"You mean like . . . " and Kochanski floundered for a moment as he tried to bring images into focus. "Let's see . . . the Rocky Mountains, or the Empire State Building . . . or the Atlantic Ocean . . . "

"Your best image was of that building: Something that your people actually built and that you have seen yourself. And then, following that picture, create a model of it here for you to focus on."

"Uh, Jartan, I'm still pretty weak on creating things. Can't I just draw it or something?"

"No. It must be an exact image. Which brings me to my second point. You need to also develop some expertise with dimensional travel into other universes, so I'm going to assign you some help from someone who has a talent for the creation of portals, among other things."

Kochanski shrugged. "Okay by me. Can he help me with those models you want, too?"

He started to feel uneasy when Jartan began to laugh.

"It's 'she,' Kochanski. And you will be surprised at what she can do."

The woman in the mirror was very beautiful, of that she felt no doubt. But how old? Leaning back in her chair, Patrice gazed at the reflection before her.

She let the image shift slightly, creasing away the first faint lines that traced outward from the eyes, erasing the darkness beneath them into a smooth glow of youth.

But the eyes themselves, she thought sadly. *I can still work subtle changes on my features, but my eyes will never lose that edge of hardness*. Never again could she look out at the world with the doelike innocence that had been such a charm thousands of years before.

She had seen far too much, and felt and lost far too much. Perhaps that innocence was lost when Kavan had so foully betrayed her. She had never meant to kill him, she thought sadly, only to let him know that it was not wise to cheat on the daughter of a god. How she had mourned her first lover. As for the young creature who had perished with him, she had no such thoughts. After all, the girl had deserved it for hunting upon someone else's grounds.

"Perhaps that was when the innocence fell away," she whispered sadly.

Was it Kavan's fault, or was it after she had truly lost count, and no longer cared? There had been that brief moment again when Traciea had been born—but then how long ago was that? Three millennia? And Traciea, who had never gained the Essence—the father's fault undoubtedly, whatever his name was. She had watched poor Traciea grow, remain barren, and in the end drift into horrifying senility. That, perhaps, was what had caused the first lines of hardness to settle in as she, still young after a thousand years, saw her child grow old, wither, and die in her arms.

She had borne no children since.

Patrice automatically locked the hurt away and moved on with her musings. There had always been other games to play; and in them there were no emotions to tangle in, no unfeeling males who would use, laugh, and drift away. Men might *try* to use her that way, but they had at least learned to fear her.

As her concentration waned, the faint lines and shadows returned to her features. Yet she could still see the cold beauty of her form. Her hair had not faded at least, flowing in an amber cascade over her shoulders to cover her full breasts, then drift over her narrow waist to end in a filigree of curls around the fullness of her hips. Smiling, her features appeared almost youthful—except for the eyes.

Ulinda's slim hand came to rest on her shoulder. Patrice looked up, smiled, and came to her feet.

"Do you bring good news?"

"Yes, my lady," replied Ulinda. "Imada, who is the younger of the two outlanders we captured, is finally ready for the next step."

"Do you enjoy your work with him?" Patrice asked with a knowing smile.

"Yes, my lady, I must admit I do. He's so gentle and trusting. The other one is taking more time, but I am gradually breaking him down too."

"Just see you don't get too attached. Nothing must interfere with this plan—nothing."

"My lady, I have served you too long and have too much to gain to allow anything, much less a little puppy like Imada, to interfere with our goals."

Patrice stared hard at her, then relaxed. Ulinda was reliable— after all, they had worked together on this plan for years.

"If you pronounce him fit to start the operation, we will begin your final transformation tonight. By tomorrow you will be Vena, the peasant girl who saved his life and became his one true love."

Again she paused. "Are you certain of your readiness also?"

"Yes, my lady. I have been assuming Vena's form on a daily basis for months now, and several teams of researchers have found no leak on any level in their probing. Only after the proper sequence of signals may I resurrect my personality."

Patrice nodded. "I want you to go through one more series of tests this afternoon. Go and set up the sequence now, and if all goes well we will begin tonight."

Ulinda bowed her head and backed away.

For a few minutes Patrice sat there, thinking hard. Then she left her private chamber and strode down the cool, marble-columned corridor, lit tastefully by high windows covered in exquisite designs of stained glass. Images of woodland glades, forests, and cliff-lined beaches shone on the highly polished alabaster floor, filling the hallway with a riot of color.

She turned down a side passage and stepped out onto a high balcony. It was so peaceful here, she thought, inhaling deeply of the salty ocean air.

Beneath her, the port was a bustle of activity, and great sailing cogs, slender clipper ships, and a fleet of warships, bronze rams polished, rode at anchor.

Here was the source of her wealth. Her capital city served as the main port for this whole region of coastline.

She had an army, to be sure, and a navy to protect against

pirates. But her main strength had always been in her hundreds of sorcerers, now including the fifteen deserters from Sarnak's ranks.

That had been a treasure haul: Almost no fighting to speak of and she had been able to snatch up a third of that fool's realm in less than a fortnight. Of course, under pressure from Allic and Jartan she'd had to retreat back to her original borders or face a war that would have interfered with her long-range plans. Still, she had gained an enormous amount of wealth and booty just from the initial assault. If only Sarnak and Allic had played themselves out against each other as she had hoped, then it all would have been hers as was her right.

She had waited three thousand years to expand her realm. Now she was tired of waiting. Soon they would know the payment to be exacted for their slights and neglect.

Turning away from her city, she stepped back into the corridor and walked farther down the hall, until she came to a broad side passage.

Two sorcerers stood before her in its darkness. Wordlessly they stepped forward, and one of them held a crystal up to her eyes and peered closely through it. A long moment passed as the sorcerer looked at her both outwardly and within.

"It is you, my lady. You may pass."

Without a word of acknowledgment, Patrice continued down the corridor. She had once challenged her way past a guard, shouting her down before she could do the inward scan. The girl had acquiesced and backed away. It had been a good object lesson for the others: The guarding of this passage must be thorough. She had not killed the young sorcerer—that would have been a waste of talent—but blinded, the girl could still be of some service in the healing arts until her eyes grew back.

The passageway was wide enough for a dozen to pass. The walls were seamless except for one faint outline just before the main entrance. That hidden side alcove was a convenient escape route if ever she should need it. She liked those little touches of plans within plans, but it was a precaution that would not be needed now.

Stopping by the door she reached out, her delicate nails tapping out a quick interplay on half a dozen raised disks of polished brass. Drawing a crystal pendant from between her breasts, she took the warm stone and pressed it into a socket that fit the crystal exactly.

The doors slipped open.

The room, over a hundred feet in diameter, was lit by the fires that came from a vast pentagram of gold and rubies set in the middle of the chamber. Within the pentagram itself was a deep fiery pit whose flames were eternally fed.

At the edge of the pentagram, she knelt on silver-embroidered cushions and removed the large sparkling crystal of fire from the sash around her waist. She gazed at it lovingly. It had been fashioned eons earlier by her father, the Creator Borc, before his death at the start of the war between the gods. She exulted in the sense of power emanating from the crystal, which even without its companion pieces made her all but invincible in battle.

Darkly, she remembered being denied the other crystals by the full council of gods, after her father's death. They had claimed that it had never been Borc's intent for her to hold all three, and in silent humiliation she had stood before them, mumbling a bitter thanks that they had at least given her the one gem. She had felt like a foolish child, forced to endure a public humiliation, while Jartan had been so pious in his mouthing of praise for Borc, even as he robbed his daughter of her legacy and locked the two other gems in his own treasure vault.

Later she had gone to him, like a low-born supplicant, to plead for a change in the decision. His words had been gentle as he'd lied and said how he could not entrust such power even to his own children, with all its potential for harm or corruption. Yet she had seen through those lies, although she had nodded and pretended to agree. He wanted the crystals for himself, it was so evident, and in the centuries that followed, when she had appeared at court functions, she had known he and his offspring were laughing at her humiliation. Now at last there would be a reckoning—not only for that, but for *all* the slights she'd endured.

Even with just one of the three crystals, she had great power. Once she had the others that were now in Jartan's possession, her power could be magnified tenfold.

Reverently, she picked up the stone and set it into its proper niche at the base of the pentagram, which began to pulse and glow, bathing the room in a twisting light.

A shadow reared up before her, towering to the height of the arched vaults a hundred feet above. Mighty arms of flame reached outward, pressing on the side of the pentagram, so that it flexed and bulged though it did not give.

She attempted to look upon his visage, but it was a face that danced and shifted in the flames. Shafts of fire snapped out, and at the end of each the image of a tormented soul appeared, shrieking in silent agony. Eyes of liquid fire, brighter than the hearts of suns, gazed down upon her. From the ends of its fangs, white-hot drips of phosphorescence rained down, forming into bodies that tore at themselves in anguish as they fell.

As it moved, muscles of glowing steel coiled and shifted like writhing snakes. Its taloned hands reached out, so that she struggled for control as it grasped toward the doomed souls, and squeezed . . .

The nightmare closed inward, pulsing, shifting. There was a flash of light and the room was bathed in a gentle brilliance, soothing to the eyes, like sunbeams glistening off the softly rolling sea.

He appeared neither male nor female to her eyes, but a fascinating, seductive blending of both.

"Gorgon," she whispered.

He smiled.

"Tomorrow I set my plan in motion. It is time for you to act as well."

There was no response, only the smile.

"When I have my father's other crystals, and Horat's portal crystal, I will have the power to break the barriers that divide our realms. With your strength the gateway can be widened for your entrance into this world, and together we shall rule."

In her heart she knew the lie. But as she looked into his guileless eyes, she could almost feel a tremor of desire. She was no fool, she knew who he was, but here in this realm, with the power of the Crystals of Fire, she knew she could bend even him to her power, once he had served his purpose.

And Gorgon, ruler of the demon lords, his features now lighting with desire to match hers, smiled yet again.

* * *

"Is that the best image you can form? Those windows are too blurry, and you don't even know how many floors there are. No wonder it's so out of focus!"

Kochanski found himself clenching his teeth and flexing his hands, imagining them wrapped around this little monster's throat.

His "help" from Jartan had turned out to be a precocious seventeen-year-old know-it-all: all boundless energy, enthusiasm, and contempt for the failings of mere adults.

Sara brushed her blond hair back from her face as she straightened up from examining the model of the Empire State Building.

"This is useless. I suggest you think of another artifact, or let me deeper into your mind so that I can help more. Why you insist on keeping those barriers up . . . it's just silly."

Kochanski's temper snapped.

"Listen, you obnoxious little twit, I don't care if you *are* Jartan's granddaughter. No one is going to rummage through my mind without my permission!"

Sara raised her eyebrows in an exaggerated gesture and pantomimed sorrow, further infuriating Kochanski.

"Jartan told me that you were still developing your powers, but I had no idea that you would be this backward. And I can't imagine how he can think that I would learn anything from you."

Kochanski struggled to think of a retort that wasn't profane and by doing so lost the exchange, as she continued:

"I guess he wants me to learn patience from working with someone so arrested in development."

She paused, then went on brightly, "Perhaps he wishes me to further my development of empathy for the unfortunate."

Sara shook her head ruefully. "It's harder than I thought, but I guess I can do it. All right, Kochanski, what other images do you want to try?"

Kochanski was fighting for control. Taking a deep breath, he managed a shaky smile, but inside he screamed, *"Why me?"*

By evening there were over a dozen models scattered about the room. With Sara's help, Kochanski had created copies of the

Washington Monument, the Capitol, and Mount Rushmore. He had even tried models of things he had seen while stationed overseas: the Tower of London, Stonehenge, and even the Chinese temple that they had been in when they were teleported to Haven.

He was exhausted, and she was as bright-eyed and enthusiastic as ever.

"You know, the last couple were much better. Why don't we try one more and break for dinner? My classmates are meeting at my house for a game—we compete to see who can create the most interesting creatures. They're not living, of course, but it's such wonderful fun. And I'm sure my friends wouldn't mind having you along."

He managed to croak a "No!" that was barely audible, but utterly final.

"Well, I guess you are a little tired. Poor man, you *are* pretty old, aren't you?"

"Twenty-three, going on nine hundred at the moment," came the numb reply.

He watched her helplessly. Her bright blue eyes now filled with the superficial, but sincere, compassion of the young.

"I understand. Don't worry, Kochanski, you're improving. And I'm sure with lots of work I can make you into a first class sorcerer someday."

She turned and walked from the room, calling over her shoulder, "I'll be back at first light tomorrow morning, and we'll pick up where we left off!"

Sara smiled contentedly to herself. His talents weren't that bad really, and he certainly was cute in a helpless sort of way.

She heard something behind her and thought to herself, *There he goes again. I've got to find out what "bitch" means in that odd language of his.*

Jartan smiled at Sara, and interrupted her. "Did Kochanski agree to this?"

"Well, no. But that's only because I didn't think of it in time to discuss it with him. Really, Jartan, I think going back to school would do him a world of good. And I happen to know that Deena is having a class on image forming and creativity for the eight-year-olds tomorrow. That's just the thing he needs help in now, and I'll be right there to help him when, uh, if he needs it."

Jartan held up his hand to quiet her for a moment and expanded his mind to pick up Kochanski. He didn't open contact from his end, just listened in on what Kochanski was thinking at the moment.

—And roared with laughter.

A few moments later he regained his poise and looked gravely down at his granddaughter.

"I'm very proud of you, Sara. You are doing an outstanding job of helping Kochanski. When you see him tomorrow morning tell him that I agreed with you, and it is my command that he is to attend this class."

"Thank you, Jartan. And you were right, too. I think I'm learning a lot about self-control and compassion from working with him."

Sara smiled at the god and excused herself from his presence.

The moment she left the room Jartan's smile widened into a wicked, delighted grin.

Kochanski sat in the class, wishing he was dead. He couldn't recall ever being so humiliated in his entire life. Not only were these little desks too damn small, but the whole class of children was trying so earnestly to help him that he hated them all at that moment.

In spite of his best efforts the pedestal in the center of class showed no distinct solid form, only a wavering image of the miniature statue that he was supposed to copy and create in solid form.

A moment later he gave up, and the whole class groaned in disappointment as even the image disappeared.

Deena, the instructor, clapped her hands to get their attention and said, "Now, children, he's still a beginner at this and he has improved, don't you think?"

The chorus of encouraging remarks and smiles made Kochanski want to puke. This really was too much. Surely Jartan had some isolated outpost somewhere that he could volunteer for.

A loathsomely cute little tyke smiled up at him and offered,

"Watch me, Kochanski, watch me!" He turned and called, "Deena, can I go next?"

Deena nodded. "Now remember, I want motion, not just a static copy."

The boy responded enthusiastically, "I'm going to try to make the model walk and then wave at me. Now watch, Kochanski."

Kochanski gazed in sullen silence as the kid created an exact copy of the small statue on top of the pedestal. Its first movements were slow and jerky, but it soon began to stroll with a fluid grace. Kochanski flicked a glance at Sara sitting next to him, and she turned to give him a blinding, reassuring smile. He hastily turned his attention elsewhere and his glance happened to settle on Deena.

Now that's some woman, he thought appreciatively. Her dark brown hair was long and shiny, and her eyes were a golden brown, warm and lively. *And that body!* He had always liked his women lush rather than slim. Her breasts must be full and soft under that gown. . . .

Kochanski was so busy undressing Deena that he hadn't even noticed that the boy had finished his turn.

Little eight-year-old Lindsey was sitting on the other side of Sara, watching Kochanski intently. She felt very sorry for him, trying so hard and coming so close, but just not being able to grasp the final stage. He was trying again; she could see the concentration on his face.

Gathering up her will she slipped a narrow probe into his mind and sent a surge of power to help.

Suddenly a solid, graceful image of Deena appeared on the pedestal. The motion of its hair and breasts corresponded exactly to Deena as she turned in surprise to stare at the statue of herself. The only difference was that the statue was breathtakingly naked.

A roar of laughter and cheers from the children brought Kochanski back to his senses. An instant later he was on his feet, red-faced and stammering.

Deena picked up the now immobile statue of herself and smiled at him.

"This is truly beautiful. If I had realized that you would respond better to living material, we would have tried this earlier." Her smile became a bit more mischievous and her eyes became more direct.

"You don't have everything exactly correct, though. Perhaps we could work on this some other time?"

Kochanski was trying desperately to find some way to get out of the situation with a shred of dignity when he noticed that Sara was no longer smiling at him. In fact, he couldn't ever recall seeing eyes that icy before.

Christ, I think she's jealous. Oh my God, do I deserve this?

Kochanski sat glumly in the Godchair.

I don't ever remember being so embarrassed before, he thought. *And what am I going to do if Sara is still mad at me? She'll probably be a nightmare at our next work session.* He shuddered at the thought.

Jartan would tell me to look at the positive, he considered. *All right, I ended up with a date with a beautiful woman, and I actually learned to create something by using the Essence.* Seeing Deena had been a truly remarkable experience, but last evening's pleasure was now in the past, and he still had to face what would undoubtedly be a jealously enraged young woman.

He stopped brooding momentarily to practice his creativity again, focusing on the model of Stonehenge in front of him. With great effort, he focused in his will, concentrating on his memories of the day he had spent exploring the ancient site while stationed in England. He pushed the image onto the model and muttered, "Change, you bastard."

And the model seemed to come alive. All the distortions disappeared and a perfect little Stonehenge was before him, this time completely intact, with all the lintels and uprights in place as it must have been thousands of years before.

I can do it. Damn!

The image almost seemed to be alive as he stared at it, and he thought, *I wish I were there.*

Instantly the Godchair reacted, and his spirit was whisked into the evening sky. He grasped the seemingly solid arms of the chair and started to order it to take him back, but then figured that he hadn't been out today; might as well give it a try.

He was astonished to note that the Godchair wasn't leaving the surface of Haven. It was headed directly east, towards one of the large islands between the continents.

A moment later the chair slowed before a large lake surrounded by hundreds of square miles of forest. There in the center of the lake was an island, and on that island was a full-sized Stonehenge.

He began to drift closer.

The old druid was in the midst of an incantation when he sensed an alien intrusion. Stopping, he turned to survey his surroundings. Nothing was in sight, but he could feel a presence growing stronger and stronger.

He switched to infrared, and then starlight vision, and still nothing. After several more attempts he tried the spirit world— and there he felt something.

Leaving his body, he could see a figure floating above, staring down at his temple. Painfully he forced his spirit upward. Very few could travel in the spirit world, and fewer yet could travel too far from their bodies.

The man in the chair was a sorcerer, and by his uniform he belonged to Jartan. Still, only those who followed the true beliefs were allowed here.

Rising before Kochanski he spoke.

"I do not permit unbelievers to watch the sacred rites. Go now before I become angry."

The sorcerer in the chair became very agitated at even being seen.

Come a little closer, the old druid thought, *and I will give you the sacred wicker death.* The time to light the fires under the wicker cages was very near.

Finally the sorcerer spoke. "How did you ever make such a good copy of Stonehenge?"

The old druid's heart started racing. The time he had worried about for two thousand years was here at last.

"You have seen the original?"

"Yes, yes. You are from Earth too?"

The druid gathered his strength as he drifted closer and closer.

He asked cunningly, "Know you of Caius Julius Caesar?"

"Julius Caesar? Sure I know of him."

"Assassin! I knew you would come someday," the druid screamed, leaping forward, propelling his strength into the spirit realm of the intruder.

The speed of the chair was amazing. Even as his fingers were about to close on the assassin's throat, the chair was gone.

Trembling, the old druid searched the sky but could find nothing.

Caesar had tracked him down at last. No matter. He had been ready for years beyond count.

He would let them come to him.

Kochanski got up from the Godchair severely shaken. Someone else from Earth was here, but was very dangerous. Maybe insane, too. Jesus, that was a close call.

He sent a call for Jartan over his communications crystal. No answer. Still, he was picking up some type of commotion in Jartan's main briefing room down the hall.

Heading down the hall, he saw great numbers of sorcerers going into and out of the main briefing room, all wearing looks of intense concern.

Entering, his first thought was the similarity to an overturned anthill. One group was preparing maps, another was entering figures on a great projection board, and another was working on two huge models of different worlds floating above the large horseshoe-shaped table. Jartan stood at the head of the table issuing commands and listening to reports as they came in.

Kochanski pushed his own concerns aside as he worked his way toward the god. As he passed he noted that the largest of the two floating worlds had numerous bright lights surrounded by circles of red, and that the smaller globe orbiting the larger one was seemingly covered with ice and snowfields with only one bright light and no red circles.

He stood beside Jartan for several minutes before the god had time for him.

"Kochanski, I've moved your training up. Sara and several others will be arriving shortly to give you lessons on portal travel in other dimensions. You've got a departure time of less than three days, so your life depends on you being a quick learner."

Kochanski's first thought was, *My life?* and then, *Three days? He's got to be kidding.*

"No, I'm deadly serious. One of our primary outpost worlds seems to be under attack. I'm sending a reconnaissance in force to check it out. You are the best sorcerer I have for the Godchair, so you're definitely going. I need information badly."

"Uh, Jartan, why? I mean . . . "

"Not now, Kochanski. There will be a briefing tomorrow after-noon when the rest of the team arrives. You'll be pleased to know that I'm sending Mark and the rest of the outlanders with you. For now, return to the Godchair. Sara and the others are preparing a training portal opening for you. You are dismissed."

Kochanski walked from the room more confused than ever. What the hell was going on?

Chapter 3

Winging in low Sarnak skimmed between the snow-covered peaks. Overhead, forward, and to either side, his escort of thirty sorcerers ranged outward, ready to react at the slightest sign of treachery.

So far it was all going according to plan. But if the roles were reversed he knew what he would do at this moment, promises to the contrary be damned.

As he swung down the side of the mountain, he felt tension knotting within him at the sight of the dozen wall crystals mounted along the upper battlements of his cousin's fortress. As agreed, they were not manned. But still, the gunners could merely be hidden.

With every sense straining, Sarnak probed for the first indicators of threat, but all was as it should be.

His lead sorcerers, following the example of the first guide, swung in over the battlements and alighted on the landing platform.

"All clear, my lord," a voice whispered through the comm link.

Sarnak looked over at the second guide sorcerer who had been flying alongside him. The path to Tor's ancient fortress was known for its difficult approach. A range of mountains nearly thirty thousand feet tall had to first be cleared; and atop those peaks were battle platforms, positioned to fire on any would-be attacker. That thought alone had sent prickles of fear running down his back.

The fortress was not built at all in the traditional sense, but rather had been carved straight into the side of a mountain, five thousand feet below the summit. Two thousand feet below the fortress was the floor of the valley, where his subjects lived, a region that could only be approached through a narrow defile.

41

For those who were condemned to travel on foot, the climb up and over the passes was a journey of seven or more days. Once over the mountains the traveler had to drop all the way down into the narrow valley below and then follow a tortuous path back up to the only ground entrance into the fortress. The valley itself was a steeply terraced patchwork of fields, orchards, and stone-walled villages stretching northward for nearly two hundred miles into the cold fastness of Tor's realm.

The main keep of the ancient palace, one of those fashioned by the creator Horat himself, was also built straight into the side of the mountain, atop a sheer rock pinnacle of smooth granite. The only way to enter it was by air—and a series of traps was studded through the narrow pass for an aerial approach. Crystals were mounted to either side in a latticework pattern, with only a narrow, unrestricted opening through the middle. Come in too high or too low and cross between two crystals, and the trap would be sprung as half a hundred energy bolts snapped out from the mountain, incinerating everything between them.

If one approached from down in the valley, the same trap awaited as the unwary victim started to climb the face of the pinnacle. A straight overhead approach and a spiral down would create the same response from an interlocking series of crystals that pointed upwards to their counterparts on the distant peaks.

Without the guides to lead them in, the approach would have been almost impossible to negotiate. Sarnak felt a twinge of jealousy for such a profligate use of the precious stones.

Following the lead of his first battle team, Sarnak turned sharply and came in for final approach. Once across the threshold of the fortress, he breathed an inward sigh of relief: The first part of the ordeal had been passed. Trying to calm the tension within, he alighted on the platform.

Around him, the rest of his sorcerers turned in sharply and, as they landed, spread out in what appeared to be a protective circle.

From the shadows of a doorway that led into the heart of the mountain, a single middle-aged man appeared. Uthul's face was angular and dark, wreathed in a beard that had already gone over to grey. The resemblance was striking, and for an instant Sarnak almost thought that he was standing before his uncle Tor. Yet Sarnak knew there was one thing that Uthul had not inherited, and that was Tor's cunning.

"Cousin, what a debacle—it was a miracle you escaped at all." Uthul strode forward, hands extended sideways in the gesture of greeting.

Sarnak looked past Uthul to see a dozen sorcerers emerge, looking warily at Sarnak's surviving retinue.

"Your father died well and with honor," Sarnak said evenly.

"At the hands of that bastard Jartan," Uthul replied, with obvious emotion in his voice. "I thought no good would come of this effort—I tried to warn him. I just knew it would be a failure."

"It was my plan, you know," Sarnak said dryly.

Uthul fell silent. "Be that as it may," he finally replied. "It's a wonder Jartan has not moved straight here to burn us out."

"I think he might have other concerns right now. He knows your father is dead; he might think that's sufficient for now."

"But it's said Allic still hunts you, and won't stop once he finds out where you have fled."

Sarnak bristled inwardly at the word *fled*. He had been forced to make a tactical withdrawal . . . but there would soon be another skirmish—that is, if his hated foe survived the threat he expected was coming.

Uthul shook his head and continued. "At least, cousin, I can give you and yours shelter for awhile here in my kingdom. But I want no part of this war if it should continue. I've already sent an ambassador to Jartan indicating my desire for peace. If he should even suspect that I gave you shelter, I know his wrath would turn on me as well. I'm surprised it hasn't happened already. That is why, when you have rested, I will have to ask that you leave my realm. There are places across the sea where I am sure you can start afresh."

"Wrong, dear cousin," Sarnak said, a thin smile lighting his features. "You see, I have a surprise for you."

As the code words were spoken Sarnak stepped back.

His thirty sorcerers turned as one, hands extended.

Thirty flashes of light snapped out. Before Uthul could even whisper a cry or begin to raise his shielding, his body had already snapped into a blinding incandescence.

A single stunned sorcerer stepped out from the doorway, hurling a blast at Sarnak, who was already prepared, his shield up to maximum. The bolt flashed, causing the shield to momentarily glow. Half a dozen sorcerers turned their attention away from the charred remains of Tor's son and slammed the one defender to the ground.

Warily the other sorcerers backed up, hands kept carefully down.

Sarnak walked up to the smoking remains and drew the signet of rule off a blackened hand. He put the signet on his finger and almost languidly looked over at the terrified sorcerers.

"He made one mistake, you know," Sarnak said gently, a sad smile lighting his features. "He just should have said the kingdom was mine and all of this unpleasantness could have been avoided.

"Are there any objections to this little change in power?"

One by one the sorcerers fell to their knees in obeisance.

"Good, very good, there's been too much bloodshed today. Your pay is doubled as of now, if that will prove any additional incentive to the lot of you."

Greedy smiles lit the faces of more than one kneeling man.

Sarnak nodded knowingly. "Excellent, gentlemen, then we do understand each other. I guess it's time that I moved in and started with my work. It's said that many artifacts from Tor and even my dear grandfather Horat are hidden within. Perhaps they can be of use in the coming struggle."

With a look almost of pity, Sarnak stepped past the corpse of his cousin and started for the entrance.

"Bala."

"Yes my lord," A sorcerer with piggy features and lifeless eyes rushed to his side.

"Be sure the body receives a proper burial."

"As you wish, my lord." and the sorcerer started to turn away.

"And Bala—one other thing. Before taking care of that, go into the private living chambers. My cousin had a wife and three small children. I would think they would prefer to join their dearly departed loved one. No sense having resentful rivals about the place."

A grin of evil delight crossed Bala's features as he motioned to several of his companions and scurried away.

"Too bad," Sarnak whispered to himself, "these family squabbles can be such distasteful affairs."

The meeting Allic had called was winding down to a close.

After the encounter with the demon Kultha in Sarnak's office, Jartan had ordered a complete investigation and sent two of Allic's sisters, Storm and Leti, to assist.

This time the search had been conducted with crystal-shattering sonics and several more traps and escape holes had been detected and dismantled. A fair portion of Sarnak's old fortress was now in ruins, torn and blasted by the thoroughness of the investigation.

The sorcerer in charge of the last area searched was completing his report, and everyone was starting to shift restlessly. It had been a long meeting and it was time to wrap it up.

Finally Allic raised his hand and said, "Thank you, Faltre." The sorcerer stopped and sat down.

Allic continued, "We are all agreed, then, that there are no more portal openings of sufficient size to be any danger here?"

There was a murmur of agreement and Leti spoke up, "I'm amazed that Sarnak could even set up what he did, much less have more than one. The years of effort to construct such a trap and the sheer power he had stored there merely to keep it in standby mode is incredible."

"Leti and I will leave at first light tomorrow for Asmara," Storm continued. "I'll report everything that's transpired here to Jartan. We can assume for now that the danger in this region is past."

"It's an old rule of war," Ikawa said quietly, "that when an enemy is stirred it might be long before he goes back to sleep. Perhaps this find here is only part of a puzzle to be unraveled, and indicates a broader plan. It could even mean that Sarnak's attack fits into someone else's designs."

Allic nodded approvingly at Ikawa's comment. On several occasions in the past, this outlander's military insight had been proven. He had learned to take any advice from this quarter with utmost seriousness.

"That will be in our report as well," Allic said. "Now, is there any other business to attend to?"

The assembly looked to each other without comment.

"Fine then, it's been a rough couple of weeks here. Let's all take the rest of the day off and try to relax a bit."

Allic looked over at Storm and Leti and smiled.

"I am certain that you two have some catching up to do with a couple of gentlemen on my staff," and his statement was met with chortles of delight from all the Americans and Japanese present.

"At least cut down on the thunder tonight," came a disguised voice from the back of the room, that was obviously Walker's. "I got my beauty sleep to catch up on."

Leaving the conference room, the group followed a narrow passageway out to a private garden Mark had never seen before, so vast was the palace and citadel complex. Though bizarre in its arrangement, Mark found the garden to be fascinating in an uncomfortable sort of way. When he had been a boy, an uncle returning from Florida had brought back a Venus's-flytrap for him. The plant had delighted him, and what he saw now rekindled those memories. Several of the plants had a strange beauty to them, with open fronds, bloodred in color, that emitted a musky cloying scent. Some were obviously traps, with viselike jaws a foot across gaping wide open. In the center of the garden was an open orchid several feet in diameter, dark yellow in color and wafting a lavenderlike scent to the breeze.

Curious, Mark started to draw closer.

"Don't," Storm whispered, coming up to his side. She picked up a clump of dirt and tossed it towards the orchid. With lightning speed half a dozen tendrils snaked out, slamming into the dirt clod, pulling it straight into the heart of the flower, which closed like a steel door slamming shut.

"Jesus," Walker gasped, looking nervously at the deadly plant.

"The tendrils are armed with poison barbs," Leti announced. "You're paralyzed before you even hit the ground, then it simply digests you. If you're lucky it starts feeding on you head-first, killing you fairly quickly. Otherwise it will slowly feed on you for days, and you're still alive, feeling everything but unable to move, or even use your shielding.

"The bastard probably kept these for the poisons." She pointed around the garden.

"And for entertainment," Allic said coldly. "Those cadonna can take a hand off as clean as a razor. You can still find them in several of the wilder places on this world; usually we destroy them on sight. It's just like Sarnak to have a garden like this. I should have destroyed them the day we took this place."

With a snort of disgust Allic brought his hand up. A slash of light snapped out, sweeping across the garden. Horrified, Mark watched as many of the plants writhed upon the ground, like snakes that had been cut in half. A sickening stench filled the air and the party drew away.

Following Storm's lead, the group left the smoldering garden, looking nervously about. Gradually the party split up until Mark suddenly realized that he and Storm were alone. At the end of a winding path, Mark was amazed by the splendor of the view before him as the edge of a sheer cliff dropped to a broad lake hundreds of feet below.

"There is a certain stark beauty to the place," Storm said, dangling her legs over the edge of the cliff.

Mark had to nod in agreement. The mountains that surrounded the inner citadel of Sarnak's former realm had the sharp, desiccated look he had seen before in southern Arizona and New Mexico. Their angles were like razor edges against the late afternoon sky, presenting a vivid contrast of dark blue against brown and gray.

"Not as pretty, though, as Homefree." Storm reached over to squeeze Mark's hand.

How lucky he truly was, he thought, letting the warmer thoughts push aside the nightmare images. It was still hard to believe that he lived in luxury far surpassing even the most palatial mansions he had visited back in England. In fact the gently rolling countryside and the orderly villages and formal gardens around his new estate of Homefree did remind him of England in the springtime.

In many ways he was now like a baron, living in splendor.

But it was a position that matched more into his American sensibilities than the old feudal system of Europe. There were eight villages in his fiefdom, each ruled by an elected town council. He could advise, and act as a judge to settle disputes, but if his decision was not satisfactory it was within the villagers' rights to go straight over his head to Allic. Though they paid him the respect he was entitled to as a warrior and sorcerer, he was expected to serve in turn. Allic had made it clear that any behavior disrupting the orderly management of his province, or any mistreatment of the people, would not be tolerated.

"We'll be home before you know it," Storm said, as if reading his thoughts. "Assimilating Sarnak's realm and following through on this latest incident will take some time, but I dare say you'll be rotated back in a couple of months and we'll have plenty of time to be together again."

Mark sat back without comment. Storm laid down alongside of him, her eyes filled with concern. But he didn't want to talk about the turmoil inside him, the gnawing fear that the hell he had glimpsed was the fate awaiting him.

"You folks care for a swim?"

Mark looked up to see Leti and Ikawa standing hand in hand before him.

"A splendid idea," Storm cried, coming to her feet and pulling Mark up alongside her.

Mark looked over the edge of the cliff to the vast lake below. It *was* hot; perhaps a good swim would be just the thing to cool him off.

"Let's do a little underwater exploring while we're at it," Leti suggested.

Surprised, Mark said, "That lake is sheer-walled and looks to be a couple of hundred feet deep."

"Silly, you can fly through the air, why not underwater?"

Now this was a twist, and the idea certainly was appealing. There had been reports that the Italians had perfected a method of underwater breathing learned from some Frenchman. They had used it to remarkable effect in sinking several British ships. He had always wanted to try it out, and now he realized there was nothing to stop him from doing it on this world.

"It's simple enough," Leti explained. "Compress your shield

in tight to your body, and allow it to be porous enough for air to get through, but for the water to stay out. Your shield will act as the gills on a fish, and your creativity will automatically make oxygen for you to breath."

"How deep can we go?" Ikawa asked excitedly.

"For now, keep it at several hundred feet. Every thirty feet is roughly equal to one atmosphere. Until you've mastered the skill you might have a leak break through when you go much above ten atmospheres. And don't let your shield rupture. Your pressure inside the shield is the same as on the surface; the sudden change would kill you. After some practice you should be able to reach five, even six hundred feet deep. Just imagine you're flying. The principle is the same."

The two men looked at each other excitedly.

"Well, let's get in the water," Storm announced.

Without hesitation she untied the simple belt around her waist and pulled her shift up over her head with Leti following suit. A moment later both were naked except for the crystal belts around their wrists and waists.

Mark and Ikawa looked at each other nervously. They had grown accustomed to the relaxed sexual mores on Haven, but since their involvements with Leti and Storm they now felt slightly uncomfortable at the naked presence of the other's partner.

A bit shyly, the two disrobed—to chuckles of amusement of the two women.

"Well, let's go skinny-dipping," Mark cried, and leaped off the cliff.

Plummeting down the face of the cliff, he snapped up his shield as Leti had told him to. Extending his arms outward, he slammed into the water, his shield protecting him from the impact. For a moment he felt a slight twinge of panic as he continued to streak downward and held his breath.

Tentatively he breathed in and exhaled. Around the edge of the shield he saw a sheet of bubbles break away and rise up.

He took another breath and exhaled, and another ring of bubbles raced to the surface.

Three dull thuds snapped through the water, and Ikawa, Leti, and Storm came streaking down toward him.

Fascinated, Mark watched as they spiraled around each other, drifting through the water with the same effortless ease as flying through the air. Yet everything down here seemed to be taking place in slow motion, with graceful, languid movement replacing the sharp, rapid-fire maneuvers of flight.

Delighted, he started to laugh and watched as the three descended past him. For all the world he suddenly felt as if he were in a vast cathedral of blue, the three other swimmers drifting down like angels dropping from heaven. The pale beams of sunlight filtered about them like light through the stained glass windows of a cathedral.

Rolling back over, he watched as they drifted down into the darkness, their halos of bubbles rising around him in ever-expanding circles.

Following his friends downward, he was fascinated as the pale turquoise blue of the upper region slowly transformed into a darker blue like the early evening sky, which interplayed with the shimmering beams of sunlight.

An iridescent column of yellow forms came spiraling up out of the depth and he almost cried out with joy as the column broke into a spiraling circle of thousands of yellow fish, striped vertically with slashes of violet.

Blending in with the school, Mark found himself surrounded in a shifting kaleidoscope: One moment the fish were all swimming end-on, presenting razor sharp images; then in an instant the school would shift, and the dark blue of the ocean would become a rainbow of color.

Downward the school turned, mixing with another column of fish. Mark followed, shifting as they did, looping and arching. Colors gradually dropped away into yet a deeper blue, as if the gentle mantle of night was washing over his world.

"Mark, can you see me?"

Snapped from his reverie by the voice from his communication crystal, he looked about. His three companions were nowhere in sight.

He felt a vague uneasiness in this twilight world.

"Hold up your offensive crystal and set it as a diffused beacon of light."

As Storm had instructed, he raised his right hand. A wide beam shot out, illuminating the fish so that their colors seemed to explode. Under the glare of the beacon, the thousands of fish which had surrounded him, and had appeared to be dark green in the muted light of the deep, suddenly stood out in high contrast, revealing a rainbow swirl of reds, yellows, and burgundy, so that the water seemed almost on fire.

Again his attention drifted as he observed the alien world about him.

"Still can't find me?" Storm said playfully, with a slight note of chiding in her voice. "It's a skill you should learn."

Mark swung his beacon back and forth but could not locate her.

"Your farseeing ability, silly."

Nodding to himself, Mark shifted his focus, channeling his attention.

The world about him seemed to shift slightly, and then from below, at five o'clock, he could detect three blips.

"Just like sonar!" he cried.

"A little sub chase," Ikawa laughed.

He rolled over into a dive, rapidly picking up speed.

Two of the blips remained motionless, but the third broke away to the left in a tight spiral turn.

Suddenly Ikawa and Leti flashed into view, illuminated by his crystal. With a cheery wave he shot past the two, who were laughing with delight at his antics.

Storm continued to dive, jinking to the left and right. Doggedly he followed, still picking up speed. He could sense the bottom racing up and, broadening his search, he could easily detect Storm swinging among the towering boulders that littered the lake bed.

In an instant he was skimming along through a swirling forest of kelp, dodging up over boulders, and traversing beneath arching caverns that plunged into darkness and then back into opaque light.

Trying to lose him in the clutter, Storm would dodge behind a boulder, out of his view, and then scurry around the far side.

Once she simply hit the bottom and remained motionless so that he shot right past her. A taunting laugh echoed through his crystal, and looking over his shoulder he saw her rise up, wave playfully and then streak away.

Grinning with delight, Mark arched straight up and over and shot back down on her tail. Gradually he closed in on her, so that he was able to track her by the bubbles given off by her rapid passage through the water.

Finally his beacon locked onto her, revealing her slender form cutting effortlessly through the tranquil depths. Tantalizingly, she stayed just out of reach as they played through the fairytale forest of boulders. Then she arched straight up, racing for the surface, sunbeams dappling her long black hair. Straight out of the water she shot, soaring heavenward. Bursting clear of the lake, he followed her upward, the warmth of the early evening air a sharp contrast to the cool waters below. At last she punched through a faint wisp of cloud and disappeared.

The cloud, rimmed with the first faint glow of pink from the setting sun, filled his view. Slowing, he drifted up and through.

Hands reached out, covering his eyes. Playfully he pulled her over and tumbled back into the puffy blanket. Her lips closed over his in a lingering kiss, their bodies intertwining into an embrace as they drifted out of the shelter of privacy back into the light below.

From far away they heard a hoot of delight, and looking down they saw several Japanese floating through the sky in their direction, laughing delightedly at the strange spectacle of the two embracing while floating in the heavens.

"Hard to get any privacy up here," Mark said, feeling a bit self-conscious about the two of them flying naked where the whole world could see them. Storm pushed away from Mark, her eyes glowing with passion. Taking his hand, she leaned over and plummeted downwards. The lake rushed up as if to hide them. Slashing through the surface, they knifed downward into its cool, protective mantle. Slowing, they looked about, like two adolescents furtively making sure that no one was watching before they kissed.

Storm drew closer, and made her shield blend into his. Eagerly they drew each other closer into a passionate embrace.

They had made love atop a cloud before, but this was the first time for them underwater. There was a wonderful sense of weightlessness as the water held them. Laughing they gradually rolled end over end, one moment prone, the next as if standing, then a moment later inverted, as if hanging suspended. And with each gentle turn and sway, their passion grew.

"Did you just hear something?" Ikawa asked, looking over at his beloved.

"Bit like thunder," she said, a wicked smile lighting her features.

"Well, at least you're quieter about such things," he said laughingly, drawing her close as if to start again what they had just finished.

"Shall we go exploring a bit first?"

He felt torn—what he had just shared with her beneath the waves was the stuff of dreams—but he could not hide the fact that he was curious to see this new world.

Giving him a playful wink, she drifted from his embrace, and, taking his hand, started downward.

Beneath them, vast schools of fish would dart away at their approach. Gradually the world grew dimmer, as the light from above shifted through the red of the setting sun, to be replaced by the golden glow of the twin moons rising together to the east. Switching on their crystals, they continued to explore the bottom, looking into crevices and then into a vast array of caverns that dropped away into darkness.

A gentle game of tag developed as the two lovers would break away and lazily chase each other. Ikawa found that he enjoyed the chase almost as much as the catch, as he skimmed behind Leti, watching her lithe naked body twisting and turning through the water.

Before them, a sheer wall suddenly loomed up. Having crossed the length of the lake, they came to a stop beneath the vast cliff, which soared straight upwards to the towering battlement of Sarnak's keep. The wall before them was dotted with caves.

"Close your eyes, turn off your sensing, and count to ten," Leti commanded. "Then practice trying to find me."

He felt a vague uneasiness, but the playful mood still held sway and he followed her command. She was gone when he opened his eyes, so he used his sensing ability to sweep the area—first out behind him, but there was no one there. He shifted his attention forward, scanning the caves.

Nothing.

Suddenly there was the slightest flurry of movement to the right, at the mouth of a cave right on the bottom.

"Got you," he cried, and zoomed for the entrance. The narrow opening closed around him, plunging him into blackness lit only by his crystal.

There was movement straight ahead, and eagerly he pushed forward. The cave doglegged to the right, and he slowed to turn the corner, ready to reach out and grab her, for he could sense her presence lingering just on the other side.

Ever so cautiously he came up to the edge, turning his beacon down to a narrow slit of light so as not to betray his presence. Lying on the bottom, he reached around to grab her by the legs. His hands grabbed something smooth, rounded, and cold.

A scream of horror escaped him: In his hands was a human skull, shreds of flesh still dangling from it's face.

The water swirled around him. Recoiling backward, he kicked out blindly, the water boiling around him in his frantic struggle.

A demon that was the sickly pale white of a rotting corpse rose above him, its phosphorescent green teeth bared and its yellow eyes glowing with malevolence.

Instinctively he raised his hand, a slash of light snapping out. The water boiled as the bolt of energy slammed through, catching the demon in the arm.

The demon roared in pain and fury, its voice hollow and ominous in the watery depths.

Pushing away, Ikawa rolled and twisted as the webbed talons cut through the water, catching him on the leg and pulling Ikawa toward his gaping maw.

Curling up in a ball, Ikawa aimed another shot, catching the demon full in the face. The booming scream abruptly stopped as the beam tore its head off. The hold loosened and he kicked away, bolting for the pale light of the cave entrance.

Half-blinded by terror he shot from the hole.

"Ikawa!"

Leti swung in alongside, a look of horror in her eyes as she saw the blood trailing from his leg.

The caverns around them seemed to explode in a maelstrom of enraged nightmares.

Leti fired three quick shots, each ripping a demon's body asunder. But still they came on.

"Can you swim?" she cried.

"I'll make it!" Ikawa grated, and the two raced through the water, two dozen or more pale forms swinging in behind them.

"Leti, Ikawa, what is it?"

"Get out of the lake!" Leti shouted. "Water demons!"

"We're coming over," Mark yelled.

"Ikawa, head for the surface," Leti cried, her voice full of concern.

Ikawa shook his head. The panic was under control and now replaced by a grim anger at having been caught so off guard.

The two continued to retreat, pulling the demons in behind them. Looking over his shoulder, he could see them swimming, their webbed hands and feet moving with smooth muscular strength, the vestiges of what had once been wings now undulating in a rippling motion like the movement of a giant ray flying through the water.

He was amazed to see that their power in the water equaled his own, and in fact the strongest of them was rapidly closing in. Clumsily he tried to aim over his shoulder and fire a bolt. The water boiled around him as the lightning shot snapped out, disappearing into the darkness, wide of its mark.

Leti swung wide, and then cut an arc across the front of Ikawa, firing twice. Her first shot missed, but the second caught the lead demon in the shoulder, sending him into a downward spiral.

The fighting here was far different, Ikawa realized, his analytical mind examining the nature of this combat even as he fled. In the air, range of firing could reach out a quarter mile or more. Down here fifty yards was probably the maximum range of an energy bolt before its power was drained off by the surrounding water. Movement was far slower as well. A close-in fight would be short and extremely deadly.

Suddenly, from straight beneath him, three forms shot up out of the depth. They had cut in front of him!

He fired a bolt at the closest demon, killing him, but could not turn back in time to handle the other two.

Swinging upward, he tried to cross above them, and they reached up eagerly to grab him.

There was a blinding flash of light, and the first demon seemed to explode. A second and third flash struck the other pursuer in the back and front at almost the same instant. The water around Ikawa was an explosion of steam and light, with the world washed in the roar of angry demons and the hissing shriek of hundreds of gallons of water vaporizing into steam.

Storm shot past, her countenance a terrifying visage of rage, with Mark at her side.

Spinning around, Ikawa and Leti now went over to the attack. At the sight of another demigod appearing as if from no-where, the demons broke away, scattering in every direction. Two more fell to her fury, the water around them boiling and foaming as her bolts shot out. Forming into a triad, Ikawa, Mark, and Leti fell in on two more demons who were madly racing back to the caverns. As if guided by a single thought, all three fired at the same time, and an instant later, Ikawa found himself swimming through the charred and boiled remains of his victim, the nauseating stench of burnt demon leaking through his shielding. The cliff wall now loomed above them, the last demons scurrying into its protection.

Frustrated, Ikawa started after them.

"Leave it go," Leti cried, swinging alongside him. "It's probably a honeycomb of warrens back there. They could lead you into a trap. I think they've learned enough of a lesson for today."

There was another flash off to their right, accompanied by an echoing shriek and the boiling hiss of steam. A moment later Storm reappeared, rage still glowing in her eyes.

"That should teach the bastards not to interrupt us," she said coldly.

Mark could not help but smile.

"We better get that leg looked after," Leti said.

Looking down, Ikawa saw that the slash was a deep one, going almost to the bone. A cut from a demon was always a tricky affair, since many times it would be poisoned. For the first time he felt pain wash through him, and a rising giddiness that was quickly turning into downright nausea.

Together, the four gained the surface. Putting a protective arm around Ikawa, Mark soared straight upward to alight on the cliff where their clothes still lay.

Leti spoke hurriedly into her communications crystal even as she bent over to examine Ikawa's leg.

"I've alerted the medical team," she said, and pulled the healing crystal from her belt, laying it on the wound to stem the bleeding.

The three dressed rapidly and were preparing to take Ikawa in when from out of the darkness a form landed beside them. Two other sorcerers quickly followed.

Without a word Allic knelt to look at Ikawa's wound.

"It could have been a lot worse," he said reassuringly, looking up at the Japanese officer with obvious relief.

Ikawa felt a swelling of affection for this man, who had come racing out to him the moment he had heard that one of his samurai had been injured. This truly was a daimyo worth serving.

Standing, Allic walked over to the edge of the cliff and looked down. "Sarnak must have kept them as pets, tossing in people he no longer needed."

A sick rage washed over Ikawa at the thought of the human skull he had held only moments before.

"A little interruption, I gather," Allic said, looking over at Storm in an attempt to lighten the mood.

"Ah, shut up," she replied huffily, and even Ikawa laughed as Allic looked over at him and winked.

The lightness of Allic's mood, however, quickly shifted to seriousness.

"You better be ready to fly tomorrow," he said to Ikawa.

"Brother, are you insane?" Leti said protectively. "He'll be laid up for at least several days."

"I need him—in fact, I need all of you." The tone of his voice ended all dissent. "Word just came from Jartan. We must report to him in Asmara at once. Gorgon has made his first move."

Chapter 4

"My lord, there is an emissary from Boreas waiting to see you."

Pina, chief steward and battle advisor to Allic, nodded to the courtyard outside the main briefing room, where a solitary figure stood in the shadows.

Since Allic's hurried return to Landra on his way to his father's court in Asmara, the audience chamber had been a swirl of activity as the business which had piled up in his absence was quickly attended to.

"He's been waiting for you for three days," Pina said evenly. "I've assured him the delay is not intended as a slight, but he doesn't looked pleased."

"Boreas?" was Allic's astonished rejoinder.

Varma stopped in his rounds of refilling everyone's drinks and interjected, "I've tried to talk to him twice, and he's the coldest, most closemouthed sorcerer I've ever met."

Allic lifted an eyebrow at Pina.

"I agree with Varma—he's one of Boreas' descendants. He definitely has a touch of the Frost."

"Interesting," Allic mused. "By all means, bring him in."

As Pina left the room Mark spoke up.

"I don't believe I've ever heard the name Boreas. Is it a place or a person?"

"Boreas is one of the oldest demigods still living. He is the eldest child of Borc, the Creator that Horat killed to start the War of the Gods three thousand years ago."

Allic drained his mug and continued as Varma refilled it.

"Boreas is my cousin by blood, but over the years he has turned into something that I can't understand. His realm is in the far north, in the icefields and fjords of the polar ice cap. He is a creature of ice and bitter cold that few would want or could stand against."

Varma dropped his facade of the jester and once again revealed the brilliant mind that he hid from all but a few.

"The histories of the Great War mention that the Frost Demons attempted to attack Haven during the conflict and confusion. Boreas and his battle team went to their universe to, as he put it, 'have a little discussion.' He decimated three worlds before they were able to buy him off."

"It has never been proven that they bought him off," Allic snapped.

"Well, be that as it may, we can't dispute the fact that something broke the power of the fire demons at the battle of Grada. It has been implied many times that Boreas has a Great Weapon that not even the gods know about. He is a demigod cloaked in legends."

Allic gave a snort of disdain at Varma.

The door opened and Pina entered with a tall, lean sorcerer. Mark was impressed. Even the comfortable temperature of the room seemed to go down appreciably.

The man was dressed in gray and white, and his face was as devoid of emotion as a week-dead fish.

He stood before Allic and bowed.

"Prince Allic, I am Traca. I bring you greetings from your cousin Boreas, Prince of the North."

Allic waved an airy acknowledgment, and responded graciously. "It is always a pleasure to hear from Boreas. Would you care to sit down and join us in a drink?"

"No, thank you. I prefer to stand."

Allic's smile became a little less warm.

"So what message forces you to journey to this land of insufferable heat and effete Southerners?"

Even Traca's smile was wintry.

"Prince Allic, we of the North are not noted for our gregariousness. But, rest assured, I meant no insult to those who have had the honor of destroying the realm of that monster Sarnak."

Mark spoke before he could catch his loose tongue.

"Does that mean that you have had contacts with Sarnak also?"

"I see your education has been sadly neglected, Outlander. The heirs of Borc will hate Sarnak for as long as the universe lasts, and beyond. It is because of him that our father, the Creator Borc, was foully murdered by Horat—may his name be cursed for eternity."

Traca returned his attention to Allic.

"We have kept the Peace as we swore, though the thought of Sarnak living has been an intolerable burden to us for over three thousand years."

"All of Haven is aware of Boreas' restraint. It saved the lives of many during the exchange of prisoners," came Allic's soothing reply. "Now. Your message?"

For the first time emotion crossed Traca's face: an almost wistful eagerness.

"We of the North hope that you might have some inkling as to Sarnak's whereabouts, since you now have access to his castle and secret papers. I am authorized to offer a score of wall crystals to replace your losses if my lord Boreas has first chance to use such information and successfully takes Sarnak."

Mark could see that Allic was furious, but did an admirable job of keeping his temper.

"Traca, inform your lord that he can keep his crystals. When and if I can find such information, all those who have cause to hate Sarnak may join me in the chase."

"Very generous. In the name of my lord, I thank you!"

For another moment the look of eagerness lasted, and then was gone.

"There is one more matter that I am commanded to discuss. It is known that you have signed all the outlanders"—and here he turned to look at Ikawa and Mark—"to contracts in your service. It is further known that several have left you and are now on the rolls as Unta."

Mark glanced over at Ikawa and knew his friend was as pierced as he was by the knowledge that two of their party were now known as unspeakable and without honor for breaking their contracts. He turned to see Allic shaking his head at them, as if to say, the dishonor was not yours.

"Yes, it is so," Allic told Traca.

"Then let me inform you that Boreas wishes to buy the contract of the one called Giorgini."

There were gasps around the table, but Allic's face was expressionless.

"I'm sure you realize the implications of your last statement, messenger."

"Yes."

"What is your offer?"

"One wall crystal."

"A wall crystal for a contract that has a little over two years left? Most impressive."

Allic then turned to Mark.

"Mark, he was one of yours. What is your counsel?"

"I don't really understand all of this," Mark said hesitantly, "but if there is a chance to give Giorgini a way to redeem himself I'd say yes."

Allic turned back to Traca. "Inform your lord that I accept."

Traca nodded. "The wall crystal will be delivered in two days. With your permission I will wait until then to take possession of the contract."

With Allic's nod of acceptance, Traca turned again to Mark.

"Know, young sorcerer, that your man Giorgini was on his way back to you when he, uh, was delayed. It is my lord's intention to put his name back on the rolls."

Allic rapped the table with his mug, and with a calm voice that belied the anger on his face said, "Unnecessary, Traca. As of this moment I have ordered Giorgini's name restored to the rolls. Now, unless you have further business to discuss, you are excused from my presence."

Traca bowed and left.

"Would someone please explain to me what is going on about Giorgini?"

Ikawa was the first to answer.

"Either Boreas or one of his people has Giorgini, and they find him valuable. The key point here is when they got him."

Varma glanced at Allic. "The manner in which the contract was offered, and the excessive price, points to a border violation. In my opinion Boreas himself flew here as soon as he knew that Sarnak had broken the Sacred Truce. Boreas would give almost anything for the chance to kill Sarnak himself. He probably got here too late for Sarnak and took Giorgini instead, to get information."

Allic stirred at that. "Yes, that is how I see it. The wall crystal is a very sutble way of apologizing for intrusion and interference."

"Does that mean Giorgini is a prisoner?" asked Mark.

Allic glanced at Varma, who responded, "I'd guess not. The offer for the contract was straightforward."

Allic straightened. "Agreed. Giorgini has obviously offered to serve Boreas. Maybe without Younger's influence he will serve him as well as you have served me. Now let's call it a night. We leave for Asmara at first light tomorrow."

"I must have been dreaming," Imada whispered, looking up into her eyes.

"Just the bad dream, my lover," Vena replied, a gentle smile lighting her innocent features. "I heard you cry out."

Imada stirred and tried to sit up, but the lightheadedness returned. Languidly, he laid back down.

The world was such a kaleidoscope of colors, of drifting images, phantasms that could be real or just imagined. But he did not even care to find out if they were real or not. One should not question this quiet paradise of love.

The bad dream again. Funny, he could barely recall it now. He could still remember his friends, the captain who had always treated him with kindness, even Sergeant Saito, who bellowed like a bull, but was more like an older brother. Even the Americans, José and Kraut. He had never wanted to be a soldier, the thought of killing anyone had been so repugnant. And the Americans had proven to be not such bad fellows after all. Yes, he could remember them, and the vague desire to return to them. He must report to his friends, but what was it he was supposed to tell them?

Something had happened to him. Something horrible. He looked into Vena's eyes. Something had happened—but what was it?

"Can you remember your dream?" she asked, her brow knitted.

Had he been swimming? No, no, it had been next to a river, hadn't it?

Leaning over, her lips lightly brushed his.

Was that part of the nightmare as well? Yet even as he wondered, he could feel the first tingle of passion as the kiss became bolder.

A hushed moan of pleasure escaped her. Sitting up, she undid the shoulder clasp of her lavender and silver-laced gown. The gown slipped away, tumbling to her waist. Reaching to her side, she snapped loose the hip clasp and the gown fell away.

Smiling she brushed back her amber curls to expose the beauty of her breasts.

Still feeling lightheaded, but this time from the joy within him, Imada sat up as Vena pulled back the covers of his bed.

Together they fell back, now joined as one, their passion rising together, then ever so dreamily falling away.

Floating in a lovers' embrace, Imada opened his eyes. She lay beside him, her eyes sparkling with love.

"Without you I would be nothing," she sighed. "Don't ever leave me."

Imada pulled her close, and kissed her lightly on the forehead.

"Can you remember the fight, my love?" Her innocent features were aglow with admiration.

The fight? Yes—that was the nightmare. The party had been on patrol when Sarnak's demons had attacked. It had been a horrific siege, pinned down in a glade with no protection. One by one his comrades had fallen. Throughout that long night he had heard their cries as they were dragged off into the darkness to be tortured and killed.

Numbed, he had waited for the coming of morning and certain death, hiding by the river bank, wounded and waiting for the end. Somehow he could remember Yoshida's screams of agony.

Imada tried to block that memory. He had been struggling. It was in the water, wasn't it? Yes, in the water wrestling with a demon. That was it. The demon had pounced on him, and they were struggling in the water when Yoshida had cried out. What had happened to that demon? He must have killed it, otherwise he would now be dead.

With the rising of the sun he had found himself alone, the only survivor of the patrol, in the smoking ruins of the glade, with bodies scattered everywhere. And the enemy was gone.

He must have been in shock, he thought. What did the Americans call it? Combat fatigue. He had wandered, lost.

Lost until the dark smoke on the horizon told him of trouble. The sight of the demons circling the burning village had been the trigger to his rage at what had been done.

He looked back at Vena.

"You're thinking of the battle, aren't you, my love?"

Imada nodded.

"I'll always remember how you came to me," she said, her doelike eyes gazing into his.

"The demons had attacked just after dawn," she whispered, as if reciting a shared memory. "They must have been the same ones that attacked you the night before. We fought as best we could. Everything, everything was destroyed. My home, my friends, and my father." Tears began to fill her eyes.

"Don't cry, dearest," Imada whispered, kissing her tears away.

"Father was ill already," she said, trying to force a smile. "He had been a warrior under our lord Allic. He had always said he wished to die sword in hand, facing the enemy, and not wasted and old. He died as he wished, slaying the demon that killed him, singing his death song. It was as he desired, and for him I should be happy.

"I was ready to die," she went on grimly. "And then I saw you flying in like an avenger borne on the wind, descending out of the sun, flame arching from your hand, your battle cry like thunder.

"Oh, how they fled before your rage," she said excitedly. "I thought first that perhaps you must be a god. Sometimes I still believe that."

Imada blushed at the open admiration in her innocent eyes.

She giggled softly. "Forgive me; I do love you so. I dream of the day I can tell our grandchildren how you came thus to save me."

Imada laughed and hugged her. Never would they be separated! "It's still kind of hard to remember it all."

She paused for a moment, looking at him with concern. "You do remember most of it, though, don't you?"

"You're helping me to," he replied with a smile.

"You fought your way to me. A demon slashed you here." She pointed to the furled scar on his shoulder. "Yet still you came for me. And picking me up, you flew off. They chased us here, into the mountains, until you finally lost them. Only then did you finally collapse, near the edge of death from your wounds, which were poisoned.

"I knew of this cave. Being on the border marches, Father had prepared this place if there was an emergency. Even as a child, I could have found this place blindfolded. He had thought of everything, hiding bedding, clothes, weapons, and food, if ever we should have need of a place to hide. And so I carried you here after your collapse and brought you back to health."

A look of concern washed over her.

"And now you seem to be healed and ready to travel once again."

"We'll always be one," he murmured.

"But you must go back to your friends, and to our lord Allic."

Yes, that was his name: Allic. Now the memory seemed so much clearer. Allic was his daimyo, his warlord, and he must obey as a samurai. There was actually a moment of pleasure in that realization. He was a samurai of Allic's. In his own world he had never wanted to be a soldier, but as a child he had thrilled with the legendary heroes of the civil wars, and the struggle for the Shogunate. Now he had powers surpassing even those of Norgunata or the forty-seven ronin. He had his duty.

Yet there was Vena.

"You can fly back with me to Landra. As I saved your life, so you saved mine. Nothing will ever keep us apart. I could not live without you."

"You seem so much stronger already, even as you talk about it," Vena said. "Think how excited your friends will be to see you. You've been gone nearly four months, my love."

"Four months!"

Startled, he sat straight up, looking anxiously around.

"The demon's poison worked deep into your soul," Vena said soothingly, sitting up alongside him. "You did not even stir until several weeks back. It took all the skill I had to bring you back to me."

How could this be? Imada wondered. They must think him dead, a prisoner, or even a deserter and coward.

"I have to get back," he said anxiously.

"Another day or two at most," Vena said.

"At least let me get up and walk about outside."

"No, my love," Vena said soothingly. "The demons know that you are hiding someplace in these hills. They have not stopped searching. I have snuck out at dusk to gather herbs for your broth, and every time I leave I can see them circling. You are still a bit shaky, you could make a mistake out there and be seen. You see, my dear, you might have the power of a god, but my father taught me woodcraft, and I think I know a bit more about such things than you."

Her voice filled with a note of pride as she spoke. Smiling, Imada found he could not argue with her.

"And speaking of broth, I've made some for you." As she left his bed, the fire's glow cast its light on her long legs and taut, rounded body. Her hair swayed provocatively as she walked across the room toward a small cauldron. She scooped out a greenish foam into a wood bowl and brought it back to him.

Playfully, he reached out to her, his arms encircling her waist as she sat down.

"My, you certainly are regaining your strength. But drink this first. It's good for you and will drive out any nightmares you might still have."

Leaning over, she brought the bowl to his lips. The drink was pungent, with a faint bitterness that made him wrinkle his nose.

Even before he had finished, the kaleidoscope of colors returned, washing over him like the lapping of waves upon the beach.

He looked up into Vena's eyes, which looked at him with a knowing gaze.

"When you wake up," she whispered, "you'll feel strong enough to travel. In fact you will find yourself already on the way home."

He could barely see her now.

"We'll always love each other, won't we, Imada?"

He tried to nod but he wasn't even sure anymore if he could move.

"You'll dream only of what we have talked about: How you fought demons in the glade and came to rescue me. And of course you'll dream most wonderfully of what we have done here alone."

He sighed and drifted away.

Standing, she swept up her gown and refastened the clasps.

She heard a door open and the echo of footsteps. A shadow appeared in the entryway, which had been so cunningly hidden to make the room appear to truly be a darkened cave.

"He's ready," Patrice said. "As soon as our informant passes the word from Landra we'll move him to the drop-off point. Until then make sure he stays drugged and asleep."

Vena looked down at Imada and smiled softly, almost feeling a twinge of regret for deceiving him.

Without comment, Patrice turned away and left the room, Vena following in her wake.

Patrice looked over her shoulder at Vena. Despite the centuries of service the sorcerer had given her, she could almost suspect the beginning of a bond between the two.

Perhaps that was for the best. Through Imada's miraculous return, Vena would be infiltrated first into Allic's circle, and from there into Jartan's court.

He would have to report to Landra itself with such information. The memory wash had been thorough, so no amount of mental probing could break that. It was Vena's cover that would still be tricky. Tonight her memory would be washed as well, her mind and identity changed over completely to the real Vena, who had actually been captured in the raid staged on the border village months ago. The girl had been difficult to break, Patrice thought dryly, but all the necessary details of her life had been wrung from her before they were finished.

Now the new Vena would assume all those memories into the core of her soul and not just act them as she had been doing the last three months. If her mind was probed, there would not be the slightest cause for concern.

Once in Jartan's court, Patrice's agents would bring Vena out of her memory wash when the time came so that she could perform her real mission—to steal the Fire Crystals, so that the set would be complete, and to take as well the Portal Gem of Horat, which would open pathways into whatever universes Patrice desired.

She looked over at "Vena," whom she had known for so long

as Ulinda. Ulinda had certainly loved the new form created for her, but then, the aging crone had always loved it when Patrice had worked her spells and made her momentarily young once again.

It was as always an excellent lever for keeping her under control.

Patrice smiled at her companion. "You seemed to enjoy your little playtime today," she said, in an open, almost humorous tone.

"It is hard not to, with him," Vena replied, her guard slipping. "He's so innocent and trusting."

"You'll learn different before this is done."

Suddenly nervous, Vena looked at her mistress. But there was no anger or jealousy on her face—only an almost wistful sadness.

Patrice's hand reached out to brush Vena's hair back from her eyes.

"Come with me, my dear. It's time we finished my work with you." Together the two slipped out of the room.

Chapter 5

He had grown to love the North, Giorgini reflected, standing at the crest of the hill overlooking the harbor. The cliffs of the fjord reflected the light of the rising sun and the interplay of reddish glow with the darkness of the areas still in shadow made it a scene of pristine beauty.

The water was still unfrozen, although shards of ice in the harbor forewarned of the coming winter. At that time the normal hulled vessels would be beached and the ice schooners would be brought out.

In many ways both the land and the people were what he thought the Scandinavian countries of his own world must be like. Although Earth never had the special crops and trees adapted to the winter climate the way this world did. Hell, even the moss that grew on the rocks was edible.

The cold wind gusted suddenly and brought tears to his eyes, and he hastily raised his shield a little. Sorcerers up here had no trouble keeping warm even on the coldest days, at least as long as they could keep power up, and their crystals were undamaged. *God knows how the normals do it,* he thought.

Still, they were probably acclimated to it. They certainly seemed to relish it.

A chill suddenly seemed to penetrate the power of his shield, but he knew by now what caused this particular cold. Turning, he saw the demigod Boreas coming in to land beside him.

Boreas was a giant of a man, as shaggy as a bear. Red hair seemed to cover practically every square inch of his body, and the flowing red beard hid his face.

The most striking thing about him, however, was his eyes. Killer's eyes, Giorgini decided once again; the eyes of an eternal hard case, who was in trouble in every sleazy bar in the universe and would never say no to a fight.

71

Boreas glanced once over the harbor as if to insure that there were no problems, and then addressed Giorgini in a voice as cold as the winter sea.

"Word has come in from Traca. Allic has restored your name to the rolls and sold your contract to me."

"Thank you, my lord. I am grateful."

"Allic has made good use of your brethren in the South, and I expect you to be of similar value to me. He certainly was none too pleased with your behavior, but said he'd let it pass since you had fought with valor and everybody was half crazed with fatigue by the time the battle ended. He stipulated that I was to 'kick your ass' for awhile to teach you a damn good lesson, though."

"I'm offering no excuses, my lord," Giorgini replied evenly. "I screwed up and I'll admit it. It won't happen again."

Boreas paused to study Giorgini, and the look seemed to read his very soul.

Giorgini had been up here for months and had dealt with Boreas many times before. He met the probe squarely, unafraid.

"You have attended enough of our council meetings to know what I require."

"Sarnak."

"You say that so lightly. Have you any idea what it means to us of Borc's blood?"

"Boreas, I don't feel it the way you and your people do, but I can understand it. And I have a score of my own to settle with him, so I will help as best as I can."

Again there was silence as Boreas turned to regard his harbor, and then glanced at his castle overlooking the city. It was made of stone, cut and polished to such a brightness that at night it seemed to be made of ice, and here in the early morning sun shimmered with the color of blood-red gold.

"Giorgini, before I decided to bring you into my service I investigated you and the other outlanders very thoroughly. I know that you are capable of the same kind of talent as Jartan's farsearch specialist, Kochanski."

Giorgini was impressed. That meant that Boreas knew he had been the radar fire control operator in the old B-29 they had flown back in China, while Kochanski was radar.

"I could direct the guns by radar. I'd track them as they came in, then use the information to train all the guns. Kochanski used long-range radar for navigation and detection. But the jobs were similar, and from what you've told me it seems that what we learned on Earth enhances certain skills here on Haven."

"I freely admit that we have already learned several things from you," Boreas replied, "although your knowledge and talents in other areas need vast improvement."

Giorgini nodded.

"However, it is your potential as a farsearcher that I require. I am assigning a team of my best sorcerers to assist you in one task to the exclusion of all others."

He hesitated as if having trouble saying the word, so Giorgini supplied it.

"Sarnak."

"Yes. He has seemingly vanished from the face of Haven. I have had scores of spies at work for months and they have found no trace of him. It was thought that he might go to his uncle Tor's realm after his death, but nothing has been heard even there.

"Giorgini, Sarnak's death *must* be at my hands. I must find him before someone else kills him—and I will do anything necessary to achieve it."

Giorgini had his shield raised to the maximum and was still being overcome by the wave of cold and hatred emanating from Boreas.

"My lord. Your aura," he gasped.

Instantly Boreas regained his control. "Find him for me, and you may name your own reward."

Giorgini nodded in an outward show of calm, but underneath he was terrified. *God in heaven,* he thought, *I don't even know how to start.* And he shivered again.

"The god, Jartan."

Mark, Ikawa, and their companions came instantly to attention, as did the eight hundred other sorcerers and demigods assembled in the vast planning room.

A pillar of light congealed at the apex of the horseshoe-shaped conference table where the demigods sat, facing the assembly.

The form wavered and coalesced into the brightly glowing image of a man.

"Be seated," Jartan intoned, and the group settled into their straightback chairs.

Already the whole operation bore in Mark's mind a remark-able resemblance to a bombing mission planning session. The walls behind Jartan were lined with charts and maps. The one remarkable new twist, however, was the three dimensional image that appeared to float in the middle of the room.

A green-blue ball several feet across occupied the center of the horseshoe. Upon it, in absolute detail, was the planetary surface of Haven. When he had first entered the room, Mark had gone up to the globe to touch it, but his hand went right through the image.

When he drew close, he was amazed to see that the fine detail was even three dimensional, showing the rise of mountain ranges, cities, rivers, and even the most important roads. Examining the city of Landra and concentrating on the image he was startled when a small pie-shaped section in the area around Landra rose out of the globe, drifted out for a foot, then increased its scale a hundred times, so that individual buildings were now easily discernable. He concentrated again on this section. Again a segment rose out another foot, expanding out a hundredfold so that the finest details of Allic's still damaged palace hovered before him.

He withdrew his thoughts and the first segment retracted to the second and the second back into the main globe. He could have spent days examining the world thus, but the room was filling quickly and there had not been time. Now he wished that he had spent more time examining a couple of the other displays.

For a while the green globe of Haven occupied the center of the display. Around it, in varying sizes, were thirty other worlds, some only a foot in diameter, one—a gas giant up toward the ceiling and orbited by a dozen moons—several yards across.

Each of the other globes had at least one green dot upon it; several had a dozen or more. He noticed a couple that had flashing yellow spots on their surfaces. But there was one, off at the very edge of the display, nearly five feet across, with a single grey moon orbiting it, that had half a dozen dots upon the surface. One dot was still flashing yellow, one dot was a steady red, the other four were flashing red.

Without asking, Mark could sense this extraordinary meeting had been called because of whatever was occurring on that world. They had rushed here almost nonstop, spending one evening in Landra as Allic called in his remaining sorcerers, then winging northward. With only the most hurried of stops for food and a snatch of sleep they had flown through the day and far into the night. There had been no rest even then, just time to change uniforms, shave, shower, and then appear for this predawn meeting. Now they would finally get some answers.

"My friends, we face a most dangerous situation." Jartan began evenly, his voice edged with concern. "Many of you might know small parts of the story."

There was a stirring in the room as the assembled men and women looked at each other. There was going to be action, that was obvious.

"Gorgon has always been a threat to our realms. For those of you with memories before the Great War, you will recall that he has been met on more than one field of action."

At the mere mention of the demonlord's name, Mark felt the cold chill of the nightmare returning. The dream was always the same, the demon closing in, leering. The horror of it was that he was paralyzed like a fly in a web, unable to move as the demon tore open his body and pulled the still pulsing heart out of his chest.

"Some of you have personally fought Gorgon and his demons. Many of you have seen the spirits of your friends dragged off to torments undreamed."

Mark nervously slipped a sidelong glance at Allic and could see the slightest of tremors crease his features. Palms damp with sweat, Mark leaned back and tried to stare straight ahead.

"Working together, we Creators have been able to erect barriers to protect Haven. A fair part of our Essence has gone into the creation of these walls.

"Yet there are ways he could enter. Small openings can be created through which he and his most powerful demons may reach out and speak to those foolish enough to hear him. Always he has been probing in such ways, ready to seduce someone into becoming his confederate. His lesser demons can even slip through such narrow openings, to act as his messenger or his instrument of terror and spying. But the walls we have generated are too strong for anyone of great power to slip through.

"But there are the outer worlds."

As he spoke Jartan pointed to the green world in the far corner. The galaxy of planets hovering in the middle of the room started to shift and spin. Rotating in a vast circle, the green planet called Yuvin, with its ominous red dots, drifted to the middle of the room.

"We must keep portals open to other worlds, to other dimensions, for trade, for knowledge. To seal ourselves off forever would cause us to grow weak, and leave us open in the end to perhaps far greater dangers.

"The outlanders present among us," and he pointed to where the Americans and Japanese sat, "are a case in point. We still know nothing of where their world is located, or even which dimension it belongs to. Yet somehow a portal was opened to them. Fortunately for us," and his voice showed a touch of affection, "they have proven to be staunch friends and allies."

Allic visibly swelled at the mention of his vassals and nodded approvingly.

"Yet nevertheless they were a surprise. It is therefore far better for us to reach out first, exploring the edges of our dimension and investigating others. Out there," and he pointed vaguely at the collection of worlds, "we can discover who our neighbors are. If we find friends, so much the better. If we find enemies, it will be on their territory and not our own beloved world.

"Thus the portals we maintain must be kept open. Now it appears that Gorgon might have broken through to such an outer world. If he is successful and masters that portal, he will have access straight to our colony worlds, and be that much closer to Haven."

"Could we not simply close off all the portals now, pulling back our outposts and settlements at once?" asked Macha from his vantage in the back of the room.

Mark looked over at he who had once been his enemy and

wished he could slide a bit lower in his seat. It was the first time he had seen the demigod since the time he had fought him in the battle before the pass. He hoped old grudges had been forgotten, but after all, during the conflict he had kicked Macha in the family jewels—an insulting blow that was now the topic of many a whispered joke.

"I'm surprised one with your combative spirit would ask such a question," Jartan replied smoothly.

"Some of the weak-livered among us might not have the courage to ask," Macha replied sharply. "You know my feelings on it, and I'd challenge anyone here who doubted my wish for an occasional good fight with that scum. I just thought I'd ask for those who don't have the courage to do the asking."

Jartan chuckled softly at the reply.

Mark shot a quick look over at Macha, who now stood tall with shoulders back, his black mane tied off in a simple queue. And Macha was looking straight back at him, his eyes cold. Squirming inwardly, Mark tried to hold the gaze, and fortunately Jartan started to talk again so he had reason to look away.

"If we abandon all our outposts, Gorgon will have won a great victory. Dozens of pathways would have to be shut down and guarded, and we would be totally on the defensive. He chose the location well: a main outpost that in turn has portals to most of our other worlds."

Jartan nodded towards the display. Suddenly a filigree of gold threads knitted the various worlds together. The greatest bundle came up from the surface of Haven, with a half dozen or more lines going straight to the world under attack. Yet from that planet, thirty or more lines arced out further, striking nearly every other world in the display.

"Take Yuvin, and he can push his way through to everything else. Eventually he would find some unguarded point and reach us here.

"That is why we must meet him there." So saying, Jartan seemed almost to reach out and cup the world in his hands.

"Once defeated, we must pursue him, through dimension after dimension if necessary, shutting down his portals, sealing him back into the hell which he came from. Perhaps then he will leave us alone."

"Let's just kill the bastard," Macha growled.

"A tall wish indeed," Jartan replied, "and a task which even I might find to be a challenge."

"How do we know it *is* Gorgon?" Cinta, one of Jartan's court sorcerers, asked. "What evidence do we have?"

As the sorcerer spoke, Mark glanced at Ikawa. The Japanese officer had met Cinta in combat for the possession of Leti's Crystal of the Sun, and had barely defeated him. The slightest of contemptuous smiles crossed Ikawa's features, and he gave a merry wink to Mark.

"I was getting to that," Jartan replied.

There was no reproach in the god's voice, but the sorcerer cringed slightly.

"There are a number of reports regarding actions here on Haven. Allic, would you please begin."

The lord of Landra stood and strode to the open end of the horseshoe.

Bowing to his father, he began, describing the incident at Sarnak's portal and mentioning as well the threat both to Mark and himself.

As Allic spoke, Mark fixed his gaze straight ahead, closing his mind to keep the memory away. Several in the group turned back to look at him with open concern. Fortunately Storm kept her eyes straight ahead as well, an action which Mark was grateful for, else he would seem her protected and worried-over lover, not a powerful sorcerer in his own right. He did notice, though, the sharp look from Macha—an almost smiling gaze that seemed to say it served him right.

Allic then went back into events covering a period long before the arrival of the outlanders: Dealings with Sarnak and vague comments from that direction which might have new meaning in light of the discovered portal. He ended with the review of evidence discovered only recently of a small village in the mountains that had been hit hard, with all inhabitants either slain or kidnapped. They had been attacked by demons, but not demons of Haven from all appearances.

After Allic, Storm spoke, and then Leti, relating events on the outpost worlds they had patrolled in the last several years. Macha followed, speaking as a representative of the god Minar, for there had been several unexplained occurrences in his distant realm as well.

"So that is the past record of evidence," Jartan finally declared. "Now to the recent events:

"Word came via a messenger ten days ago that an outpost had detected a disturbance indicating that a portal of some significance had been opened.

"I sent a messenger to bring me a standard report. He did not return.

"Three days later I sent out a triad, led by one of my best sorcerers, Suda Codi."

There was a murmur in the room. Mark remembered the woman from his first visit to the city. She was a vivacious character, full of life, and with a reputation as a voracious lover—an experience he had never sampled, though Walker had strutted about for days with a grin of delight after an alleged meeting.

"There was no report from them as well. Finally I sent three more. One came back and died within minutes of his arrival."

Mark could see Walker leaning forward anxiously.

"Four of the six outposts had been overwhelmed and destroyed. A vast and impenetrable energy field had been erected about the fifth and sixth, through which nothing could pass. The fifth outpost was already in flames and aswarm with demons.

"The messenger told me that he had personally recognized one of the leaders of the attack. It was Jujatag, third demon lord of Gorgon's realm."

An angry stir swept the hall.

"And Suda Codi?" Walker asked nervously, coming to his feet.

"I'm sorry, but there is nothing to report on her."

Walker sat back down, his countenance grim. Sergeant Saito leaned over and put a hand on his shoulder, while Shigeru, the wrestler and staunch follower of Walker's, growled darkly at his friend's pain.

"This, therefore, is the plan," Jartan continued. "I will send another recon team in."

"But two have been annihilated already," Storm interjected.

"What hope will a third have unless it is a significant part of our strength? If that's the case, then we should send everything in an all-out sweep."

"We still aren't sure of what we face. It could be a mere strike by one of the minor demonlords either as harassment or as an outright bid. If that is the case, then several of our demigods can handle it. If it is Gorgon, I want to know before we go in."

"And if it *is* Gorgon?" Storm asked.

"Then we must strip our defenses dangerously thin. I myself shall go, leaving my realm in the hands of the gods Chosen, and Minar. Macha will act as liaison to Minar through this crisis."

There were nervous mutterings in the room. Jartan's leaving would leave his realm underprotected in case of attack from another quarter. Though he was not yet sure of all the implications of power, Mark nevertheless grasped the fact that if Jartan had been away when Tor and Sarnak had struck, the end result of the last war might have gone differently.

"To go myself if there is merely a diversion would leave us vulnerable here. To send my sons, daughters, and sorcerers without my support could result in a disaster if Gorgon himself has passed through. We must know more first.

"That is why I have gathered all of you together: to be ready at an instant's notice. I am now declaring a full state of emergency. Know that my security teams have already gone to operational status.

"I know this might be rough on some of you, being called in without any explanation to your families. I'm sorry for that, but the situation demands it. All of you will be required to stay within the confines of my palace, and I have made every effort to see to each of your needs."

He paused for a moment, the pulsing glow of his form now tinged with blue.

"Though I loathe to say this, I must. Any attempt to communicate with anyone outside of this palace or to leave the grounds shall be punished severely. I know we are all comrades here, but the wiles of Gorgon are legend. If you detect the slightest oddity in behavior, even of your closest friend, I regret to say you must report it immediately. I would rather have my security people track down a thousand false leads, than to discover too late that one of you revealed what has been said here this morning."

The room was silent, with many sorcerers looking nervously at each other.

"We understand each other. All of you are dismissed; clear this room at once. If we mobilize, you must be ready with full fighting gear in a quarter turning's time.

"I want Allic, Storm, Leti, Macha, and the offworlders to stay here."

"Uh-oh," Goldberg exhaled softly, "I think we've drawn the shit detail."

Mark looked over at his old flight engineer and smiled. He hadn't seen Goldberg since after the battle of Landra. Once he'd recovered from his wounds, Goldberg had been sent out on an embassy and reparations team to help settle the costs of damages and injuries during the brief war between Macha and Allic.

Mark came up to Goldberg's side and shook his hand with obvious delight.

"I think you're right," Mark said quietly as they walked through the stream of sorcerers leaving the room. "How was the assignment?"

"Great," Goldberg grinned. "Macha sure can throw one mean party when he sets a mind to it. I was living better than Errol Flynn and Cary Grant rolled up in one. I'll tell you about Macha's granddaughter when I've got the time—in fact I might even be an in-law before long."

Mark grinned in return. He'd always had a special fondness for Goldberg.

"But let me tell you something, boss," Goldberg went on, "Whenever your name comes up around Macha, boy does his blood boil. He heard a couple of his guys cracking a joke about what you did to him. Why, he tore off his crystals and fought both of them bare-knuckled, not a lick of magic or crystals in the fight—and beat them to a pulp."

Mark looked over at Macha, who was moving up to the half circle within the horseshoe.

"What a fight! It was better than Louis and Dempsey—and I was at that fight. Macha could put Joe Louis on his back and out for the count with a single punch."

"Great, glad to hear it," Mark replied dryly.

"But what the hell," Goldberg continued, "from the sound of things I've got a gut feeling we're in the barrel again and no mistake. So why worry about him? Anyhow, let's go hear the bad news."

Falling silent, they joined the rest of the group.

Jartan drifted over to the table, and his pulsing image dropped to almost human height.

"This I wanted to share only with you alone," he said quietly. "There has been some concern about security here. In fact, some of this is a test. The information I gave out was important, to be sure, but if Gorgon should hear of it, it will not be devastating. This part of the briefing, however, could only be shared with the team that will have to take direct part in it."

The offworlders looked at each other nervously and Goldberg nodded at the correctness of his prediction.

"Kochanski, would you step forward please."

Feeling a little shy, Kochanski came up to stand by Jartan's side.

"Your friend has mastered some rather unique skills in the time he has spent with me. He can tell you about the Godchair later and what he has learned and can do. He is the best I have seen with it in many a century. Though I am loath to send him into peril, there is no other way."

The note of concern in Jartan's voice was obvious to everyone. Kochanski looked over at Jartan with open affection.

"I am sending Kochanski and Leti in as a team using the Godchair. Kochanski will guide it; Leti will reconnoiter, and if need be, defend against any assault. First I want confirmation of Gorgon's whereabouts. Beyond that I need to know the size of his forces and what we shall need for an effective counterstrike.

"Though it was not revealed during the briefing, I have a secret outpost on the moon orbiting the world under attack."

As he spoke, the planet drifted before him. A green light appeared on the surface of the icy moon.

"I am sending the rest of you in under Allic's command as a support team for Kochanski and Leti in case of trouble. You are to establish your base there in secret, and then the two of them will venture down to where the attacks are taking place. Macha, you will stay here as a direct liaison to your father. Storm, you will serve as a liaison from the team to me. Position yourself in the hills beyond their outpost in case they are suddenly cut off."

Kochanski stood before the group, proud of the trust placed in him, yet obviously nervous as well.

"My tactical officers will brief you on the details. There are other issues I must attend to now. Good luck to all of you."

Without waiting for a response, Jartan simply disappeared.

"The shit's gonna hit the fan," Goldberg whispered.

Chapter 6

"Allic will be leading what is believed to be a reinforced reconnaisance team out before daylight tomorrow. Jartan has brought his people to the highest state of readiness; his sorcerers and allies are standing by to leave within a quarter turning's notice. Jartan further stated that they will either be facing Gorgon or his lieutenants."

"Are you sure this report is accurate?" Patrice inquired sharply.

"Yes, my lady," the sorcerer said evenly, her eyes lowered. "The proper security combination code was included."

"Excellent! Have the team pick up Imada and meet me here." She dismissed the messenger and walked back into her private suite.

Drawing close to the raised dais in the center of the room, she paused a moment to admire her creation.

Ulinda no longer existed. She had indeed become Vena in body and soul. The innocent-looking girl was still in the magically induced slumber that was required for the final mental implanting. After awaking, and until such time as the proper code words were spoken to her, she would appear to the world as a twenty-year-old girl, daughter of a dead border guard. Once the hidden Ulinda had been activated, she would already have passed through the rigid security checks, and from there the slipping into Jartan's crystal vault would not be too difficult, especially when the majority of his forces had been diverted elsewhere.

Patrice felt a ripple of pride. Not many others could work such a transformation, both inwardly and outwardly. And there were not many who could have conceived of a plan so simple and yet so cunningly elaborate. Even that fool Gorgon was playing his part and could be controlled.

A gentle sigh escaped Vena, as if she was lost in a pleasant dream.

Almost lovingly, Patrice brushed the hair out of her eyes. She had been drawn to the real Vena. There was a combative defiance to the girl that she had found all too appealing. The draining away of her memory and spirit had been in many ways a painful task. She had been glad in the end to slip the poison into the girl's drink and end the ordeal.

She leaned over, brushing her lips against Vena, and lingered for a moment. The girl sighed, a smile lighting her features. Patrice felt a rising temptation to continue, but finally drew away.

A moment later there was a knock on the door: the four sorcerers who would escort Patrice's spy. One of them carried Imada, who was still in a drugged sleep. She felt a slight wave of revulsion at the sight of the outlander dressed in Allic's livery.

"Pick up the girl," she commanded. "It's time to move." Then she waved the team of sorcerers into her private bedroom balcony.

"Send the security team up," Patrice whispered into her communications crystal.

A moment later she saw a dozen shadows rise from a lower battlement and spiral upward through the darkness.

"All clear," a voice whispered back.

"Let's go then," Patrice commanded.

Four sorcerers, two to each sleeping burden, lifted into the sky, with Patrice in the middle.

Once clear of the city, they would follow her plan, which had been rehearsed half a dozen times. The party would skim low over the hills and mountains as they skirted what had once been Sarnak's realm, and reach their destination—the charred remains of Vena's village—before dawn.

Once there, Patrice would lift the sleeping spell and withdraw before the two woke up. She would have a long day of hiding in the hills, to avoid the chance of being spotted. Strict communications silence would have to be maintained throughout the day, but once darkness settled again she could return home.

The plan was now begun. She felt a swelling of confidence for what would be an almost inevitable victory.

*   *   *

Kochanski was waiting when Allic and the others came out of Jartan's briefing room. The moment the Americans saw him there was a round of good-natured greetings and back slaps.

"Must be tough to be permanently stationed here in the lap of luxury," teased Goldberg.

"Hell, Kochanski. Who was it who gave that assistant of Colonel Guest's back in China a hard time for being such an asskisser?" added Walker.

Kochanski's face started to flush and Mark interrupted smoothly, "In case you clowns don't remember, it was Kochanski who discovered the existence of Sarnak's tunnels and saved our collective butts."

Walker winked at Mark and continued, "Sure, Captain. But what's he done since then except lay around here, chase women, and pull soft duty?"

There was a roar of laughter which even Kochanski joined.

"Damn, I missed you guys," Kochanski choked. "How about we go get a drink?"

Then all eyes were on Sara as she entered the room, earning an appreciative whistle from Walker.

Sara gave the others a casual nod, but all her attention was on Kochanski.

Eyes filling with tears, she burst out, "Jartan won't let me go with you. I've told him that I was the best one to mindmesh with you during the recon, but he says I'm too young and he's going to give the job to Leti."

Kochanski was horrified at the mere thought of Sara going into danger. Thank heavens Jartan felt the same way. He looked at her appreciatively. There was only a six-year age difference between them, but that was a hell of a gulf when it was the difference between seventeen and twenty-three. Still, in another year or two . . . He pushed the thought aside. In another day or two he might not even be alive, let alone a year or so. Their eyes held for a second, and then he resumed his gruff attitude towards her.

"Good. Because no way would I risk your life like that."

At this Sara burst into tears. "Kochanski, what if I never see you again?"

He patted her shoulder clumsily.

"Hell, don't worry about me. Didn't you once say that the gods seem to protect the ignorant, or something like that?"

Tears still flowed over her cheeks, but Sara regained her composure somewhat.

"Jartan had agreed to let me have part of my dowry early. And I am giving this to you." Handing Kochanski the large portal crystal they had been working with, she continued, "This crystal is already attuned to both our Essences, and I have lowered the detection ratio to as small as possible. Wearing this, you should be almost impossible to be found and . . . and . . . "

Breaking into tears again, she gave Kochanski a hug that damn near broke some ribs, then ran from the hall.

Kochanski stared after her a moment, glanced down at the crystal in his hand, shook his head, and turned around.

Facing him was a sea of broad grins. His face immediately turned bright scarlet, and the grins widened even more.

"I'm going to beat the shit out of the first one of you filthy minded idiots that says something," he grated.

"Hell, Kochanski, none of us here would dream of saying a word. Would we, guys?" responded Walker.

The overdone chorus of *Noooooos* frustrated him even more.

The old druid had never relaxed his vigilance. He who had opposed Caius Julius Caesar for so many years was aware of the almost superhuman competence of the man. When the druid had talked the various nations of Gaul into supporting Vercingetorix's revolt against Rome, he had assured them of Caesar's defeat. That Caesar had won after being outnumbered by over ten to one was beyond belief.

With the price that Caesar had put on his head, he had fled to the western isle to try and stir up support for their Celtic brothers in Gaul.

While there he had heard reports that Caesar was preparing an army and an invasion fleet to folow him.

It was while performing a ritual at the ancient, sacred temple of the old ones called Stonehenge that he had been transported here.

The old sorcerer who had brought him to Haven had been

delighted at his catch, since he had been merely fishing, as he called it, in his exploration of the various universes.

They had taught each other much over the years, and the druid had quickly become a master sorcerer. When his friend eventually died, the druid used his talents, knowledge, and love to create a realm of forest and water. Within a few years he had built the kind of enchanted kingdom that was his version of the Blessed Isle.

But, always aware of Caesar's undying enmity, he had suspected that Caesar would petition the very gods themselves to follow him. Apparently the bastard had finally found him.

Calling in his descendants and the tribes of his nation, he informed them that Caesar had come at last. War was coming, and all those who were prepared as spies and informers knew their assignments. The moment any strangers arrived on the Isle, he was to be informed.

"I believe they will not come openly as assassins, so do not be taken in by any stories they might tell. All know what a death-trap our forests are to those who fly above, so look for them to infiltrate by land.

"I have promised that they shall die the sacred wicker death, so great care must be taken to capture them alive. Their blackened skulls will serve as a token of the greatness of the true faith!"

And the assembled nation rose to cheer their Messiah.

"All right, let's take this from the top of the list."

Jen Valenta, Jartan's master armorer, stood before the reconnaisance team. Though a sorcerer of less than fifty years of age, she had a remarkable skill with weapons and phenomenal memory for detail, combined with a beautiful physique, wavy dark hair, catlike eyes, and a stunning ivory complexion.

"Let's start with defensive crystals." So saying, she lifted her left hand.

The group followed suit and snapped their shields up to full intensity. A half dozen of Jen's assistants walked down the double line of offworlders. One fired a quick shot at Kraut's shield, intently studying the flash of light and its dissipation.

Motioning for Kraut to shut his shielding off, he reached into a pouch and quickly replaced Kraut's gem. Stepping back he motioned for him to power up again. There was another shot, the assistant nodded with satisfaction, then continued down the line.

"Next, offensive crystals."

One by one, the group stepped up to a firing line to one side of the vast armaments hall and fired off a rapid series of shots, ending with Allic and Leti disintegrating the stone target which the offworlders had merely chipped.

"Now check that your communications crystals are properly linked."

One by one the group patched into Allic, who had stepped to the far end of the room while Jen watched intently.

"All your primary weapons check out satisfactory. Next, check that your emergency backup crystals, offensive, defensive, and communication, are securely hidden and tied."

Ikawa bent over, and slipped his hand inside his right boot. Pressed up against either side of his Achilles tendon he felt the small leather pouches which held the precious reserves.

"Your medical emergency kit, locator beacon crystal, emergency rations, and survival blanket should all be secured to your backpack harness. Please check your combat partner."

Ikawa turned to Mark, who gave him a grim smile.

"It's almost like the old days, just before a raid," Mark said, as Ikawa opened the backpack and checked to make sure all items were in place and secured. Mark in turn reviewed Ikawa's equipment.

"Team leaders and section leaders should have destination maps secured to their belts. All members should have escape rendezvous maps, wrapped around an acid vial. If you fear capture, be sure to strike the vial. Remember the vial will also shatter if your shielding goes down and you are hit by an energy bolt."

Ikawa reached into the pouch about his waist, drew out and checked the small leather bundles, and gently resecured it.

"Finally, all of you have a poison pellet attached to a left upper molar."

Nervously, Ikawa let his tongue run against the projection.

"I know it must make all of you nervous to have it there. Believe me, it is secure—no amount of chewing, or any type of normal mouth movement, will disturb it."

"If you're wrong, lady, I'm coming back and filing a complaint," Walker retorted, but his humor fell flat, so tense was the group at the prospect of what was ahead.

Jen smiled at Walker's bravado. "To activate the pellet you must stick a finger into your mouth and scratch it as hard as you can with your fingernail. Two seconds after you do that, a highly potent poison gas will be released. If an enemy is close by, you can take him with you by simply exhaling. The poison is quick and painless. Ten seconds after you activate it, you will be gone."

The group looked nervously at each other.

"This is not normal procedure. Quarter is usually given and sorcerer prisoners accorded some rights, since guild laws are so strong, and not even a demigod would want a guild to blacklist him. But believe me, you do not want to be taken alive by the demon lords."

Her words were sharp and forceful. The demon lords could kill your body, of course—and death would be a blessing. But if their hatred for you was strong, they would work their incantations over you as you died, then capture your soul before it fled to the Sea of Chaos and hold you in their torment for eternity.

It was a power that even the gods of Haven had not mastered—nor desired to control.

"If all equipment is in place," Jen continued, "you should now don your cold weather gear."

Going over to a long rack of clothing, Ikawa pulled down the fur-lined parka, hood, boots, and leggings, all of which were camouflage white, that had been tailor-made for him only hours before. He found it unusual to be in heavy clothing again, for with his shield he could go out in any type of weather. Yet it might be necessary to hide from a sweep, and shielding could reveal their position.

Suited up, he went back to stand before his men and give them a final check-through. Then he turned about and came to attention, his men following suit, with Mark's contingent falling in alongside.

Jen made a final inspection, nodding her approval, and then, with a salute to Allic, Storm, and Leti, she stepped back to the corner of the room.

"We will depart as soon as Kochanski arrives with the God-chair. You've all been through a portal before, so you will remember the sensation."

Several of the men grimaced at the memory and Allic smiled.

"You'll get used to it. Remember, we *jump* through. I'll go first and Storm will bring up the rear. We will be landing at a hidden outpost on Uye, the only moon of the world under attack. The air there is breathable, but the temperature will be cold enough to freeze off certain of your appendages. Once we have secured the base, Kochanski and Leti will depart, via the Godchair for a reconnaisance of the battle zone. If the demons are gone, we'll jump down after them. If the demons are there, a full evacuation will be made. If they are detected, we either go in to get them out, or they fall back to Uye."

There was a stir at the far end of the room as Kochanski floated in, astride a magnificent throne that was carved in a stunning and intricate display of crystals and polished wood.

"We're ready to go. Let's move to the portal." Allic strode down the length of the armory, his sorcerers marching behind him in a double column, Americans and Japanese mingled together, with Kochanski bringing up the rear.

Ikawa felt a swelling of pride as he looked over his shoulder. The soldiers behind him, though nervous, were tough and proud, bonded together in a comradeship undreamed of only a year ago.

Following Allic's lead, the party passed through the armory and then into a vast colonnaded staircase that descended into the subterranean corridors of Jartan's command center. The area had been sealed off hours earlier as a security measure, and the once bustling section was cloaked in an eerie silence. Allic went up to what looked like an ornately paneled wall, which slid back at his approach.

In the center of the vast room there was a pulsing white glow, which immediately sent a prickly feeling down Ikawa's back. It had the exact same appearance as the portal opening in the Chinese temple, which they had fallen through what seemed like a lifetime ago.

Allic turned and looked back at the offworlders.

"Don't hesitate, just step briskly through. On the other side, quickly move out of the opening to make way for the next man.

It has been known for a person to materialize on the other side in the exact same space as another—with, I might add, unpleasant consequences for both.

"You all know the drill. There is a chance we might be jumping straight into a fight, so have your shields up, and deploy at once into a defensive perimeter.

"Now take a final minute to recheck your equipment, then let's move out."

Ikawa felt a certain reassurance in Allic's tone. There were times when the demigod could appear to be nothing more than a good drinking partner in a bar, but at moments like this he projected the command presence of a seasoned combat veteran.

Ikawa turned to Mark. "This time we go through the portal as comrades, a prospect that is a pleasant change," he said calmly. Ever since the incident in Sarnak's chamber, Ikawa had sensed the fear eating at his friend's soul. He had already resolved to stay close to Mark at all times. If Mark should break, no matter how understanding the men would be as to the cause, he would be finished as a combat commander.

It was a situation Ikawa knew would destroy his friend forever.

Mark smiled wanly and extended his hand, which Ikawa gripped firmly, focusing his thoughts as if to communicate inwardly that Mark could rely upon him no matter what happened.

"Ikawa."

Looking over his shoulder, he saw Leti and Storm standing behind them.

Without a word Leti reached into a pouch hanging on the outside of her parka and drew forth a black leather belt, in the center of which was the sparkling glory of the Crystal of the Sun. She slid the belt around Ikawa's waist and cinched it tight.

Her eyes glowing with love, she kissed him on the cheek and drew back. "It will serve as a protector for you and your friends."

Storm stepped past the couple and reached into her tunic to produce another belt of leather, this of supple whiteness into the center of which was set a large crystal of lightning. With a light kiss she handed it to Mark.

"Just burn their damn hides off with it," she said with a smile.

"Well, as I always said," Goldberg interjected, breaking the embarrassed silence, "It's good to have friends in high places."

Smiling, Storm shot a gentle bolt at Goldberg, who staggered backward in a mock display of pain.

"It's time," Allic said quietly, nodding to the circle of sorcerers around the pentagram.

The men fell silent, except for the sing-song murmuring of the portal weavers.

The room started to pulse with light that shifted through a wild kaleidoscope of colors, twisting and turning upon each other. A shower of hot white sparks soared to the ceiling and hovered above the group, to be joined an instant later by tendrils of forest green, which changed in a moment to an icy polar white. The white held, absorbing, washing out the other colors, dropping downward, becoming a glaring intensity that seemed to hold before them as a solid wall.

One of the sorcerers around the pentagram looked over to Allic and nodded.

"Follow me," Allic shouted, and with a wild cry of delight he leaped into the pentagram and disappeared.

The head sorcerer pointed at the next man in line.

"Go!"

Kraut leaped into the void.

"Go!"

Saito followed.

"Go!"

"Banzai!" and Shigeru disappeared into the light.

"Go!"

"Oh shit!" and Walker jumped through.

The line quickly moved forward, and soon Ikawa stepped up to the jumping-off point.

"Go!"

Taking a deep breath, Ikawa ran headlong into the light.

The world disappeared, and he felt a dropping away as if all gravity had been nullified. There was an eerie sensation of falling away into the heart of a sun, as if he was riding a comet that in an instant would traverse the entire galaxy.

Lights snapped past, like a shower of stars racing towards him, violet in color and soaring past to shift to the darkest red before disappearing. He felt godlike, soaring through the universe on wings of fire.

The cone of light bent and shifted, dropping away around him with yet more speed—a racing tremor of power pulsing into his very heart. *Not even a god*, he thought, *could know such power, such limitless joy as this*. A glowing barrier appeared, which stood like a cascading wall of fire. He snapped through it with a jolt, as if an invisible hand had stunned and slapped him.

Dimensional gate, he thought.

The falling away continued. He could now hear a distant shout ahead, like the delighted cries of a companion who in a boat farther ahead was already shooting the rapids.

More lights shot past the tunnel, twisting and turning, and then a darkness was before him. At first it was only a pinprick in his field of vision, racing up like the mouth of a tunnel.

He hit the ground hard, knocking the breath from him.

"Move out and away," a voice called.

Rolling over sharply, he tumbled out of the narrow confines of the portal onto a field of ice.

There was a thump behind him. Looking back he saw Mark standing in the narrow cone of light.

"Keep moving," Allic shouted.

Jumping high in the moon's low gravity, Mark landed beside Ikawa.

"Better than the Cyclone at Coney Island," Mark said, forcing a grin.

"That ride made me sick," Ikawa replied, remembering his student days in America. "This one was far better."

Together they raced out for several dozen yards, their shields snapped to highest intensity, and crouching defensively they concentrated on farsearching, scanning the snow fields for the slightest sign of movement.

There was nothing but the icy darkness.

More and more came through the portal, until nearly a score of warriors stood in a circle facing outward.

"Respond if you sense anything," Allic called.

The group was silent.

"Maintain position once the portal's closed, and dampen your shields to avoid detection."

Ikawa spared a quick look over his shoulder.

Suddenly the Godchair appeared with Kochanski and Leti aboard, and under his skillful guidance it gently came to a stop an inch above the ground, then sharply veered off to one side. Behind them, Storm came through. Without hesitation she rose into the air and soared into the darkness, disappearing from view.

Allic extended his hands and then brought them together. The portal flashed down, lingered for a second, then disappeared.

Darkness returned to the frozen steppes of Uye. As his eyes adjusted to the darkness, Ikawa looked around.

He could barely see the skillfully camouflaged buildings set into the side of a frozen glacier.

"It was open for less than two minutes," Allic said, coming over to the chair and looking at Leti.

"You shielded it as soon as you got through?" she asked quietly.

"Yes, but they might have detected it when the portal first snapped open. We didn't have anyone on this side to shield it before I arrived."

"We knew the chances of that," she said evenly.

Allic looked around once more, as if to reassure himself.

"At least we timed it right. The planet is just rising." He pointed to the far horizon.

Far faster than any sun or moonrise on Earth, the vast green planet rolled above the horizon, a massive crescent. Its forested surface reflected the red light of the system's star with a ruby glow.

The sight was awe-inspiring, and for the moment the group's anxiety was washed away in silent admiration.

"If we survive this, I want to come back here," Saito whispered, coming to Ikawa's side.

"Worthy of a hundred Hykos," Ikawa replied.

"Hell, I'd pay fifty bucks for another ticket on the ride we just had," Walker said, approaching Mark.

The planet continued to rise before them, the group whispering to each other in awed tones, even as they tried to concentrate on scanning the ground and sky for danger. The glare from the planet now lit the snow field and cast shadows of lavender darkness.

Suddenly, at a ninety degree angle from where the planet was rising, a red shimmer filled the sky. For a moment it appeared as if a storm of fire was rolling across the horizon, and Ikawa prepared to leap into the freezing air, to gain altitude for a strike.

A long red band of light shimmered in the morning air, and, with dull flaming glow, a red, giant star broke the horizon.

"Look over there," Kochanski called, pointing to the planet. "On the darkside, near the equator and ten degrees in from the terminator line."

Straining his eyes, Ikawa scanned the planet's surface—and then he saw it.

A glow of fire pulsed and wavered.

"The last base is under attack," Allic said quietly. He looked at Kochanski and Leti in the Godchair. "You know what to do. Get ready."

He turned back to the rest of his command.

"The last fortress is already under siege, and shielded by an enemy field. Getting in and out without detection will be almost impossible. I want the defensive perimeter of this base manned and ready; we can expect company before this day is out."

Chapter 7

Pina glanced again at the report, before continuing to interrogate Imada.

"The medical diagnosis shows you've been through a lot, young man. You were given up for dead months ago."

"I never would have made it without Vena here," replied Imada, gesturing to the girl beside him.

"Yes, so you've told us," responded Pina dryly. "You seem to have had a very harrowing time of it."

His glance fell on Vena, who stood a little behind Imada, her head slightly lowered, obviously unused to being in a palace and addressing such high ranking sorcerers. Even as he watched, Imada reached out to grasp her hand in a gesture of reassurance.

Pina carefully kept his face blank, but inside he smiled. How long had it been since his first case of puppy love?

Still, the story was almost too pat, and he was responsible for the realm during Allic's absence. Making a decision, he turned his glance to Valdez, who was standing over to the side. "I'd like you to escort these two young lovers back to the healers for a more complete check."

Valdez nodded approvingly.

Imada started to look a little flustered, as if unsure what to say, so Valdez said diplomatically, "There is no way you can join your friends at present. They are on a mission for Jartan. So, we have the time to make sure you are totally fit before we restore you to duty." He motioned for them to follow him and walked out of Pina's office.

"My daughter is about your age and has heard of your arrival and adventures. She pointed out that with all the outlanders gone, you two wouldn't really know anyone here, and has asked if you would care to join us for dinner."

Imada hesitated, but Vena said smoothly, "Thank you. It

would be nice to have another girl to talk to right now. I'd never dreamed that I would ever be in a palace, and even with Imada's support I feel almost lost."

Valdez nodded absently, letting her prattle on.

"You're doing fine, Kochanski, just fine," Lefti said.

He smiled and gave her what he hoped was a confident wink.

At least this approach was much easier. Before, he had traveled to places he could not see, guided by symbolic logic, or wherever his imagination might take him. Now Kochanski could clearly see where he was going. The forest world seemed to fill the entire sky; and since there was no sensation of movement, the vast planet appeared to be racing up to smash them.

It was strange, he thought. He knew space was a vacuum. Yet there was no sensation of the absolute cold. He still found himself breathing and even hearing Leti as she spoke softly, giving him directions.

Of course, only their spirits were riding the Godchair toward the planet. When they had departed, he had even looked back to his "real" self, who sat as if lost in a deep slumber, with Saito and Shigeru standing to either side of the chair as guards. He knew that if any harm came to his body, or to the actual physical presence of the chair still resting on Uye, then he would be forever doomed to be a wandering spirit. There was also the risk that his spirit could be injured by forces unseen. At that moment his real body would simply cease to breathe.

"The battle's reached its climax," Leti whispered.

Directly below, Kochanski could see what appeared to be a wall of fire encasing an inner shield which was glowing white hot.

"Let's speed this up a bit," Leti suggested.

Nodding, Kochanski let the directions pass through his mind. Their speed instantly doubled. The world came racing up, the lit crescent marking the approaching dawn shifting to the edge of the globe and disappearing over the horizon.

The vast red orb of the star shifted over the horizon as well, passing in an instant through a spectacular sunset that sparkled through the upper bands of the planet's atmosphere.

The pair dropped through the upper atmosphere, Kochanski slowing the chair as they swept in toward the planet's surface.

"Shift us over behind the mountain range north of the base," Leti said, pointing to the high peaks about ten miles away from the battle.

Kochanski spared a quick look down at the fighting, a hundred miles below. Bright flashes illuminated the dark sky, the shield snapping white hot with each impact, so that it seemed like brittle glass about to burst under the strain. There was a blinding flash. For a brief moment the shield went dark, then came back up, smaller than before, and obviously weaker.

Kochanski knew there were people dying down there, sorcerers of Jartan's that he had most likely never met, but comrades all the same. His fear was gone, burned away by the grim determination to finish the recon as quickly as possible so that a relief force could be dropped in before all was lost.

Turning his thoughts from the battle, Kochanski guided the chair toward the towering mountains silhouetted with the lavender glow of the approaching dawn.

"Between those two peaks, a bit off to our right," Leti whispered. Kochanski propelled the chair forward—but felt the slightest of tremors, a vague uneasiness as if someone were standing behind him and looking.

"You felt it?" Leti murmured.

Kochanski nodded.

"Get us behind those peaks." Her voice held a controlled urgency.

The mountains now filled their view: Peaks sheathed with mantles of ice, carved by the ceaseless winds into a wild cathedral of fluted columns, soaring arches, and high vaulted caverns illuminated by the crystalline red of dawn.

Kochanski focused on a narrow cavern near the summit of the mountain, and soon the icy walls embraced them into their protective folds. With a sigh of relief, Kochanski brought the chair to a halt and settled it down on the cavern floor.

"Did they see us?" he finally asked.

"Something out there swept us," Leti said, and Kochanski realized that even this demigoddess had known a moment of fear. "It didn't lock onto us, though, so I think we got through without any problem."

The two smiled at each other with relief. Then Leti said, "Let's take another look," and Kochanski slid the chair forward to the edge of the cavern.

Far below, in the distant valley, the battle continued to rage. From a hundred different points, sheets of fire and energy bolts slammed into the shimmering defensive shielding.

"Can they hold out?" Kochanski asked.

Even as he spoke, a blinding hot flash snapped across the field. Leti was silent, grim-faced.

"Over there," she whispered finally, and Kochanski looked to where she was pointing. A thin point of white light, tinged in red, was pulsing and glowing inside the fold of a crevice that flanked the main battlefield.

"Their portal jump point?" Kochanski asked.

"I want to get a closer look at it," Leti replied. "Bring us in underneath it, then rise slowly. We'll break the surface for a quick look and pull back down if threatened."

"That's right on top of them," Kochanski replied, trying hard to sound matter-of-fact, but knowing that his fear was evident.

"They'll be sweeping a lot farther out, expecting an approach to come in from a distance. If we're in almost on top of them, we'll have the element of surprise. Besides, this chair and its abilities are a well-kept secret, so they won't expect it, or be looking for it."

"All right, then," Kochanski replied, swallowing hard. Focusing his attention, he gazed at the jump point, calculating distances, and in his mind drew an imaginary line which terminated farther up the crevice.

A shudder passed through the Godchair, and the ground rose to swallow them. Kochanski guided them through the darkness by probing forward with his mind through a shadow realm of projected image and phantomlike echoes of energy.

"Can you sense where we are?" Leti asked cautiously.

A bit shocked, Kochanski realized that what he had already come to take as second nature was a complete mystery to the demigod by his side. The realization gave him a sense of satisfaction with his ability, but it was slightly unnerving to think that a being of such power was now totally dependent on his ability for guidance, and for survival.

A ripple of energy swept past him.

"There is something powerful, malevolent out there," she said nervously.

In the blackness he could see, as if with other eyes, the goal looming closer, the pulsing energy of the portal, surrounded now by other forms, radiating power. They were unlike anything he had encountered in his practice sessions back on Haven, or even in his encounter with Sarnak. These forms emanated a darkness deeper than the blackness of the rock through which his spirit form drifted. Occasionally the darkness would swirl outward, probing, and for a moment he would feel cornered, his heart freezing; then the probe would sweep on. As he drew closer, though, he could feel his confidence growing. They were constantly sweeping the area, but had not detected him.

The energy glow of the portal now filled the world before him. Shifting to the left, and judging that the place he had selected was directly overhead, Kochanski cautiously guided the chair upward. In an instant the blackness gave way to a blue, opaque light. He felt a momentary thrill over the precision of his approach. Exactly as planned he had emerged inside a ridge overlooking the portal.

Leti gave him a nod of approval.

Carefully, Kochanski edged the chair forward to breach the edge of the hill, projecting outward just far enough to see the world before them.

Not a hundred yards below, the portal stood revealed, surrounded by a hundred or more demons, while a larger circle of demons faced outward, watching intently.

Kochanski tried to suppress a ripple of fear by forcefully reminding himself that he was only here in spirit, and thus invisible to normal eyes, and that Leti was bending all of her tremendous power to blocking out unseen eyes as well.

"Why such concentration around the portal?" Leti whispered through the mind link.

Kochanski could not answer, and after a moment of watching he lifted his gaze to the battle raging not a mile away. The glow of the shielding was up again to white hot intensity, and there was another explosive snap as the shield overloaded. Wild howls of delight burst from the demon host as it winged over the besieged outpost. The demons were unlike any he had ever seen before—

bigger, darker, and all of them frighteningly capable of wielding the Essence for the casting of bolts in battle. The demons he had first met and feared on Haven were mere children to the power he now saw.

The defensive shielding of the outpost came up again, this time as a small cone of light not a hundred yards across. The outer buildings of the fortress city were now beyond protection.

"Inner defense line," Leti said grimly. "They're down to the end."

White-clad figures emerged from the unprotected buildings. Several lifted into the air. But a rain of fire arced down and in from every side. The white forms crumpled, fell, those in the air flashing into incandescent brilliance before tumbling away, trailing fire and smoke.

"For Christ's sake, can't we help them?"

"No."

Kochanski's sense of fairness rebelled, although he knew the correctness of what she was saying. Gathering intelligence *had* to come first; then it would be up to Allic to evaluate and consider the possibility of a sortie to take the pressure off. But the screams could still be heard, and the lurid light of the flaming city cast an ugly glow across the morning sky.

"I estimate over seven hundred of Gorgon's demons here." Leti's voice was cold, and her tone snapped Kochanski back to the harsh reality of what had to be done.

Tearing his gaze away from the destruction, he looked over at the ghostly image of his companion and saw that though her voice might seem detached, her face was contorted with pain and rage.

"Don't look at me," she said softly. "Keep watching the portal for anything that comes through. I've got to determine who is leading this assault."

Kochanski followed her orders, but there was nothing to report. The portal was still surrounded by the demon host, yet nothing was coming in or out. Long minutes passed, and then ever so slowly the portal started to pulse with a deeper intensity. The inner circle of demons began to nod excitedly, their guttural growls echoing up the narrow valley, momentarily blocking out the roar of battle.

"Something's up," Kochanski whispered.

The light of the portal shifted suddenly to the deepest of reds, and doubled in size so that the host had to step back or be pulled in.

"What in the name of the gods?" Leti whispered.

An expectant hush came over the assembly below them. As one, the demons went to their knees, taloned and winged arms stretched forward, fanged heads lowered.

The portal snapped and flared again with a blinding intensity, turning into a pillar of flame half a hundred yards across. The battle beyond came to a stop, and Kochanski spared a quick glance up to see that the enemy host had broken off its assault and was pulling back toward the portal. Feeble shouts echoed on the wind, the defenders crying out in triumph at the apparent retreat.

The sky above the crevice was darkened by the wheeling circle of retreating demons who were arcing in and out, their harsh cries filled with a chilling note of lust and joy.

"It's not a retreat," Leti whispered softly. "Something else is pulling them back here."

The ground trembled and shook, the trees surrounding the deep ravine swaying, branches rattling. Hosts of birds and reptilian creatures soared into the air, scattering madly, their panicked calls counterpointing the mad shouts of the demons.

The trees nearest the portal started to smoulder, and roiling clouds of acrid smoke coiled off the branches. With thunderous cracks, the forest exploded into flames, the heat spiraling upward to jostle the demons above, who now cried out in triumph.

The trembling of the ground shifted, became deeper, with a booming, thunderous roar.

"Something's coming through," Leti cried, and Kochanski could sense the fear in her voice.

The portal started to swirl about itself, taking on the appearance of a maelstrom. The vast circle of demons came to their feet, arms extended, the power of the Essence emanating from them, drawing the portal ever wider, while overhead the hundreds of demons circled in tighter, forming a living wall about the opening.

"They're ripping the portal wide open!" Leti shouted.

"Maybe we should get out of here," Kochanski whispered.

"Wait. We have to be sure it's him."

The dimensional gate flashed white, then black as night. Kochanski felt as though he was staring into the blackness of infinite space, or into the darkest pit of hell.

Yet even in the darkness there was a deeper blackness that oozed upward, sickening and vile as a noisome pestilence; as if the rot of decay had taken form and now crawled out into the realm of the living. Formless, the darkness slithered upward through the blackness of the portal.

The wheeling host and those upon the ground fell silent, and from a thousand demons Kochanski sensed a redoubling of effort.

The darkness exploded. With a blinding rush, the blackness soared upward, wreathed in blood-red flashes of light, cloaked in steam and oily smoke. Mighty arms stretched outward, taloned hands reaching up as if to snatch the very sun from the sky. A grim visage took form, fanged mouth open. A booming roar echoed across the hills, drowning the delighted howls of the assembled host.

"Gorgon," Leti whispered in terrified awe.

The head turned slowly, deliberately, eyes of fire scanning, and Kochanski's heart turned to ice as the sweeping gaze fixed upon him and his companion.

"Yes, Gorgon," and though a whisper, the words seemed to have form and weight, crushing Kochanski.

"Get us out!" Leti yelled.

Instinctively, Kochanski willed the chair straight up. Looking over the edge of the chair, he was horrified to see the entire side of the hill sloping downward in a wild explosion. And out of the explosion a dark form soared upward, hands reaching as if to grab him.

"A little toy of Jartan's, is it not?"

The voice was no longer dark, but rather almost gentle, chiding.

"I wish to see it," Gorgon continued. Kochanski hesitated. The voice whispered through his mind, cutting into him. He felt his limbs grow weak, his resolve melting as the form raced closer.

"Wait for me," Gorgon said softly.

Wide-eyed, Kochanski saw the form grow closer. The screams of Leti were audible, but somehow the words simply did not come through. And then he remembered.

"Kiss my ass!" Kochanski roared.

The ghostly image of the chair soared straight up into the heavens, even as the talons closed over, the world rocking beneath him with curses of rage.

"Hang on!" Kochanski shouted.

The planet dropped away. Within seconds the curve of the horizon was visible, the angle growing sharper, the disk of the planet taking form. Kochanski could see the moon hovering above him, its icy form reflecting the dark red of the sun which filled half the sky.

The moon's surface rushed into sharp focus. Swinging in, the couple instinctively braced for what was surely going to be an impact. Kochanski felt the now familiar sensation of a slowing down, a merging. Momentarily, he closed his eyes and then opened them.

Allic stood before him.

"It's Gorgon—he's following us," Leti cried, leaping from the chair.

Weak-kneed, Kochanski stood, not embarrassed by the fact that he was visibly trembling.

"Circle in and form a shield around the chair!" Allic roared. White-clad figures emerged from the concealment of the hidden buildings, heading toward the point where the portal had been formed. "Get that portal ready to go. The moment Storm returns, we're out of here."

Still numb, Kochanski could only look around as his comrades came racing toward him.

Allic grabbed Kochanski by the shoulders and looked into his eyes.

"Are you all right?"

Leti turned and came to Allic's side.

"He was wonderful. Gorgon came on so fast I was damn near paralyzed. If he hadn't thought quickly, we would have been taken."

Kochanski was unable to respond. If he had acted, as far as

he could remember it was from instinct driven by fear.

Then Leti raced off to organize the defense.

"Stay in the Chair," Allic commanded.

"Why?"

"Because it's Gorgon that we're facing now."

Kochanski sensed what was being said, but still couldn't quite form the implication clearly.

Allic drew closer. "If the shield goes down, destroy the chair to keep him from getting it."

He clapped Kochanski on the shoulder and turned away. But there was a look in Allic's eyes that Kochanski had seen far too often: the look of a man who knew that chances were he only had a short time left to live.

Kochanski sat down and turned his gaze heavenward. But there was no need to project outward to search; the blackness was already sweeping down from above. The demon lord had crossed over space itself, leaping from one world to the next, an action only a god or one of equal power could perform.

"Here he comes!" Allic cried. "Throw your power into the base's defensive shield. Alone, we'd be picked off one by one." Allic was silent for a moment, then gave an anguished scream: "Storm, where are you? We're going to be cut off!"

The darkness filled the lavender sky, swirling and turning, and a shout of rage thundered across the landscape.

Then darkness coiled inward, taking a manlike form, with twisting fire for eyes and teeth of molten lava. Allic raised his hand to slam off a bolt that would have shattered the shielding of any mere mortal.

The bolt struck the figure in the chest. Kochanski watched as the form shrieked and seemed almost to burst apart. It tumbled to the ground, trailing fire and smoke, and the ice about Gorgon turned instantly to scalding steam.

Incredulous, the offworlders looked at Allic.

"Is that all there was to him?" Walker laughed, his voice cracking with nervousness. "I damn near pissed my pants and then he falls apart after a single bolt. That's one shitty demon."

"It was too easy," Allic whispered cautiously. "He's playing with us."

Suddenly, from the boiling column of steam a cloud raced out to skim across the ground—which rippled and exploded beneath its passage.

"Get ready!" Allic roared, crouching and forcing his shield to its maximum level.

The cloud slammed into them, and from within a darkness leapt into the air. Bolt after bolt slashed out of its hand, overloading the defenders' shield, forcing it to glowing whiteness. Kochanski felt as if a weight was pressing down on him, and stunned, he watched as his comrades struggled to keep their defenses up. Steam filtered through the screen, prickling his skin, turning the battlefield into an opaque realm of shadows, fire, and mist.

Allic raised his hand to fire another bolt. It struck the demon lord in the chest the same as the first.

Gorgon appeared to stagger for a moment, and then a taunting laugh boomed out. The look of pain disappeared, to be replaced by the sardonic visage of someone who was merely playing.

"Allic, your power is like the spit of a child," the demon mocked, hovering above the party. "Go on, try it again. I need some entertainment before I drag you away."

His face contorted with rage, Allic raised his hand and slammed out another shot, joined by Leti. The combined blow struck Gorgon and seemed to simply glance aside.

Gorgon roared with malevolent delight. "Now receive something from me!"

A tornado of fire slashed out from his hand. Kochanski could feel the power draining away from them as the group struggled to hold their collective strength together. For long seconds the contest of strength swayed back and forth, but with the combined strength of Leti and Allic, the buckling shield gained power, and then firmly held.

Gorgon broke off the attack and drew back.

"So you have enough slaves to hide behind this time," he said, his voice almost chiding. "Well, we shall even that."

Gorgon raised his hand again—but this time a shielding formed, encompassing the defensive one.

"No way to escape now," he laughed.

With the wave of his other hand, a portal snapped into shape. Within seconds, the first demon appeared, followed by another and another. Forming a circle around the portal, they turned their own powers in and the portal broadened, so that a continual stream of Gorgon's followers was soon rushing out.

Kochanski, knowing what was about to come, stood and stepped down from the chair. He saw his comrades looking to each other, and in their eyes was a grim determination, but also nods of farewell. Leti moved from Allic's side to stand by Ikawa, and their hands touched momentarily. The portal broadened once again, and from out of the host of demons a dark shape appeared.

"Ah, Kultha," Gorgon roared, "that one you told me about—is he here?"

Kultha swept forward, coming up to the edge of the shielding, his gaze focused on Mark.

"My lord, you can have anyone else," Kultha cried, "but leave this one for me. I want him alive!"

Allic stepped out from the center of the group, and Kochanski followed, to stand beside his old commander.

Mark's eyes were filled with terror, but he forced a wan smile and shook his head, as if to say that he was still under control.

Gorgon again roared with delight as Allic looked up at him and slammed off several shots which were simply absorbed by the demon's shielding.

"It's almost time to test our strengths again," he screamed.

"When the shielding goes, take out as many as you can," Allic shouted, "and remember what to do last."

Kochanski ran his tongue against the back molar and looked over at Mark. His old friend seemed petrified by fear. Then Kochanski looked at Ikawa, who nodded with understanding. When it was lost, one or the other of them would kill Mark if he could not do it himself. Turning, Kochanski stepped back to the chair.

The outer shield flickered, and from Gorgon's hand, and from his assembled demons and warlords, an all-encompassing sheet of flame slashed out.

The defensive shield flared up, sparkling to white heat. Kochanski could feel the pressure grow as he added his own strength to the unequal contest, focusing his offensive crystal into the defense as well. But the difference in strength was simply too much. Like a dam of rotten ice giving way before a spring flood, the shield flared and with a blinding flash snapped away in a thunderclap roar, counterpointed by the demons who, howling with delight, swarmed forward for the kill.

Chapter 8

Patrice paced back and forth, inwardly cursing, her gaze fixed upon the pit of fire that was the communications link to Gorgon's realm. Stopping momentarily, she waved a hand, sending an interrogative into its depths. Nothing.

How dare he keep silent, she raged. *Without me he wouldn't even know they were coming. Surely he must have captured or killed them by now*!

She raised her hand to brush back her hair, and only then noticed that her hand was trembling. Turning her palm over, she stared at the tremors. Some moments later, she shook herself back to reality.

What is wrong with me? I haven't been this nervous for centuries.

Patrice again glanced at the empty flames and walked over to the thronelike chair facing the pit. Picking up an ornate chalice from the small table, she settled herself into the chair and sipped her wine.

I will be patient, she told herself. *This wait is nothing. If need be I will wait twice as long, and then twice as long again. What is time to a demigod but a means to an end?*

And she felt her strength returning. Soon she would know, and at long last start her plans to achieve her proper destiny.

Sighing contentedly, she put her wine chalice down and laid her hands on the arms of her chair, staring firmly into the flames.

Ralnath strode into the map room looking for Sarnak and found his master overlooking the section denoting Jartan's capital of Asmara. He knew better than to interrupt Sarnak's train of thought, so he waited silently at his side. Glancing at the map, he saw a bright flashing light that denoted a major portal opening right in Jartan's palace. Now what is going on? he wondered.

A few moments later, Sarnak straightened and nodded for Ralnath to proceed with his report.

"We have run another check on our security system using an outside source and it is secure. The other courts still believe that Uthul is still alive and in control."

"Which guild did you use this time?"

"A new one. A bastard of one of Macha's cousins started an off-shoot of the sorcerers guild in one of those southern city-states. We led him to believe that it was a secret assignment from Macha himself, and suggested that you were hiding right here."

"Well?"

"Very impressive effort. I suggest we use his organization again. He used that trade mission of two weeks ago as the primary vehicle to infiltrate a team and went through at least two other levels before concluding that your imitation Uthul was legitimate, that Uthul intended to have your head if you ever did show up, and that you had never been here. We paid him the agreed fee and told him we would be back in touch. I've taken the liberty of putting him on a retainer to pass along any information he might pick up. The trade mission was monitored by one of Leti's people. We made sure they caught wind of it as a cover operation. Her counter operatives are good, they'll penetrate this group, get the official report, and from Leti it's straight to everyone in Jartan's court."

"Excellent work, Ralnath."

"It had a side benefit as well. Several people in Uthul's old circle who are unaware of the change spilled some information."

"What kind?"

"Nothing serious. It was the usual false leads we've been setting out and declaring as secret information. It came straight back to us through the report. I already know the people, they're being arrested right now and will be awaiting your examination."

Sarnak smiled. "Good, I need the diversion."

"Uh, unfortunately, Sire, there is something else. One of the sensitives in the detection section has been claiming that there is some kind of vague probing going on he has never encountered before."

Sarnak seemed to grow before his eyes as the total power of the demigod concentrated upon him. When he spoke, his voice carried a sentence of death if the answers were not correct.

"Probing from where?"

"Impossible to tell, Sire. I have assigned an entire team to assist in tracking and analysis, but so far all we have been able to come up with is a sense of uneasiness on the part of the sensitive. The problem is that it is occurring with increasing strength and regularity."

Sarnak turned back to the map. His next comment was in a calm, matter-of-fact voice.

"Jartan is apparently sending a force via portal to one of his buffer worlds. That damned Kochanski and the Godchair are part of it, so we can temporarily drop the screening on that sector. It could be anyone doing this other probe: Minar, Allic, even Boreas. But whoever it is, I want increased protection against these probes.

"Something is up," Sarnak continued. "There have been indicators that most of the sorcerers in Jartan's realm and his vassal states have been pulled in. Then this portal opens. What is going on?"

Inwardly he cursed. Only months ago he could have been a mover in this game, ready to pounce at whatever advantages were opened. Now he was the hunted, his legions reduced to a handful of loyal followers. Yet he was alive, could still plot, and in the end might still have an opportunity to gain the advantage.

He gazed at the map for long minutes. Ever so gradually, a smile crossed his features.

"What about Patrice?" he whispered, looking at Ralnath.

"Patrice, my lord?"

"Call it an instinct," Sarnak went on. "Just an instinct. She never had the courage to act on her own the way I did. But there is a vacuum now where I once held power. I can't place the intuition, but it's there. Our team in her capital—is it still loyal?"

Ralnath hesitated. "My lord, we haven't dared to make contact with any of our operatives. You yourself wanted to leave all communications cold in case after our defeat someone turned sides."

Sarnak cursed softly. "I'm blind," he hissed. "Damn them all, I'm blind."

"A suggestion, my lord," Ralnath said carefully.

"Go on."

"Use the organization that checked out our security. Send them into Patrice's capital. Let them contact our people and try and get them to turn. If they betray you, we'll remember them later and pay back in full. If they don't turn, we can safely reestablish contact."

Sarnak smiled. "Most ingenious. Let it be done. If they check out correctly I want an observation team reporting on Patrice. If something is happening, we might turn it to our advantage."

Ralnath stood a little straighter, trying to disguise his fatigue. "At once, my lord." He turned to leave.

"Oh, one other thing. The prisoners—do they have families?"

"Yes, my lord."

"Arrest all of them," Sarnak replied evenly, "but do it discreetly. We'll arrange it later to look like all of them died in an accident."

Ralnath bowed low and withdrew.

Sarnak calmly watched him leave, then returned his attention to the map beneath him. To all in the command center he was in total control, the master tactician. Inside, his thoughts weighed odds and calculated chances, barely holding his fear in check.

His enemies were legion, and to be found by any of them before he could consolidate his power would mean his death. To be found by Allic or any of Jartan's brood would be bad enough. It was Boreas, though, who he was most afraid of. For with Boreas it would be far worse than death—it would be an eternity in an icy hell, tortured by a creature—an implacable force—who across these eons still blamed Sarnak for the death of his father.

Those in the map room were startled by their master's abrupt departure.

Where can I run if he finds me? To whom can I turn to with the strength to resist him? Once again Sarnak considered the unthinkable.

Mark felt as if he was staring into the very heart of hell. Kultha hovered above him, laughing darkly. The thin shield, now glowing white-hot, was all that protected him from the creature's malevolence.

Somewhere in the back of his mind he remembered the poison capsule, yet such was his terror that he felt as if his arms were made of lead and he could not move for the blessed release contained within.

Never had he known such intensity of attack. The shield strained, snapped up to what he thought was maximum, and then kept right on going.

A tremor ran through him, and then with a blinding flash he was on his back, shield gone, the nightmare of Kultha, with talons outstretched, swooping down from above.

A mad rage filled him, and a sense of self-loathing. Now, at the end would he die as a frightened rat?

Screaming, Mark came to his feet, and aimed a bolt at Kultha's face. A bone-numbing thunderclap snapped through the ground, which sent Mark staggering. Glancing up, he saw Kultha's gloating look change in an instant to stunned surprise.

Swinging around, Mark stood transfixed.

The entire glacier behind him had simply disappeared, blown apart. Hunks of ice larger than a house soared heavenward, tumbling end over end. Debris arced across the sky, a wild torrent of ice, smoke, and steam.

From out of the heart of the explosion Jartan emerged.

The god who Mark had stood before in awe back in Asmara was nothing now but a pale comparison to what a god could be in the rage of battle. As he ascended, his visage was as blinding as the sun, wreathed in light, so that Mark had to avert his eyes from Jartan's face.

Debris rained down, and snapping up his shield for protection, Mark crouched low. As if from a great distance he heard commingled the roaring defiance of the demons, the cries of hope of his own comrades, and now the screams of a host of sorcerers who swarmed out by Jartan's side.

"Mark!"

The warning snapped him into action and he rolled sideways and then swung up into the air. He felt the brush of Kultha's talons as they closed over the spot where he had just been.

Ikawa swung up alongside and within seconds the old group started to form: Walker behind him, Saito beside Ikawa, the rest of the offworlders trailing into the growing cluster.

Never had Mark seen such madness of aerial combat as Jartan's thousand-odd sorcerers swarmed into the demon host.

"Go for altitude!" Mark shouted. "We'll climb out and then pick our targets. Now move it!"

He looked over at Ikawa and saw the concern in his friend's eyes disappear as the instinct for air combat took over. Mark jinked the group left, looking over his shoulder for Kultha, but the demon chieftain had disappeared in the confusion. Bodies tumbled past, demons trailing fire and smoke, and, tragically, sorcerers as well. So tight was the crush of battle that antagonists actually slammed into each other and fell tumbling, trading blows at such close range that shields overlapped, so that strikes would literally rip an opponent in half in one blinding flash of death.

"Gorgon!"

The anger in Jartan's voice was like a physical blow, but it filled Mark with a wild joy and desire for vengeance.

A demon loomed before him, intent on striking a sorceress from behind. A bolt shot out from Mark's hand, joined in an instant by twenty other strikes from the group. The demon's shield exploded, and the group, pushing through the oily smoke, climbed out to the top of the fight, which was now a thousand feet in the air.

"Gorgon, meet me!"

Mark looked to his right and was stunned to see Jartan towering above him, wreathed in lightning, his image a hundred or more feet in height.

"All you, clear this area!" Jartan roared, and Mark realized that the god was looking at him. Suddenly Mark felt small, insignificant. A sheet of flames snapped past him, and looking to his left he saw the darkness of Gorgon, flame foaming from his mouth, charging across the sky.

"Get us the hell out of here!" Walker screamed.

Mark needed no persuading. Jackknifing over, he headed back into the maelstrom below, though his attention was riveted by the battle between a god and demon lord.

The icy air rippled with flashing shields, crackling bolts of light. Jartan moved as if made of light itself, shifting, dodging, while Gorgon came on relentlessly. A bolt of Jartan's went wide, slashing through a score of demons behind their lord. No broken bodies trailed away; rather they simply snapped out of existence, leaving nothing but glowing filaments of settling dust.

A formation of demons slashed up from the writhing combat. Like falcons leaping upon their prey, Mark and his command pounced and sent their opponents tumbling to their deaths, shrieking and writhing as their wings trailed fire and smoke.

"Take their portal!" Mark shouted.

Goldberg, picking up Mark's command, signalled it to other sorcerers around them, so that as the group swept downward it soon numbered more than fifty organized attackers who swept all in their path.

And then Mark saw him. Next to the portal, Allic and Kultha swirled in ever-tightening circles, trading blow after blow, both of their shields glowing white-hot. The terror of the demon returned, yet even stronger was Mark's rage.

Focusing his power through Storm's crystal, he dove straight downward. A blinding flash snapped out, catching Kultha on the chest, sending him staggering.

"He's mine!" Mark screamed. "Ikawa, lead the rest to the portal."

Allic spared a glance back and grinned with delight.

Above Allic, three demons swooped in, pouncing on the demigod. Allic turned toward them—and in that moment Mark found himself facing the source of his dread.

A slash of fire swept out from the demon's hand, staggering Mark in his flight. Raising his hand, Mark knew he was in a balancing game as he slammed a bolt toward the demon. Power between offense and defense had to be carefully matched. The decision would be realized when one or the other finally had to shift his offensive power to defense, because at that instant the other could start to increase the pressure until the defender's shield was shattered, or he attempted to flee.

Mark felt himself channel the maximum Essence, yet still his opponent slashed out, circling ever tighter in an attempt to catch Mark from behind, and thus place him at a disadvantage for the attack.

Jinking to the right, Mark soared straight up, exposing his back for a moment. Kultha fired a bolt which staggered him, yet still he continued up and over in a classical Immelmann turn. Rolling out, he was directly above Kultha, and dove, slashing a shot straight into the demon's back.

In that instant, Mark felt the balance shift. Kultha rolled over, aiming a shot up, but it went wide, giving Mark's shielding a momentary respite so that even more Essence could go into the next offensive shot. Kultha turned away, diving. Screaming with triumphant rage, Mark focused his power through Storm's crystal, and a blue-white slash slammed into the back of Kultha's head. The demon tumbled, slamming into the ground—but rolled and came up to his feet as Mark landed not a dozen feet away.

Kultha crouched low, slamming out another shot. Laughing maniacally, Mark stood motionless, absorbing the bolt. In a wild show of contempt he extended his arms wide, not bothering to fire back. For the first time he saw terror in his opponent's eyes.

Then Mark brought his right arm up and fired. Kultha's shield overloaded and snapped, and the demon went staggering to his knees.

Kultha threw his arms up to the heavens. "Spare me!"

The slightest of contemptuous smiles lit Mark's features. "Eat shit and die."

Kultha's head exploded as Mark's bolt slammed into it, and the decapitated body was flung end over end.

"Gary Cooper couldn't have done it better."

Mark looked over to see Kochanski astride the Godchair.

"Good fight," Allic shouted, flying to Mark's side.

"You saw it, then?"

"Most of it. I figured you could handle him on your own so I just killed a dozen or so demons who wanted to interfere with your revenge."

Smiling, Mark nodded his thanks and looked about them. The battle was still on, the demons swirling in a great protective arc around the portal, holding back the advance, while their luckier comrades fled through it. A concussion swept over him, and looking skyward he was stunned to realize that Jartan and Gorgon still wrestled for control. Mark suddenly knew that only a minute or two had passed since the first appearance of the god, and that the battle was still in doubt.

"Allic!"

Mark turned to see Storm, her countenance grim, coming in low with Leti and a dozen sorcerers. Between them was a great sling in which nestled a round object, covered by silken blankets.

"Against the portal!" Storm cried, and ripped back the protective cover.

Though he had never seen it, Mark knew that he was gazing upon the legendary Heart Crystal. Nearly eight feet in diameter, it flickered and glowed as it rested upon its carved stone base.

Allic grinned wickedly. "Clear the portal, break off the attack!" he roared, his command instantly picked up and relayed throughout the attacking sorcerers. Hundreds of forms dove in every direction, with Ikawa and the offworlders cutting back toward where Mark stood.

"Focus on the Heart," Allic shouted. "Everyone stand clear."

Turning, Mark snapped his energy into the Heart, augmenting it with Storm's crystal. Allic, Leti, and Storm stood together, hands extended to the great crystal, barely touching it. The inside of the great gem seemed to swirl in a mad kaleidoscope of color. Mark suddenly felt as if his own power was out of control, as if he was driving a car and the accelerator had jammed. The Crystal seemed to suck the Essence out of him in one great torrent.

The ground trembled beneath his feet. A cone of fire, as hot as the core of a sun, snapped out, slamming into the portal.

The booming explosion turned the ice a hundred yards around to steam. A massive fireball rushed heavenward, spreading in a cloud of flame.

—And suddenly it appeared as if the explosion was rushing back in upon itself.

Demons tumbled through the air, swept into the heart of the firestorm as the portal imploded. Horrified, Mark saw more than one sorcerer dragged to his doom among the hundreds of foes.

The explosion snapped inward, and then simply disappeared. A ghostly breeze smelling of charred flesh, steam, and sulphur washed across the field, and as it passed, Mark stood awestruck by the carnage. Hundreds of writhing demons cluttered the ground, shrieking and tearing at their wounds, where the portal had once been.

"Look!"

Mark glanced where Kochanski was pointing. A thin snap of light glowed on the surface of the besieged planet above them, spreading outward, and Mark was startled to hear Allic's laughter.

"The shot from the Heart passed through the portal and detonated the one up there. They must be frying, too!"

Mark knew he would have felt sickened by the carnage if these had been human foes. Against these incarnations of evil, though, he could only feel a grim sense of satisfaction.

There was another snap of light, and a hot blast rolled against the glacier-clad hills—but this time it came from above. Looking straight up, Mark saw Gorgon reeling backwards, clutching his shoulder, a torrent of fire pouring from the wound. Jartan, grim-faced, shot another bolt into the demon lord.

The image of Gorgon suddenly stretched outward, filling half the sky, and like a vapor of fog slashed by sunlight he disappeared. Jartan swung about as if searching, and in a blinding flash soared heavenward towards Yuvin. In an instant he was lost to normal sight.

Mark looked back to where the focus of the battle had been around the portal. All that was left was steaming wreckage, yet hundreds of demons had survived, cut off now from all hope of retreat back to Yuvin. In terror they fled, desperate to escape the wrath of Jartan and his followers.

Focusing a blast from the Heart against an enemy cluster, a score or more were felled; yet more streamed off in every direction, pursued now by Jartan's triumphant sorcerers.

Mark looked about to rally his command. "Stand down," Allic said, coming to Mark's side. "We've had enough for one day—let the reinforcements mop up what's left."

Still eager for vengeance, Mark started to bridle.

"We've done more than enough already," Leti said, putting her hand on Mark's shoulder.

Suddenly he realized how exhausted he really was. Though the battle had been brief, the terror of what had seemed to be inevitable defeat had worked its effect, and he realized that he was giddy with relief and exhaustion.

Glancing around, he saw Ikawa and the rest of the offworlders come swinging in from the far side of the ruined portal. Slowing, the group dropped down and alighted. Fear gripped him, and he did a quick scan, counting heads. Ikawa, seeing his concern, nodded that everyone was all right, then rushed to his side.

The two held each other's gaze for a moment, and then Ikawa grabbed Mark and embraced him.

"I didn't want to leave you, but I knew you had to face him alone."

Unable to respond, Mark only nodded.

"A hell of a fight," Ikawa announced, walking over to Leti. "I thought we were finished."

"So did I," Allic said coolly, forcing a smile. But his hand trembled slightly as he pulled a flask out and drained its contents.

"Just what the hell happened?" Walker asked, coming up to join the group. "One second I'm getting set to scratch that damned tooth and finish myself, and the next thing all hell breaks loose."

"We were simply bait, it seems," Allic announced, gazing over at Storm. Mark could see a look of reproach in his eyes.

"I'm sorry, brother, neither you nor Leti could be told. Gorgon might have been able to probe your thoughts," Storm said quietly. "We've had a portal hidden inside that glacier for some time." She pointed to the shattered mountain.

"Once I came through, it was my job to open it up, shield it, and guide Jartan and his forces through. Jartan was hoping to catch Gorgon and all his demons here on this moon, and hold him inside a massive pentagram hidden beneath the ice, right beneath our feet. But the bastard wouldn't alight where we wanted him to. If he had, Jartan would have had the field up, and we could have pinned and destroyed him. We waited as long as we could, but when your shield went down, we had to save you."

"Thanks for the late rescue," Allic said, trying to sound philosophical though his annoyance was obvious.

The offworlders looked at each other, realizing that if the rescue had come mere seconds later, most would have committed suicide rather than run the risk of capture.

"Jartan's returning," Kochanski announced quietly, as he sat astride the chair looking upward.

There was a swirling rush of wind, a coalescing of light, and Mark looked up to see the god hovering above them.

"Get him?" Allic asked.

"The bastard escaped through a secondary portal and pulled it down behind him." There was a chilling note of exasperation in Jartan's voice. "Everyone all right here?"

"Shaken but alive," Allic replied coolly.

A thin smile creased the god's face. "Couldn't be helped. Anyhow, it put a little excitement into your lives."

"That type of excitement I can do without," Allic said in a low voice.

A rumble of laughter came from Jartan.

"You did well, my children—and you offworlders, too. We'll talk later; I think I need to vent some rage, and Gorgon's trapped demons are as good a target as any."

The god formed into a swirling torrent of flame, and snapped across the sky, disappearing from view.

Incredulous, the offworlders looked at each other, none daring to admit the fear they had just felt, nor their frustration at realizing they had simply been bait to pull the enemy in.

"Anyhow, we won," Saito announced philosophically. Leaving the group he went over to kick the headless corpse of Kultha, rolling the body over for a closer look.

"Better than the blow from a headsman's sword."

"Yeah, will you look at that?" Walker said excitedly, coming up to stand by Saito's side. "Who kicked this guy's ass?"

"Mark did," Allic announced proudly.

Walker looked at Mark with open admiration. "No shit?"

Mark nodded.

A hand slipped into his. Turning, Mark looked into the admiring eyes of Storm, and the sight of her filled him with such warmth that he smiled. It almost felt as if he had just kicked the butt of the town bully, and now his girlfriend was coming forward to show her pride. He realized the notion was absurd, but nevertheless, at the moment it felt pretty damn good.

Chapter 9

It was the aftermath of battle. Jartan had brought the entire group of demigods, sorcerers, and captured demons down to the surface of the planet. Without the restraining powers surrounding the base, the main portal was operating nonstop. Groups of fresh sorcerers, ranging from healers to administrators, were arriving regularly and moving swiftly to their appointed tasks. Mark had seen it often enough before: the tail of an army catching up to the vanguard once a position had been secured.

In a pavilion on a nearby hillside all the outlanders, along with Allic, Storm, and Leti, were watching the activity with an exhausted apathy.

Allic seemed to show the most energy, quaffing cup after cup of wine and glaring at the tall column of light on the plain that was Jartan.

Transferring the glare to Storm, who was sitting next to Mark, he grated, "I still can't believe we couldn't have been told!"

Storm glanced at him wearily. "We have been over this before, brother. I was under orders to keep silent and prepare the other portal for Jartan and the rest of our forces. Your job was to do a reconnaissance, and if detected, to be very convincing bait."

Leti agreed with a nod. "Allic, it was only our obvious vulnerability and terror that drew Gorgon and all his demons into Jartan's trap. A major invasion of our forces from the moon to here would have played into their hands. You've seen the defenses they had prepared here."

She paused for a moment, and continued, "I'm not ecstatic at being kept in the dark either, but our casualties were very light, Gorgon severely wounded, his forces either killed or captured, and we kept the damage to this world to a minimum. You cannot argue with success like that."

"Thank you, daughter."

125

A glowing figure began to materialize in the pavilion. The Americans and Japanese all began to stand in the presence of the god, but were waved back to their seats by Jartan.

Mark glanced out onto the plain and saw that the figure in the massive column of light was still out there, directing incoming traffic and ordering the establishment of a defensive perimeter.

Now how the hell does he manage to be in more than one place at a time? he wondered.

A voice in his mind answered: "It's a very handy talent. Not only can you accomplish a lot more, but it makes assassination attempts much harder. Though for someone like you to do it might be viewed as a bit of a mental aberration."

Mark froze. He glanced back at the Jartan in the pavilion and noticed that the god was smiling at him.

"You are to be congratulated, young sorcerer. Kultha was no mean foe, and your courage in conquering your fears is worthy of note."

Jartan leaned back and favored them all with a smile.

"In fact, all of you did very well. This whole operation went far better than I had expected. It is an ancient axiom that no battle plan ever survives contact with the enemy. But this one went too well: Gorgon should have anticipated our counterstrike and yet it appears he didn't. Perhaps I am being too suspicious, but it seems as if everything went too perfectly—and when dealing with Gorgon, that makes me worry."

Kochanski was so thankful to be alive that he wasn't even resentful, and burst out, "I don't care about the whys so much as being glad that I'm still in one piece. I've never been so scared in my life—and that includes any of the bombing missions back on Earth, including Schweinfurt. Those demons freeze my very blood."

"That's why they're called demons," growled Allic. "I suppose I have to agree with the tactics, Jartan, but I don't have to like them."

"Storm said it best when she said convincing bait. The key word is 'convincing,' son. Without that, Gorgon would never have committed his forces to a place where we could ambush him. So think of it as a means to an end and move on."

"Right," responded Allic dryly. "So what's next, Jartan?"

"Well, I've been in touch with my siblings back on Haven and we have decided that since Gorgon and his realm seem to be in disarray, we should repay his aggression with a little maneuver of our own. Minar and Chosen are coming here with their own forces and we are going to use this world as a jumping-off point to take at least two more buffer dimensions. We just might have a real opportunity to get that scum."

He hesitated before continuing, "If we do have the advantage, we'll go over to a full offensive and push in as far as possible. With luck we might even strike into the heart of his realm."

Storm gave a low whistle. "That's a tall order."

"What's the matter, sister?" Allic said peevishly. "You want to live forever?"

"I'm not taking any risks that aren't worth it," Jartan replied with a slight edge of rebuke. "It's just there might be a chance here to push Gorgon's weakness to our maximum advantage. We would be remiss not to take it. He's been a threat for far too long."

"Just as long as there are no surprises from my own side," Allic retorted.

Mark cringed inwardly, waiting for an explosion. He could sense there was a silent conversation now raging between Jartan and his son.

After several tense minutes, Allic finally nodded and sat down.

"Every family has its little spats," Leti sighed, forcing a smile in an attempt to break the tension. Allic grinned back at her, and Mark could sense that his liege lord had won some face-saving point and was now satisfied.

"As I was about to say," Jartan continued as if nothing had occurred, "if the campaign is successful it means we can develop this world as a settled colony, rather than as a military outpost, since it will no longer be a buffer area.

"Therefore, in reward for your services I am awarding all members of the first assault landed estates here, to be held in perpetuity by you and your children. The area that each offworlder will hold here will be larger than entire provinces on Haven. Granted, it is a wilderness now, but in times to come this world will grow and prosper, as will your families and descendants after you. Allic, Leti, and Storm will jointly administer this world and it will be considered part of their realms."

The offworlders grinned at each other, their weariness forgotten. Mark looked over at Allic and smiled.

"That headstrong son of mine had nothing to do with this decision. I had formed it before I sent all of you out," Jartan's thoughts whispered to Mark, "but I should add he argued for it on your behalf, so let's just have him think it was he who pushed it through."

Mark chuckled inwardly.

"Take a few days to rest up, go visit your new lands, and then we'll gate you back to Haven. All of you offworlders have done enough campaigning for now. With the reinforcements coming in from Minar and Chosen I'll have more than enough sorcerers."

"Well, I'll be damned if I'm going back," Allic replied, "I've got some personal scores to settle with Gorgon, so don't ask me to play palace guard."

Jartan chuckled. "Still trust me enough to fight by my side?"

"Come on, father," Allic laughed, "please spare me the injured parent routine."

"It's just that you need a rest. A lot has happened to you over the last several months."

Mark watched Allic closely. Had it been up to him, he would have ordered the demigod to stand down. He'd seen too many men get pushed to the edge by combat. Allic's recent near-fatal injury and the shattering battle before Landra had been bad enough. The battle fought only hours before seemed to have put a cap on it. He could sense the brittleness in Allic, the jerky edge to his movements, the exhausted look in his eyes. The demigod was a classic case of combat fatigue.

"Don't let him go," Mark whispered inwardly, forcing his thoughts to Jartan. "Find an excuse."

"He's still a bit sensitive over the last issue," Jartan replied silently. "Though I thank you for the concern. But if I send him back now he'll lose face, and some might think I'm displeased over his emotional outburst. Don't worry, Mark, I'll try to keep him close by my side."

"This does upset my planning a bit," Jartan said aloud. "Leti, would you mind going back and acting as steward till my return?"

Leti looked at Ikawa. "I think I could find it in me to follow this obviously unfair order," she replied with a grin.

"Figured you would."

Storm gave Leti a slight, petulant frown. "You always get all the fun assignments. I always said he liked you more," she whispered, and her gaze focused wistfully on Mark.

"Enough of this!" Jartan laughed.

"If you, Minar, and Chosen are going on this assault, who will be in charge of Haven?" asked Leti.

"My sister Aleena will be nominal leader, but I am not expecting much to happen. If there's an emergency, attempt to contact her. You don't necessarily have to stay in Asmara—my people there will keep things running. Just stay in touch, and see what you can do for Aleena. We've all been neglecting her; I can understand her mourning, but a long time has passed since the Great War."

"It'll be tough. You know how she is."

"Well, I'm not anticipating anything serious, and we won't be gone that long."

Mark remembered what Kochanski, who was fascinated by the history of Haven, had told him about Aleena. The goddess had been mated with the dead god Danar and was still mourning his death, isolating herself almost completely from society.

"She can't be relied on if something unexpected comes up," Storm interjected.

"Don't worry," Jartan replied. "This campaign won't take long. Sarnak seems to be out of the picture, and Boreas will assist you in case he should finally reappear. As for Patrice— I doubt she would dare to act up while we're gone."

The flames in the pit seemed to come alive as Gorgon's presence filled the fire.

"You're hurt!" Patrice cried, stepping forward. Again, his visage was almost gentle, innocent, with soft features and rounded eyes. A jagged wound cut across his shoulder, oozing what appeared to be blood, but shimmered like molten steel.

Gorgon's image shook his head. "It is but a trifle. I almost forgot that I was supposed to lose when I closed with Jartan."

He bared his teeth, as if suppressing rage and frustration.

"The plan worked better than you can imagine. Without it I would have not prepared such an escape beforehand and he would have killed me. Who would have thought that he could have prepared such an elaborate ruse. And the power he was able to focus!"

"He has lost none of his cunning. That's why"—and at the last second Patrice stopped herself from saying "my"—"our plan is so brilliant. We use his own strengths against him."

The image in the fires seemed to study her for several moments.

"I have given up much already. My armies on the outer marches have been crushed, and I'll loose a dozen or more outposts as they move to take advantage of my supposed weakness. But each step in will draw them further into the web, and further away from Haven. Now, what of your tasks?"

Patrice felt his almost overpowering will focus on her. His eyes were mesmerizing in their power. Pulse racing, she felt an almost sexual charge course through her, and she fought desperately to master herself.

Gripping the arms of her chair tightly, and a little short of breath, she responded with an attempt at a sneer.

"Armies decimated. Outposts lost. Gorgon, your 'armies' undoubtedly included most, if not all, of the demons that are useless or potentially troublesome. When you have taken Haven there'll be other servants who are far more pleasing."

There was a roar of laughter from the demon lord, but the pressure of his will upon hers did not lessen, it merely took a different path.

"Most astute, Patrice. There were several in the unfortunate assault whose ambitions might eventually have become a nuisance. And I have very carefully blocked the portals to my key dimensional points. The outposts that are open to attack will fall, but are not critical."

Again his attention on her intensified.

"I am fortunate in my ally. Perhaps your cunning can equal Jartan's. However, you have not answered my question. How goes your plan to infiltrate Jartan's treasure vault? Without the portal crystal of dead Horat we can go no farther."

Patrice felt like she was losing control, and with an almost physical jerk she tore her gaze away from his, her aura almost blinding as she fought his mental assault.

Taking deep breaths she fought to get her racing heart under control. Then her temper snapped, and her aura became flame and she a creature of living fire. Surging to her feet, she flew to the edge of the pentagram and screamed, "This is my plan, and I can carry my part of the bargain. But I will not be trifled with or I'll call more than your image through this gate and teach you the lash of my power."

Gorgon lowered his gaze. "It is our way to push and dominate. You look so helpless when you are human that I sometimes cannot help myself."

"The gate will be ready when the time comes," she snapped, and with a wave of her hand broke the spell that kept the narrow portal open, and Gorgon faded from view.

Shaken by the encounter, Patrice entered the pit of flames to relax and cherish the fires, being very careful not to overstep the boundaries of the pentacle that opened the gate.

There was no doubt about it: Gorgon was too strong for her. She probably could beat him if he were restrained by the pentacle, but would not be able to withstand him in open combat. Again she felt the desire within her building. To mate, to consummate, with a demon lord like Gorgon—what would it be like?

Reason returned. *I must have the remaining Crystals of Fire. Only then will I be strong enough to control him.*

She spoke aloud amidst the roar of the fires, "And then I will do what I want!"

The light from the moons came through the open window of Imada's quarters in Jartan's castle, setting up a gentle cross-hatching of silvery hues. Almost spellbinding in intensity, the moonbeams crept across the floor as the moons glided across the sky.

When they touched the figures in the bed, there was a sigh and the woman stirred.

Carefully, the sorcerer within Vena stripped aside the layers of pain that hid her. Vena's memories, the anguish of remembering the screams of her parents as they were burned alive by

Sarnak's assault of their village, and her own rape, became a gossamer web that the sorcerer peered through cautiously.

A moment later, she emerged. The body was still Vena, but the spirit that guided it was Ulinda; over 900 years old, filled with the inner cunning that had caused her to rise into Patrice's most trusted circle.

With a touch of her hand she sent Imada into a deeper sleep, and rose from the bed.

Moving gracefully to the open window, she gloried in her new youth and beauty, standing naked in the moonlight.

She raised her arms over her head as if to absorb the light, and triumph raced through her. *To be young again*, she exulted. *No matter what happens, I feel young again.*

Dressing quickly, Vena left their room and went down to the garden in the courtyard below. There she walked around as if unable to sleep.

Stopping to sit on a bench under a tree, she seemed to relax while watching the beauty of a large fountain that poured forth water in majestic blues and white. Opening the case that she always carried with her, she took out a harp and began to softly strum a song.

Even the sorcerers on watch thought nothing of her presence, and other than an occasional check to insure her safety, ignored her.

Feeling the touch of the sorcerer on duty move on, Vena seemed to gesture to a bird on one of the lower branches of the tree. Moments later, the bird alighted next to her hand as it stretched along the back of the bench. A short hop to her shoulder, the exchange of the message telling her to proceed, and it was gone.

So. It is time at last, she thought. Fear of what she was about to undertake threatened to overwhelm her, and for a moment she considered the possibility of remaining as she was. But the bonds that were upon her were unbreakable, and she found her body moving toward the passageway even before her thoughts on the matter were finished.

Realizing the futility of attempting to fight the compulsion, she accepted the course of action and became one with her goal.

Ten minutes later she was at the door of Enaar's room. Very

carefully, she probed the latch and entered silently. There she breathed a sigh of relief. Once inside a private apartment she was safe from the scrutiny from the sorcerers on watch.

There on the bed lay Jartan's chief custodian of the treasure vault. Recently widowed, he seemed to radiate such torment even in his sleep that Vena had no trouble assimilating his thoughts.

His late wife had become accustomed to shopping in a store outside the protection of the palace over the last several months. There she had been finding rare and wonderful manuscripts that were of particular delight to her husband, at almost unbelievably reasonable prices. Even the store mistress had become a friend.

The tragedy that had occurred just five days ago had been almost unheard of. The explosion at the lamp oil shop next door had burned down almost half a block and caused a dozen deaths.

The shop mistress' testimony, and Enaar's identification of his wife's scorched crystals, were proof of an unfortunate accident that had shocked the court.

Standing in the bright moonlight, Ulinda used the data she had recently gotten from Patrice's agents in the city, who had interrogated the unfortunate—and still alive—wife, to carefully infiltrate Enaar's subconscious.

Only after about half a turning was she able to start to direct his thoughts. Years of similar efforts in Patrice's pleasure gardens stood her in good stead as she began to exert more and more control over his subconscious.

Stripping off her gown, she crawled in his bed and began to caress him, keeping him in a deep enough sleep that he would not awaken, but alert enough that she could control his dream.

Ten minutes later she had the information she needed. A simple dream of his wife trapped in the treasure vault had revealed everything. Not only did she have the code words to silently open the doors and put the ever-alert guard demons to sleep, but she knew the location of Enaar's private passageway.

A touch of her hand and Enaar's sleep deepened, his breath coming slower and slower. There was the faint whisper of his lost love's name, and then the breathing stopped.

It was best, she thought, though to her own surprise she felt a faint touch of pity. She could sense the agony of his loss, and it would appear that his old heart had simply given out from the pain of what he was enduring. Besides, only he and Jartan knew the codes by heart. It'd take time for someone else to get in to run the routine security check, and by then she'd be long gone.

An hour later she was back in her bed beside Imada. The two Crystals of Fire and Horat's massive portal crystal were now hidden in her harp case. There had still been room in the case, so Vena had taken something for herself, too. After all, with the risks she was taking, she deserved some extra compensation.

Carefully she retreated back through the veils of Vena's subconscious until only Vena was left, sleeping the sleep of the innocent.

Disappointed, Ikawa saw the portal's exit point looming up. If given his own way, he would have gladly embarked on an endless tour of Jartan's far-flung outposts, if only for the sheer joy of the jump-throughs.

The sensation of free-fall now gave over to a sense of returning weight and of a slowing down. The cone of light closed in, enveloping him, as if it was now swaddling him in a soft cushion to deaden the fall. He felt his feet touch ground. Rolling aside, he hit the cool turquoise floor of Jartan's main portal room. The glow was behind him now. Hands reached out, helping him to his feet.

Smiling, Ikawa looked around. Shigeru stood to one side, green-faced, looking about anxiously as if in sudden need of a bathroom. Walker was by the wrestler's side, unable to contain a teasing smile.

"I love that part when we slammed through the dimensional gate," Walker chortled, holding his hands up and waving them about as all flyers do. "It's better than pulling off a power dive."

"Do you want me to change the color of your tunic?" Shigeru groaned. "My stomach will be happy to oblige."

With mock horror Walker stepped back, to the good-natured laughter of the Japanese and Americans who stood clustered together.

Ikawa strode up, still smiling. It was hard to believe that only three days ago they had stood here, tension knotting their bodies, prepared to jump into what had nearly been their end.

"First thing I want," Saito announced, "is to get this damn poison capsule removed from my mouth. I haven't been able to eat right since they put it in."

"Ditto on that," Goldberg rejoined. "That, a hot shower, and a good rub-down by Shara, that masseur on Jartan's staff."

"You mean the little blond," Walker laughed. "I wanted a rub down from her myself, and not just a back rub if you get my meaning."

"What would that sorcerer, Suda Codi, say?" Goldberg interjected playfully. "The reunion you two had was rather audible to all of us last night."

"You should talk," Walker snapped, smiling wickedly. "You're talking about getting that rub down—what about this granddaughter of Macha we've been hearing about? Hell, Macha's got a grudge against Mark as is. I'm tellin' ya, he won't take lightly to your two-timing his precious granddaughter."

"Let's just get to the showers," Ikawa announced. "You fellows can sort out your little rendezvous later."

There was a chorus of agreements and the group headed off. Ikawa noticed there was a certain swagger to them, and as they passed out of the portal room and back up to the readying area, everyone they passed nodded respectfully, calling out greetings and compliments which the party revelled in. Laden down with battle gear, unshaved, and obviously a bit gamey, Ikawa felt a certain pride in the image they must project of hardened warriors back from a short but brutally tough campaign—an image that would be talked about throughout the palace and enhance their prestige even further.

Discarding their gear in the readying room, the men smiled with relief as the poison capsules were defly removed.

"To the shower and steam room!" Goldberg cried. "Last one there gets Matan's sister for the rub-down."

Matan was near legendary back at Landra: a two hundred and fifty pound bath attendant with hands like bear traps and a look to match.

Pushing and laughing, the group poured into the hallway, Ikawa in the lead. Stunned, he came to a stop, and was nearly bowled over by the men pushing in from behind.

"Imada!"

Unbelieving, Ikawa saw the young soldier standing before him, a lovely wisp of a girl standing protectively by his side, looking a bit fearful at the sudden rush of men moving toward her.

The boy nodded, trying to force back tears, and coming to attention, he saluted and bowed.

"Private Imada reporting, sir."

Grinning with delight, Ikawa returned the military salute he had not given now for what seemed like a lifetime, and then rushed forward to grab Imada by the shoulders and shake him with delight. The rest of the Japanese swarmed around the two, laughing and shouting, while the Americans stood to one side, grinning at the joy of their friends for the return of a comrade given up for dead.

"Now, how did you come back? What happened?"

Imada looked at the circle of his friends. "I'll try to explain what I can remember," he said shyly, "but it'll have to be Vena who does most of the talking." He nodded to the girl who still clung to his arm.

As if noticing her for the first time, the Japanese stepped back slightly, smiling at her, respectfully mumbling their greetings.

"And Yoshida?" Ikawa asked softly.

Imada lowered his head, and shook it sadly.

The group fell silent.

"Well, at least one of us has come back," Mark said softly, coming up to shake Imada's hand. He looked at Vena closely, smiling a greeting and noticed how she looked to Imada with a loving gaze. Yet somehow there was the ever so faint sensation that the gaze was a bit *too* intent, as if she was putting it on for the group's benefit. Their eyes locked for a second, and Vena quickly looked away.

"The showers can wait," Ikawa announced. "Let's go back to our quarters, I want to hear everything that happened to you."

"I'll be happy to share our story with you, Captain Ikawa." Vena whispered softly. "Imada has told me so much about you."

The group gathered in around Imada and Vena and continued down the corridor while Mark and the Americans fell in behind.

"Lucky guy," Walker said, coming up to Mark's side. "The

kid must have been through hell, it's been months since he disappeared."

"Yeah, a long time," Mark replied quietly.

"Allic!"

The demigod strode into the lounge area, nodding good-naturedly at the enthusiastic greetings. He could not help but feel a ripple of pride at these warriors who had added so much to his power and prestige, besides proving themselves loyal friends as well.

Inwardly he still rankled at how his father had used both him and these men. Even gods can make mistakes, and his timing for the counterstrike had been a little too close for comfort; it was still a wonder to him that at least one of the men had not broken and poisoned himself the moment the shielding went down.

Mark strode forward, hand outstretched in greeting. Allic looked at him closely—yes, Mark had recovered from his fears, and inwardly the demigod felt a sense of relief. He would have always protected the man, out of memory of his service in the war against Sarnak, but a proud warrior, if broken, would have continued on as merely a shell.

Allic thought on that for a moment, and how too often of late he needed yet another drink to steady himself. It was just a phase, he kept telling himself. But for one who could live for thousands of years, he knew far too many such as he who lived out a long twilight hidden away, lost in memories of other ages, burdened by life from which escape came all too slowly.

The burden of life: one too many lovers gone old and dead, too many offspring aging before him, too many battles fought on the razor edge of terror. He sighed inwardly, chasing the dark thoughts away. Varma, his jester and counselor, was always good for these moments, but the little man was back at Landra.

"Enjoying the rest?" he asked.

"Delightful," Mark said, though his voice betrayed a certain restless edge.

The rest of the group came up behind Mark, eager for news.

"Jartan has agreed to let you investigate the copy of Stonehenge that Kochanski found," Allic said, trying to force a smile. "Perhaps there could be a link back to your home."

A delighted whoop went up from Smithie, Kraut, and several of the Japanese, the rest smiling with varying degrees of pleasure.

Allic carefully watched the shades of reaction occuring around him, and knew that his feelings about this project were mixed as well. It was the natural desire of all men to return to their homes, and for those with strong attachments and families it was only natural. Though honor-bound to help these men, Allic knew that if they were successful, and this strange druid somehow knew a way back, he would lose not only his friends, but the strongest contingent of sorcerers it had ever been his fortune to recruit. For these men had already been a team before they had come to him, and fought with a skill and remarkable innovation that was stunning to behold; without them, the war against Sarnak might have gone very differently.

He looked closely at Mark and Ikawa, who in turn exchanged an uneasy gaze. They were comrades here, and sworn enemies back in their old world. If a way was open for them to return, Allic knew they were honor bound to go back to serve their countries, though it would mean giving up their power, titles, the women they loved, and perhaps their friendship as well.

Allic wished inwardly that this chance had never come up. In fact, if it had been up to him, he might have been tempted to hold them to their three-year contracts. But Jartan had overruled that, stating that such exceptional service had to be exceptionally rewarded in turn.

"What's happening with Jartan?" Ikawa asked, breaking the painful silence.

"We move out in a couple of hours. Jartan sat down and had a little chat with several of the demons we captured and managed to persuade them to reveal the portal they used to gain Yuvin and how to break through it. From there we'll be inside Gorgon's outpost realms. Hopefully, the challenge will bring him up. If not, we'll consolidate on that world, then gain the next portal in. At the least we'll pull a half dozen worlds into our sphere of control, and with luck we might just gain a final confrontation."

"Sounds like a hell of a good fight to me," Walker said softly, looking wistfully at the floor.

"You sure you won't need us?" Ikawa chimed in.

Allic smiled at this display of loyalty. He could sense that more than one sorcerer on the expedition was wishing to be anywhere but on a drive into Gorgon's realm, but here these men were still offering to volunteer. He knew some of it was sheer naivete over what might still be faced, but on the whole they were a group that was confident, tough, and did not like being kept out of a fight.

"It's not the fight to get yourselves tangled up in. Jartan wants people a little more seasoned in demon lore for this one."

"In other words, we're not good enough?" Ikawa asked.

Allic shoke his head. "In other words, you're too valuable to waste in this type of fighting. You've done your part; let the others do theirs. We need some reliable backups down here anyhow to keep an eye on things. Jartan feels your expedition can provide a valuable service just by checking out an area he has had no contact with or ventured to in quite some time. Besides being a reward, your trip will serve the broader plan as well."

He saw that this comment placated them, and provided an honorable way to be out of the next fight. If only they really knew how terrifying going into the demon dimensions would be. Just once before had he penetrated into the outer reaches of Gorgon's realms. It had been a travail of horrors. The human inhabitants, if they could be called such, were demented creatures who seemed to live merely for the slavery and sport of the demons. One could not move, drink, eat, or it seemed, even breathe without fear of a trap cunningly laid to catch the unsuspecting. Over everything there hovered a dread, a dark coiling fear that crept into the soul . . .

Noticing a carafe of wine on the table, Allic strode over and poured himself a drink. Taking a long pull, he finally turned back to face his comrades, forcing a smile.

"It'll be a picnic, so don't think you're missing anything we can't handle," he said evenly, clapping Walker on the shoulder. "Besides, the way you fly, you might be a danger to the rest of us."

"Ah, go on, sir, I can out-fly any of the old geezers you've got with you," Walker shot back.

"That's just the problem. They might want to burn your ass for your arrogance."

Walker broke into a grin at the compliment.

"How soon can you leave?" Allic asked, turning to Mark.

"We could be on our way as early as tomorrow. Leti has already gone over the route with us. I'm curious to see these floating islands that I've been hearing so much about."

"They sound like aircraft carriers from back home," Ikawa interjected.

"Aircraft carriers?"

"Large ships that we used back on Earth to carry and launch the airplanes that we told you about," Ikawa replied quietly, looking over at Mark.

"In the war your people were fighting with each other?" Allic inquired.

"They were proud ships," Shigeru said. "I had an uncle on the *Kaga*."

"You never told us that," Smithie said cautiously. "That was one of the ships that hit Pearl Harbor."

"And was lost at Midway," Ikawa added quickly.

"It's in the past now," Mark responded sharply, looking at Smithie.

The group fell silent, and Allic could sense that with even a remote prospect of returning home, old memories and possibly old antagonisms could again be stirred. He had warned Jartan of this but the god had insisted that it was a risk that had to be taken if the offworlders were to be fairly rewarded.

"It should be a pleasant enough trip," Allic went on. "The floating islands should make your journey an interesting and pleasant jaunt. Some of them date back to the Great War, when they were built so we could quickly move sorcerers from one continent to another. They are now a chain of free city states, so remember you will be outside both my jurisdiction and Jartan's.

"I don't want you cracking any heads in tavern brawls the way you did last month," Allic said with a smile, slapping Shigeru on the shoulder. "I won't be able to bail you out if you do."

The wrestler broke into a shy smile. "They started it," he whispered.

"Five to one odds against you hardly seems fair, though," Allic replied, his visage suddenly grim though his eyes betrayed a certain pride and amusement.

"I'll try to stay out of trouble, sir," Shigeru replied uncertainly, apparently unsure if Allic was angry with him or not.

"Come on," Allic laughed, "I'm going to miss you scoundrels. Let's have a couple of drinks and then I'll be on my way."

The crowd gathered around Allic, in front of a long table which was already strewn with half-empty bottles. They were soon laughing uproariously at Walker's latest round of crude jokes, but stopped to cheer enthusiastically when Leti came in.

"Having a night with the boys?" she asked, coming up and putting her arm around Allic.

He looked at her and forced a smile. He knew that she was fully aware of what could be faced on Gorgon's outpost worlds in just a matter of hours, and knew as well that his sister, if anyone, could see through the forced bravado.

"Just a couple of quick ones to see you folks off on your expedition."

"I wish you were going with us, my lord," Ikawa said, coming up to stand next to Leti.

So do I, Allic thought.

Scanning the faces of his men, he noticed that Imada, unlike the others, was not into his cups and sat quietly to one side. Taking Leti's arm and putting it onto Ikawa's shoulder, he broke away from the group and went over to the corner of the room. Nervously, the young offworlder came to his feet.

"It's a pleasure to have you back with me," Allic said cheerfully, looking straight into the boy's eyes.

"Thank you, sir." The boy fell quiet.

"I only had a couple of minutes to scan the report from Valdez and Pina. You went through a tough time, but you seem to have handled yourself quite well."

"If it hadn't been for Vena, I would never have made it back."

Allic was silent. At the mere mention of the girl's name he could see the wistful light in Imada's eyes. It was a remarkable story, and he knew Valdez to be thorough, but still he wished he had time to sit down and talk to this miraculous girl. One did not long survive as a demigod without being suspicious of anything that seemed to be too good.

"Sir, if it's all the same to you," Imada ventured quietly, "I'd rather not go on this expedition."

A little surprised, Allic looked closely at the boy.

"Not afraid of a little adventure are you?" he asked, feigning annoyance.

"No, it's not that at all," Imada replied, with a touch of indignation.

Allic smiled knowingly. "It's the girl—is that it?"

Imada smiled bashfully.

"I'm still ordering you to go on the trip, though," Allic said sternly.

Imada started to say something, thought better of it, and came to attention. "As you wish, sir. I'm sorry to have troubled you with it."

Allic started to turn away. Then, looking back at Imada, he felt himself soften. The boy was the youngest of all the offworlders, not even eighteen years old, yet if the reports were true his actions were those of a seasoned veteran. He hesitated, then called, "Leti, could you come over here for a moment?"

She broke away from the raucous crowd, Ikawa by her side.

"I think we have a little problem here," Allic said evenly, still looking at Imada.

"What is this about?" Ikawa said quickly, gazing at Imada, who now stood rigid.

"Leti, we've got ten of our older sorcerers going out with the group to handle the equipment and baggage, don't we?"

"There's a lot going with us," she replied, her voice edged with curiosity over why her brother was concerned about such a detail. "There's our personal equipment, clothing, some trade items, gifts for the island rulers and for this druid character. It's quite a load."

"Think they can handle another hundred pounds or so?"

"I guess so. Why do you ask?"

"I heard she's nearly as slight as you are," Allic said, still looking at Imada and breaking into a smile. "I think a hundred pounds or so would be just about right—though don't ask her. Women are all so damn sensitive about their weight."

Confused, Imada could not reply.

"Damn it, lad, the girl goes with you, if that's the problem. I think you deserve this little reward. In fact, I'm ordering her to go along to keep you out of trouble."

Unable to contain himself, Imada let out an exuberant whoop.

"Hey, what's going on?" Walker shouted, coming over to join the group.

"She's going with me. Vena's going with me!"

"I heard you like this woman called Watan," Leti said, looking at Walker with a mischevious grin. "Shall we bring her too?"

A look of mock horror lit Walker's features.

"Like hell, your ladyship. But if you could arrange for Rita Hayworth . . . "

"Or Suda Codi," Mark suggested.

"One is enough," Allic replied. "This is supposed to be a military reconnaisance, not a floating love trip.

"Now go tell this remarkable girl of yours that I'm ordering her to look out for your health during the trip—and damn it, the two of you better get a good night's sleep. Now, get out of here."

"Thank you, sir, thank you," Imada said, bowing low. Turning, he dashed from the room, followed by the delighted catcalls of his comrades.

Allic turned away and started for the door.

"My lord, forgive me for asking, but why?" Ikawa said, coming up beside him.

Why indeed? Allic wondered. He wasn't quite sure himself. If anything, the boy probably needed to be separated from her for awhile to reestablish his own sense of independence. Yet something in the back of his mind had whispered for him to do this. There was no logical reason, but Allic had found through long experience that at times his intuition could take what appeared to be the most inconsequential of events and turn them into a path that would later be more significant than he had ever anticipated. Doubtless this was only an indulgent whim, though, and smiling, he let the thought drop.

"Let's just say I can half remember a time when I was seventeen," he told Ikawa. "Anyhow, it's best that I be going. Take care of yourselves, and we'll see each other again shortly."

Allic was surprised when Ikawa suddenly extended his hand and grasped him by the forearm.

"Take good care of yourself, my lord. Our thoughts will be with you." Then, pulling back, Ikawa bowed.

Unable to reply, Allic merely nodded. Looking up, he caught Mark's gaze, and the outworlder, as if understanding something, wordlessly saluted.

"Take care, beloved brother." The thought whispered through his mind and he glanced over to see Leti staring anxiously at him.

"I always do," Allic thought in reply. She tried to smile, but didn't quite manage it.

Before the rest of the group had even realized it, Allic had slipped through the doorway and started down the corridor. Passing through the high-columned chambers of Jartan's audience halls, he looked about. All was silent and empty. With his father gone, followed by nearly all the sorcerers of his realm, Asmara seemed empty and still, like a tomb. The comparison troubled him as he continued on.

The few aging sorcerers who had been left behind to manage the portal nodded a wordless greeting as he entered the chamber. The glowing gateway shimmered before him.

"Any word?" he asked.

"The advance team hit through several hours ago, and gained a foothold inside one of Gorgon's dimensions," a white-haired sorcerer whispered. "We've taken some casualties, and Qubathin, Minar's youngest son, was killed."

"Damn it," Allic sighed, desperately wanting a drink. His hand drifted up to his tunic, and then he remembered that he had left his flask back at the party. The thought made him nervous.

He hesitated, tempted to go back and retrieve his talisman, but to do so now would look rather foolish.

"Are you ready, my lord?" the sorcerer murmured, nodding toward the portal.

He looked at the old woman and tried to smile.

"No," he whispered, "this time I'm not ready at all." Closing his eyes, he stepped forward and disappeared into the light.

Chapter 10

Overwhelmed with the sheer pleasure of flying, Mark dove ahead of the formation, banking in a tight downward spiral. The coastline of Jartan's realm had long since dropped astern, and for several hours they had made their way eastward, flying high to catch a strong tail wind. Kochanski had already reported sensing the first artificial island just beyond the horizon, and all were eager for the first view.

"Hey Captain, wait up!"

Mark looked over his shoulder to see Walker dodging in behind him, like a fighter rolling in to wax his tail. Laughing, he cut a sharp split S to the left, and Walker, catching on to the game, held tight, closing the range.

"Behind you, Walker!"

Saito swooped down, cutting a tight arc, and reached out to slap Walker's feet.

"I'll be damned!" Walker roared, his pride wounded. Jack-knifing over, he went into a vertical dive, with Saito hot on his heels.

The pair dropped away.

Mark watched the mock combat with interest. Saito had obviously been practicing. Walker continued his dive toward the ocean, and Mark felt a faint ripple of concern as his young tail gunner pulled out at the last second. Saito dropped below him, and a faint line of spray kicked up as he skimmed the water, wobbled, and then finally recovered to cut up and slap Walker's feet again. The action was greeted with a shout of delight from the Japanese.

Walker, not to be outdone, went into a vertical climb and finally his superior skill allowed him to pull ahead. Coming up nearly to Mark's height he flipped over and dove straight back down on Saito. Mark held his breath as the two closed with terrifying speed. At the last possible second Walker broke left, rolled, and snapped in behind Saito. There was a faint crack of light and a yelp from Saito as the gentle bolt brushed his backside.

Slowing, Mark looked back at Ikawa, and for a moment he felt the tension again, unsure of how the group would react. He could see the concern in Ikawa's eyes as well. There had been an undercurrent of nervousness between the two groups now that the prospect of a way back home had been offered.

Climbing again Saito and Walker flew side by side. With a mock show of pain Saito rubbed his rear end, then broke out laughing.

"Next time, my friend," he chuckled. Walker, grinning with delight, and as usual completely unaware of the others' concern, fell in alongside the sergeant, and the two traded a round of good natured jibes.

Mark looked over at Ikawa and forced a smile. "Saito's getting damn good."

"Your Goldberg's been giving him some pointers."

Your Goldberg. The way it was said struck Mark as strange. What was happening here? he wondered. Here on Haven he had found everything he had ever dreamed of having. Storm was a wonder of love that was beyond imagining. He held the power of a lord, and beyond that he could truly fly, a thrill still so intoxicating that for a moment his thoughts drifted again to the wonder of it all. About him were all his comrades, Americans and Japanese, weaving back and forth across the sky, racing ahead, climbing, dropping, chatting, and laughing as they leisurely floated through the air.

At the center of the group was a circle of ten of Jartan's sorcerers carrying a tightly woven net in which was piled their supplies, and the rather frightened Vena, with Imada floating by her side. In a way Mark felt sorry for the men and women who were assigned to be their bearers. They were a strange breed of sorcerers; never having mastered the lightning reflexes and offensive striking power for combat flying, they had instead developed the ability to carry heavy burdens through the air, and thus were always useful. They put him in mind of military transport pilots, absolutely essential to any endeavor, yet never knowing the ultimate challenge. They had developed their own guild, and looked at the single combat flyers around them like an adult troubled by a brood of boisterous children. Like transport pilots, they were the unsung heroes of any military operation, and in times of peace, they were in many ways far more important than the aerial combat flyers of Haven who could barely get off the ground with the burdens these sorcerers moved vast distances with ease.

What would happen to all of this if a gate back home was found? He tried to imagine life back on Earth and knew that he would be forever haunted by this dreamlike world. Yet he felt honor-bound to return; he had taken an oath and his country was still at war. What would it be like to return to that war? It was hard now to even imagine the sensation of holding a yoke in his hand, the whispering of the wind replaced by the roar of four Wright Cyclone engines. And the flak, the damn flak bursting ahead, with the Zeroes swinging in so that he felt small and naked as their cannon fire slashed through the plane.

Mark looked at Ikawa. They would have to kill each other back there. The two of them, who had more than once saved each other's life would be enemies again. Yet they were both honor-bound to go.

"Will you go back?" Mark asked, unable to contain the question any longer.

Ikawa tried to smile. "I have the same oath as you."

"We would be enemies again," Mark said sadly.

"That would never happen," Ikawa said, reaching out to touch Mark on the shoulder. "I would rather die myself than hurt you."

"I know that, my friend."

And Ikawa *was* his friend, the closest he had ever known.

"What about the others?" Mark asked.

"I think our oaths as officers are different," Ikawa replied. "I will not order any of my men to return. Here they are warlords; back home they would be nothing but numberless bodies. Yet even so, I think quite a few will go. The ties of their families are strong for them."

"I think Smithie might go back, maybe Kraut as well," Mark said slowly. "The others I'm not sure, but you're right, it will be up to each individual."

"You two seem awfully glum." Leti drifted to Ikawa's side.

"Oh, just chatting," Mark said, a little too quickly. He knew what Leti must be feeling; he had seen it in Storm's eyes when he had first told her about Kochanski's discovery of the druid. There had been no scene, she had carried herself as always with the mature bearing befitting her station. Where was she now—and Allic as well? Mark breathed a silent prayer for their safety. Here he was worrying about what was just a slim possibility, while his lord and the woman he loved might even now be in combat, or worse.

"The island should be just over the horizon now." As she spoke, Mark could discern a faint smudge of white.

"Tulana, we have you in sight now," Leti announced into her comm crystal.

"Good to hear from you, Leti, you lovely old wench."

Startled, Ikawa looked at his lover.

A faint blush tinted her face. "Tulana's an old friend," she explained. "He owns the central chain of islands. We've known each other a long time."

"I see," Ikawa said evenly, trying hard to hide any jealousy.

"Your bottom still as lovely as ever?"

She held the crystal away and said quickly, "He never got that far."

"It's all right," Ikawa replied, trying to stay calm.

Mark struggled unsuccessfully to suppress a grin.

"Well damn me, woman, tonight will be like old times, so hurry up and get down here, I've been waiting all day. In fact I've been waiting for nearly a damn decade to see you again."

"We'll be down shortly, coming in out of the southwest." Then Leti touched Ikawa's hand and said. "He can be a little tiresome."

Ikawa merely nodded.

Feeling it best to leave the two alone, Mark swung away and climbed through the light scattering of clouds. The air was warm and pleasant, the ocean below a splendid turquoise glittering in the late morning sun.

Still riding the easterly wind, the group held formation a mile above the ocean. At first it appeared they were approaching an anchored ship, floating in the middle of the sea, but as they drew closer the sheer size of it all started to set in.

"Damn thing must be five thousand feet across," Goldberg shouted, coming up to fly beside Mark.

"Makes a carrier look like a rowboat!" Kochanski called.

Amazed, Mark felt as if he was flying over a 17th century fortress town in Europe. The island was laid out in a star pattern, the five points resting on massive circular pontoons, dominated by spirelike battlements which tapered upward into towering masts. Each of the five points was obviously a bastion with crenellated walls and a central keep. The five bastions were free-floating, linked back to the central island by broad triangular drawbridges, with the points reaching the bastions, and the bases linked firmly to the main island.

The central part of the star was more than six hundred yards across, resting on a circle of pontoons. From the air it looked like a crazy patchwork quilt of narrow streets, warehouses, homes, and even several small temples. Bobbing at the tip of each bastion were glass-covered stills, which converted the sea water, through evaporation by the sun, into drinking water. On the leeward side of the island, the open space between two of the bastions served as a harbor for what appeared to be half a hundred fishing vessels and a score or more heavy oceangoing sailing ships.

The sailing ships captivated Mark's attention almost as much as the island city. The largest one, nearly a football field in length, was reminiscent of the classic clipper ships of McKay which had raced the famous China route a hundred years before. The ship was twin hulled, its lines sleek and graceful, with masts a hundred yards or more in height.

"Damned if that one over there doesn't look like a trireme," Kraut shouted, pointing to an arrow-sleek vessel that was cutting through the gently rolling sea, its oars rising and dropping in unison.

"Time to go down," Leti called, and winging over she started into a nearly vertical dive

"Look, I'm a dive bomber," Walker shouted, and extending his arms like wings, he rolled up and over. Laughing, the rest of the group fell to imitating him. Mark joined in the fun, arms extended, plummeting straight down.

The star city filled the world beneath him, rushing ever closer. Following Leti's lead, they dove directly towards the central part of the island, to an open platform atop a pyramid-shaped temple. Mark cut his speed and swung out, then circled in and lightly touched down, the rest of the group alighting around him. The platform was empty except for the new arrivals. Looking up, he saw the transport sorcerers making a far more stately and workmanlike approach, Imada still hovering alongside them.

"Leti darling!"

Mark turned to see a huge, shambling bear of a man, nearly seven feet in height, with shoulders as wide as Shigeru and a flowing auburn beard that swept down past a broad leather belt which seemed ready to burst due to his tremendous girth.

The giant strode forward and with a single hand swept Leti into the air, as if she were a toy. With a display of bravado he loudly kissed her on the cheek and then made as if to kiss her on the neck.

"All right, Tulana, put me down, damn it!" Leti shouted, but Mark could hear in her tone that she was delighted to see him.

The huge man dropped Leti and surveyed the group.

"So where's this great warrior that ruined my chances for you?" he roared.

Leti nodded toward Ikawa who stepped forward. Mark could see that his friend was anything but pleased at the reception they had received so far.

Tulana extended his hand, his eyes aglow. Ikawa took it, and there was a moment of silence as if the two were sizing each other up.

A grin finally creased Tulana's face.

"You're all right, my man. Though when I first heard about you, I had a mind to look you up and tear your head off out of sheer jealousy—till I heard the particulars. Anyone who could win back Leti's Crystal of the Night is a better man than I, and damn my eyes and teeth, I don't admit that very often."

Ikawa finally relaxed, and Leti, with perhaps a little too much show, slipped her hand into his.

"By Jartan's bloody eyes, I'll bet you offworlders have never seen a floating city like mine," Tulana shouted.

Surprised at the blasphemy, the sorcerers looked nervously around.

"Oh, don't worry yourselves none. I got some of the codger's blood in my veins. I'm a grandson of Boreas and a great-grandson I am of Jartan's on my mother's side. I'm a favorite of Jartan to boot, so I'll swear by the old goat as much as I like, damn me. I guess that means I was just making a pass at one of my great aunties." Tulana roared at his own joke.

"Come on, I'll show you the sights and then it's time to break open a barrel or two of beer."

"Did you say beer?" Walker shouted.

"The best to be had."

"Say, I think I'm gonna like this place." Eagerly he fell in alongside the ruler, who, still shouting imprecations, started down the steps of the pyramid.

Mark walked over to Ikawa, who smiled and said, "I thought the son of a bitch was going to break my hand."

"I think he likes you," Leti ventured, unable to keep from grinning.

"Well, thank God for that," Ikawa replied. "I certainly wouldn't want to upset the family."

"You know," Mark said, unable to contain himself, "if you two ever make some sort of formal marriage out of this, that guy's going to be your nephew-in-law."

"Just what I've always wanted," Ikawa groaned.

After several hours of crisscrossing the city, which Tulana was showing off with evident pride, Mark found himself to be captivated by the place. Even in the unique world of Haven, it ranked as one of the more bizarre regions he had ever seen.

Tulana's island of Salemar was over three millennia old, and as far as he could guess, the giant had been ruling it and eight others like it since their creation during the Great War. The islands had originally been created as rest points for sorcerers crossing the ocean and afterwards evolved into major trade ports linking the continents. There were now four such chains crossing the ocean and from each of the chains, like spokes on a wheel, dozens of minor centers radiated outward so that no point on the ocean was more than half a day's flying time from a safe haven. Tulana kept boasting that his system was the first, and that all the others were but minor systems controlled by rivals who at best were simple-minded incompetents.

Mark found that there was a certain organic quality to the arti-

ficial island, like an ever-living organism that was forever building itself, wearing down, and replacing parts at need. It was,
Mark felt, as if a great ship from the time of Alexander had
somehow survived across the ages, due to constant maintenance,
and through time had acquired the architecture and design of
every ship that had been built afterward, so that in the end the
vessel was an historical melange.

The floating island was built on a series of pontoons, which
in turn were anchored by heavy cables to the ocean floor. Each
island was located above a relatively shallow spot in the ocean,
so the depth here was under a thousand feet. All elements of
its design had been engineered to ride out the roughest storm.

But the city's understructure was what held his attention the
most. A vast interworking of pegged timbers, ropes and iron
beams, it set up a cacophony of creaks and groans as the island
rolled in the sea.

The city supported nearly ten thousand inhabitants and was
far more than merely a port of call for sorcerers flying across
the ocean. It served as a trade center and safe haven for ships
as well, but gained most of its livelihood from the shepherding
and harvesting of fish.

"I've got millions of tons of food growing out there," Tulana
boomed, pointing expansively to the shimmering ocean. "I'm
prince of a chain of nine of these islands and control most of
the central ocean. It's the best damn realm in this world!"

Tulana looked back at the weary travelers who sat about his
long table in the main feasting hall, which on all sides was open
to the pleasant afternoon breeze, offering an uncluttered view
of the sparkling ocean in every direction.

"A beer would sound mighty good right now," Walker said,
looking hopefully up at Tulana.

"Ah, damn me, I've been neglecting you." Laughing, Tulana
clapped his hands.

A doorway into the floor opened and half a dozen servants
appeared, dragging up a heavy barrel which they deftly cracked
open. Heavy leathern flagons were filled and passed around,
foaming amber brew dripping down their sides. Without waiting
for the others, Tuluna swept up a flagon in his beefy hands
and drained it off. Expectantly he looked over at Walker who

tentatively sniffed the brew, brought it to his lips, and took a short pull. A look of delight lit his eyes.

"This stuff is great!" Kochanski called.

"Now for some mituni," Tulana shouted, and servants appeared carrying trays of golden fish, sliced into thin strips. The Americans looked at each other in confusion.

"Sushi!" Shigeru cried and, caught up in the informality of his host, the lumbering wrestler stood, scooped a handful of raw fish from a passing platter, and downed it in a single gulp.

"Excellent!"

"Jesus Christ," Smithie mumbled, looking at Mark. "Is that stuff what I think it is?"

"Raw fish," Mark said, trying not to appear nonplussed, while around him the Japanese eagerly dived into the repast.

"How the hell can you eat that stuff?" Walker asked Saito, while trying to keep a look of disgust off his face.

"It's delicious," Saito replied, spearing a long golden sliver on the end of a fork and passing it to Walker.

Walker wrinkled his nose.

"They say it makes you a better lover," Shigeru growled. He leaned over Walker's shoulder and dangled a piece in front of Walker's face.

Walker tentatively sniffed it. "I don't want to tell you what it reminds me of," he said quietly, and Mark couldn't help but break into a laugh.

Tulana, surveying the scene with obvious amusement, clapped his hands again.

"Bring in the zah!"

"Damn it, look at the size of that lobster!" Kraut shouted. The room broke into a round of excited cries as four servants appeared, carrying a monstrous, four-clawed creature, steamed red and nearly the size of a man.

Laying the creature before Tulana, one of the servants handed him a heavy mallet. Tulana brought the weapon smashing down on a claw, which cracked wide open to reveal a mass of creamy white meat. Pulling a knife from his belt, Tulana sliced out several pounds of flesh with deft strokes, speared the chunk on the end of the blade, and leaned over the table to offer it to Mark.

"Go on, take a bite, and pass it on."

Mark bit and was stunned by its sweet richness. Grinning, he passed the blade to Kochanski.

"Better than Maine hardshell," Kochanski replied with delight.

The servants now fell to, wrestling the claws free, smashing them open, and passing the meat about, while Tulana buried his face in the first claw, so that his beard was soon coated with juice and meat.

"See why you didn't have to worry about me being interested in him?" Leti said quietly, smiling at the Japanese captain, who was fastidiously cutting a large piece of zah into more manageable slices.

In the distance a horn sounded, counterpointed by a rolling of drums.

Tulana tossed the half-devoured claw onto the floor, his eyes afire. "Damn them, they're at it again!"

Cursing, he walked over to the edge of the pavilion and leaned over the side.

"From what direction?" he bellowed.

"Northeastern quadrant. A patrol ship just relayed the message," came a voice from below.

"How many?"

"Three, possibly four. They're Cresus—we know that for certain."

"I'll bet my pouches they're the same ones hit us last week and killed old Gupta. Well, make the ship ready, I'm getting sick of these bastards.

"All right," Tulana shouted, walking back into the center of the room, "feasting's over for now. We're going hunting!"

"These men have never done something like this before," Leti said anxiously. "Maybe they should sit this one out."

"What the hell—they're sorcerers, aren't they? Come on, a little hunting will do them good.

"What say you," Tulana yelled to the assembly, "you're not afraid of a little fishing expedition, are you?"

"Fishing? I'd love to!" Shigeru cried, lumbering to his feet and tossing a handful of sushi aside. "Let's get going."

The group, carried away with the feasting and Tulana's half angry, half excited mood, shouted approval.

"To the ships, then!" Tulana stormed over to the trap door, followed by a boisterous mob.

"Just what the hell are Cresus?" Mark asked, falling in beside Leti, who was obviously less than pleased.

"They're fish," she said quietly.

"What kind of fish?" Mark asked, although he really didn't want to know.

"Carnivorous, and bigger than a house. They're a constant problem for the sea shepherds."

"You mean like a shark?" Ikawa asked.

"I don't know the word," Leti replied, "but if a shark can swallow an entire ship, you've got the right idea."

"Here we go again," Ikawa said, trying to smile.

Following Tulana's lead, the party poured into the street, which was aswarm with several hundred men racing down to the boats docked on the lee side of the island. The atmosphere was strange: grim, but with a wild note of excitement. Above the general confusion, Tulana's voice could be heard booming out oaths and commands.

Reaching the harbor side, Mark was delighted to see that they were going to board the large clipper-type ship he had seen from the air.

"What do you think of her?" Tulana called, pointing expansively. "*Cloud Dancer* is the finest one afloat!"

Not waiting for a response, he turned away, and with a good deal of cursing and shouting, ordered the ship to depart.

"I think we're going to be swimming underwater," Leti announced. "The rest of our group hasn't had a chance to practice so I'd better give them some pointers right now." Calling the offworlders together, she hurriedly started to explain the techniques of breathing beneath the waves.

Mark and Ikawa broke away from their men and wandered astern to where Tulana stood by the wheel.

"We've got four of them out there for certain," Tulana announced. "One is old Naga—he's been a thorn in my side for years. Wait until he finds out I've got over a score of sorcerers and another demigod with me this time!"

"It sounds like it's going to be exciting," Mark said tentatively.

"Exciting? There's nothing like it! I hate the damn things. They can swallow a hundred tons of the finest mituni in a single pass and be out again in an hour. This time of year they cruise the western end of my chain; later in the season they'll shift further east. And the gods help us if they ever got to one of my cities— they'd make splinters of it in the flash of an eye. But damn my soul, if they weren't here to pester me, I'd die of boredom, I would."

"All's ready!" came a cry from forward.

"Cast away, then," Tulana shouted. "Hoist all sails."

"Why don't we just fly out to where they are?" Ikawa ventured. "It'd be faster."

"I'll need the rest of the men when we get them to breach. But you'll see, we've got a broad reach today, we'll be there in no time.

"Clear away!"

A curtain of white canvas thundered down from above, filling the masts. The crew, cursing and shouting, worked the sheets, pulling the sails in, while from above came a wild litany of shouts and chanties as the men let out yet more sails.

A shudder ran through the huge vessel as Tulana guided it out past the star point bastions.

"Now hang on," Tulana shouted, a delighted grin on his face.

Spinning the wheel hard over, he pointed the ship north. The canvas sails snapped and thundered, bellying out with the wind, and the deck started to heel over. Nervously Mark looked around for something to grab on to.

The vessel lurched and the deck canted even higher, while the crew strained at the windlasses, hauling the sheets in tight, cranking the vast fore and aft sails down to form winglike airfoils.

"We're flying a hull," Tulana cried as the canting continued so that Mark felt as if the entire vessel would roll straight on over. Unable to contain himself, he lifted off the deck.

"A land walker to be sure," Tulana shouted good-naturedly. "But go on, fly out a bit and see me beauty sail."

Mark looked over at Ikawa, who flew up to follow Mark through the rigging. Sailors waved to them as they rose above the ship.

"It's magnificent!" Ikawa cried.

Cloud Dancer cut through the water like a knife, its massive fore and aft sails pulled taut as drumheads. It sliced easily through the waves, kicking up curtains of spray and leaving a rooster tail plume fifty feet high in its wake. The curtains of water caught the early afternoon sun in a rainbow wash.

"She must be doing close to thirty knots," Ikawa said. "It's just amazing."

Together the two swooped down, racing along the downwind side, slicing through the salty spray and then arcing back up again. Pointing to the foremast crow's nest, Mark raced through the rigging once more and alighted next to several sailors who were anxiously peering forward.

"A good day for a hunt," one of the sailors cried.

Forgetting what Leti had told him only moments before, Mark smiled in agreement and settled back to enjoy the invigorating roller coaster ride.

"There they are!" one of the lookouts shouted at last, pointing to several small boats on the horizon.

Cupping his hands, the sailor leaned over the railing. "Straight ahead," he roared.

Tulana came floating up through the rigging to hover next to the crow's nest. He brought up his communications crystal and listened as a report came in from the ships ahead.

"Four of them to be sure—it'll be a hell of a hunt. Get your people ready!" he shouted.

Rising from the crow's nest, Mark and Ikawa followed Tulana back down to the deck.

"Clear the boats," Tulana ordered, and the deck crew, racing to the port and starboard railings, pulled the canvas clear from a dozen sleek, two-masted catamarans. At the bow of each of the boats was a massive catapult armed with a twelve-foot spear tipped with a razor-sharp barb, and stacked alongside each weapon were a dozen more bolts. Forward on the main deck, a battery of four more catapults were revealed that stood nearly fifteen feet high, armed with twenty-foot bolts.

"They've got double torsion catapults," Kochanski said excitedly. "It's like an ancient navy going to war."

In spite of his earlier trepidation, Mark found himself getting caught up in what was happening.

"Gather round," Tulana commanded, and for the moment the giant became serious and grim-faced as the offworlders clustered around him.

"We're gonna have a grand time in a couple of minutes. Leti's told me that except for your leaders, you folks have never been underwater before."

The men exchanged nervous glances. Mark could see that besides the underwater briefing, Leti must have been filling them in on what they would be facing, for their previous childlike enthusiasm had definitely been tempered.

"Now the Cresus is a terrible big beastie, not very smart, but nasty when he gets riled. We'll pick up our ladultas once we get near, and then we start in."

"What are ladultas?" Ikawa asked.

"Friends of ours—you'll see. Hopefully there'll be enough to tow us all in; I sent word ahead to get extra mounts for the rest of you. Now, once we start to close, the trick is to get underneath a Cresus and then start hitting him with your energy bolts. Aim for the ass end of the damned things, they're real sensitive there, but watch out for their tail flukes. Have you got all of that?"

"I think so," Mark replied, though he wasn't quite sure what had just been said. "You mean we just shoot to kill them and that's it."

"Kill them?" Tulana roared, looking over at the two sorcerers from his island, who started to laugh uproariously. "Kill them, he says!"

"What's so funny?" Mark asked, looking at a short, barrel-chested sorcerer who had stripped to nothing but a loin cloth.

"It's just to get the damn things moving," the Sorcerer told him. "You see, we want the things to breach."

"What the hell is breach?" Goldberg asked.

"You know, like in *Moby Dick*—to get them out of the water," Kochanski responded. "I guess the catapults are to finish them off."

"Aye, you've got it, laddie," Tulana rejoined, slapping Kochanski on the back and knocking the wind out of him. "We want the damned things to breach, and by Jartan's hairy ass it's a sight that'll make a god tremble. When you got one heading up, get out of the water ahead of it, so the boat crews know what's coming. If it looks like the thing is going to hit a boat, it's your job to go back in and divert it a wee bit."

"And how do we do that?" Ikawa asked nervously.

"You go back in and give it a couple of strikes along the head to steer it in the opposite direction, then get the hell out of the way and watch the show."

"In range!" came a shout from above.

"Helmsman, take her into the wind and clear away the boats. Sorcerers, follow me, and by the gods don't let any of them get near this ship. Old Naga would just love to eat this thing for dinner."

Pulling off his tunic, Tulana quickly stripped down to skin and crystals, all the time giving Leti a lascivious grin. The goddess slipped out of her tunic and flying breeches, but shaking her head at Tulana, she modestly left her undergarments on.

"Let's go then," Tulana ordered, his disappointment obvious. He flew across the deck and out over the ocean toward a light catamaran that was running close hauled before the wind.

Leti and the offworlders followed him, the men quiet for a change.

"There's our ladultas," the barrel-chested sorcerer called, pointing to what appeared to be a boiling foam of water, laced with fins.

"They look like sharks to me," Walker said nervously.

"More like dolphins," Shigeru said excitedly.

Slowing, the group drifted down to the water. Tulana plunged right in, disappeared for a moment, and then surfaced, while the offworlders hovered nervously above the waves.

"Come on in, the water's great," Tulana shouted. A fin came up alongside him and several of the Americans shouted warnings, to which Tulana replied with laughter. "They're friends," the prince roared. "Now get your asses in the water, damn it."

Setting the lead, Mark plunged in. When he resurfaced, he saw a lithe torpedo-shaped creature that looked a bit like a sailfish circling tight around him. Mark gazed suspiciously at the ladulta. Its eyes were large and round, almost like a baby seal's. Drawing closer, the creature gently nudged him.

"Air breather, friend?"

Startled, Mark could only swim down to look at the ladulta.

"Friend, airbreather kill Cresus?" Like a Tal, the ladulta was telepathically communicating with him.

Smiling, Mark reached out to touch it.

"Friend," he thought, "never fight Cresus before. Will you help me?"

"Help good. I am Sul named; take hold my top fin. Cresus bad, kill our young, try to smash cities of airbreathers. We teach them lesson today."

Tentatively, Mark grabbed Sul's dorsal fin and let the ladulta pull him back to the surface. It came nearly out of the water, blowing air. Taking a throaty breath through a breathing hole in the middle of its back, it dove slightly.

"Say, these things are like Tals!" Imada shouted.

"There's enough here for all of us," Tulana shouted, as the off-worlders floundered around the water, getting oriented. "Trust their judgment; they know this game better than you. We'll stick together as a group—if you get separated from your ladulta, just call his name and keep calling it till he picks you up."

"Worg, stay on the surface and direct the action up here. Mark and Ikawa, keep track of your people and I'll call the commands in to you. Shift your crystals accordingly."

The barrel-chested sorcerer mumbled a curse, but nodded in reply.

Tulana disappeared below the waves, then surfaced again. "I've got one. Follow me."

"Hold tight," Sul commanded, and together he and Mark plunged beneath the waves.

"Check in," Mark called through his comm crystal.

"Smithie here."

"Goldberg here. This is great, Captain."

"Walker. I don't like this underwater shit, captain."

"Kochanski here. Everything's all right."

"Kraut here. Captain, I'm sensing something really big up ahead—make that two, no, *four* images forming."

Mark turned his attention forward and sensed a vast moving wall straight ahead.

"Ikawa here. My people are all right."

"Hang on, my friend, something damn big ahead."

"I've got it, Mark." Sul surged forward with remarkable speed and Mark was thrilled by this strange charge into the sea. Propelled by the ladulta's powerful undulating action, Mark rode above the creature, hanging on with his left hand so his right would be free to fire.

A dull flash lit the ocean ahead, followed an instant later by a deafening roar.

"Tulana hit good," Sul whispered, and Mark could sense the delight in the creature's thoughts.

"I'm on to one," Tulana's voice roared through the crystal. "Close on me and let's get him up."

Sul, as if having heard Tulana's voice, swam forward. In spite of the shielding which protected Mark from the drag of the ocean, he found himself struggling to hang on as the ladulta charged in.

Looking around, he could see the other ladultas closing in, each towing an offworlder. More than one sorcerer was gripping his ride with both hands and cursing wildly.

Suddenly the ocean before Mark turned a darker blue, and then went black.

"Hang on!" Sul called, and instantly he snapped over, diving straight down.

"Holy shit!" Walker screamed, and the comm crystal was suddenly overloaded with shouts of panic, matched by Mark's own cry.

The ocean before him was a vast cavern of darkness half a hundred feet across, surging in his direction. The circle of darkness was rimmed with teeth, each of which was the size of a man.

The darkness surged past, buffeting Sul and Mark. Behind the mouth was a great dark bulk that seemed to stretch off into infinity.

Tulana appeared straight ahead, racing beside the creature. Turning, he swung in next to Mark.

"I figured I'd stir him up for you first," Tulana roared. "It's just a little one for you folks to break in on. Now let's get him upset!"

"You crazy bastard," Mark yelled, but his words were drowned by the shouts of his companions.

"Start fire," Sul whispered.

Mark pointed his hand at the massive bulk gliding above him and fired. His shot was followed instantly by a score of others.

A deafening roar boomed through the ocean, and the Cresus kicked and rolled, buffeting Mark and his ladulta.

"Again!" Tulana ordered.

Another volley laced out. Suddenly the creature's tail loomed straight ahead, flukes slashing back and forth as the Cresus turned and started up.

"He's breaching!" Tulana shouted. "Everybody out of the water!"

Sul cut away from the Cresus and raced straight upward, rocketing past their prey.

"Release," Sul called. "I wait in direction of sun."

Mark let go and, clearing the surface, he flew into the sky, blinded by the afternoon glare. Around him the water seemed to explode as the offworlders soared into the air. Several launches stood by not fifty yards away, their aft catapults pointed to where the sorcerers had emerged.

"He's breaching," Tulana roared, exploding out of the water below Mark. "Everyone get your asses clear."

Directly beneath Mark the water suddenly turned black. A geyser exploded under him, threatening to tumble him as he shot away.

And then the Cresus appeared.

The mouth, its teeth glinting wickedly in the sun, rose heavenward, higher and higher into the air. Transfixed, Mark floated above it.

Yet still it came upward—fifty feet, then a hundred feet, the water exploding around it like a tidal wave.

A glint of light shot past, and the creature gave a bellow and seemed to rear even higher.

Another glint, and a catapult bolt snapped past Mark to bury itself in the creature's head.

A third bolt shot out, catching the creature in the middle of its body. A geyser of hot blood sprayed the ocean in rivers of red.

The Cresus shrieked and kicked, and then like a mountain it fell on its side. As its body hit the water, a towering wall of water and foam kicked into the air.

"Good shooting!" Tulana cried.

The Cresus rolled and kicked on the ocean's surface, while the three launches crested the tidal wave and circled in, slamming three more shots into its head.

Tulana soared to Mark's side. "Fun, isn't it?"

Stunned by what he had just witnessed, Mark just looked at the prince.

"Now let's go for a big one," Tulana yelled. Turning, he dove westward to where the ladultas circled, waiting.

"Fun, he said," Walker called to Mark. "If I hadn't been swimming naked, I'd still be cleaning the shit out of my pants."

"Well, let's get after them," Leti shouted, and Mark could see that she was caught up in the excitement of the hunt.

"In and after them," Kochanski screamed, swinging in behind Tulana. "Thar she blows!"

Shigeru roared with joy and dove past Mark. Finally caught up in the thrill of the chase, Mark followed, plunging into the ocean and calling Sul's name. Within seconds his companion appeared, joyfully spinning through the water in a series of loops before coming up alongside Mark.

"Good kill," Sul called. "Now let's get big one!"

"Lead on!" Mark shouted.

As they dove, the world started to turn dark, the visible reds near the surface shifting in the water through green and into an ever-darkening blue.

"I've got him," Tulana called through the comm crystal. "Tell your ladultas to track on me!"

As Mark relayed the command, Sul made a sharp banking turn and raced away.

Mark turned his senses forward, probing, and picked up the images of Tulana and Leti ahead of the group.

"Naga! It's him, damn it!" Tulana screamed.

The effect on the ladultas was electric: A series of throaty growls echoed through the water in a strange harmonic chorus that shifted and wove itself in a multivaried interplay of minor chords.

"What the hell is that?" Mark thought.

"Battle chant," Sul's thought returned. "Let Naga know we come, that we come to kill. He take many young, many herd brothers, many mates. Now we fight again."

"Thar she blows," Kochanski cried through the comm. "The damn thing's a monster!"

Mark strained his attention forward, and suddenly the image formed. His first instinct was to recoil, but the wild charge through the ocean and the ladultas maddening song overcame him.

"Bugler sound charge!" Kraut yelled.

"Banzai!" came Shigeru's growl as his ladulta pushed forward. Naga's massive bulk grew ever wider. The sorcerers were coming in on a broadside strike, and Mark, scanning back and forth, could barely sense either end of the creature.

"The damn thing's at least two hundred yards long!" Ikawa shouted.

Tulana and Leti, forcing their ladultas to slow, waited for the rest of the group to catch up.

"We're near the bottom. It's one of his old tricks, so watch out," Tulana shouted. "Everyone fire on my command!"

In a tight formation the group surged in. At the last possible second the team jackknifed straight down to the creature's side. The Cresus was simply gliding along as if his tormentors were only a minor annoyance.

Sul jackknifed once again, turning directly underneath the massive beast.

"Fire!"

The water crackled into steam. Unable to miss, Mark pointed and let go with a fiery bolt.

"He's crushing down!" Tulana roared. "Break out!"

Horrified, Mark saw the monster's bulk come dropping.

Sul spiraled down and out, skimming so close to the sandy bottom that he sent up a wave of silt. Alarmed cries drowned out the comm link, ladulta shrieks filled the sea, and over everything else was the insane trumpeting of the enraged Cresus. Sul pulled away at the last possible second, as the mountain of flesh slammed down on the ocean floor. A tidal surge stormed out, and to his horror Mark saw more than one of his comrades torn free of their ladultas by the turbulence. But their mounts heroically circled back to pick up the dismounted sorcerers.

The ocean around Mark went black. It seemed impossible, but sweeping around him was a massive tail fluke, bigger than the side of a hanger.

At Sul's command, Mark slammed out shot after shot, though the ocean around him was a wild confusion of energy bolts, darting ladultas, and—filling his vision—the writhing form of Naga, bent on crushing them.

Sul pulled up over the fluke and raced down its backside, expertly rolling with the turbulent wake.

"Keep shooting!" Sul kept calling.

Mark, grasping at last that Sul and he were a team, finally started to block out the flow of the action, trusting to his companion to safely guide him through the battle and focusing only on placing his shots.

Shigeru banked in alongside Mark, exuberantly firing at the massive underside of the tail.

Suddenly the Cresus rose from the ocean floor and surged forward, his two hundred foot wide tail slamming up and down. The ladultas broke away, avoiding the turbulence, and with what Mark thought was incredible bravery started to dart underneath the creature. More than one of the offworlders, simply overwhelmed by the battle, was still not firing. Sul cut down and started a run, straight up the length of Naga's body, and Mark slammed off a series of bolts, unable to miss.

"Wonderful strikes, wonderful. We finally getting him mad," Sul cried.

"I thought he already was mad!" Mark called.

"Just getting started. Hang on!"

The creature surged downward again and Sul darted away. There was another boom as the Cresus slammed into the bottom, and then it was up again.

From the corner of his eye, Mark saw a ladulta spiraling upward, pushing a limp form. It was Goldberg!

"One of my men is hurt!" Mark cried.

"My brother Gavd, he take him up. Airbreather not dead, just knocked asleep."

Anxiously, Mark looked around, unable to see more than a

handful of his companions. Another ladulta spiraled by, swimming spasmodically in a jerky spiral, with Saito no longer holding its dorsal fin, but now swimming alongside as if trying to help the creature to the surface.

Sul let out a cry of rage and turned to go back in.

"He's going to breach!" Tulana roared through the comm link. "Everyone up and clear!"

Sul leaped through the water, rocketing straight up into the light.

"Meet in direction of sun. Release!"

Mark cleared the surface and was stunned to see *Cloud Dancer* less than a hundred yards away.

"Break him east!" Tulana roared. "To the east, the bastard's after my ship again!"

Turning, Mark arced back into the ocean, even as his other comrades were coming up out of the water.

"Sul! Damn it, Sul!"

The ladulta surged in and, without slowing, Mark grabbed his companion's fin.

"Naga is wily one! Go for ship," Sul cried. "We must aim for Naga's eye."

The darkness was coming up with blinding speed.

Now trusting Sul's judgment, Mark hung on as the ladulta darted back and forth.

Leti surged past, hanging on to her companion, but Tulana, bellowing with rage, swam alone.

Mark and Shigeru followed in their wake. The Cresus's gaping mouth filled the ocean before them.

"Jesus Christ!" Mark screamed, as Sul seemed to swim straight into the jaws of death. With deft turns, Sul cut in front of Naga, turned away, then darted back in.

"Now fire. There eye!"

Mark saw the orb, as big as the side of a house. A bolt shot past him, Tulana's, and drawing aim he fired. The ocean boiled with steam. Both shots hit, but it was as if they had struck a steel wall, and Mark saw that the lens was pockmarked with scar tissue. A traplike lid slammed down and the creature shifted away.

"Keep firing, we going up!" Sul cried.

The ocean color was shifting, growing lighter. Mark, hanging by Tulana's side, kept firing bolt after bolt into the protecting lid.

Suddenly they were out of the water, Sul arcing into the sky. "Release!"

Mark let go, hovering by Naga's side, still firing away. Over his shoulder he could see *Cloud Dancer*, its crew desperately working to turn the ship around.

"You bastard," Tulana roared. "You scum-eating spawn of hell. Damn you, I'll kill you this time!"

Shouts echoed up from below. Looking down into the torrent, Mark saw a light catamaran tumbling end over end through the air, the crew shrieking. Shigeru darted in, so close that he actually slammed into Naga's closed eye. Pointing down with both hands he fired off a brilliant flash of incandescent heat.

"That's it, damn my hairy ass!" Tulana roared, and dove to Shigeru's side. Mark hovered above them, incredulous, as Tulana landed on Naga's closed lid and continued to fire.

A bolt slashed past Mark, and then two more, the steel-tipped shafts burying themselves into the monster's grey side not a dozen feet from where Tulana and Shigeru continued to fire. The creature started to arc even further away.

"He's falling!" Leti screamed, coming up beside Mark. "Get back!"

Mark followed the demigod up and away from the creature. Now several hundred feet in the air, he looked down—into Naga's mouth. Like some pit of hell, the mouth was a hundred and fifty feet across, and ringed with row after row of teeth that marched downward into a fetid darkness. The creature seemed to be nothing more than one vast eating tube, capable of swallowing anything in its cavernous maw.

Unable to resist, Mark fired straight into the darkness.

A thundering boom echoed up, and the air filled with the stench of rot and decay. The creature seemed to surge in his direction, and Mark soared upward as the massive gullet slammed shut in a vain attempt to devour him.

Naga started to fall away in the opposite direction from *Cloud Dancer*. The creature slammed back down, sending a plume of spray half a thousand feet into the air. A great tidal wave surged out and the great ship appeared to rise straight up into the heavens, hovering for a moment and then sliding back down the face of the wave, the crew shrieking and yelling, some with fear. But to Mark's amazement, most of them seemed to be enjoying the ride.

The ocean surged and boiled, the dark bulk of the monster turning, and with amazing speed it raced eastward.

"Damn him, the bastard's running away." Tulana shook his fists in impotent rage. "Come back and fight me, you thieving, shit-eating coward!

"The thing's so damned big you could put fifty bolts into him and he'd still keep fighting, but he never gives us a chance. He'll run at top speed for a hundred miles," Tulana said dejectedly, coming up to hover by Mark's side. "He always does that just when we really get going. We'll never catch him now."

"Thank the gods," Mark said, in an awestruck whisper.

"Yeah, damn the bastards." Tulana's disappointment was obvious. "Well, let's get back to the ship, rescue our people, and tow the dead one in." Without waiting for a reply, the prince dropped and swept across the ocean surface to where ladultas were busy picking up the survivors of the wrecked launch.

"What a fight. Best time of my life!" Shigeru cried, rising from the spray.

Ikawa cut a path from the wrecked catamaran to draw up alongside Mark. "It's a miracle no one got killed. A lot of broken bones, but those ladultas picked up every man."

"Goldberg—anyone see him?" Mark called out.

"Back on the ship already," Leti announced, swinging in to join the group.

Saito, coming up from the wrecked launch, was the last to rally.

"How's your ladulta?" Mark asked.

"Broken fin and some cracked ribs," the sergeant said with tears in his eyes. "I fell off and he went back in to save me and got hit by a fluke. They're taking him to the healers in Tulana's city. Damn, those creatures are grand." His comment was met with a chorus of agreement.

"You know," Leti announced with a smile, "Tulana's been fighting with Naga for the last two hundred years. If he ever actually killed him, I think he'd be secretly heartbroken."

Incredulous, Mark looked over at her.

"I think it's sport for both of them," she explained, shaking her head.

"Well, next time," Walker said quietly, "I'll stay home and listen to the game on the radio."

"It's been great, come back soon," Tulana roared, staggering under the effect of an all-night drinking bout.

Mark looked around at his companions. More than one of them was leaning over the side of *Cloud Dancer*, gasping in the cool early morning light.

"Christ, Mark, do we gotta fly?" Walker begged, his face a pale shade of green.

"It'll clear our heads," Mark said evenly, not really believing his own words. His nausea was not helped by what was going on astern. The massive bulk of the Cresus they had killed the afternoon before was hooked to the stern by a cable, so that the vessel had barely crawled halfway back to the floating island during the night.

Hundreds of ladultas surged around the half-submerged corpse in a wild frenzy of feeding, their calls counterpointing the feasting aboard ship. To Mark's amazement, he had discovered that the ladulta loved beer, and he had shared an uncounted number of flagons with Sul, to the point that the two had babbled telepathic endearments of undying friendship.

For the ladulta this was the grand payoff. A hated enemy was dead, there'd be food enough for weeks, and in return they'd help their surface friends by herding fish into nets and bringing up zah from the bottom.

In celebration, the ladulta of Tulana had called in their neighbors from several hundred miles around to join in the festival, so that the ocean was awash in blood, Cresus meat, beer, ladultas swarming about and tearing off hunks of meat with their razor-sharp teeth. It was a party Mark knew he would forever remember with either fondness or disgust—he wasn't quite sure which.

"Time to be off," Leti announced. The transport sorcerers, who had sat out the battle at the city and flew out after the fun was over, nodded their good-byes to Tulana and lifted into the air with Vena, who seemed anything but pleased with Imada's condition. With teetotalers' disdain for their less disciplined companions, the sorcerers quietly grinned at each other.

"All right, I hate these damn good-byes," Tulana growled, casting his eyes over the group.

"Shigeru, anytime you want to come out for a good hunt, you're my honored guest."

"With pleasure, my lord," Shigeru slurred happily as Tulana slapped him on the back. Ignoring propriety, Shigeru slapped the prince in return, so that Tulana staggered and broke out into a delighted grin.

"You're all welcome back, and maybe we'll kill that bastard for sure!" Tulana roared. "Why, by my hairy jewels, it was the best hunt in years!

"So long, you beautiful wench." Reaching out, he grabbed Leti's backside and squeezed. Playfully, she slapped him across the face and finally he let go. Ikawa, still uncomfortable with the attention Tulana had been showering on his lover, tried unsuccessfully to force a smile.

"He actually took the crystal back all by himself?" Tulana asked, looking at Ikawa.

Leti put her arm around Ikawa and smiled at her lover with an admiring gaze.

"Then maybe I'll be your nephew, too," Tulana shouted with a grin, and gave Ikawa a bear hug.

"Now get the hell out of here. I think I'm going to throw up again and I don't like my guests to see it."

"There's some other good-byes to attend to first," Mark said.

Tulana smiled indulgently. "Yeah, they do grow on you. If ever you need their help, just let me know." Turning, Tulana staggered away, bellowing an obscene chanty which was quickly picked up by the crew.

Mark leaped over the side of the ship and his companions followed. The cool water felt good and he found it cleared his head somewhat. He let his shielding down so the water soaked through his garments to rinse out the after effects of the feast, then switched the shield back up again.

"Sul, Sul."

A ladulta darted past him, homing in on Shigeru who, bumbling out a string of endearments, embraced his companion.

"Still drunk like me," Sul's thoughts whispered through Mark's mind.

Turning about, Mark saw his friend hovering in the water before him.

"I came to say good-bye," Mark whispered.

The ladulta drew closer and nuzzled him like an overgrown puppy.

"We good battle team, good friends. You come again we swim together, I show you my world. You need me, I come, anywhere ocean flow."

Mark reached out and gave him an affectionate embrace.

"You need me, I always come to help," Mark replied.

Sul hiccuped and rolled his eyes.

"Try Cresus meat with me. We make room for you beside body."

"Some other time," Mark groaned. He found it strange to hear laughter echoing through his mind.

Sul spun around him in a tight arc, his tail gently brushing across Mark's chest, then the ladulta darted away.

Mark rose from the water and saw his companions forming up, looking at each other sheepishly.

"Well damn it, they're like underwater Tals, like damn puppies," Goldberg sniffled.

"All right, let's get going," Mark growled, trying to hide his emotions.

Cursing and groaning, the group lifted into the air and winged over the Cresus, which was surrounded by ladulta still gorging themselves, while others floated lazily alongside, their bellies distended.

"Lord, what a stink!" Walker said, wrinkling his nose.

"My ladulta said they really love it when it's aged for a couple of weeks," Goldberg rejoined.

Walker, leaning over, lost what little breakfast he had vainly struggled to hold, to the delighted hoots of the ladulta circling below.

"Do you really expect me to believe this?" Patrice yelled.

The messenger cowered. "Your ladyship, I am only reporting

the information sent back from Asmara. It's already been cross-checked with another source. She is traveling with the group, and by now she's halfway across the ocean, with little or no hope of breaking free."

"Get out of here," Patrice snapped.

The messenger, bowing low, scurried out of the room without looking back.

"Damn them," Patrice snarled, slamming her fist on the table before her.

I've got to get control, she kept trying to tell herself. She could feel the spasmodic trembling of her hands, knowing that the terrible stress was finally taking its toll.

How am I going to break this to Gorgon? The thought made her stomach turn into knots. Already he was roaring about the damage done to his realms, the ever increasing pressure of Jartan, and the fact that so far he had borne all the burden of the struggle.

That had always been her intent on this campaign: to let him take all the risks while she reaped the greater share of rewards. There had been the slightest of hints from him that if there was treachery involved, that if she was in fact secretly allied to Jartan, he would have his vengence. Would he assume that now, even though she was innocent in this delay?

"What am I going to do?" She reached over to a side table and refilled her goblet yet again, watching as the trembling of her hands eased ever so slightly.

If the girl was trapped in close proximity to Leti, the strain of keeping up her false identity must be crushing. And the slightest mistake or dropping of her guard would be fatal to all these long years of planning.

Would Vena have the strength and resourcefulness to somehow slip away? Even if she did, Patrice thought dejectedly, there was no possibility of her ever being able to outrace Leti.

"I'll have to get her out," Patrice muttered.

Sitting back, she extended her hands, and the tile-covered surface shimmered with a pale light, the small crystals at the four corners glowing brightly. A milky filament appeared, and the surface of the table became wrapped in a fine mist that quickly formed into a map of the ocean.

Patrice stood up, hands still extended, and the map moved, the projection and scale changing to reveal the northern chain of floating islands ruled by Tulana. She shifted the perspective around, scanning the distance between each. The measure of flying time appeared between each island, the figures adding up and appearing in one corner.

Suddenly the images moved yet again, growing smaller. A map of the entire ocean again filled the table as she studied the chains of floating islands farther south, marking off distances and tracing out routes, calculating move and counter move.

She guided the image back to Tulana's chain, this time focusing the map in so that a relief of each island filled the entire table. Yet more figures appeared beside each of the images, showing the strength of the islands' fortifications and garrison, information updated regularly by her so-called merchants.

Gradually the plan started to form.

With a wave of her hands, the image on the mapping table disappeared. She touched her communications crystal.

"Inform my guards and first battle team to prepare for an immediate departure," she commanded sharply. "They are to report to me in one turning."

Without waiting for a reply, she snapped the crystal off.

First, though, she'd have to tell Gorgon about the delay. As she contemplated the promises and lies necessary, she had another long drink, but the trembling would not go away.

Chapter 11

Mark looked around suspiciously, feeling a tingle of discomfort running down the back of his neck. Back in Landra, he had become accustomed to the open friendliness of the people; after all, the "offworlders," as they were still called, were acknowledged heroes of the realm. He realized now he had become spoiled by the treatment.

While serving with the occupation force in Sarnak's old realm, he had also known a wariness and sullenness that was to be expected from a conquered people, and had gone out of his way to show the common people there a certain understanding. Perhaps it was being an American, he thought. Even when they'd beat a people, they'd wanted to be liked by them. But it was different here.

It seemed as if these folks, at best, simply didn't give a damn who they were. They just wanted to fleece them of their money and make life as difficult as possible.

The only positive thing about this was that the city of Portus, an independent city-state bordering the druid's forest realm, was unsurpassed in beauty.

They had flown in the evening before and the first sight of land from over a hundred miles away had been the high snow-capped mountains catching the golden-red hues of the early evening sun. The city flanked both sides of a narrow fjord, and the mountains beyond the town were covered with a forest which had left him awestruck.

The trees would have dwarfed the towering redwoods he had once seen north of San Francisco. Some rose over half a thousand feet into the air, their trunks nearly fifty feet across. The town itself was actually part of the forest, living trees supporting a spindly latticework of buildings that arched from trunk to trunk.

The tavern they had stayed in had actually been carved into a trunk with rooms suspended around the outside like barnacles on a rock.

"I hope this one pays off," Ikawa growled, his bad temper starting to show.

"We've got to be patient with these people," Leti replied, trying to smile.

Mark looked over at Ikawa, who was still bristling from their last rejection, the fifth of the day. The last merchant they had talked to in hope of obtaining equipment and a guide into the druid's realm had laughed them out of his office, calling Leti a spoiled brat of Jartan's who had no business in the area to start with. It had taken all of Ikawa's self-control, along with a restraining hand from Saito, to keep him from decking the man.

Leti paused for a moment, looking around as if lost. There were no streets in the traditional sense in this town, since the town was actually part of the forest, each trunk a building unto itself.

A burly man walked by, a heavy pack on his shoulders, and Leti hopefully stepped up to him.

"Excuse me, I'm looking for the traveling merchant Deidre."

"How come?" the man replied, as if annoyed at the interruption.

"We have business with her."

"What kind of business?"

"Private," Leti said quietly.

"Then she should have made better arrangements for you to find her," the man said, stepping past Leti.

"We'll pay you to take us there," Mark said, stepping in front of the man and holding out a silver coin.

He paused and looked up at Mark. "You're the folks interested in going inland, aren't you?"

Mark nodded.

The man laughed. "The only ones who go in there and come back are the ones the old man of the forest invites. Do yourselves a favor and go home."

"How do we get invited?"

"Listen, sonny," the man said evenly, "we make our living by trading with the old man. We're the only ones allowed in and back. No one's going to give away our secrets, and you can be damn certain no one's interested in getting the old man angry at them. And when it comes to Deidre, your best bet is to skip it. So just buy what you want here, and go home."

Without even asking, the burly man took the coin out of Mark's hand.

"Payment for some excellent advice," he said almost cheerfully and made as if to continue on.

"Damn it, I've had it with this shit," Walker snapped, coming up to block the man's path.

"Walker, don't," Mark commanded.

"Ah, so the mighty sorcerers are going to gang up and threaten me, is that it?" the burly man said, raising his voice. "An excellent display of Jartan's so-called sense of fair play."

"All we want to do is find Deidre," Walker snapped.

"Find her yourself." The man shouldered his way past, not bothering to look back.

"If you're looking for Deidre, I'm over here," a high, clear, and very amused voice called.

Mark looked up and saw a thin, almost childlike woman leaning over a balcony that arched between two trees. Her waist-length brown hair floated in the cool forest breeze, and her freckled face and green eyes were alight with laughter at the scene beneath her.

"I've been waiting for you," she said, and beckoned to the group.

"Is there something wrong?" Imada asked nervously, reaching out to touch Vena.

She flinched, drawing away as if his hands were poisonous. His heart breaking, he pulled away from her. She had been like this since they had left on what he had thought would be an exciting trip, one which for a girl who had grown up on a border outpost would be filled with wonder.

"Why won't you talk to me?" Imada sighed.

"There's nothing to say," Vena whispered, and she smiled, though somehow it looked brittle and cold, as if she was hiding something.

"I think I'll go for a walk," she went on. "Sitting in this room is bothering me too much."

She paused, looking into the mirror. He watched her closely. Funny, he never remembered her doing that when they had been in Landra and first come to Asmara. All her attention had always been focused on him. But now, he noticed, she could not pass a mirror without pausing, staring at her reflected image, sometimes drawing close to it as if she was gazing at an interesting stranger. She noticed him looking at her and turned, the smile in place.

"Why are you watching me like that?" she whispered almost accusingly.

"Because I love you."

She smiled and drew closer, but in his heart he sensed that it was an action that was being forced. She kissed him lightly on the forehead.

"I'd like to go out for a walk," she said.

"You remember Leti's orders, we're to stay here, and I know she means that even more for you."

"I can take care of myself," Vena snapped.

"Maybe back along the border," Imada said, drawing closer and tentatively putting his hands on her hips, "but this town seems dangerous."

She pulled away from him and started to the door.

"Vena, you know the rest of the men will stop you from going out."

"And what's wrong with you?" she snapped. "Aren't you man enough to tell them different?"

Stunned, he looked at her, unable to speak.

She seemed to hesitate and then turned back to him.

"I'm sorry," she whispered, and he felt as if somehow his old lover was now back. "Oh, I'm so sorry, Imada, it's just that I don't like this place. I wanted to be alone just with you for a while, and then they made you come with them. I guess I'm just angry."

"It's all right," he sighed, coming up and hugging her. "You haven't played your harp since we left," he continued, brushing her cheek with the back of his hand. "Why don't you sing me a song?"

"The harp? I don't feel like it." He felt as if her response was just a little too sharp.

He looked over at the battered case, resting by her side of the bed.

Suddenly her lips brushed against his ear.

"Let's do something else," she whispered, and though at the mere suggestion he felt his passion taking hold, still he could sense a strange distance within her, as if her body and mind were two separate beings.

"So that's the arrangement," Deidre said, motioning for a servant to pour another round of drinks.

Mark took the goblet appreciatively. The wine seemed to have been made from a fermented honey, yet it was light, even slightly dry instead of cloyingly sweet, with a curious flowery aftertaste.

"I'd still prefer to fly it," Walker said.

"Go ahead and try," Deidre replied. "Above that forest canopy you could crisscross the old man's realm until you were damn near as old as he is and not see anything. Fly under the canopy and you'll be lost inside the first hour.

"Riding is the easiest way. Each of us who has permission has our own private trail and markers. So you go my way or not at all." She smiled sweetly at Walker, who shook his head and said nothing.

"One thing," Leti said evenly.

"Go on."

"No one else wanted to take us in, they said the old man would be angry with them. So why are you doing it?"

"I'm his granddaughter," Deidre replied. "If he doesn't like me bringing you in, I'll just get yelled at. Whether he kills you or gives you a feast will be your problem, not mine."

"But I'm the daughter of a goddess," Leti replied, "with some of the best sorcerers in all of Haven with me."

"If you're telling me that as a threat," Deidre replied, "rest assured, Grandfather can take care of himself even against you. Your father rules an ocean away, not here. These are free city-states, under no god or goddess, so your name and lineage count for little."

"I still don't understand why you're bothering with us," Mark interjected. "No one else would give us the right time of day."

Deidre laughed. "Because I'm good-natured."

Walker looked at her suspiciously.

"And besides, I'm a merchant. Your price is a good one, believe me. Finally—let's just say I'm a bit bored."

"Bored?" Walker asked.

"I'm curious as to what the old man will do when and if he finally agrees to see you."

"I don't like this one bit," Walker snapped.

"If we want to see him," Leti replied, shaking her head, "this is the only way."

She paused and looked at Ikawa. "That is, if you really want to do this." Mark could sense the hopefulness in her voice. He knew if Storm were here the two of them would not do anything to get in the way of this venture, yet at the same time both would hope that in the end nothing would come of it and that there was no way to ever return to Earth. He found he was half hoping for the same result. The thought of having to make a choice was becoming a nightmare.

"I'm sorry," Ikawa replied. "We have to find out."

Leti forced a smile and looked at Deidre. "When do we leave?"

"This afternoon. There's no time like the present to get started."

At the sight of the coastline, Patrice felt as if energy had coursed into her. The land was as beautiful as she had remembered it, the vast trees cloaking the mountainside, the sparkling snow-capped mountains, the deep crystalline blue of the ocean. It was so different from the rolling hills and pastoral splendor of her own land.

She looked over her shoulder, scanning the world. It was as if the sky were hers alone, and she the only person soaring above the world.

Her guards and battle team were far behind her now, resting on one of the floating islands, concealed under the garb of guild sorcerers going east to work for a prince half a world away. They would continue on slowly, awaiting her word for the right time to strike.

They must be in Portus, she realized. The trick would be to sneak in without being detected. If the party was still there, getting Vena and the stolen crystals out might be difficult, since no matter what her guise Leti would recognize her on sight. She would need an ally in this; and she smiled at the memory of an encounter she'd had when had been younger.

"There are times I think we're just riding in circles," Ikawa said, looking to Leti as if for confirmation.

She smiled, shaking her head.

"I'm every bit as confused as you are. I've never been in a realm like this before."

If he had not felt there was an ever-increasing danger to what they were doing, he would have been enjoying this trip like no other he had ever been on before.

In the four days since leaving Portus, he had sat astride his Tal, dumbfounded by the wonders of the forest. Deidre had explained to them that the great woods they were traveling through were not made up of individual trees as all had at first assumed but a single vast living entity—each "tree," as it were, a single stem of an organism which she believed had an intelligence as well. The forest, which covered tens of thousands of square miles, had six separate trees growing in district groves. The border regions between them were areas of tangled conflict as roots and stems struggled for dominance and to push their neighbor back.

The second day out from Portus, they had crossed such a region, dividing the forest of the ocean, the Portus Woods, from that of the Druid Woods. Ikawa had been filled with a dark foreboding at the sight of it.

It seemed as if the trees were locked in a slow-motion combat. Roots reared up out of the ground, drilling straight into the hearts of rival trunks; branches snaked upward, struggling to block the light of their rivals, winding in to strangle and choke. The forest was a vast litter of dead limbs and broken trunks piled up like jackstraws. As they took a break from their march, Ikawa had nicked a trunk around which a root from a rival was trying to curl, and in their one hour stay he was amazed to see the root had grown several inches.

There was even a strategy to this slow motion struggle: Roots came up around an attacked trunk, reaching out to coil around the offending limbs and strangling them in turn. It was a region he was glad to flee.

Though all the trees were of the same species, there were many trunks that were different, as if they were manifestations of different organs. Some had silvery bark, the bottom sides of their leaves nearly mirrorlike, projecting bursts of light downward into sections of the forest where new saplings were arising to replace trunks that had died.

Sections of the forest were covered with spindly vines which Deidre carefully guided the party around, warning them to stand far clear of any of the vines' golden orchidlike blooms, which contained a pollen that could induce a paralytic state. The vines were parasitic, moving through the forest like some strange disease, their needle-sharp tendrils driving into the trunks of their host, draining out the life-giving nutrients, and then quickly moving on through the branches when the tree reacted and attempted to strangle the invader.

Ikawa looked back up again, trying to somehow judge the direction of their travel, but with little success.

Mark, urging his mount forward, came up to ride beside his two friends.

"If I knew the old coot was going to be friendly, I think I'd actually enjoy this place," Mark said, looking over his shoulder at a vast pulsating array of mothlike insects which had started to gather behind the party nearly an hour back.

"Say Deidre, what are those things?" Mark asked, pointing back to the moths.

"Just what they look like," she said with a smile, and then turned her attention forward.

"A fountain of information," Leti whispered.

"You notice there's been a hell of a lot more of them following us?" Mark said. "They've been coming in from every direction."

"Other things, too." Saito came up to join the conversation, pointing to a large flock of grey birds that kept circling and filtering through the trees, winging in low over the party, moving as silently as bats in the night.

"Something's building up," Leti said, keeping her voice pitched low.

Ikawa nodded in reply. He kept looking about, yet was so confused by this strange world that he could make no sense of what he was looking for. All he could tell was that somehow the forest had become watchful.

Deidre put up her hand to motion for the party to stop.

On the ground before him Ikawa saw a shard of white sticking out, covered by a latticework of roots that had a curiously disquieting appearance to them.

"I'd suggest we stay straight on the trail here," Deidre said softly, "and pass the word back to the rest of the party to keep quiet—and for heaven's sake, don't drop anything."

Ikawa sensed a ripple of conversation going through the Tals, and several of them whined softly like puppies that were suddenly afraid.

"Say, Captain," Walker hissed, pointing to the ground, "tell me I'm wrong, but those roots look like they're shaped like skeletons."

"You know, he's right," Ikawa whispered, looking at Leti.

The floor of the forest for several hundred yards ahead was torn and convoluted by roots that seemed to come together to form skulls, limbs, and entire bodies, both human and Tal. Scattered here and there and covered with a sprinkling of leaves, white fragments of bone were evident.

"What happened here?" Leti asked, her voice low but insistent.

Deidre, without looking back, pointed up. "See those white sacks in the branches?"

Ikawa followed where she pointed and saw dozens of great white globes, like inverted parachutes, hanging several hundred feet above him.

"Doiga—large stinging insects," Deidre whispered. "If something upsets them they come out by the millions and swarm over their victims. The roots of Uldrasill take what is left. Somebody from the last party through here most likely upset them.'"

"Upset them?" Walker whispered.

"Laughed too loud, or jumped on the ground and they felt the vibrations. Sometimes they'll attack because they simply feel like it."

Walker for once said nothing, looking straight up as they passed through the danger zone. The scene of the struggle was finally behind them, and Ikawa felt he could breathe easier again when the white nests were no longer in sight.

"I'm going to swing out to the back of the party just to keep an eye on things," Ikawa whispered. "Imada, come along with me."

Imada started to protest, looking over at Vena, who rode quietly by his side, but the look in his commander's eyes told him that it was an order.

Leti and Mark nodded as the two pulled over to let the others pass.

"Imada, you're fairly good with things of nature," Ikawa asked softly. "Tell me what you're feeling."

"We're being watched, Captain. Those grey birds, for one thing; and have you noticed the pleasant chatter of the forest has died away?"

Ikawa paused, realizing that Imada was right. The wonderful singsong cries and woodland sounds had dropped away into an oppressive silence.

"Even those clouds of moths," Imada continued. "It feels like they're part of something as well."

The party continued past, and as each rider drew abreast, Ikawa whispered a warning.

"I think we'll walk for a stretch," Ikawa announced, swinging down from his Tal, who looked at him curiously.

"Legs hurt," Ikawa said, looking into the creature's eyes, knowing that the Tal would undoubtedly announce what was being done to his comrades, and to Deidre as well.

Kochanski, the last in line, drew abreast of the two and swung down off his mount to join them.

"I hope you don't mind, Kochanski," Ikawa said quietly, "if Imada and I speak in our old tongue."

Kochanski, understanding immediately, said nothing.

"That's better, I feel we can talk freely now," Ikawa said in Japanese. "I don't trust the Tals, or anything else around us at the moment."

"It feels strange to hear our language again," Imada replied with a smile.

"Your lady—is she well?"

Imada slowed his pace. "Why should you ask?"

"Oh, just that Leti has been concerned for her. She senses some sort of distance on Vena's part, a drawing away."

"There's nothing wrong," Imada said, a bit too forcefully.

"There *is* something wrong, my young friend, otherwise I would not be hearing such defense in your voice. Would you care to talk about it?"

"Just a lovers' spat," Imada said, and Ikawa could sense the lie.

"I think it's more than that. Leti feels there is something not quite right about Vena, but she can't seem to place a finger on it."

"It's none of her business," Imada replied sharply, and then, embarrassed at his outburst, he looked away.

So something is wrong, Ikawa realized. Imada had always been the most gentle-spoken of all his soldiers. Granted, he had grown since their arrival here, but he was still more of an innocent child than a man.

Ikawa could tell as well that this was no lovers' spat. The Vena that Imada had described so enthusiastically was not the woman riding up front, not even the woman he had met so briefly upon their return from the raid. He felt somehow that Vena was made of glass, and one sharp blow would shatter her to reveal something underneath. It was Leti who had first voiced the thought, and he found now that it was even taking hold in him as well. He knew that Imada was hiding something, a deeply troubled feeling that there was something wrong with the girl he loved so passionately.

"There—do you hear that?" Imada hissed, stopping and looking off to his left.

"I didn't hear anything," Ikawa said, suddenly alert, but seeing nothing in the gloom.

The druid smiled as the head of the party drew past. How blind they were! Not fifty feet away, and all of them so totally unaware.

His granddaughter flashed a bright smile. *The little fool. Her arrogance will be the undoing of her yet*, but he could not help but shake his head affectionately. She truly had the spirit of an imp, almost flaunting a warning to the others and laughing that they were not even aware that since crossing under the Doiga the group had been surrounded by his sorcerers.

The girl was right, though. There was a demigod with them, one of Jartan's brood to be sure, and he felt a bitter wave of disappointment. Killing them would have been such interesting sport. Perhaps he would have thrown several to the Doiga; his pets must be hungry again. Of course it would be amusing as well to take others to the border and tie them between a trunk of his beloved Uldrasill and watch as his own tree and the next tree, Bughala, wrestled over the tidbits. Or even better, he could train a root to enter his victim through the soles of his feet, gradually growing inside the man's body, tracing its way up through the veins, slowly eating him alive until the root finally tangled the beating of his heart.

Haven had given him so many amusing ways of dispatching his foes. Now they had found him out, and Caesar had finally sent his assassins to finish the battle started two thousand years ago.

The Druid chuckled softly at how innocently they were walking into the trap, following his granddaughter like little lambs to the slaughter.

He felt the demigod's gaze sweep past him, probing into the gloom, pause but for a second, and then continue on.

No, he couldn't tangle with an angry Jartan, damn him. If he killed this woman—and it would be so easy to do—Jartan would come storming over here and tear Uldrasill apart. He patted the hollow trunk he was standing in with affection.

"No, my beauty, we can't let him hurt you." It would be like Jartan to rouse the druid's rivals—the accursed Vir, master of Bughala, and Wormteeth, master of Wilvika—to join him, to press Uldrasill back and destroy the kingdom he had built. Those two ungrateful bastards! Turning on their own father and moving away, like his other sons with the Essence, each to a separate tree.

So he'd have to take them alive for now and find out who the real assassins in the party were. Maybe then this demigod would realize the nature of the company she kept and get the hell out of where she didn't belong.

Smiling, he softly whistled.

*   *   *

Kochanski stopped.

"I just heard something."

"It was a voice," Imada announced. "No, not a voice, more like a bird call, but a voice as well."

"Don't move," Ikawa whispered.

A fluttering of wings snapped overhead and a blizzard of white engulfed Ikawa, blinding him. The moths that had been following them flooded the trail and then swept past them.

A loud shout echoed from the front of the column.

"Into the trees," Ikawa hissed, and he leaped straight upward, soaring for the high canopy of the forest, Imada and Kochanski following him.

It seemed that in that instant the forest, which had been brooding in silence, exploded into life.

Part of the canopy overhead, adorned with the mirrorlike leaves, shifted, sending a blinding column of light into the middle of the party. The group was shouting, covering their eyes for protection. The vast column of moths circled in upon the group, joined by birds which added to the confusion. Other birds swooped in, holding sections of flowering vines and dropping them into the confused mass.

It happened with such stunning quickness that Ikawa could barely believe that the struggle was over. His comrades tumbled from their Tals, convulsing from the effects of the paralytic vines and then lying still.

Gaining the high branches, he motioned for the other two to join him.

Only one rider remained upon her mount: Deidre, who sat at the head of the column looking back at the fallen group and laughing softly.

From out of the shadowy forest several dozen forms stepped into the light, led by an old man leaning on a staff.

Ikawa felt himself trembling with rage, though he was still not quite sure what had happened. Never had he been so surprised by an attack, and never so completely overwhelmed by it before he even had time to properly react. He could see Leti lying by her Tal, and in rage he raised his hand, pointing it at the druid.

"Tie them up carefully. I want no accidents," the druid said. Ikawa hesitated. So they were still alive.

"Vena!" Imada hissed.

"Shut up," Kochanski whispered, putting his hand over Imada's mouth.

"It was too easy, Grandfather," Deidre said, jumping off her Tal and coming up to hug the old man.

"They must have suspected," he said curiously. "Either that or they're incredibly dumb."

"They kept wandering about the town, harassing everyone about wanting to see you. One of them was overheard saying they'd come from your old world."

"There, that's it," the druid shouted. "I told you about Caesar. He finally found me, poor old me all the way out here. That bastard never could forget a grudge."

"They really don't seem all that bad," Deidre replied.

"They'll condemn themselves to the wicker death with their own words, you'll see," the druid shouted. "And besides, an old friend is here to help me prove it!"

Ikawa looked curiously at Kochanski, who still had his hand over Imada's mouth.

"Wicker death?" Ikawa whispered.

"You don't want to know," Kochanski sighed.

The druid turned away from Deidre and started to walk down the path, looking at the prostrate forms which his assistants were already picking up and carrying down the trail. The druid hesitated.

"Three are missing!" he roared.

The forest seemed to explode with activity. Shafts of light swung around like searchlights, and flocks of birds exploded outward. A beam of light snapped through the high canopy and the druid, with staff raised, looked straight up.

"Come down here!" he roared.

"Time to leave!" Ikawa shouted, bursting straight up through the branches. Imada struggled to return, waving his hand down as if to strike the druid.

"You'll hit our own," Kochanski cried, and the boy relented, following Ikawa.

"Come back here!"

Breaking clear of the forest, Ikawa paused for a moment, and, pulling his trouser away from his leg with his left hand, he cut a long length of fabric away with his right. He looped the light blue material around a branch and then continued to fly straight up toward the clouds, Imada and Kochanski following him.

Upward they climbed through the cool afternoon air, the canopy below like an endless sea of green. To his left he could see the high mountains marking the shoreline that they had passed through the day before. But in the other three directions as far as he could see was the high plateau of the forest which appeared to go on to the end of the world.

Gaining the protection of the clouds, he turned to look straight back down. His two comrades swung up beside him.

"We're in our element up here," Ikawa said. "They won't follow."

"And they're in theirs down there," Kochanski said bitterly.

"And they've got Vena," Imada cried.

"Don't forget the rest of our friends," Kochanski said, his voice cold, "and Leti as well."

Embarrassed, Imada lowered his head.

"I don't see anything," Ikawa said, scanning the forest thousands of feet below.

"So what are we going to do now?" Kochanski asked glumly.

"Wait till it settles down and then go back in," Ikawa told him.

"Back there," Kochanski said, "we're likes babes in the woods."

"Any better suggestions?"

Imada and Kochanski could only shake their heads.

"Then we better get comfortable, and stay up here over this one spot."

Wiping the sweat from his brow, Allic collapsed wearily to the ground.

"You look played out," Storm said, her voice edged with exhaustion, as she came to sit by her brother's side.

"Won't this ever end?" Allic's voice was distant and shaky. "We've hit five worlds in six days, each one a jump through into battle. I don't even know where the hell we are any more."

"A good choice of words," Storm said, looking about at the shattered landscape. Each step into Gorgon's territory was like a journey into the heart of desolation.

She leaned back to look at the twin red suns hovering malevolently overhead, their heat blasting the shriveled land. The air was dry and dust swirled about them in dark clouds, hiding the ruins of the fortress they'd just stormed.

Snaps of lightning arced overhead, but as Storm watched the discharges they gave her no pleasure. To her, lightning could be a weapon, but it was also a thing of beauty, snapping out of dark clouds, pregnant with life: giving rain. The lightning above crackled from dust cloud to dust cloud as they swirled and eddied over the planet's cratered surface. The scent of sulphur hung heavy in the air, billowing up out of ugly fissures. Numbly she took the mask away from her face, wiping the buildup of dirt out of the inside, rubbing her eyes, which instantly started to tear as the stinking clouds seemed to assault her.

"Why in the name of all the gods would Gorgon ever want a place like this?" Storm sighed.

"It fits his personality," Allic said dejectedly.

Storm leaned against a mud-caked boulder and looked around. The ground was carpeted with corpses which were already starting to bloat in the heat. In an hour or two there'd be another stench in the air, and she forced the thought away to keep her stomach from rebelling.

Many of them were Gorgon's demons, their blackened faces contorted in the agony of sudden death. Some had been hit on the ground, so brutally swift was the surprise of the attack; others had been caught in the air, their burned bodies breaking on the boulder-strewn land.

She looked at them with disgust. They were not human or demon, to be sure, but they were not animal either. Her flesh crawled with the thought that somehow Gorgon might have found a way to blend the two together, creating horrifying caricatures of mankind. She felt no remorse for the killing she had done here, as she gazed upon bodies with extra limbs, grotesque faces covered in scales, bodies with normal human faces but with four legs and no arms that were obviously used as beasts of burden, torsoes with two heads, and others, male, female, with horrifying exaggerations of sexual organs.

"It's like he's created a nightmare and we're trapped in it," Storm whispered.

"I just wish we could corner the bastard, have it out and then go home."

"So do I."

Allic looked up at the column of light that suddenly appeared before him.

"The few prisoners that talked said he pulled out just as we jumped in," Jartan said coldly. "We know which way he went, so we follow."

"Damn it, Father, we're running into a web," Allic replied. "This world has half a dozen jump points to other worlds; so did every other place. There's no logic to it. We can't chase them all down. We seem merely to be following him where he wants us to go."

"Sooner or later we'll hit a nerve, a place he values too much to let go without a fight. When we do, we'll close in for the kill."

"At the time and place he chooses," Allic replied.

"Minar and Chosen agree with me in this. We will press in for the kill. We're going to finish this war, and when we pull out we'll smash everything behind us. I intend to wipe these places clean of portals, fortresses, everything. Even if he survives it'll take him eons to work his way back to us."

"We've only got a single line back to home," Allic pointed out. "He could always cut in behind us. And cutting that line would slow us up for days if we needed to retreat."

"I've already thought of that," Jartan said, "and that's why you're staying behind here."

"Now wait a minute," Allic protested, wearily coming to his feet.

"You're finished, son. You've lost your edge. I saw you in this fight—you let a demon lord hit you from behind. He might have killed you if your sister hadn't been there to protect your back. I'm leaving you here with a garrison of forty sorcerers, to maintain a strong point to our rear. If he tries to cut us off with a raid, it'll be your job to keep it open."

"Listen to him, Allic, you can't keep it up anymore."

"Damn all of you. No," Allic snarled.

"Allic, shoot first!"

As he started to turn, Storm snapped off a weak bolt, knocking him in the side and slamming him to the ground before he could even react and bring his shield up.

Angrily he rolled over, raising his hand.

An impenetrable barrier formed between him and Storm as Jartan came between them.

Allic looked coldly at his sister, who cautiously came forward once Jartan floated back, and knelt by his side.

"Are you all right?"

"Side hurts like hell," Allic said, struggling to breathe.

"When we were children and played that game you could beat me every time," Storm said gently, laying her hand against his chest.

His ragged breath came easier and he forced a smile.

"Except I at least aimed for your backside."

She hugged him affectionately. "Brother, if it had been a demon lord I'd be singing your death song now. To tell you the truth, I've been protecting you for the last three battles. You need a rest, you've lost your edge. Sooner or later, and I fear it will be sooner, we're going to get hit hard at a jump and they'll tear you apart."

"I'm not sending you home, at least," Jartan said. "I need all my strength out here, this is where the threat is. Now listen to your sister and me and agree to run this garrison for awhile."

Trying to force a smile, Allic shook his head ruefully. He started to cough hoarsely as he pulled his mask aside for a moment to clean it out.

"Don't leave me here for long," he told them. "This place could drive even a sober man to drink."

Storm looked worriedly to her father but said nothing. Then she glanced back at the grotesque corpses around her. All she wanted was to get this over with and go back home to a world that was still sane, a place that Gorgon would never lay his hands upon and destroy as he had this desolate land.

Chapter 12

Something cold splashed against his face.

Startled, Mark Phillips opened his eyes. They were riding, weren't they? He must have fallen asleep, and he tried to sit up.

He couldn't move. Yet he already was up, on his feet.

Gradually he started to focus, and noticed the sound of laughter echoing in the air.

Shaking his head, he tried to reach up to wipe his eyes, but he couldn't move his hands.

Damn it, I'm tied.

The focus finally returned and he saw a wizened face peering up at him, green eyes dark with suspicion.

"You're the druid," Mark whispered.

"The speech of Jartan's realm," the druid replied, his lilting accent difficult to understand. "Yes, I'm the druid you sought."

The man stepped back and Mark could see Deidre standing by her grandfather's side, her rough leather riding breeches and tunic replaced now by a flowing linen gown of green, her brown hair swirling about her like a curtain of filmy gauze.

"Well, Mark, I did as you asked and brought you to him," she said with an almost sad smile. "So don't blame me."

"This is one hell of a reception."

"Better than the one you planned for me," the druid cackled as he walked away.

Mark tried to move his wrists and instantly realized that all his crystals had been taken. Yet he could still focus his power to a limited degree. As if reading his mind, the druid looked back at him.

"I wouldn't try anything—not a single word of command," the druid laughed. "My friends over there might get upset."

The druid pointed over his shoulder to half a dozen sorcerers, dressed in dark green livery and brown capes, who were sitting around a campfire looking over at their captives.

"The slightest sign of magics and my friends might use theirs on you."

Laughing, the druid continued to where Shigeru was tied up next to Mark, and scooping his hand into the small silver bowl Deidre carried, he splashed Shigeru, who groaned and opened his eyes.

They were in a small clearing, illuminated by the reflected light of a circle of mirror branch trees. In the center of the circle was a vast trunk nearly a hundred feet in diameter and rising straight as an arrow, its great form punching through the canopy of surrounding trees.

Somehow, Mark knew this must be the heart of the forest. In the distance he could hear scatterings of conversations filtering through the woods. Overhead he saw several people leaning over the side of a platform, looking down at the prisoners with open curiosity. If he wasn't in such a wretched situation he felt as if he could actually be captivated by the sylvan tranquility here.

The harmonics of songbirds echoed from the high trees, and multihued butterflies, some as large as his hand, others so tiny they seemed like motes of dust, filtered through the clearing. The patterns of light reflected down from above seemed to counterpoint the bird songs, and Mark realized that in fact the two were linked, the light shifting subtly to the rising and falling tempo of music.

A gentle breeze stirred through the woods, carrying with it the pleasant scent of the ancient woods, mingled with a near cinnamon odor which he finally realized came from some of the butterflies that would wing in close to his face and hover before him, as if curious about the strangers.

"Say, Captain, where the hell are we?"

Mark leaned over to see Walker tied up farther down the line.

"Ask him," Mark growled. "He's the one holding the cards."

The druid came walking back up the line of captives and stopped again before Mark.

"It seems you're the leader of this group. At least the leader that's awake. For now, we'll keep that daughter of Jartan asleep."

So he had captured Leti as well.

"How is she?"

The druid laughed. "To think I actually captured a demigod," he said shrewdly. "Always thought it'd be an interesting challenge, them with their high lording ways. She'll be the joke of everyone now, the great daughter of Jartan captured by bent over, old me." There was a hysterical edge to his voice that Mark found disquieting.

"If you know she's a daughter of Jartan, then you know as well how he'll react to this treatment of his own blood and those who serve him," Mark retorted.

"Ah, but the great god isn't even on Haven right now," the druid snapped. "You know he might never come back."

Then: "I have friends, I do, certainly they are true friends, they are," the druid teased, hopping back and forth like an excited child.

Over by the fire, a tall, slender form stood, threw back her hooded cape, and walked to the druid's side.

Mark knew at once that here was someone with a power as potent as Storm's or Leti's, perhaps even more so. Her gaze made him nervous, but he returned it without flinching.

"I'm Patrice," she said quietly, "and it's time we had a little talk."

Ikawa stopped. There—he had heard it again: a voice.

The chase had been a hard one and in the beginning he had despaired of ever finding his friends. After waiting an hour, they had dropped from the cloud and found the blue scrap that marked their escape. Within minutes of their return to the forest, Ikawa had noticed that the sounds had changed, as if the woods was again watching, and then the idea had formed.

Focusing all of his strength through the crystal Leti had given him, he formed a shield around himself and his companions, but suppressed the flickering glow of it, altering its light, blending it into the twilight colors of the forest floor. It was something he could never have done with an ordinary crystal, but this one came from the demigod of the night and seemed strangely adaptable to this purpose.

They had moved forward, floating through the woods, drifting from shadow to shadow, Ikawa subtly altering the shielding to match the ever varying interplay of shadows. The effort had drained him to exhaustion, but he had to press on to find his friends and get them out. If he should stop even for a moment to rest, to let the shield down, he knew they'd be discovered and lose what little hope was left.

Drifting through the shadows, he guided his friends on, feeling Kochanski's hand on his left leg, and Imada's on his right.

He heard the light crunch of a footfall and looked straight down to see two men walking past. One paused, and looked up straight at him. Ikawa felt the sweat beading out on his forehead from the strain of keeping the shielding up and from the knot of fear. He avoided looking straight at them, watching instead from the corner of his eye. The man hesitated briefly, then continued on.

"Jesus Christ, that was close," Kochanski whispered.

"Keep your mouth shut," Ikawa hissed.

He heard the voices again, this time closer, one of them a woman's.

Cautiously he drifted around the side of a trunk and saw, directly ahead, a shimmering of light. Several trunks away, a platform hung out from the side of a tree nearly on a level with himself. Several children stood on the platform, their backs turned to him, leaning over the side as if watching something.

Well, we're here, Ikawa said to himself. *Now what the hell am I going to do about it?*

"So you came from the same world as I did?" the druid roared.

Mark felt as if he was shadowboxing with a madman. No matter what reassurances he gave, the old man would lapse into a near-maniacal fear.

"Can I say something?" Sergeant Saito cried, and Mark laid back against the post.

The druid turned to face him.

"You can see we are different races, can you not?" Saito asked, and the druid nodded in agreement.

"Deidre, would you agree that though we are of two different races we behaved as friends?"

"It's true," Deidre said sympathetically, and Mark sensed that this girl was not entirely on her grandfather's side. And she kept looking at Patrice with outright suspicion.

"Back on Earth we were hated enemies, Mark's country which was America, and mine. And America was allied with Britain in this war against us. But now we are friends. I want you to know that at least the Americans are from your blood."

Mark realized the jeopardy Saito had put himself in, but saw his line of reasoning as well, shifting the argument away from shouted accusations and denials. Thank God someone was thinking clearly, Mark thought, cursing himself for trying to argue the facts on the surface.

The druid hesitated, looking over at Saito.

"Where is this America?"

"Across the great ocean, thirty days' sail to the west," Mark said quickly. "Your descendants found the land and settled it. Britain is where my people come from. I have the same blood as you."

"You were fighting against Britain," the druid said.

Saito nodded.

"Who else was Britain fighting against?" the druid said quietly.

"It doesn't matter," Mark snapped quickly, realizing the trap Saito might be walking into.

The druid looked back at him coldly.

"Caesar is dead," Mark told him. "He was stabbed by the Roman Senate.

"Thirty years back," Mark announced loudly, trying to improvise so that all would get this new history straight, "Italia had a new leader called Mussolini. All of us, including Saito's people, fought him and destroyed his power and turned Rome back into dust."

The men around him nodded vigorously in agreement.

The druid seemed to hesitate.

"Remember, Grandfather, they're Jartan's sorcerers," Deidre said, her voice showing the slightest touch of concern. "If they really intended to hurt you they would have come in far greater strength."

"Then why are you here?" the druid asked.

Mark sighed with relief. Perhaps they were finally getting through.

"Because we think you might know how to open a portal back

to our own world so some of us might be able to return home."

Patrice looked over at Mark with evident surprise.

"You're neutral in all of this," Mark said to the demigod. "You know how we came here and what we've done since. Can't you explain that to him?"

Patrice smiled—and in that instant he knew without doubt that she was an enemy.

"I've followed the story of these outlanders closely," she said, resting her hand lightly on the druid's shoulder.

The old man looked up at her with a gap-toothed grin.

"Has anyone else of the gods or demigods ever even bothered to visit you here?" Patrice said with a husky whisper.

"Only my lady here," the druid shouted. "No one else."

"That's why I rushed here to warn you," Patrice went on. "These people only want to see your temple, to smash it down, and then to kill you."

Mark looked at Patrice with a cold fury.

"Castrating bitch," Walker snarled.

"Perhaps we can arrange that treatment for you," Patrice retorted.

"Shut up!" the druid roared, and raising his staff he snapped out a bolt, knocking Walker unconscious.

"They kidnapped one of my friends, and then were coming here to kill you," Patrice continued.

"Kidnapped who?" Mark asked in surprise.

"See how innocent he sounds. Why, poor Vena." Patrice broke away from the druid's side to go kneel over the unconscious girl lying next to Leti.

"That's a lie!" Mark shouted. "Vena was with us, she's the companion of one of our men."

"She seemed perfectly content traveling with us," Deidre said inquiringly, looking at Patrice with a growing suspicion.

Mark shook his head.

"Which man was she with?" the druid yelled.

Mark remained silent.

"One of the three that escaped," Deidre said quietly. "The young one."

"Wake her up," Patrice asked, her voice pleading. "She'll tell you."

The druid turned away from Mark and, going over to Vena's side, he scooped a handful of the liquid out of the bowl that Deidre brought over and splashed it into the girl's face.

With a groan, Vena stirred and Patrice helped her to sit up.

"Vena, dear," Patrice whispered, her voice breaking with emotion. "Vena, I've come to rescue you. You're safe with me now."

"Let her talk for herself," Deidre snapped.

Patrice looked up angrily. "The girl's frightened. These animals kidnapped and bewitched her for heaven knows what purpose. I've been frantic trying to reach her."

Vena opened her eyes and looked about.

"Tell her the truth now, Vena," Patrice said quickly, looking up at Deidre as if the girl had injured her by a false accusation. "Tell her how I've come to rescue you."

"This is disgusting," Deidre snarled. "Grandfather, that woman's hiding something."

Vena looked up at Patrice and then reached out to hug her. "Thank the gods you found me."

Ikawa looked sharply at Imada. His features seemed to have gone blank, as if the pain of betrayal was far too much to bear.

He leaned in to Imada, his lips touching the boy's ear.

"Don't move, don't make a sound, son. I'm counting on you as a soldier."

Imada looked at him, the tears streaming down his face.

Goddamn it, something was horribly wrong, far more than the fix they were in now. Patrice had added an element Ikawa just could not understand.

What am I going to do?

"I'm glad I could help you, my old friend," Patrice said to the druid as she helped Vena to her feet. The girl was now sobbing uncontrollably, screaming that she had been raped.

"Hush, child, we'll go home now," Patrice whispered, patting her on the shoulder.

Mark looked at the girl with disgust and then his gaze shifted back to Deidre, who was staring straight at him as if trying to decide.

"I think it best that I leave now," Patrice said smoothly. "You can entertain your prisoners as you wish. I'd love to stay and watch, but this poor child needs familiar faces and a quiet place to heal. Also, I believe some of her property is stacked up with the captured booty."

Deidre looked sharply at Patrice as the demigod suddenly let go of Vena as if she did not exist and walked swiftly over to the pile of packs, saddlebags, and accoutrements taken with the party.

"Why such a rush?" Deidre asked quietly. "Vena's been through a terrible ordeal. Perhaps the two of you can be our guests for a couple days. Let her regain her strength. After all, I know Grandfather would love to visit with you again."

The druid, who had been watching the little drama with interest, perked up at his granddaughter's suggestion and came up to Patrice's side, swiftly putting his arm around her waist.

"It *has* been a long time," he cackled. "The last time, we were both young, but my dear, I'm still young inside—and in other ways, if you get my meaning."

A spark of impatience lit Patrice's eyes as she said, "I think I really should be going." She forced a smile and kissed the druid on the cheek. "Though I'd love to stay, I want to take Vena home. Now, if you'll help me find her pack and harp case, I'll be on my way."

She broke away from the druid's embrace and bent over the pile of goods, reaching in greedily and pulling the bags aside.

"Why the rush?" Mark called. "It seems like you want to get away before the truth is learned!"

The druid seemed to hesitate.

"It would be an insult to my grandfather if you didn't at least share a meal with us," Deidre said sharply.

The druid looked craftily back at Patrice. "Yes, at least eat with me first."

She ignored him, fumbling over the goods with increasing agitation.

A muffled shout of triumph escaped her lips as she pulled a battered harp case from the pile. Clutching it tightly, Patrice turned to look back at the druid.

"I'm leaving now," she announced. "Come, Vena."

"What's in the harp case?" Mark shouted, his suspicions at last taking concrete form. Vena had clung to it in the same way, and he now cursed himself for not taking more of an interest in her behavior.

"Yes, my dear," the druid whispered. "Why not play us a song first? I'd love to see the instrument, and hear it."

The tableau seemed to hold before Mark: Patrice seemingly pulling in some vast hidden power, the druid looking up with all his attention focused upon her.

Deidre slowly backed away, coming up by Mark's side. He felt her hands brush against his, and the cords separated.

"Don't move," she whispered, and he felt the coolness of two crystal bands slip into his palms.

"Please forgive me," Patrice said, smiling. "I'm just upset over Vena. I'd be delighted to stay the night with you."

Mark felt Deidre's hands suddenly grab his as if to take the crystals back. He clenched them tightly and said nothing.

The druid came up to Patrice and kissed her, his one hand running up her side, lingering over the swelling of her breasts, while his other hand still clenched his staff. Mark kept his eyes on Patrice and could see the sudden loathing in her eyes.

"Something's going to happen," Mark whispered. "Get ready."

The druid, crackling with delight, turned and started to walk away.

Patrice's shield snapped up to full.

"Grandfather!" Deidre screamed.

Mark was amazed by the old man's agility as he fell to the ground rolling, his shield going up as the place where he had just been standing exploded in flames.

Patrice fired off another bolt. Staggering, the druid came to his knees, trying to point his staff at her. The six sorcerers who had been standing around the fire, snapped off a volley of shots at Patrice.

Screaming, Patrice turned to face them, knocking the first one on his back, his shield disintegrating under her powerful blow.

Laughing, she looked back at the druid, hitting him again even as he fired a bolt which set her shield glowing but did no damage.

Patrice started to turn, looking at the row of offworlders still tied, shorn of any shielding.

"What pretty targets!" Patrice raised her hand.

Mark leaped away from the post, his shield up, and aimed a bolt at her which he knew was useless.

"Deidre! Wake Leti!"

The girl darted low, flying through the air. For the first time Mark realized she was also a sorcerer, and had been concealing it all along.

"Come on, you whore!" Mark shouted.

His words hit home. With a scream of fury Patrice turned her attention fully on Mark, oblivious of the druid's strikes and the helpless targets, many of whom were using their power to burn their bindings off, their faces contorted with agony.

A searing blast struck and sent him staggering.

"Lousy bitch!" Mark screamed, firing back.

Another blast struck him, knocking him down, his shield barely holding. He knew that this fight was futile, and the next strike would kill.

A dazzling snap of light crackled overhead, striking Patrice from above.

Startled, she looked up.

It had to be Ikawa using Leti's crystal.

"Storm," Mark screamed, hoping to confuse her, "finish her!"

Patrice hesitated and looked over to see Deidre, shield up, pouring the reviving liquid over Leti, protecting her with her own shielding.

"Vena!" Patrice shouted, reaching into a fold in her dress and pulling out a set of crystals. She tossed them to Vena, then, holding the harp case tightly, leaped into the air.

Several blasts hit Patrice at once. She fell back, the harp case bursting into flames and falling into the pile of baggage.

With a shriek of near panic Patrice turned, smashing her fist into the burning case. For an instant Mark saw a sight which made his stomach turn to knots: In Patrice's scorched hands were three great crystals.

Roaring with triumph, she rose into the air, oblivious now to the bolts hitting her.

"Storm!" Mark screamed, hoping that Patrice would be

unnerved by fear, thinking that there were two other demigoddesses present, yet feeling foolish and weak at the same time as he called out his lover's name like an incantation to protect him.

"Patrice, face me!"

Leti was on her feet, tearing the small crystals from Deidre's wrist and setting up a far stronger shield over the two of them.

Another blast came out of the trees from above, blinding in its intensity.

With a wild curse, Patrice soared straight up, Vena struggling to keep up with her.

A form burst out of the treetops.

"Vena!"

Patrice continued into the canopy, but Vena hesitated.

"Vena, don't leave me!"

Mark looked up, heartsick at the anguish in Imada's voice.

A cold laugh escaped Vena's lips and she raised her hand to strike Imada, who floated before her, his shield down.

Before she could strike, a slash of bolts came up in every direction. Vena exploded into incandescence and plummeted to the ground trailing flames.

Small fires crackled all around the glade, and the druid, roaring with anger and ignoring everything else, ran over to the large trunk of Uldrasill which had been scorched by a bolt. Rising into the air he patted out the flame with his hands.

Mark suddenly became aware of the fact that the forest was alive with motion, the trees swaying, yet there was no wind.

Crouching low, he waited for another strike. With the huge crystals she had just taken, Patrice could easily best all of them. But there was no sign of her.

Kochanski suddenly appeared, hovering just below the green canopy. "She's gone, heading southwest like a bat out of hell."

Sighing, Mark flew back to the ground and snapped his shield down. Looking up, he saw Imada kneeling, rocking back and forth and sobbing over the smoldering remains of his lover.

Leti started to go to his side.

"Leave him be for a moment," Mark said quietly. "He has to understand it alone."

Leti stopped and looked at Mark, and he could see the sadness in her eyes.

"Sometimes this world is an ugly place," she whispered.

Surely by all the gods this can't be my beloved, Imada thought numbly. The world seemed to have gone out of focus, the enormity of what had happened so vast that all the thoughts, all the realizations could not force their way into his mind at once.

He looked at her face, strangely peaceful, leaned over to kiss her lips, then leaned back.

Something was changing. Lines started to crinkle out from the edges of her eyes, racing across her face like frost lacing a windowpane on a cold winter night. The lines deepened, her face turning brittle, the color of old parchment. Her eyes started to sink into dark hollow sockets, and the fine gossamer hair changed to white.

Numbed with horror and loathing, he watched as the truth of Vena was revealed in death. In that moment Imada lost his youth, his innocence, all that he had ever believed was possible in the dream world he had thought was real.

Still smoldering beside her was the harp case, its side smashed in.

Yes, he had seen Patrice take something out of it. That must have been why Vena had clung to it so. Yet there was something else in there, and reaching in he grabbed a lump of clay, a bit larger than his fist. As he lifted the object a fragment of clay fell away, revealing a dark flash of red underneath.

This would be his, he thought coldly, and slipped the crystal into his tunic.

Mark came to his feet, and smiled wearily as Ikawa and Kochanski landed by his side.

"Good shooting," Mark said, grasping Ikawa's hand.

"It's not often I appreciate being called a woman," Ikawa replied, "but I'll let it pass, and damn good thinking on your part. It scared her half to death."

The druid, who by now had stopped the burning of Uldrasill's trunk, came over to face Mark.

"You mean that other demigod isn't here?"

Mark nodded.

"Good," and he puffed himself up, the nervousness in his eyes gone. "Who released you and gave you weapons?" He waved his staff toward Mark.

"I did," Deidre snapped. "And you can thank me for it right now!"

"Just because that woman did what she did, doesn't change my opinion of you one bit," the druid roared.

Leti came over to stand beside the druid and put her hand on his shoulder. "Do you know who I am?"

"Who woke you up?" the druid cried.

"I did, Grandfather," Deidre said, her patience obviously at an end.

"I'm as strong as Patrice," Leti whispered, forcing a tight smile. "So let's look at it this way. If it was our intent to harm you, I'll kill you right now."

Before the druid could react, Leti grabbed his staff. Mark watched as the two seemed locked in a bitter struggle. The staff started to glow, and the entire forest seemed to be in renewed turmoil, the trees swaying, the reflected light from above snapping back and forth. He could almost sense a nearly audible groan running through the woods.

With a startled cry, the druid fell back, the staff in Leti's hand.

Deidre came protectively to her grandfather's side, raising her shield to cover both of them, and looked at Mark with hate-filled eyes.

A sad smile crossed Leti's features. "We came here as friends and want to keep it that way," she said. To Mark's surprise, she bowed her head, dropping one knee slightly—an action he had only seen her and Storm do in Jartan's presence.

She held the staff out to the druid.

"Please forgive my impolite actions, but you just didn't seem to want to listen."

Puffing hard, the druid snatched the staff and then looked around, his pride obviously wounded.

"Well, next time just explain yourselves and we won't have all this fuss," the druid snapped.

Exasperated, Deidre dropped her shield.

"Would you mind if we gathered our things?" Leti asked politely. "I'm afraid we are going after Patrice immediately."

"Wait a minute," Kochanski said. "After coming all this way?"

"Did you see what Patrice took from the harp case?"

"Three damn big crystals, two of them a match for the one that was belted at her waist—the third was much darker," Saito said, rubbing his burned wrists and coming to join the group.

"She now has the complete set of the Crystals of Fire," Leti said coldly.

"Crystals of Fire?" Mark asked.

"They were forged by her father, the Creator Borc. Upon his death, the council of gods decided that for the time being she would only inherit one of them. The others were to be put in safekeeping until such time as she had matured and proven herself to be trustworthy. She never has, and has always bitterly complained of that decision.

"Maybe it was the wrong one. Maybe if they had given them to her then, she would have demonstrated her ability to handle such power wisely—for the three together give her more power than anyone on Haven except the gods themselves. Perhaps that is why she has always been so sullen and withdrawn from the rest of us.

"Regardless of that, though," Leti went on, her voice betraying her anxiety, "she's obviously gone through some elaborate plot to obtain them."

She paused, looking at Imada, who was still kneeling by Vena's side.

"And it was done when three of the gods are away fighting Gorgon," Ikawa said quietly.

Startled, Leti looked at him. "I hope not even Patrice would be insane enough to seek such an alliance." She hesitated, then snarled, "By the gods, that must be it. Why else would she also have stolen Horat's Portal crystal?"

"Say, what the hell is going on around here?"

Mark looked over to see Walker, who had been knocked unconscious by the druid, starting to stir.

"There's been a fight and we're free," Saito said, going over to cut him loose.

"Damn. I miss *all* the fun," Walker complained, his voice still groggy.

"Maybe not for long," Leti said bitterly. "Anyone with burns, let me take care of them. Get our gear together—we're flying for home within the hour."

"Are you going after her?" the druid asked.

"That's the plan, once we find out what she's doing."

"I don't take getting cast aside like that lightly. I'm going with you."

"Grandfather," Deidre said quietly.

"Now don't go grandfathering me, you brat. Uldrasill can take care of herself for now. I haven't been out of these woods for a couple of thousand years. It's time I had a little adventure."

"We'll be flying hard," Leti warned.

"Do you need a couple extra sorcerers, or not?" the druid snapped, his pride obviously still smarting from the treatment he had received.

Leti smiled and nodded.

"Then we'll get some food and be on our way." The druid laughed.

"If we've got an hour, can I at least ask one favor?" Kochanski said nervously.

"What is it?"

"The Stonehenge, the great circle."

Startled, the Druid looked over at Kochanski.

"Now I know you," he shouted. "You're the one who tried to sneak up on me, you, you . . . "

"Grandfather!"

"It's right over there, just on the other side of Uldrasill," the druid said, looking at Deidre.

"Should have strangled her at birth," he whispered as she took Kochanski's hand and guided him away.

"If you'll excuse me," Ikawa said, and he left the group and cautiously approached Imada. His heart tightened at the sight of the corpse.

The boy had been in love with a sorceress perhaps fifty times his own age. Realization of the horrible treachery that had been played upon his innocence made Ikawa want to scream with rage.

What could he ever say to comfort him now? If the girl had truly been his lover, it would be one thing. But not this—the treachery of betrayal compounded by the obscenity of a cruel seduction of youth.

Ikawa scooped up a blanket laying beside the pile of baggage and, kneeling by Imada's side, he covered the corpse.

"Come on, son," Ikawa whispered, taking Imada by the shoulders and helping him to stand.

The boy turned to him, and there was a cold bitterness in his eyes.

"There's nothing to be said, so don't even try." Imada's voice was flat and distant.

Pulling away, he turned and walked into the woods.

Slipping through the streets of Portus, Patrice ducked into a narrow doorway and slid the bolt shut behind her.

Three men stood, poised to strike, but as she threw back her cape they bowed low.

"Everyone in position?"

"As you commanded, my lady."

"I was successful," she whispered, and the three sorcerers grinned with delight.

"Are the communications crystals in place here?"

"We smuggled them in. We haven't tested them yet, as you ordered."

"Good. One never knows who's listening."

One of the men nodded to the back corner of the room, and she walked over to open a plain wooden chest. As she put her hand into it, a faint glow filled the room.

She quickly spoke a string of code words, waited for a response, then closed the chest.

The message would be leaped across the middle chain of floating islands, from agent to agent. Once it reached home, nearly half of her sorcerers would bend their strength to jamming all means of communication, cutting off those left in Asmara from news of the events here. Within minutes, her battle team would be taking off from a boat anchored north of the middle chain of floating islands. She visualized the charts of the region, calculating the distance to be covered and the times of arrival.

In an hour it would be time to leave. For now, she had a few moments to relax.

She had flown for hours, filled with a deep fear that Storm and Leti would be in close pursuit. Yet the sky had remained empty, and the fear had gradually dropped away. The enemy would be hours behind her.

Yet why? Surely they would have had the advantage; they were fools not to press it. Whoever had reported that Storm had left Haven would pay for it when she returned.

"A messenger flew in from Asmara this evening," one of the sorcerers said, coming up to offer Patrice a goblet of wine.

"Who?"

"We think one of Jartan's granddaughters."

"Were you able to get to her?"

"We think she's hiding somewhere in this town. We're making inquiries."

A granddaughter? Could she take the time to hunt her down? She pondered the course; it'd only take an hour or two, but there were things far more pressing, and besides, whatever news she carried was not worth the bother of torturing out of her now.

"Let her go. Now bring me something to eat, and then we leave."

Struggling with exhaustion, Kochanski groaned with relief as his feet touched solid ground in front of Stonehenge. Deidre had guided him around the huge tree and into the clearing while he babbled excitedly, telling her of the famed history of the artifact back on Earth.

And yet it was not exact, he suddenly realized.

All the lintels were in place, the circle truly complete, the outer ring of stones all standing as well. The stones were covered with swirling designs made of chalk and blue paint. There were other differences as well: two smaller circles of upright wooden posts were in the middle, one inside the other, each the height of a man and with holes carved, apparently at random, through the posts.

He had never thought that the Stonehenge the druid would create would be the one he remembered from two thousand years ago, and not the one that was on the Salisbury Plains of today.

Making a link between the two would probably be impossible unless Kochanski could convince the crazy old man to knock half of his structure down. And the thought of making his own full-sized Stonehenge now seemed foolish. Even if he did, what chance would there ever be of success?

Dejected, he sat in the middle of the circle, pouring out the story to Deidre. She agreed with his analysis, telling him that her grandfather had tried many times to find Earth, and had always failed. She then got Kochanski to talk about himself, and sat with rapt attention until Leti and the others arrived to announce they were leaving.

Stretching, Kochanski looked over at the dark-haired girl, who shook her head and forced a smile.

"A long flight," she sighed, and then to his surprise, she drew closer and slipped her hand into his.

"Kochanski!"

"Oh, shit," he whispered. "I know that voice."

He looked over his shoulder and saw Sara flying in from the west, escorted by two of the druid's sorcerers.

"And here I fly across a damn ocean looking for you, worried sick, and I find you with this . . . this cheap woman!"

"Now Sara," Kochanski said, looking from one girl to the other.

"And who is this loud-mouthed child?" Deidre retorted.

"I'm his lover," she snapped. "His *ex*-lover."

"Lover?" Deidre looked at Kochanski with wide-eyed shock. "So you seduce girls barely old enough to know better, is that it!"

She slapped him hard across the face and stalked away.

"I've never touched her!"

Deidre stormed off without replying.

Kochanski gave Sara a withering look. "Get out of my sight," he hissed.

"With pleasure, you cheater," she replied haughtily. "Now where's Leti?"

Kochanski nodded to where the rest of the group was landing.

"I'll never let you touch me now," she snapped, her voice choking.

"That's fine with me. I'd kiss a snake first."

She slapped him across the other cheek and stalked off.

Dazed, Kochanski stood in the darkness, swearing softly at whatever evil-minded god had ever conceived of the idea of creating women.

From out of the shadows Mark appeared. "Getting punched around a bit tonight, aren't we?"

"They can all go to hell."

"Both of them will want you even more now, if only to beat the other one." Mark smiled.

"God spare me." Kochanski rubbed his jaw. "Just what the hell is Sara doing here?"

"She was sent by Pina. I was just talking with her and Leti. It took them over a week to crack the security code into the treasure vault. They wanted to double check, just to make sure. And they found what we already know—some very valuable crystals were missing.

"Pina tore the place apart with a security check. Vena came up as a suspect so Sara was sent out here to tip Leti off and run a check. The girl was seen in the area the night before the keeper was found. No one ever suspected that he had been murdered until they got the vault open."

"Kind of risky, sending a kid out like that," Kochanski replied, unable to hide his concern.

"She can obviously take care of herself. And don't forget, she is pushing eighteen," Mark replied.

"Too bad she didn't get here a couple of days earlier."

Mark nodded in agreement. "There's something else, though."

Kochanski could sense his fear. "Go on."

"Gorgon cut behind Jartan's forces three days ago. We haven't heard a word from them since."

Kochanski was silent, knowing something more was coming.

"It was the confirmation for Leti," Mark replied. "It's no coincidence; she's convinced Patrice is in league with him, that this whole thing was planned, and the only glitch in it was our forcing Vena to come along."

"Then what the hell was she up to?"

"With the power of the three Crystals of Fire, and the portal crystal, she could break the barriers the gods have set about this world to keep Gorgon out. It looks like the entire war was a feint to draw the three most powerful gods away from the true threat. Patrice is going to open a portal and let Gorgon in. If she succeeds, he'll have his armies in Haven, perhaps even take Asmara and the Heart Crystal before Jartan can get back."

"Jesus Christ," Kochanski whispered. "If only we had known before Patrice got to us."

"Sara's trip wasn't all a waste, though," Mark said quietly. "At least now we know how bad things are. Patrice will probably try to cut us off," he went on. "We'll take enough time to eat, but exhausted or not, we've got to try and catch her, or get back to Asmara and organize an attack before she opens the gate into hell."

Chapter 13

"Jesus, Captain, I think it's burning," Kochanski called, coming up to fly by Mark's side.

Anxious, Mark tried to focus his attention through the thick overcast; he could sense the image of the first floating island off the coast, but beyond that—nothing.

There was nothing on the comm link crystals, either, and since leaving the mainland, the group had maintained a strict communications blackout to help avoid detection.

"He's right," Leti shouted, swinging up beside Mark and Ikawa. "They're in trouble."

"Let's get below these damn clouds. Maybe we'll see something."

Mark weighed the decision. Flying through the thick overcast hid their movement, since it was still unknown if Patrice had support, yet he didn't want to drop down on the floating island without knowing what was going on.

Mark looked over his shoulder. He could barely see Saito, who was directly behind him, and the rest of the group was strung out beyond in the clouds with Sara bringing up the rear.

At least he had convinced the druid and Deidre to rest overnight in Portus. Considering the grueling punishment of this flight, the old man would have been in the ocean by now.

"All right," Mark called, "let's dip out of the clouds and take a quick look. If we're heavily outnumbered, we'll pull back up."

Slowing he started to bleed off altitude, the rest of the group following suit. The thick overcast held for long minutes, until he felt as if they'd fly right into the ocean before they'd drop out of the storm.

Slowly, the greyness broadened out, there was a faint glimpse of dark rolling seas, then clouds again, then more sea, a wisp of tangled grey, and they were clear.

"Goddamn it," Mark groaned.

The horizon ahead was awash with flames, reflecting luridly against the low overcast.

"That bitch destroyed the city," Leti screamed in rage.

Mark drew his thoughts forward, scanning the sky for any movement of flyers. It was empty.

"I'm not picking up any combat," Kraut shouted, "just the city in flames."

"Standard battle approach," Mark called, using his communications crystal. "Remember, they have wall crystals. I'm calling in our arrival so they know we're friendly, but look out anyhow; they might be trigger-happy."

Mark tried repeatedly to raise the island's command center but was greeted by silence. As the group winged closer, to his horror he could see why. The entire core of the city was a sea of flames. The drawbridges to the five bastion points were up, but two of them were in flames as well. Several miles out, they passed over a sinking ship with dozens of survivors clinging to its sides.

"Shouldn't we help them?" Shigeru cried.

"Not yet. It could still be a trap, and we've got to find out how bad the city is first. We'll send somebody back later."

Drawing closer, Mark was sickened by the horror of what he was seeing. Scores of boats dotted the water, dozens of them overturned, flame-scorched and sinking. Hundreds of people clung to wreckage, crying for help, raising their hands to the group which now passed overhead. An explosion shook the air, and ever so slowly the vast center core of the city started to settle down, like a wounded beast sinking into the sea.

Steam shot heavenward, filling the sky with a dirty mist that blended in with the rolling clouds of black smoke.

The city kept settling farther into the sea, and then, ever so slowly, the distant edge rose into the air.

"She's going down!" Leti cried.

Horrified, Mark watched as ant-sized people leaped into the sea, while others, caught in the flaming streets and collapsing buildings, screamed in terror.

Higher and higher the city rose, while the eastern end started to slide downward.

Mark cursed with impotent rage as the vast structure seemed to hover for a final moment before starting its long slide to the ocean floor. Huge sections broke away, crushing those unfortunate enough to be floundering in the dark waters below. Explosions rent the air as buildings crashed into each other. There was a last convulsive roar, and then, as if a hand had swept over the ocean, the fires went out. The only light in the wreath of smoke came from the now feeble-looking torches of the two burning bastions.

Flying with maddening speed, Mark winged into one of the three surviving bastions. Screams of panic cut the air at his approach, and a shower of arrows rose to greet him. Pulling up, he hovered in the air, the rest of his comrades forming around him.

"We're friends," Mark roared. "Stop shooting, we're friends!"

"Stop shooting," came a distant voice from below. "It's the offworlders."

Mark waited for a moment, then slowly began to lower himself, keeping his shield at full strength. There was the slim possibility that it could still be a trap—or the other chance, equally dangerous, that someone might have a red crystal affixed to an arrow, which, if it hit his shielding, would destroy him in a fiery detonation.

Several arrows still came up, which Mark and the others easily dodged. Cautiously, they settled atop one of the fighting towers to be greeted by a motley assortment of grim-faced fishermen with bows, women, children, and a single soldier.

"Thank the gods you're here," the soldier cried, trying to hold back tears of rage.

"What happened?" Leti asked, even as she bent over to help a badly burned woman who laid on the bastion floor in numbed shock.

"We picked up a brief warning from the next city westward that they were under attack by a dozen sorcerers," the soldier said quietly, his voice edged with shock. "That was it; we heard nothing more. Oplin and Uyl, our two sorcerers, called the alarm. Before we were even half ready they came in low from the south, undetected."

"We didn't stand a chance," a woman cried angrily. "There

were thirty of them, and a terrible one that suddenly appeared from the east shot bolts like the sun itself."

"Patrice." Leti whispered the name like a curse.

"They knew our weak points," the soldier continued, "went under the city, hitting the pontoons, knocking out the fire pumps. Oplin and Uyl were dead in the first minute, fighting with our wall crystal. They got two of them, at least, but once they were dead, we were defenseless. My comrades fought for the city; I was sent out here to organize the defense of this bastion.

"I can't believe I'm the only one left."

"We begged for quarter," the woman shrieked. "We begged them to let us at least go to the boats, but that woman—that woman told her followers to keep firing. Even some of them were sickened by the slaughter and drew back. I heard her scream that she wanted everything sunk before the offworlders got here."

"She wanted to deny us quick access back," Leti said, her voice cracking with rage. "Wipe out two jump points and we'd have to detour far to the north, adding days to our return."

"If you hadn't been coming here, this never would have happened. My husband wouldn't be dead!" The woman leaped at Mark, tearing at him, pounding him with her fists.

Mark didn't resist but let her vent her rage. Suddenly the woman dissolved into tears, and tenderly he put his arms around her.

His visage dark, Mark looked at Leti. "We stay here the night to help these people."

Her thoughts drifted into his mind.

"Far worse will happen to them if we don't get back. If Gorgon breaks through, all Haven might look like this. Patrice did this to cut us off. She must have boats positioned back to the southward island chain, and then she'll leap westward. We've got to keep moving; maybe the next island out is still intact."

"Damn it, Leti, they need our help now! The next island might be entirely gone, and we'll drop into the sea from exhaustion."

The demigod hesitated. "An hour to help, then no matter what we rest for awhile and push on. I can't go it alone. Patrice could be waiting with her band, I need your escort. We'll have to take the chance that part of the island, or some boats, survived."

Mark struggled for control as she continued, "Do you want me to tell these people that by helping to save them, the entire world might become a nightmare? Do you want me to force them to make that choice?"

"Damn you," Mark hissed out loud. Ikawa, whom Leti had allowed to hear what she was thinking, looked in Mark's direction. From the anguished look in his friend's eyes, Mark could see that Ikawa had been arguing the same point.

The woman in his arms, still sobbing, was pulled free by several fishermen and led away.

"Who's in charge here?" Leti asked quietly.

"I guess I am," the lone soldier said wearily.

"We'll rescue who we can. I'll try to heal as many as possible over the next hour, then we need a place to rest before we leave."

"What?" the soldier roared. "You're going to leave us? We need your help now."

Mark was startled to see tears forming in Leti's eyes.

"I can't tell you why," she said softly. "Please believe me, we wish we could do more."

"Here we get caught in your sorcery wars, we pay the price, and then you leave." The soldier's voice was bitter with rage.

"We're wasting time," Leti said. "Bring your most injured people to me. Mark, Ikawa, start pulling people out of the water."

The group leaped into the air. Spreading out over the darkness, they scanned low over the waves for victims.

Mark could see a number of ladultas coursing back and forth, calling excitedly, pushing exhausted and limp forms toward the bastions. Working in teams, the offworlders would dip down, scoop a person up, and carry him or her in. Yet Mark felt frustrated, sensing that hundreds of people were in the water, and in the short time available only a handful would be saved.

"It's time," Leti suddenly called over the comm links, her command flooded out with shouts of protest.

Mark looked over at Ikawa, who had been working with him, and could see the anger and resignation in his eyes.

"In a moment!" he called, and keyed into the Americans' commlink, while Ikawa did the same with his men.

"This is a direct order," Mark whispered sadly. "We've got to go in now and rest before pushing on."

"Bullshit, Captain," Walker replied.

"Goddamn it, I feel the same way," Mark said wearily. "You know why we've got to go. We might save hundreds here, but uncounted thousands of others might die if we delay. God help us all. I'm asking you as my comrades to go back in now."

There was a moment of silence.

"You heard him," Walker finally whispered. "Let's go in."

Mark turned and started back, and then, on an impulse, he dived into the sea.

"Ludalta, pack leader."

He could hear a rippling cry cut through the water as he kept repeating himself.

In the darkness he sensed a form coming up which suddenly brushed alongside him.

"I Omna. Airbreather, fire maker?"

"Yes," Mark thought, "friend of Tulana."

"What happen?" the ladulta asked anxiously. "Airbreather city burn, many dead, many hurt, crying for help. Why?"

"Enemies of Tulana do this, make war on Tulana."

"We see her in air, not friend of ladulta to do this. She kill two of us. Never in memory airbreathers hurt ladulta."

Mark could sense the confusion and rage in Omna's thoughts.

"Other herds to south of floating cities far away. Are there ladulta there?"

"Cousins distant herds," Omna replied. "Why ask?"

"War come between airbreathers," Mark responded.

"All ladulta friends, ocean big enough for all. Why not same for airbreathers?"

Mark was unable to reply.

"Do you know Sul?" he finally asked.

"Sul mate kin, we hunt Cresus together, you hunt Naga with him?"

"Yes, we hunted together."

"I know of you, then."

"Tell him I wish him well and always his friend," Mark replied. "Firemakers must leave now to fight evil woman who hurt your kin. We must fly to next island west."

"No good," Omna replied, "totally destroyed. It was smallest of floating cities, less than thousand airbreathers there, it sink."

"How do you know that?"

"Ladulta call to each other through water, pass word across sea. Calls reach back and forth ten times quicker than you fly."

What are we going to do? Mark thought to himself.

"You sound sad, afraid," Omna whispered.

"We must go to western lands. Without island we might not be able to fly."

"I call to friends west see what can be done. You fly, we will help you. Ladulta wait for you there."

"Thank you, my friend. I'm leaving now. Please try to save as many as you can."

"That we already wish to do," Omna said. "Others call, have found more. Farewell."

Omna slipped away and Mark rose back into the air. Back at the darkened bastion, he settled to the ground and looked around at his grim-faced comrades.

"Let's try to get some rest. We push on in three hours."

The men looked at him darkly, knowing he was right but unable to respond.

Sleep was impossible. The night air was rent with a cacophony of curses, screams, and maddening confusion so that Mark felt as if his soul was being torn out of his body. Huddled together in a room, the men tossed back and forth, more than one stepping outside with the excuse that he was going to relieve himself only to return a half hour later soaking wet.

"Even if the next island out's intact," Ikawa finally whispered, coming to sit by Mark's side, "I think we'll be too damned exhausted to fly to it."

"It's been sunk," Mark said grimly.

"Where did you hear that?"

"The ladulta told me, but they said they'll help us when we get there."

For the first time since arriving, Mark saw Ikawa smile.

"We'll just have to trust them, I guess."

"Let's hope so."

"Leti's exhausted herself with healing," Ikawa sighed. "She'll be weaker than we are."

"We've got to keep moving."

"I know that, damn it," Ikawa replied.

"Come on, it's time to go." Mark and Ikawa looked up to see Leti framed in the doorway, her tunic and breeches brown with caked blood.

The men filed out of the bastion and back to the open platform. The storm had cleared enough to reveal the twin moons of Haven riding high in the midnight sky.

The lone soldier stood before them, rage in his eyes.

"Someday you'll understand," Leti whispered sadly. Rising into the air, she turned westward. The offworlders mumbled their apologies and followed her.

Mark, unable to stop himself, looked back and knew that he would be forever haunted by the lone soldier's gaze: the look of an innocent man caught in the wheels of war.

Stretching her weary limbs, Patrice strode to the edge of the dock and looked out across the empty sea, tinged now with the first faint light of dawn.

Never had she pushed herself so hard, and she felt herself trembling with exhaustion. The flying had been tough and seemingly endless through the night. Two of her sorcerers had disappeared, plummeting into the ocean; a dozen others had been left behind on the boat which had been their launch platform. Yet it had worked. The two strike forces had hit with devastating effectiveness, and she smiled inwardly, knowing that the goal was now almost within reach. All communications were being jammed by her sorcerers positioned off the coast in small boats, blocking the offworlders from any hope of sending a message.

It was regrettable that there had not been enough time to finish destroying everything. But the carnage would undoubtedly stop the offworlders in their misplaced desire to help save her victims. There was nothing left of the next city out, and jumping the distance from Tulana's city to the mainland would be nearly impossible even for a sorcerer who was well rested.

The destruction bothered her slightly. Killing in battle was one thing, but the slaughtering of women and children had been rather distasteful.

"My lady, your breakfast is ready."

Patrice looked back at Leona. In some ways the young sorceress reminded her of Vena.

Poor Vena, she thought sadly; but the girl had served her purpose well.

"I'll be along in a second, dear," Patrice sighed.

With a flash of red, the ocean before her turned scarlet with the first light of day. Breathing deeply of the morning air, a sad smile lit her features.

Several hours of rest, she thought, and then to the mainland by dawn tomorrow. Safely into her own territory, she could leave the escort behind and fly with the power and speed of a demigod, far ahead of Leti and her escorts. By the time the forces of Asmara were stirred, the portal into Gorgon's realm would be open to receive him.

The water rippled, and with a light splash a slender form darted through the golden depths. Half curious, she watched the creature streak away. There was something about the creature's eyes that bothered her—as if it were somehow accusing her.

Vaguely uneasy, Patrice followed the shadowy form as it popped out of the water again, held in the air for a second, and then turned over and plunged into the depths.

"They're beautiful, aren't they?" Leona said, coming up to stand beside Patrice.

"Beauty can hide an enemy," Patrice replied. "Stay here. If you see it again, strike it."

The girl looked at Patrice with shock. The demigod had seen Leona refrain from striking the boats and people in the water as ordered. She wanted to say something, but thought better of it. For the moment, she'd need all her people. There'd be time enough for punishments after the campaign was finished.

She touched the girl on the shoulder.

"He could be a threat to us," she said with a smile. "Better to take no chances."

Leona merely nodded in reply.

There was another splash, and without turning her gaze from the girl, Patrice raised her hand. A slash of light snapped out; the water foamed and tumbled, stained red with blood.

"Like that," Patrice said quietly, and walked away.

"Over there," Leti cried, her voice trembling with relief.

"They did it," Shigeru roared. "I knew they would."

After Regensburg, his last mission in Europe, Mark could remember such a moment—with two engines out, and fuel nothing more than vapor, he had cleared the cliffs of Dover and finally saw the landing field ahead. It felt the same now. There were no engines this time, but exhaustion had taken him to the limits of endurance and beyond. To splash down would have been useless, for he'd still have to swim on the surface, draining his strength further, and to go below the water would require concentrating on shields. If they didn't have something to land on, further flight would be impossible.

Now there was a place to land and rest, thanks to the ladultas. Dozens of the creatures were slashing about on the surface, and in the middle of their circle was a roughly piled assembly of planks, boards, and fragments of wreckage. It wasn't much, but at least it was a place to lay down and sleep.

Dropping out of the sky, Mark winged over the raft and saw ladultas pressing in on the sides and from underneath to keep the platform afloat. He touched down lightly and felt the boards bucking and swaying. One by one, his comrades winged in to land. More and more ladultas appeared, pushing up against the raft, keeping it above the water.

"They're amazing, just amazing," Ikawa whispered in awe.

Walker looked nervously around, lying stretched out on a plank that rose and fell with the waves.

"Just hope I don't puke," he groaned. An instant later his loud snores echoed across the water.

"Wish I had something to eat first," Shigeru moaned.

"Always your stomach first," Ikawa sighed, but he could not help but agree.

"Captain, look!" Saito cried, pointing to the edge of the raft.

A ladulta appeared, holding a kicking putta in its mouth. Shigeru took the proffered fish and tenderly patted the ladulta on its flank.

"It said they're getting more fish right now." Shigeru grinned. Reaching into his tunic, he pulled out a knife, quickly cleaned the fish, and sliced off a long strip of golden flesh.

"Care for some, Captain Phillips?" he said with a weary smile.

Hunger finally winning out, Mark took the strip and tentatively tried it, while the other Americans watched him suspiciously.

"Not bad," Mark said, to his own surprise. "You all better eat. We need our strength to push on."

"Captain, I'm picking up someone coming in from the west," Kochanski announced, coming to his feet.

Mark looked up and turned to scan westward. Kochanski never ceased to amaze him with his special ability, which now even seemed to outstrip Leti's.

"I've got it, too," Leti said quietly, wearily standing.

"Get ready—it could be her." Trembling with exhaustion, Ikawa started to rise into the air.

"Jesus Christ," Kochanski whispered. "If it's her, I think our shit is cooked."

"It's Tulana," Leti cried with a smile.

Mark could now see half a dozen forms cutting so low across the ocean that they rose and fell with the rolling sea.

The forms grew larger, coming on hard.

"Damn that bitch's hide to hell!" Tulana's voice boomed as he drew in to hover above the raft.

This was a different man than the one Mark had seen less than ten days before. His eyes were livid with rage, his features purple, as if every vein in his face was about to burst.

"Why in the name of the gods did she do this?" Tulana screamed. "I found the wreckage of my city just over the horizon, and ninety percent of my people were dead. Damn her, I'll draw the bones out of her living body, I will. My ladulta tell me she destroyed Valna as well—nearly four thousand dead."

He looked at Leti, as if hoping against hope that the underwater messages were mistaken.

She could only nod sadly.

Tears of rage clouded Tulana's eyes. "Why?" he asked hoarsely.

Quickly she explained all that had happened, and his features grew pale.

"She's mad," he whispered; and the sorcerers who had accompanied him looked to each other with fear and confusion.

"We need to get a message back to Asmara at once," Leti said, "but she's jamming our communications crystals."

"I noticed that, it started yesterday," Tulana said thoughtfully. "The Cresus had moved again. I had *Cloud Dancer* two hundred miles west of what was left of my city"—he pointed vaguely back to the horizon—"when I lost contact with my capital. Thought it was the atmosphere or some such thing. Then I caught a garbled distress call and nothing more.

"I've been trying to save some of my people all night. The ladulta told me you were coming up, so I waited here till dawn, hoping I could rescue some more victims and then link up with you and get some answers.

"If she wants a war, she has one," Tulana finished darkly.

"We've got to get back to Asmara and organize," Leti said. "Once she's home, I think she'll open a portal that we will not be able to contain."

"She's halfway back already," Tulana told her.

"How do you know that?" Mark asked.

"A ladulta died to find out for me. Damn it, she murdered him. His mate called the news up to us; it came in just as I got word that you had landed out here." Mark felt a ripple of anxiety, and Tulana shook his head.

"Sul's with the ship. They've got their blood up, I've never seen them this mad before. In my realm, to kill a ladulta is a capital crime. They've never had anything like this happen to them before.

"It's *still* a capital crime," and as Tulana spoke, the ladulta circling the raft started a bone-chilling chant.

"Can you people fly another hour?" the prince asked. "*Cloud Dancer*'s closing in from the west. Once we land on it, we could come about and get another hundred and fifty miles closer to the coast while you rest."

"We could try," Mark replied, feeling for the first time in two days that perhaps they might have a chance after all.

Mark woke from a dreamless, exhausted sleep to see Leti kneeling beside him.

"Time to move," Leti whispered, smiling wanly at him.

Mark could not help but notice that she had seemed to age overnight. Her features were drawn, her eyes red-rimmed and bloodshot from exhaustion and fear. Standing, she stepped to Walker's side and gently touched him on the shoulder.

Blinking the sleep out of his eyes, Mark stepped out of the cabin he had been sharing with Walker and Kochanski, and climbed the ladder onto the windswept deck. Ikawa was already awake, looking toward the sun which now hung low on the western horizon.

"Sleep well?" Ikawa asked, holding out a flask of wine. Mark took a mouthful, swished it around, and spat it over the railing.

"I could sleep for a week," he said.

"When this is over with," Ikawa replied, trying to smile.

"It always seems that there's a next time, though. On Earth there never seemed to be enough time just to sleep. Then the war of Sarnak, and now this. Damn it, can't we just have peace?"

"You have to play the cards life deals you, unfortunately," Ikawa said quietly.

The response caught Mark off guard. Yet as he thought, he knew that it was moments such as this that somehow gave a purpose beyond life itself. He still did not know what had happened to Allic, to Jartan, and to Storm. Was she still alive, or was this action of Patrice's tied into a far broader plan which in a matter of days could spell his doom and the end of all he had so come to love? Never had her love for him seemed so precious. If only he could be with her, he thought wistfully. If only he was sure he would see her again.

"The samurai understands the intertwining of life, of death, of peace and war, and how one does not exist without the other," Ikawa whispered. "Chances are we have already lost. Tulana just told me that the ladulta say she has almost reached the mainland. We will not be there for another day."

Mark could not respond.

"Yet we still have this moment," Ikawa continued, "and we will still try."

"And if we lose?"

"Then it is all gone—this world, this beautiful world which I love now far more than where we came from. Knowing the evil we are about to face has made me love this place far more than I could ever have imagined, because I realize how fragile it truly is. I think I understand how the gods who created this must feel, why Jartan will die himself to protect it. Because if it was never threatened, we would not know how precious it truly is. Your Norsemen knew this in the Dark Ages, when even Valhalla would have its final day, and thus the moments of goodness were all the more precious. If we understand that, then how precious those whom we love and call our friends truly are. And how terrible the burden we now carry to protect it for others, even if it means that we shall die and never know its pleasures again."

Ikawa looked over at Mark as if suddenly embarrassed.

"We better get the men ready to move out," he said evenly.

Unable to reply, Mark smiled. Their gaze held for a moment in mutual understanding.

The rest of the men came up from below, some cursing and groaning, others quiet, all with anger in their eyes as Tulana broke the news that Patrice was even now reaching the mainland.

"Well damn it, let's get some flying done," Walker said, rising into the air.

Together, the group ascended into the afternoon sky, Leti and Tulana in the lead. Turning westward, they disappeared into the clouds.

"Just what the hell am I going to do now?" Allic muttered to himself, peering up over the lip of the cave where he had remained hidden for the last two days.

The fortress was aswarm with Gorgon's minions. Where they had come from he had no idea. They must have remained hidden on another part of the world and come back.

The attack had been brutal and stunningly swift. Half of his garrison gone under the swarm of the first overpowering strike. There was nothing to do but run and hide.

He looked at the rest of his men. Dejected, they sat huddled in the darkness. He could hear the rasping wheezing of their breath.

There'd been no water since this morning. The filters on their masks had long since clogged and become next to useless.

His fantasies floated now between the nightmare bodies and a cold glass of water—it wasn't even wine anymore or brandy, it was simply water. There was nothing here at all to work with, nothing he could coax and change with his powers into something they could drink. Perhaps Jartan could have pulled it off, but where the hell was he?

"My lord."

Allic looked back.

"Edwinna's dead."

He looked into the shadows where a sorcerer sat, still cradling the woman's head in his lap.

There was nothing Allic could have done to save her. He had drained what little strength he had left into her, but the horrifying burns had simply been too much for him to master. In another time, another place it could have been done all so simply—but not here.

He cursed silently at his impotence.

A shadow winged through the blood-red sky, and he froze.

The demons were still looking for them. Yet it was not those searches from above that worried him. As long as they kept their shields off and hid in the cave, they would be safe; the landscape was a massive catacomb of such warrens. Yet there were other searches as well.

Cautiously peering over the rim again, he saw a team attempting one.

A demon stood on a low rise not half a mile away. Beside it was one of the nightmare perversions of humanity, a man with four legs, but no arms. Its head was bent low to the ground; then it rose, hesitated, and turned to one side. The creature moved into a hollow and disappeared from view, the demon following behind it.

It had taken Allic a while to realize that the creature was trying to find them by scent. Ever so gradually, the demon—and their monstrous slaves—would close the circle around them, flushing the sorcerers into the air where the finish would be short and deadly.

Allic slid back into the darkness of the cave.

What would kill them first—the demons, or the lack of water?

Jartan must know by now what had happened. What the hell was delaying him?

At the moment, Allic almost didn't care. They were going to die, and when the time came, he would lead one last sortie and take some of Gorgon's minions with him.

Chapter 14

An inner thrill of warning coursed through Patrice's mind, but her plot was now too far along for caution. Yet his presence was almost soothing; gentle in visage, and so carefully crafted in its seductiveness.

"I sense fear," Gorgon said quietly.

"If we should fail," Patrice replied, almost too quickly, to cover her misgivings.

His laughter echoed through the empty chamber. "We fail? Together we shall rule Haven."

"Yet I turn now even against the gods."

Even Patrice was amazed at her own indecisiveness. She had been divorced from the circle of gods since the Great War, and they in turn had ignored her. Now they would know the folly of their slights. . . . Yet still there was that sense of fear.

"The gods," Gorgon laughed, his voice like that of a delighted child pulling a prank on unsuspecting elders. "What are they? Why are they known as gods? Because they stole Haven from the Old Ones and abrogated the power unto themselves. We and they are cut from the same cloth."

"Yet they are gods."

"And you shall be a goddess. My goddess and consort."

Patrice hesitated. "But they are immortal, and even a demigod like myself will know age in the end."

Gorgon's laughter echoed through the night. "I shall make you immortal also."

Incredulous, she looked at him.

"Can I not steal souls bound for the Sea of Chaos and bend them to my bidding? If I have such power over death, then know that you, too, shall be immortal when my hand stretches across Haven."

His image pulsed and glowed, shaping and reshaping, hovering for a moment as a seductive woman/child, then as a man, then as a strange shaping of the two, which held Patrice spellbound.

"It is but a small matter," Gorgon whispered. "Remember, you now hold the Crystals of Fire, except for the Heart the most coveted of Jartan's gems."

"Jartan?" Patrice asked. "Where is he now?"

The image of Gorgon rose high in the pillar of fire.

"He has taken much that is mine," the demon lord boomed. "Thousands of my servants, a score of my lords have fallen into the Sea of Chaos by his hands. Even now his forces storm the very gates of my inner realm. Yet he has paid as well, for by my hand even Minar was injured. I have slain their sons and daughters, their children's children, and their host of followers."

Patrice could sense the rage in his voice and knew that Jartan and Minar had dealt Gorgon a severe setback, despite of the cost he'd exacted.

"Yet it shall be as nothing," Gorgon went on, dropping into a thin pulsing flame. "For when my servants have passed through to your realm, the work shall begin. With Horat's Portal crystal, I will be able to break through the barriers and step into Haven, making it ours. Jartan and Minar know not the threat. Already we have slipped past them, destroying the portals back to this world. It will take them days to cut their way back here—and by then it will be too late.

"It is time we begin," Gorgon whispered soothingly.

Patrice looked at him, her features fixed in a smile. How long she had planned for this moment, she could no longer recall. She could not even say when the turning away had first begun; how many countless nights she had savored the anticipation of this moment, though her heart had stayed her. Could it be that the mere anticipation had kept her alive, kept her dreaming and plotting?

She watched him closely, and the clarity of thought returned. He would try to destroy her in the end, she knew. Could she ever control him?

"You are not afraid of me, are you?" Gorgon purred, and again his voice was like that of a young woman's.

A dark smile flickered across her mouth. No; she could control even him—or it—or whatever it was that floated before her.

When his work here was done she would bend him to her will, or drive him back into the darkness. It had gone too far already, she realized. She had taken action which would force Jartan to strike her—if he returned—and that thought filled her with a sudden edge of fear and at last pushed the caution aside.

"Afraid of you?" she whispered. "I fear nothing."

Her right hand pointed downward, and the dark portal crystal by her feet flared into brilliance.

The portal widened, deepened, pulsing bright red. Shafts of light snapped past her, so that the room appeared to be engulfed in an inferno. From out of the flame five forms drifted upward, their taloned wings beating darkly against the light.

Arcing outward, they spiraled down to land by her side, their coal-black eyes like pits of eternal night.

"Your servants," a demon lord growled, bowing.

"Then begin your work," Patrice said coldly, stepping back from the pentagram.

Forming a circle around the pillar of light, they raised their winged arms, their cries renting the air.

Then one by one, from out of the light, yet more appeared, broadening the circle, drawing out the legion of their warriors and magic users, and preparing for the arrival of their master.

Exhausted, Patrice turned away, and a gentle laughter washed over the room. She looked back to see the image of Gorgon, still barred from her realm by the power of the Essence laid down so long ago. But here at last she was cracking the final barrier, and she could see the lust of anticipation in his eyes. He looked over at her and smiled again, the smile of an innocent child. She smiled back to him, the smile of an innocent woman.

"There—do you sense it?" Leti whispered softly. The Heart crystal in the center of the conference room glowed and flickered, bathing those in the circle with a gentle lavender light. "She's doing it; she is actually cutting the fabric of the Essence, laying our world bare to him."

Ikawa looked across the room at her, and though for a moment their eyes caught and held each other, he felt so very distant from her. She was now a demigod burdened with an awesome responsibility to protect the realm, while he was still merely a sorcerer, the holder of a minor fiefdom.

Boreas, who had arrived only moments before the war council had begun, shifted in his chair and glared with a cold anger. "She's opened the gate."

"How long do you think we have?" Leti asked, looking over at the only ally whom she and Tulana had been able to summon. Communication had been next to impossible, so thorough had Patrice's jamming been. If not for Tulana's strength, and the crystal shard forged by his grandfather, they might not have reached even Boreas. All attempts to reach Aleena had failed, and Reena, whose realm was on the other side of the world, would not respond, so distant was she now to the concerns of others.

"The barriers are the strongest bonds ever forged," Boreas said darkly. "Even with Horat's crystal it will take days. She needs to bring through hundreds of his demons first; they in turn must channel all their energy back into the portal to stretch it wider. We have three, maybe four days before Gorgon himself can cross through."

Leti settled back in her chair and sighed. Boreas was silent, while Tulana, sitting next to him, pulled on his beard and cursed.

"And Jartan?" Mark asked.

Leti shook her head and looked at Pina, who was now in charge of the gateway portal.

"Jartan's forces have gone through fourteen jumps on this campaign, eleven of which are into Gorgon's outer realms. Picture it as a long thread leading into an unmapped darkness. Two days ago the thread was cut at the fifth jump point inside Gorgon's territory.

"It was a perfect defense," he said evenly. "The deeper in Jartan went, the more he had to leave behind to protect each point in our communications line. I would assume that after the fifth jump point was outflanked and taken, Gorgon's people followed up the line, cutting point after point."

"So Jartan's still cut off and there's no hope of contacting him?" Tulana asked.

Pina nodded. "Jartan might not even know yet that he's been

cut off, or could assume that it's a minor harassment to his rear and continue to press forward. It could be weeks before he comes back. If he followed standard battle doctrine, he would have kept a strong point midway on his communications line. Hopefully that point will hold, but even it could be outflanked and cut off."

"A masterful deception," Boreas commented.

"Obviously well planned," Pina replied, with a slight hint of admiration for the professional skill of his adversary. "I suspect Jartan will perceive this merely as a delaying and harassing action and will continue to press his attack into the heart of Gorgon's realm."

"And we lose Haven," Leti said grimly. "The whole thing fits together so nicely. Lure the gods off Haven, lead them on a wild chase, then cut straight into the heart of our realm."

"But it hasn't all gone according to plan," Ikawa replied, the slightest edge of rebuke in his voice.

Boreas and Leti looked up at him.

"Vena was supposed to steal the Crystals of Fire without our even being aware that they were gone. The portal would have been opened, again without our being aware of it. If our attention had not been drawn to it, and at least some of her shielding penetrated by the power of the Heart"—he pointed to the massive gem glowing before the group—"Gorgon might already be among us.

"There's been a delay of nearly ten days as well," Ikawa continued forcefully. "I dare say that Gorgon's forces have taken a terrible beating from the gods while he waited for the crystals to be retrieved."

"We must fight our way through," Boreas pointed out. "It'll take us three days to reach her realm. We'll have no levies of armed men available—there is no time to march them down there. I am bringing all my sorcerers; when I left I had already passed the word to marshal here."

"How many will that be?" Leti asked.

"Just under seventy with warrior skills—and that will strip my realm bare. Twenty are already here with me"—he paused—"including Giorgini."

Ikawa looked at Mark, who stiffened, but did not comment.

"We have only a hundred or so from Jartan's provinces," Leti said, "and most of those are not of the top echelon. We can get another forty or so from the free guilds and minor fiefdoms."

"I brought up ten from Landra, and we can pick up another ten from occupation duty in Sarnak's old territory," Pina interjected. "Those of Minar's provinces closest to us can throw in another forty or so."

"Twelve from my territories," Tulana said coldly. "I had to leave seven behind to protect my cities from the Cresus."

"And there's us," Ikawa said.

"Around three hundred then, who can make it here in time," Boreas said. "Calling up transport people and other nonmilitary sorcerers, we might get four hundred total."

"And the gods know how many hundreds of demon warriors and lords will have already passed through by the time we get there," Leti pointed out.

"It doesn't look good," Valdez grumbled.

"There's nothing else we can do," Boreas snapped. "We have to attack."

"Frontally," Valdez said, "against a fortified position with wall crystals, and the odds already against us?" He gave a snort of disdain and walked around the Heart crystal to face Boreas. "We'll be slaughtered on the first assault."

"So we stay back here and hide, like frightened children?" Boreas growled.

"Are you accusing me of cowardice?"

"If your people had done their proper job, that woman never would have infiltrated our ranks."

"I take responsibility for that," Valdez snapped.

"You damn well should."

"If you want satisfaction, I'm ready to meet you any time," Valdez shouted.

Boreas leaped to his feet. "Here and now, if you don't like what I said."

"Damn you, we're suppose to be fighting on the same side," Ikawa roared, coming up to stand between Valdez and Boreas.

Leti came up beside Ikawa and angrily put her hands on Boreas shoulders. "Valdez is the best security advisor in Jartan's realms. He's better than mine, he's better even than your Farnak. If she got past him, she'd have gotten past any of our people."

"I don't need you to defend me," Valdez said slowly, his voice brimming with rage.

"I need all of us to work together," Leti shouted. "If you two want to kill each other later—if there *is* a later—then go ahead."

Ikawa took Valdez by the shoulders and gently pushed him away from Boreas. "Not now," he whispered. "First Patrice, who has insulted you far more by what she did."

"But I must redeem my honor," Valdez whispered, torment in his eyes.

"You've never lost it."

Valdez was silent, and Ikawa felt his throat tighten. He could understand the torment of this man. Through an unprecedented security breach, an enemy had stolen into the heart of Jartan's realm and opened the way for attack. The guilt was slowly killing the man.

"For the common good of us all, don't cause a breach between our people and Boreas."

Valdez looked into Ikawa's eyes, and for the first time since coming to Haven, Ikawa could see confusion in the old warrior's face.

"We settle it later," Valdez growled, breaking free from Ikawa and looking back at Boreas.

The demigod merely nodded.

"Yet I still say that a frontal attack on Patrice's city is suicide," Valdez told the council. "She might believe that word has yet to reach us of the danger and it'll be several days before we can respond. But nevertheless her defenses will be deployed. Hours before we hit, she'll know we're moving in. In fact, she'll fully anticipate our arrival."

The room was silent for a moment.

"There is no other way," Leti said finally. "Perhaps with the Heart crystal we can cut our way in."

"The damn thing's a wonderful weapon," Boreas replied, "but cumbersome. It'll take my strength, and yours as well, just to move it. In an air battle it'll be next to useless, and we'll have to fight our way across twenty, maybe fifty miles, before we even reach the walls where the power of the Heart can be brought to bear in its full strength. Even if we breach the walls and knock out her heavy crystals, we'll still have to fight our way over and into the palace, cut our way through, and then finally smash the portal down—a position which will be swarming with Gorgon's denizens."

The room was silent again as everyone in the chamber considered his words.

"Then we'll have to try from another direction," Tulana said quietly.

"I figured we'd get around to this sooner or later, and I didn't feel like wasting my breath first," he went on. With a snap of his fingers, one of his sorcerers stepped forward and unrolled a chart on the table before the Heart Crystal.

"My forces are already moving. Just remember I'm the one who thought it up when it comes to reward time later."

Chapter 15

"This is Red Team calling in," Walker said, breaking comm link silence. "I've got many, many bandits coming up at twelve o'clock."

"Fifty at least," Kraut shouted, winging up alongside Walker. "No, make that seventy-five plus."

"Seventy-five plus," Walker repeated into his crystal.

"What are bandits?" a voice crackled through the interference that Patrice's defensive teams were putting down.

Walker looked over at Kraut and shook his head.

"The guys in the black hats. The enemy!"

"Acknowledged," came the curt reply.

"They're coming up through the cloud layer," Kraut shouted, pointing forward and below.

Several miles ahead, Walker could clearly see the first specks, flying in a loose weaving formation. More and more appeared, coming up on an intersect path with Walker, Kraut, and their thirty companions.

"Christ, will you look at those demons," Walker yelled.

Behind the first wave of enemy sorcerers, half a hundred forms appeared, black and red against the early morning clouds, their mighty wings slashing through the air.

"Magic users all, I bet," Walker said coldly.

"White or Black leader?" the comm link asked.

"Negative on that," Walker replied. There was no sign yet of either Patrice or Gorgon, at least.

The two groups continued to close.

"I'm sensing more coming up out of the city," Kraut announced. "Maybe fifty—more like sixty, at *least*."

"They must have picked up the main van of our attack group," Walker shouted. Looking back over his shoulder, he tried to pick out where Leti and the other one hundred and fifty sorcerers were keeping to the upper cloud bank ten thousand feet above him. He focused his attention for a moment, scanning. There—he could barely sense them. Leti was cloaking the group well, but at this range they might be noticed.

"Let's keep acting like the bait that we are," Walker said, avoiding the comm link. The enemy would know that this small formation was a forward recon and bait—thirty sorcerers approaching Patrice's city could be nothing else. The trick was to make the bait so enticing that they'd make a stab nevertheless, and then get jumped from above.

"They're breaking into two groups." Kraut pointed forward.

The range had closed to less than two miles, and Walker could now see that the demons were spiraling upward in tight circles, going for the upper cloud bank, while sixty sorcerers were banking out in a wide circle, holding the same altitude as the "bait."

One of Jartan's elderly sorcerers came up to hover by Walker's side, giving him a nervous glance. Walker smiled. "Let's get closer in."

The sorcerer said nothing, but it was obvious that he wasn't happy.

"Come on," Walker shouted. "It's gonna be a good scrimmage!"

Judging carefully, he watched as the sixty sorcerers continued a wide banking turn, positioning themselves to come in on Walker's right, while the demons continued to spiral up.

"Something on our left—they're coming straight up from the ground below," Kraut yelled.

Walker looked down. A quarter mile below, he saw scores of demons breaking through the scattering of clouds and ground fog.

"Imada, how you doing?" Walker looked at the boy beside him. He would have preferred if the lad had stayed with Ikawa, but he had insisted upon being in the front of the action, and Ikawa had finally relented.

Imada said nothing, but his eyes were cold, as if eager for contact. There was something about him that gave Walker the chills.

He looked forward again. A couple more seconds, just a couple more, and then break and head straight back out, pulling the attackers in under Leti, who could hit them from above.

"Contact—we have contact!"

Stunned, Walker looked back over his shoulder.

A ripple of fire slashed through the clouds above.

"Damn it, they were in the clouds, shielded and waiting for us," the voice over the comm link screamed. "We're getting hit on . . . " The channel went dead.

Several bodies came tumbling out of the clouds, trailing fire and smoke.

"Break, left and down!" Walker screamed. Winging over, he started into a near vertical dive. When he looked back, the rest of the group was following, and Kraut was closing in alongside. Farther back he could see the demons who had been spiraling up now cutting over, knifing through the air, while the group that had been circling to the right started to dive as well, coming in behind them.

"Stick to me like glue," Walker shouted to his group.

Damn them, if only his own people were around him, he wouldn't be so worried, but there was only Kraut, Imada, and the rest were aging warriors from Jartan's and Storm's courts. The outlanders had introduced a whole new level to aerial warfare here on Haven, flying in tight formation, jumping, slashing through, and then pulling out as a team. They had won Allic and his warriors over to this system, but few others understood the tactics, and he feared that once combat was joined they'd follow their old instinct to break apart and engage in individual combat.

"Don't mix it up. Hit them, then go for the clouds and fog bank!"

The range closed with frightening speed. Walker lined up his shot on a demon who, roaring with battle lust, was winging up to meet him.

A ripple of bolts shot up from the enemy, several striking Walker's shielding so it glowed white-hot.

Damn, they've got power, he thought grimly. Snapping through two hundred yards, he continued his dive straight at the enemy. Half of the demons were already jackknifing over, building up their own speed to cut in alongside Walker's group as they cut through.

Walker lined up his foe and slashed out with a bolt. Kraut hit the same demon as well, loading his shield. Walker fired again, diving so close that he could have touched the demon as he dived past. The demon's shielding exploded, and his wings went up in flame. Trailing oily black smoke, he tumbled out of the sky.

They cut through the group, a number of demons swinging in to race alongside, trading blow for blow.

Walker jinked left, sparing a glance back. The swarm of enemy were streaking in from behind. To his horror he saw four of his companions twisting to engage in single combat.

"Stick to me!" Walker screamed.

A white-haired sorcerer scored a killing shot, knocking his demon over with a blinding flash. At the same moment his shielding snapped, hit by three bolts from above, and the man disappeared in an explosion of fire and smoke. The other three, helplessly caught, were swarmed under as the groups closing in from behind cut through them, hitting with half a hundred bolts.

"Keep moving—don't stop!" Walker shouted. The rest of his group, with an almost equal number of demons dogging their flanks, raced downward. The low clouds and fog seemed to race upward with terrifying speed. He hit the cool blanket of mist but continued his dive. The trick now was to out fly the enemy. The plan had been blown. Leti and her strike group were going to have to be on their own for the moment. But at least Walker could tie up six or seven times his own number, trying to kill as many of Patrice's allies as possible without losing any more of his own sorcerers.

. ."Don't slow down and hang on my tail!" Walker broke through three hundred feet, then a hundred. Pulling out at the last possible second, flying through the heavy fog, he skimmed through the edge of an open field.

A horrifying scream rent the air. Sickened, Walker looked back to see another of his sorcerers smashing into the ground at top speed. The demon who had been trailing him, too intent on his prey to notice, also slammed into the ground.

Twisting and dodging, Walker flew full-out, cutting through the field. He spared a quick look back and saw Kraut and Imada and most of his surviving sorcerers still behind him. Directly ahead he could sense a forest. A demon cut out of the mist, trying to swing in front of him. They traded bolts; then Walker sensed a narrow trail into the woods and raced straight at it. A grim laugh escaped his lips as the pursuing demon slammed into a tree.

"Hang on!" Walker screamed as he swept down the path at top speed, sensing rather than seeing the twists and turns of the trail. Bolts of energy slammed through the forest, exploding the trees into balls of fire.

"Red Leader, Red Leader, situation?" It was Leti.

"A little tight at the moment!" Walker cried.

"Same here. We need your support."

"I think it's the other way around!" he shouted.

His attention shifted for a moment as he looked up. His heart felt like it was surging into his throat as he jinked left at the last possible second, cutting so close to a towering pine that a shower of branches and needles exploded around him.

"Take care of yourself, Walker!" Leti cried.

He found himself laughing. "What else can I do?"

The path before him split into even narrower trails. There was no time to choose, so he cut left. If he dared to slow down, the demons, who were probably flying above the forest, would get ahead and into position to pounce whenever he and his group finally emerged from the woods.

"Green Leader, Green Leader, initiate now!" Leti's voice crackled, stunning Walker with its intensity. She must have focused her strength through the Heart to send out such a strong signal, which could cut through any amount of jamming Patrice had put up.

"Good luck, Captain," Walker whispered. Suddenly the trail before him went dark, and he realized that he was flying straight into a cliff wall that cut straight up out of the heart of the forest.

"My lady, we've just got a report. The Heart Crystal has been sighted in the group."

Patrice looked up to see the sorcerer in charge of battle communications standing before her.

Stunned, she came to her feet. The Heart Crystal—at her very doorstep. Was Leti mad? Or was there a plan within the plan which could still be dangerous for her?

The comm link by her side crackled with battle reports and the booming shouts of triumph from the demons.

No battle discipline with those bastards, she thought darkly.

"It's hard to figure out exactly what is going on, though," the sorcerer ventured. "The demons keep blocking our communications crystals with their talk."

"They're exuberant, that's all," Patrice replied. The sorcerer hesitated, then went back to stand over the map. But she could sense his misgivings—and for that matter, the misgivings of all her people at the emergence of hundreds of Gorgon's demons.

No one of her realm had known of the plan, not even her most trusted battle advisors. When the first demons not needed to expand the gateway had at last come out of the portal rooms, there had been cries of consternation. Two of her sorcerers had been killed in the corridors—along with several demons—when a fight had broken out. She suspected that more than one of her followers might consider turning against her, but before they could marshall such a plan the battle would already be won.

Leti's attack, days before expected, at first had alarmed her, but now in retrospect Patrice thought it was the best possible thing, turning her people to a common defense, diverting them from what was no longer a secret: that Gorgon would break through to Haven before the day was out.

"Green Leader, Green Leader, initiate!" slashed through the comm link.

Patrice looked over at one of her battle advisors, who was flanked by Takgutha, fourth demon lord of Gorgon.

"White must refer to you," Takgutha growled, "black to my lord. We know there are two battle teams out there. Green must refer to yet another group."

Patrice did not respond, feeling a ripple of anger at Takgutha's impudence for speaking when not asked to, as if he were controlling the battle.

"We estimate nearly all their forces are either in the clouds or on the ground," Patrice's battle leader hissed, glaring at Takgutha, who smiled with barely concealed disdain.

"It could be a false signal."

"Or Boreas," Takgutha snapped.

There had been no reports of him, Patrice thought. If he had been at Asmara or flown south with his people, her spotters should have picked him up.

"The offworlders?" Patrice asked, looking at her communications sorcerer. The man whispered an inquiry into his crystal and a moment later looked back.

"We think two were with the group that we've cornered on the ground. In the air only one has been spotted."

Boreas and the offworlders: There was the puzzle. She still had a reserve of sixty sorcerers and two hundred sorcerer demons under her command, with another twenty arriving every hour. Where was he—and the offworlders—or were they even here at all? Surely Leti would not be so foolish as to split an already inferior force before charging in.

"Commit the reserves of my followers to finish off those pests who bother us," Takgutha growled. "Capture the Heart. It's a prize worth half this miserable world."

"*I* am in command here," Patrice raged, coming to her feet.

Takgutha, without dropping his smile, bowed low in obeisance. "But of course, my lady. Forgive me."

The rest of her people looked at her in stunned silence.

The Heart, she realized, masking her thoughts, not sure if Takgutha could somehow reach into them. Leti had the Heart with her. If Patrice could gain that before Gorgon came through, then surely she would be his superior in strength. It was almost as if Leti were offering it straight to her. In the air, the weapon was too unmanageable, except in the hands of a god, but if Leti could bring it close enough to the city, it might cause trouble for Patrice.

But the Heart could be hers. . . . She looked up at Takgutha and smiled.

"You stay here in command of the reserve," she said coldly. "I'm taking my people in to finish Leti off."

"I humbly advise that I and my warriors should go with you." Takgutha replied softly.

And capture it for your lord, Patrice thought darkly.

"Stay here and manage the defense. I want all flanks covered as originally planned. Fail, and you are responsible. I'm taking my people to finish Leti off." And she swept out of the room.

"And if they come by sea?" Takgutha growled. "You know we are ill used to that realm."

"I already have my plans for that," Patrice snapped, "but they'd be fools to try."

How long he had been underwater, Mark could no longer calculate. Somehow he had even mastered sleep while keeping his shield up against the crushing weight of the four hundred feet of ocean above him.

Tireless ladultas by the thousands had swarmed around him and the other sorcerers, towing the humans in relays. Tulana had even devised harnesses that tied to the ladultas' dorsal fins and hooked to each of the humans so they would not have to hold on during their three-day, thousand-mile underwater passage. Mark could only hope that the diversion had paid off; that through some miracle they had successfully—and secretly—been brought to the gates of the city without Patrice being aware that Boreas had entered the fray.

Yet it was a grim chance they were working on, the hope that Patrice, detecting Leti and the Heart Crystal, would send everything against them and leave the back door open for a lightning strike into the city to smash the portal.

Now there was only the waiting in the darkness. Boreas drifted past Mark, with Tulana by his side. Boreas looked spent. Since creeping to the outer approaches of the city, he had bent his entire strength to chilling the water above them, stating that the cold blanket would reflect any probing from above and thus mask their position.

"Another hour and we'll be there," Tulana said, coming up to float by Mark's side.

Eager to rise out of the tomblike darkness and begin the assault, Mark grinned in reply. He could barely discern Shigeru's shadow on his left, and Goldberg on his right. The rest of his command were strung out in a single line to either side, steadily drifting forward with their ladultas.

"Green Leader, Green Leader, initiate!"

Startled, Mark looked at Boreas.

"Damn it, we're not quite there yet," the demigod growled; then:

"Ladulta battle mounts! All riders get out of those harnesses."

Reaching over to the strap around his chest, Mark hit the release plate and broke free from the creature who had been towing him for the last hour.

The ladulta circled away to form in with the hundreds of his companions, who would come in the support wave. A ladulta cut in close, brushing Mark's side.

"Ready for battle again, Mark friend?"

"Sul! I didn't know you were here," he cried with delight.

"My herd arrive just before sky become bright. Not miss this fight with you."

Eagerly, Mark reached out to grab his dorsal fin, while affectionately patting his companion with his other hand.

"We avenge death of comrades today."

"You ever fight against men before?" Mark asked.

There was a moment of hesitation. "No."

"Listen to my directions, then," Mark said. "I'll get us through this."

"Group commanders, check your communications crystals," Boreas ordered.

"Saito, run down your list," Mark said quickly. "Remember, gentlemen, report to your group leaders only. We fight as a team; Goldberg and Shigeru will act as our sonar.

"Follow Tulana straight into the harbor. If not detected, we'll run all the way in, come out of the water, then go for the palace. We'll provide air superiority while Boreas and his people break in to smash the portal. If they detect us coming in, we'll provide near-surface support to Boreas, who will continue to run deep.

"Any questions?"

"Yeah, Captain," Smithie interjected. "When the hell are we gonna see sunlight again?"

"Soon enough."

"We've got to go immediately," Boreas called. "Now, attack!"

Sul leaped forward, his lithe body slicing through the water at top speed. Mark tightened his grip and hung on.

Long minutes passed. Though he probed in every direction, Mark could sense nothing—just the open sea and the long lines of sorcerers, their mounts, and the surging school of ladultas following in their wake.

"Bottom contact," Kochanski announced. Looking down, Mark finally sensed the ocean floor shelving upward out of the depths. Boreas and his battle team dove to hug the bottom, while Mark and his battle team pushed straight ahead, following Tulana.

"We've cleared the outer harbor," Tulana whispered, coming up to Mark's side. "Just a couple more minutes."

To his left and right, Mark could sense the jetties that guarded the approach into Patrice's citadel. They had originally planned to be well inside the harbor and to spring out the moment Leti called. He could only hope the delay was not fatal.

"Something ahead," Sul's thought whispered through Mark's mind. "Human moving away."

Mark looked over at Tulana, who nodded and picked up speed. With his attention focused forward, Mark could vaguely sense a shadowy image ahead of them. The image turned into two forms, and then four.

"Going to surface," Sul whispered.

Tulana curved upwards, and Mark and the rest of the team followed.

The ocean started to brighten, shifting from indigo darkness to a twilight blue. The four forms suddenly disappeared.

"They left the water," Sul called.

"They're on to us," Tulana shouted. "Keep moving!"

With an incredible burst of energy Sul slashed through the water at breakneck speed, pulling up alongside Tulana, the other sorcerers spreading out into a two-hundred-yard front. In spite of his fear, Mark felt a wave of exultation. It was like some mad underwater cavalry charge, as the ladultas cut through the water at more than thirty knots, their riders hanging on and shouting war cries.

A booming ripple of echoes and high pitched pings came through the water.

"They've dropped in behind us," Sul whispered.

"Keep pushing forward," Tulana cried. "They're trying to divert us. Let the ladulta cover us!"

Mark looked over his shoulder and could sense half a dozen forms dropping in behind the group from above. There was a splash almost straight overhead, and he could see the shadowy form of a sorcerer cutting down.

An energy bolt slashed past, making the water boil and hiss. Two more bolts snapped out.

"Christ, Captain, we're getting jumped," Kochanski cried.

"Keep moving in," Tulana called.

Another bolt shot past, nicking Shigeru's shield. The wrestler let out a startled grunt.

"Don't turn back!" Tulana ordered.

Mark looked over his shoulder. Three sorcerers now rode on his tail, not more than a hundred feet behind. Sul started into a wild series of jinxes and swerves, yet continued to follow Tulana's lead.

Suddenly half a hundred ladulta emerged from the shadows. Surging in, they charged the enemy sorcerers, their booming chants rumbling through the ocean with a bone-chilling pulse.

Unbelieving, Mark watched as the creatures slammed into one of the sorcerers at top speed, knocking him over. Like sharks in a feeding frenzy, the ladulta lashed into him, slamming him again and again.

An energy bolt snapped out, cutting a ladulta in half, and at that moment Mark saw the true savagery of the creatures when aroused. Thundering screams rent the ocean, and the creatures crashed into the sorcerers. Bolts continued to flame, killing half a dozen more, yet still they continued to strike. A sorcerer's shield went down under the repeated blows. Sickened, Mark could see the man flailing under the inrush of water, desperately trying to swim to the surface. The ladulta circling above him rammed his body, forcing him ever deeper until finally he went limp. His two companions panicked and thrashed toward the surface, firing blindly into the herd. Their shields snapped off, and with savage cries the ladulta pushed them into the darkness below, tearing their bodies to pieces.

Stunned, Mark looked at Sul. Three sorcerers had been killed in a matter of seconds.

"Now we are truly angry," Sul whispered coldly, and surged forward.

More splashes vibrated through the water ahead.

"Enemy forward!" Tulana cried.

Mark could sense them: a dozen sorcerers.

"They're holding tight together, and going down!" Shigeru cried.

"Follow them in!" Tulana ordered.

Sul cut downward. With the advantage of speed the ladulta offered, the group quickly started to close.

A blinding flash snapped through the water ahead, and shouts of rage echoed up from Boreas' group, still hugging the ocean floor.

"Christ, they've got a wall crystal with them," Mark called.

The group loomed into view, hovering above Boreas' group, which was still charging forward. Another bolt slashed out, and the scream of a ladulta echoed through the ocean. Sickened, Mark knew that without shielding, his mount was totally defenseless. He might possibly survive a strike, but Sul would be dead in an instant. He wanted to tell Sul to drop him off and he'd swim in alone, but without the ladulta's added speed, he doubted if they could effectively break through.

"Hit them hard then keep moving!" Tulana cried.

The group surged in, closing ranks. The shadowy images resolved into a dozen sorcerers in a tight circle, shields up, surrounding a wall crystal.

A ripple of light snapped up from the ocean floor, striking into the enemy sorcerers. Shields glowed white-hot, water boiled away in steam, and cries of panic and rage counterpointed the wild battle chant of the ladulta.

A bolt snapped out from Tulana's hand, followed an instant later by shots from his team, cutting straight into the circle of sorcerers. A single form snapped into light, and one shattered body fell away.

Another slash of energy arced out from the wall crystal, cutting into Boreas' attack group, killing a man and his mount.

Tulana, with Mark at his side, charged straight at the enemy, who now turned their attention to the upper group. Dozens of bolts slammed back and forth. With a wild curse, Kochanski tumbled free from his mount, who simply disappeared from the violent impact of half a dozen hits. Saito fell away, his shield glowing hot, his ladulta crippled and circling blindly.

Suddenly, the enemy surged straight upward, racing for the surface.

Mark could see the wall crystal tumbling into the depths, and in that instant he saw the glow of a red crystal, locked inside a glass tube tied to the side of the massive gem.

"Break, break!" he screamed. "It's gonna blow!"

Tulana screamed out a warning as the wall crystal tumbled straight into the mass of Boreas' warriors, still charging in along the ocean floor.

The ocean snapped into a dazzling brilliance. The shock wave slammed into Mark, knocking him free from Sul. Horrified, Mark could see half a dozen sorcerers below floating limp in the water, their shields gone. Crippled ladulta spiraled upward by the dozens, struggling to gain the surface; others, torn apart, hung motionless. Wild screams rent the ocean, and a man came shooting up past Mark, his left arm gone, trailing a dark cloud of blood. Vainly, the sorcerer kicked for the surface through the wreckage and boiling steam. A ladulta surged past Mark with lightning speed, slamming into the man and, without slowing, pushed him straight up.

The attack had simply ground to a halt.

"Rally and keep moving!" Boreas' command boomed through the water. "Keep moving, damn it. Tulana, get above the water!"

"Rally on me!" Tulana called.

Scanning, Mark could see the prince floating near the surface.

"On Tulana!" Mark called through the comm link.

Through the shadows, Mark could see his companions moving in, some still on their mounts. A form brushed past: Sul. To Mark's horror, he saw a red slash on his friend's side.

"You're hurt!"

"Steam burn!" Sul whispered grimly. "Still fight, though."

Saito came in without his mount and trailing his left leg; Kochanski and the others reappeared circling in. All around them the ocean was a horrifying confusion of bodies, bubbling steam, and wounded ladultas.

"Another one!" Shigeru cried. A small crystal dropped past the group, a red crystal tied to its side inside a bottle. Suddenly a dozen more dropped in around them.

"Out of the water!" Tulana screamed.

"Get your herd out of here!" Mark called to Sul. "Stand clear and get out of the harbor—you'll be slaughtered in here!"

Mark let go and surged upward; Sul, calling to his companions, cut out and away.

A thunderclap washed over Mark as the first crystal detonated. Shooting out of the water, he was blinded by the sun, but dodged instinctively back and forth, trying to find his foes. Below him, a dozen columns of water shot heavenward from the depth charges.

A bolt slammed into his shield. Turning, he cut around and scanned the ocean. The heart of Patrice's city was straight ahead, not half a mile away. The vast circular harbor spread out around him, and the sky was swarming with demons. Even as he watched, he saw ten of the creatures cut across the front of his formation, each dropping a crystal. Seconds later the ocean seemed to explode.

"We've got to break them up!" Tulana cried.

Twisting and turning, Mark fought for altitude. "Formation, damn it, get in formation!" he screamed.

Goldberg was the first to gain his side, followed seconds later by a dozen sorcerers trailing in behind a grim-faced Saito.

A band of demons cut down and through the group, trading shots. Mark aimed a bolt, hitting his target, yet still the demon surged in, talons extended. Mark cut sideways and the demon shot past, his face contorted with rage. Two more bolts slashed into Mark, stunning him, as the battle broke down into a wild melee. From above he saw three demons winging downward, carrying a net that cradled a wall crystal.

"Break them!" Tulana screamed. The prince cut inward, firing bolt after bolt. Shigeru surged ahead, then suddenly drew up, coming to a complete stop and raising his hand. A slash of light cut out, hitting the net and smashing the bottle that held the red crystal.

The wall crystal detonated with a thunderclap roar, and the three demons disappeared in the flames. The shock wave washed over Mark, but he could see the flame of the explosion engulfing a dozen demons and sorcerers who had been flying close to the group.

"That's it!" Tulana screamed. "Now through the hole!"

Charging forward, Mark cut through the expanding fireball, his companions behind him.

The maneuver threw off their pursuit, and Mark saw that they were nearly to the city wall, with Patrice's palace not a quarter mile ahead.

Then crisscrossing lights slashed out from the palace and the walls surrounding it.

"Wall crystals!" Tulana hissed. "They must have a dozen of them!"

The water below seemed to explode as Boreas emerged, cutting straight up, the first of his companions following in his wake.

"In on them!" Boreas shouted. "We've got to close and finish it!"

A bolt from a wall crystal cut into the group behind Boreas, knocking two back into the sea, yet still the attackers kept emerging. Mark spotted Giorgini in the group, and inwardly breathed a sigh of relief.

"Above us!" Saito cried.

From out of the boiling cloud of smoke, still expanding outward from the detonated crystal, a dozen demons were charging straight down.

"Block them!" Boreas cried. "My group follow me!"

Mark turned to meet the attack. Relentlessly the demons swarmed in, the leader disappearing when hit by half a dozen shots in the mad confusion.

"A wall crystal!" Shigeru cried.

Two of the demons in the center of the group had folded their wings and were plummeting, holding a crystal between them. Desperately Mark fired again and again, but the two shot straight past him. Winging up and over, Mark followed—straight at the water where Boreas hovered, rallying his sorcerers as they surfaced, and pushing them into the attack on Patrice's palace.

"Above you!" Mark screamed.

Boreas raised his hand and fired, and one of the demons exploded. Desperately, the other clutched the crystal to his chest and continued the fall.

Mark fired at the demon's back while trying to follow him down. He could see the flash of red as the demon reached into a pouch by his side, while still clutching the massive wall crystal within the folds of his wings.

"No!" Mark screamed. Boreas tried to cut in front, to stop

the creature in his suicidal plunge.

The demon slammed full force into the ocean. For the briefest of seconds Mark thought the creature had failed. And then, with a blinding flash, the world before him seemed to disappear.

Chapter 16

"It sounds like they're getting swarmed under in the harbor," Ikawa cried, his voice edged with exhaustion. The interference that Patrice had been sending out had disappeared only moments before, and now Ikawa could clearly hear the shouted battle commands.

Straining his gaze forward, he could discern the outline of Patrice's city through the dissipating clouds and the flashes of combat on the far side.

"There she is," Leti cried, pointing.

For Patrice was winging up through the clouds with yet more reinforcements spread out behind her.

Desperately Leti looked around. After the initial onslaught, her sorcerers had managed to hold their own, trading nearly equal losses as the combat weaved back and forth across the heavens. Yet the defenders had fought with masterful skill, always keeping between Leti and the city, gradually forcing her group to curve off toward the shore—and away from the palace.

"Coming up from below!"

Ikawa looked straight down, and through the wisps of fog he saw scores of demons and a dozen sorcerers rising up. "Walker, Walker, where the hell are you!" he cried, but there was only silence.

Grimly, Ikawa looked at Leti. "Walker must be finished!"

"There's too many," she shouted. "We've got to get the Heart down on the ground where we can fight with it.

"To me," Leti roared. "Break off combat and to me!"

Motioning for the dozens of sorcerers surrounding the Heart to follow, she started to dive, cutting in toward the coast on an oblique away from the group coming in from below and Patrice's advance from the city. Leti's assault team broke away from their combats, turning to follow their leader, the enemy they had been battling swinging in to dog their flanks.

"That hill looking out over the city!" Leti shouted, pointing forward.

Ikawa judged the distance and could see that they were falling miles short of their target. He could only hope that the assault wing from the ocean would somehow gain the citadel after all.

The ground raced up to greet him and he landed alongside Leti, rushing over to where the team carrying the Heart settled in to land. Frantically, they cast aside the nets to free the crystal.

A shriek rent the air, and looking up Ikawa could see Patrice streaking in.

"Leti, come and meet me!"

"Like hell, you bitch," Leti growled, focusing her attention on the Heart. Extending his hands, Ikawa joined her, while the sorcerers who had carried it formed a circle about the two, putting up a protective shield.

A bolt of light shot out from the Heart, slicing past Patrice and cutting two of her sorcerers in half.

Ikawa felt drained, as if the Heart had somehow seized and drawn every ounce of his strength outward.

Gasping for breath, he staggered. The Heart was too powerful for him; he feared that to use it without Leti by his side might very well kill him.

Patrice stormed overhead, a brilliant slash of fire cutting from her hand, slamming into the protective shielding, the energy around the group snapping and glowing.

"Again!" Leti screamed. More of her sorcerers were now winging in, even as the enemy closed. To his horror, Ikawa watched as stragglers were cut off, overwhelmed, and sent tumbling from the sky.

He turned back to the Heart. Another snap of light, and several more of the enemy dropped from the sky, but Patrice dodged the bolt at the last second.

Swinging outward, she circled wide, her followers forming up into a massive cloud of attackers.

"Again!" Leti screamed.

A dozen sorcerers shouldered in around Ikawa, extending their hands to the glowing Heart. He felt his vision dropping into blackness as another explosive shot cut through Patrice's attack formation.

"They're coming in!" Leti roared as a hundred or more forms dived from above. Bolts of energy slammed out, rippling through the collective shielding, turning it white-hot. Stunned sorcerers fell screaming to the ground.

Leti, extending both hands upward added her power to the shield, bolstering it, her dark hair swirling about her in the incandescent storm.

Exhausted, Ikawa slumped to the ground, unable to continue. The balance seemed to hold, a struggle between the offense and defense, each side shifting more and more energy in. Patrice dropped her own shielding, shouting with triumph as she slammed bolt after bolt into Leti's group.

"Hey, bitch!"

A high, clear voice rang out over the battle. Ikawa looked up to see a sorcerer, dressed in the flame-colored livery of Patrice, swing in behind the demigoddess and slam a bolt into her head.

Stunned, Patrice fell away.

"How 'bout another!" A second sorcerer fired straight at Patrice, burning her arm.

With a shriek of rage, Patrice fell backward, her hair smoldering. Turning, she looked through the swirling confusion for her tormentors, her protective shielding snapping back up to full. Ikawa could feel the strain on the defense dropping away.

"Time to get the shit outta here!" the first sorcerer screamed, diving straight toward the defensive circle.

"It's Walker!" Leti cried. "Let him in!"

The shielding snapped down for a second, as Patrice's forces, stunned by what had first appeared to be a betrayal, broke off the attack and scattered.

Laughing, Walker alighted beside Leti, who embraced him and turned to kiss Kraut on the cheek as he landed next to his companion.

"Almost had her," Walker said ruefully, looking over towards Patrice who, still stunned by the double blow, had cut away from the group, her battle team following.

"Just how the hell?" Ikawa asked, coming to his feet.

"I thought our shit was cooked," Kraut said, beaming, though

Ikawa could see that the man was trembling from the strain of what they had just pulled off.

"Anyhow," Walker interrupted. "There we were flying straight into a cliff. There was no way out, so I went to ground.

"He actually flew into a narrow crevice and stopped cold," Kraut interjected. "I thought we were dead. Well, it drove them crazy, it looked like we just disappeared. We stayed there for a good ten minutes, and finally they broke up and started filtering through the trees looking for us. It was easy pickings then, we jumped them as they came through."

"What about the others?" Leti asked quietly.

"We lost most in the fight and the chase," Walker whispered, the exhilaration of the moment before gone. "Two more hit the cliff. We lost the others fighting in the woods. Finally there was just Imada, Kraut, and me.

"Anyhow, Imada, he's the one that thought it up. He said why the hell don't we strip their dead and see what we can do. Ain't that right, Imada?"

Walker turned around, smiling. The group surrounding them was silent.

"Say, where the hell is the little guy?" Walker asked nervously. "He was right behind us when we jumped that old witch.

"Imada?"

"He didn't come through," Leti whispered.

Stunned, Walker looked around the battle-scarred group. "Goddamn it."

"I think they're forming up again!" one of Storm's sorcerers cried.

Turning, Ikawa saw Patrice skimming low around the base of the hill, swinging in and out through the scattering of trees.

Ikawa watched her intently as he stepped up to the Heart to concentrate for another blast.

"Get ready," Leti shouted.

"For Christ's sake, it's Imada!" Walker shouted, pointing to a lone sorcerer who rose from the ground a hundred yards away and streaked towards Patrice.

The lone figure climbed up, shield off with arms extended.

"What the hell is that kid doing?" Walker shouted. "Imada, get your ass in here."

The boy continued on, not looking back.

"He's surrendering," Kraut said, his voice edged with disgust.

Ikawa watched in unbelieving silence. Imada hovered in the sky, the demigod winging in towards him. The boy continued to float in the sky, and then with a dramatic flourish fired a bolt back toward his comrades.

"The bastard's turned traitor," Walker snarled.

Ikawa was silent, unable to comprehend that one of his own would do this. Leti hovered before Imada for a moment, and in his heart Ikawa found himself praying that she would strike him down and thus end his disgrace. She suddenly pointed back towards the city, and two sorcerers fell in on either side of Imada and started off.

"Traitor!" Ikawa roared. He concentrated on the Heart and sent out a blast, but his shot went wide and he staggered back, drained.

Suddenly, in the distance a brilliant flash snapped through the sky beyond the city.

"What in hell was that?" Walker whispered.

"Maybe they got through!" Kraut cried.

Struggling to control his anger, Ikawa returned to his primary responsibility and focused his attention on his communications crystal. Instantly he picked up the wild shouts of a battle in progress.

"A wall crystal"—it was Shigeru's voice—"they're going to blow another wall crystal!"

Shouted commands slashed through the command link.

"I'm on him, I'm on him." Ikawa recognized Mark's voice.

Seconds later, a brilliant flash lit the sky, and a towering column of steam and fire mushroomed into the heavens.

"Green Leader," Leti screamed. "Green Leader, what's happening?"

The comm link was overloaded.

"Green Leader!"

The distant thunder of the exploding wall crystal rumbled across the plain.

"Green Leader is down," a shaken voice reported. "Repeat, he is down."

Horrified, Leti turned to look at her companions.

"In and on them." It was Tulana, his voice washing through the confusion.

"It's finished," another voice cut in, and then faded.

"She's pulling back!" Walker shouted.

Patrice, turning, started back toward the city alone. The rest of her sorcerers fanned out and pulled back beyond the range of the Heart, where they went to ground.

Leti watched with cold interest.

"Shall we go in?" Ikawa asked.

Leti looked around at the battle-worn group.

"The Heart's the only thing that's giving us the edge at this point," she said quietly. "We go into the air, we lose its firepower. We've made it as far as we can. Whoever is left over there will have to finish it. We're fought out."

Another thunderclap and burst of light snapped through the sky, engulfing one of the high pinnacles of Patrice's palace, and the massive tower collapsed into ruin.

Ikawa, heartsick and exhausted, looked over at Leti, who wordlessly shook her head.

"She's coming back."

Takgutha looked over at Patrice's battle commander and smiled. "Whatever for?" he said hoarsely. "She wanted the Heart, she should be able to take it."

"Not at the price of our wall crystals," the battle commander hissed. "You have no authorization to take them. And you killed some of our people doing it."

"It was an emergency," Takgutha snapped. "I heard how the offworlders introduced this little trick. I felt they should get a taste of it themselves."

"She wants to talk to you. You are ordered not to use any more crystals," the sorcerer growled.

"I have no time now," Takgutha roared. Turning away, he barked a series of commands into his own crystal.

"They still might break through," Takgutha snarled.

"We have enough firepower to block them!"

"I want them dead now, so their bodies can be laid before my lord as an offering."

"Not at the price of our crystals!"

With a curse, Takgutha raised his hand; the battle commander snapped up his shield in response. The two looked at each other warily.

"Later, little one," Takgutha laughed. "I'm going out now to draw some blood."

"She wants you here when she gets back," the battle commander shouted, though the fear was evident in his voice.

"Tell your," and he paused, "tell my lady she can find me fighting, where anyone who is a warrior should be."

With a cold laugh, he swept out of the room. Half a dozen demons greeted him by the door, carrying between them three wall crystals in slings.

"Boreas!"

His shield gone from the blast, Mark found himself in the water, unsure how he had fallen, or where he even was.

"Boreas!"

Mark, his shoulder numb, looked up at the vast pillar of fire and steam that rose heavenward and saw Tulana hovering above him. Feebly he rose upward and looked around. Bodies lay scattered on the water: ladulta who had stayed with the assault floundered on the surface, stunned by the blast or lying still in death. Mark felt as if he was somehow caught in the end of the world.

"Over here!" It was Shigeru, Giorgini by his side, holding Boreas's senseless body.

Mark flew down to join them.

"I think he's still alive," Giorgini said grimly, his face a vision of horror from the blood pouring down from a torn scalp.

"You two get him out of here," Tulana roared. "I'm going in and finish this!"

Mark looked at the warrior with disbelief, and then started to rise.

"You're out of this," Tulana ordered. "Your arm, Mark!"

Numbly, Mark looked over at his right arm and for the first time realized that it was broken, saw the shard of bone sticking out from a wound that pulsed with blood. He suddenly felt giddy.

"Organize a rear guard with your offworlders. I'm going for

the palace," Tulana said, and soared upward, a scattering of sorcerers winging up around him.

Mark tried to follow. But Goldberg cut in front to hold him back.

"You heard him," Goldberg shouted. He grabbed Mark's good arm and fumbled for his communications crystal.

"Mark and Saito battle teams, this is Goldberg. Tulana's battle orders rally on me, rally on me."

"I've got to go in!" Mark cried, struggling.

"You're finished, Captain." With a violent pull, he streaked down, wrenching Mark so that he felt he was going to pass out.

"Anyhow, it's finished," Goldberg whispered.

For a moment, there was silence. The demons that had been circling above swung about to pursue the attack group.

"We better get organized," Goldberg shouted.

Rising above the water, he called out a series of commands, and Mark could see Saito coming in with the rest of the Japanese, Kochanski by his side. Smithie appeared from the water, blood pouring from his nose and ears.

"I can't hear," Smithie screamed. "Damn it, my ears."

Kochanski settled by Smithie's side and finally calmed him down.

A series of bolts snapped down from above. Looking up Mark saw a covey of demons cutting low across the water.

With his right arm gone, all he could do was snap up his defensive crystal and hope for the best.

"Come with me, Mark friend."

Looking down into the water, Mark saw Sul hovering by his side.

"Not yet," Mark whispered, unable to stop watching Tulana's mad rush for Patrice's palace. The sky rippled with light as the attack force doggedly pushed in, dodging and weaving through the interlocking blasts of half a dozen wall crystals, the pursuing demons breaking off to hover above. Onward Tulana pushed.

"Goddamn it, he's gonna make it," Mark said.

And then the group seemed to disappear as three explosions ripped across the face of Patrice's palace.

"Damn it, damn them all," Goldberg hissed. The explosion roared across the harbor, echoing and re-echoing.

THE CRYSTAL SORCERERS   261

From out of the boiling maelstrom, lone sorcerers appeared, staggering, pulling back. The last to emerge was Tulana.

"Pull out," Tulana's voice cut through the comm link. "Get out, we're finished."

"Maintain fire," Saito shouted, and the group laid down a protective series of bolts over Tulana who, cutting low, streaked down the main boulevard of Patrice's city, a half dozen survivors around him, while from behind a host of demons led by a towering form closed in.

"Get in the water, break and run!" Tulana shouted. "We can't fight them anymore up here!"

"Go!" Sul called, pushing up by Mark's side.

"We're out of here, Captain!" Goldberg shouted, diving into the water.

Grabbing Sul's dorsal with his left hand, Mark dipped below the waves.

With powerful kicks, the ladulta pushed away, going deep. All around him Mark could sense or see his battered companions, surging due west, racing for the narrow harbor entrance.

"Ahead, crystal!" Sul called and cut a sharp right angle. A flash snapped through the water, the shock wave ripping through Mark. Two ladulta surged past, Shigeru on one, Giorgini on the other, between them Boreas, protected by their shields. Mark could see it was a dangerously close thing—they were desperately overextending themselves. A close hit would overload them. Then they disappeared from view as Sul pulled ahead.

For long minutes the group surged through the harbor, unable to gain the surface against the combined strength of the wall crystals and demons above. Their only hope was to zigzag through the water, dodging the depth charges.

"The harbor entrance is just ahead," Sul called.

This was the tough spot, Mark realized. The demons would be surging into this point to block their retreat and force them to the surface.

"Not much farther," Kochanski called. "Two hundred yards and we're out."

A booming echo snapped through the ocean, half a hundred ladulta picking up the call.

Sul slowed.

"What is it?" Mark cried.

"Cresus," Sul hissed.

"Merciful God," Mark groaned. The entire group seemed to pause. Snaps of energy flashed ahead, and the shadowy forms loomed larger.

"They must have kept them off to one side on the bottom while we swept in, and then herded them in," Kochanski cried. "We've got to go up!"

"Stay down and get through them!" Tulana roared through his comm link, and pushing forward he let go of his ladulta. "Get between them and then out."

With a wild shout, Tulana charged straight in.

"Hang on," Sul called, and drove forward.

Mark could sense half a dozen of the beasts, filling the harbor entrance from one side to the other, being driven forward by teams of sorcerers who kept striking their flanks and their tops in order to keep them from breaching.

Tulana slammed out a series of bolts to the left and right, and a gap between two of the beasts started to open.

Sul cut straight in.

"Crystal behind us!"

Mark looked back and could sense the energy of a small gem as it dropped.

A snap of fire slashed out and Tulana, caught by the blast, rolled out of control.

"Tulana!" Mark screamed.

The maw of a Cresus swept past him. Horrified, Mark watched as Tulana struggled weakly to get out of its way.

"I'll see you in hell!" Tulana roared.

The maw closed over him and he was gone.

Ladulta charged past Mark and Sul, shouting their rage, pulling the battered survivors out. A bolt of energy snapped past Mark and, uncaring, he looked up to see an enemy sorcerer hovering above a Cresus. Mark waited for the death blow, but Sul cut downward in a twisting spiral, racing for the ocean floor.

The Cresus surged past them, its massive tail flukes creating a swirl of turbulence; then suddenly it was behind them.

Sul's voice boomed through the ocean, calling to his companions, and Mark could sense the cries of grief as the shattered remnants of the attack force retreated into the open sea.

Beyond caring, Mark hung on as Sul dodged among the depth charges. Gradually, the concussions dropped away, the only sound the calls of wounded ladulta echoing feebly through the water.

"Rally on me," a faint voice hissed through the comm link. It was Saito.

Mark roused from his lethargy and looked around.

The clicking call of a ladulta snapped through the water.

Sul turned and pushed on, and gradually Mark could sense other forms moving in the water.

"Rally on me." The voice was stronger now.

Several dozen forms were in the water ahead, and Mark forced himself to regain his composure. For the first time since the explosion in the harbor, he became aware of the throbbing pain in his right arm, and of the thin swirl of blood streaming from it. Looking down at Sul's side, he saw a similar trail welling out from his companion.

"We're a fine pair," Mark thought.

"At least we survived," Sul replied sadly as they joined the exhausted remnants of the assault team.

"The captain made it," Goldberg called, dropping away from his ladulta to come up and float by Mark's side.

Mark could feel his world going dark. "How bad?"

"Half the assault team is gone," Saito replied.

"Our people?"

"Not sure yet," Saito told him.

"Green Leader, Green Leader," an insistent voice whispered through the comm link, and Mark finally realized that it had been calling for several minutes now.

"Green Leader here," Saito called.

"Did you smash the portal? We saw a tremendous explosion," Ikawa asked.

Saito hesitated. "Negative, it was only their wall crystals. The attack is finished."

There was a moment of silence.

"Is this Saito?" Leti called.

"I'm in command now."

"Mark—where is he?" Ikawa cut in, his voice edged with panic.

"Wounded." Saito looked appraisingly at Mark with the cold gaze of a combat soldier judging the condition of another. "He'll pull through."

"Rally in to us," Leti whispered. "The sky is clear."

"Here comes Shigeru," Goldberg announced, pointing downward.

From the murk, Shigeru and Giorgini emerged, still towing Boreas. Alongside them was Kochanski pulling Smithie, who was now unconscious.

"We better get in to Leti before they pick us up again!" Saito announced, leading the way straight up.

"I leave you now," Sul whispered.

"You and your herd are true warriors," Mark replied sadly, and let go of the dorsal to gently stroke Sul.

"We stay to keep fighting?" the ladulta asked.

Torn, Mark looked at his friend. How could he tell him the battle was lost, that Gorgon would break through and that Haven would be devastated in the wars to come?

"Go out to sea. If we should win, we will call you. But if you hear no more of us, know that we died to help preserve your world. Avoid all humans who are left, for they will be servants of the evil one and might harm you."

"I will wait for your call," Sul whispered, nuzzling up by Mark's side before turning away and swimming off into the darkness.

At last Mark broke clear of the ocean. Northward on the distant horizon he could see the outline of Patrice's city, a towering pillar of smoke above it. Saito circled for a moment above the group, then pointed back toward a hill half a dozen miles from the city and winged off.

Struggling, Mark tried to keep up. He spared a glance at the bedraggled survivors. Barely a man was uninjured, and clusters of sorcerers clung together, helping to pull their unconscious and badly injured companions toward safety.

"Here they come again!"

Wearily Mark looked up and saw a scattering of dots straight ahead in the sky.

Grimly he tried to force his shield up. The world seemed to

close in as if he was looking down a long dark tunnel swirling with dancing spots of light. The tunnel closed into blackness, and he felt himself falling away into night.

"Just what in the name of all the gods did you do?" Patrice stormed through the shattered wreckage of her audience chamber to confront Takgutha, who stood defiantly in the middle of the room, surrounded by a dozen of his companions.

"They were breaking through. I used the wall crystals to stop them."

"Breaking through!" Patrice screamed. "You destroyed half my wall crystals, you shattered my palace, hundreds of my people are dead in the streets. Damn you, it looks like they *did* break through!"

"I stopped them," Takgutha growled.

"How did they get this far by sea? Was the harbor entrance blocked as I had arranged?"

"The command was not properly passed," Takgutha said coldly. "The creatures were not in position, but they did finish them off on the way out. It was a good plan; we wiped them out."

"Where's Kuthna? I want to hear his side of this."

"He was killed in the explosions, my lady. I am sorry—he was a good battle commander." A thin smile crossed Takgutha's features.

Wild with fury, Patrice whirled around. The bastard had set her up. He had undoubtedly blocked the order to move the Cresus in. He wanted an attack from sea to get this far and to use it as an excuse to smash most of her wall crystals.

"You wanted this battle to prove yourself to your lord!" Patrice snarled.

"I am a warrior," Takgutha said matter-of-factly.

"Then prove it!" Patrice raised her hand and slammed a bolt into Takgutha before he could respond, knocking him off his feet. Snarling, his companions started to snap up their shields.

"Don't move!" Takgutha roared, coming to his knees. A torrent of blood poured from his right arm.

Patrice struggled for control. "We'll have a reckoning on this." She swept out of the room, Takgutha following her with a hateful gaze.

Down into the heart of her palace she stormed, cursing inwardly at the wreckage—and cursing herself. The Heart had been tantalizingly within her reach until the offworlders had struck her. Now she channeled her energy to the ugly scorches on her side and the back of her head. The pain eased, though true healing would have to come later.

She was tempted to gather her forces and strike Leti again to finish it off. Too much time had been wasted, though, and again she upbraided herself. So what if her palace, her crystals, even her city was destroyed? She could have had the Heart. Yet Gorgon was now so close to coming through. She had to be present. Was Takgutha a portent? she wondered darkly. Would Gorgon betray her?

Her mind swirled with the contradictions arising to what she had felt to be such a seamless plan for success. And she felt an inward chill now—for after all, the one thing she could never truly read was what lingered in Gorgon's heart.

She had to be present at the moment he came through, to judge him. Yet he had promised so much, his voice whispering to her across the centuries, promising all when this moment finally arrived.

Takgutha would pay for this; his blood would cement the bond. She wanted to see Gorgon flay the living flesh from his vassal's body, and then she would know. Patrice turned to one of her companions.

"Tell that bastard Takgutha I want him in the portal chamber."

The sorcerer looked at her coldly, and bowing, turned away.

Two sorcerers stepped from a side alcove and bowed low. "The traitor you wanted," and they pointed to where Imada stood.

Patrice stopped and gazed at the boy, who looked at her with innocent eyes.

Her features softened. "Why did you come to me?" she whispered, probing inward, searching his mind.

"My Vena served you," he replied. "I did not know it, but you had bonded me to you as well. When I saw you, I could not harm you."

The boy fell to his knees and abased himself before her.

She did not know whether she felt disgust or something else at the sight of him, so totally vulnerable, totally willing to do anything she might wish. She hesitated. After all, he might be an amusing plaything. Reaching down, she gently grasped his hair, raising his head and gazing into his eyes before letting him go.

"Bring him along," she said softly, and proceeded on. She'd have to think about him when there was time. If she decided not to accept him, at least Gorgon would be amused to have an offworlder to examine.

The doors to the portal room were wide open, the corridor lit with a lurid blood-red glow. Demons lined the corridor and at her approach bowed low. Without slowing she entered the chamber.

For an instant her senses recoiled at the raw power in the room. Two hundred demons stood in a vast circle, arms extended. The crystals to either side of the pentagram glowed with such blinding light that Patrice averted her gaze.

Gorgon hovered in the middle of the pentagram, his form rippling with power, his body taut, as if straining against an unseen barrier that was gradually falling away.

At the sight of Patrice, a smile crossed his features.

"Soon, very soon," Gorgon laughed, his chilling voice booming and echoing.

Patrice gazed at him, probing, unsure.

"I have heard one of my warriors displeases you?" Gorgon whispered, his voice now soft, melodious.

Patrice nodded, struggling to remain detached, to judge his inner thoughts.

"I will reward him properly for you when I emerge," and his voice was like the promising sigh of a lover.

"Soon you shall have Haven at your feet, the Heart Crystal in your hand, and I shall defeat Jartan, who has ignored you far too long."

Patrice felt an inner voice calling to her, as if warning her to step back from the edge of the abyss. She looked into Gorgon's eyes and his smiling gaze washed over her.

"It is time now that I come through and join you, my lover," Gorgon called, and the room surged with light.

Chapter 17

"There's nothing else to be done," Leti said grimly, looking around at the assembled group.

Ikawa stood by Leti's side, his gaze on the ground. He knew she was right, but the finality of it was still so sudden. Only an hour ago, when he had seen the explosions ripple across Patrice's palace, he had thought for sure that the mission had been a success. Wild cheering had broken out. And then the garbled battle reports had come in—the obvious cries of an army defeated and in retreat.

At that moment he had looked to Leti and had known what she had quietly formed in her heart and had been carrying since the meeting in Asmara, the true reason why she had insisted on bringing the Heart Crystal. She was going to destroy the Heart, Patrice's city, and herself.

"Do you see any hope of pulling back toward Asmara?" Pina ventured.

"Hopeless," Valdez growled. "Gorgon and his host will explode out of there soon—damn soon. Even I can sense the power surging out of that hellhole. We'll be overrun before we even get started. Leti is right. It's the only chance we have to stop him."

The group was silent again.

"I agree with Leti." Boreas, his features grey and drawn, limped into the circle of sorcerers surrounding the Heart. Ikawa could see that every step for the demigod must be an agony.

"I sensed this was Leti's final plan, but I did not speak since I believed we could break through from the sea. It worked at Baltaman during the Great War; I believed it would work again here."

"And Patrice fought at Baltaman, and helped lead the attack

by sea," Valdez said quietly, the slightest edge of reproach in his voice.

Boreas looked at the sorcerer and nodded.

"There is no time now for recriminations," Leti said quietly.

"When I go forward, I'll not look back. I am not ordering anyone to do this, though I'll need all of you if there is to be any hope of getting close enough. If you should decide to turn away, I will not see it, and there will be no shame. We've got to get close, right up to the wall at the very least. If there's time, I'll give the word to run, but if not, if it seems they're about to overwhelm us, I'll do what has to be done without warning."

"What will happen when she hits the Heart with that red crystal?" Shigeru whispered to Ikawa.

"Boom," Walker said evenly, coming up to stand next to the wrestler. "You saw what a wall crystal can do when it goes. When that big baby lets go, it'll flatten everything for miles. It'll blow that city apart, and take the portal with it."

"Those poor people in that city," Goldberg sighed. "They had nothing to do with this."

Leti nodded at Goldberg.

"I'm truly sorry about that, it is not in our creed to harm innocent people in war. But if we do not do this, millions will die, for Haven will become a battleground when Jartan returns. And if he should not stop Gorgon, this world will become a nightmare."

"What about those too injured to move?" one of the healers asked, motioning to more than thirty sorcerers who lay under the shade of a nearby tree. Mark was among them, as was Smithie and Kochanski, who had suffered a severe concussion and collapsed after the group had made it back to land.

"If we succeed and smash the portal, then look after them," Leti whispered. "If not," and she paused, "then I think you know what you'll have to do for them."

The healer seemed to struggle with her inner feelings, and then wordlessly she stepped back to the wounded.

"Are there any comments? Though I ask you make them brief—even now the portal is bending outward, almost ready to burst. We must move quickly."

No one spoke.

"Then I give you five minutes to prepare as you see fit."

The group broke up, most of the sorcerers going off to be by themselves.

The offworlders came to circle around Ikawa.

"Let's go see Mark," he said quietly.

"He just came to," one of the healers said quietly, rising from Mark's side.

Ikawa knelt beside his friends. The healer had closed the wound, but was unable to expend more energy to knit the bone since so many required her attention. The arm was padded and bound tightly in a splint.

"I heard what she said," Mark whispered.

"So you know."

Mark nodded.

"You gave me a scare," Ikawa said, trying to smile. "We were flying out to give you cover and some of your folks thought we were the enemy."

"That's the last I remember."

"Walker saw you fall. You took a little water before we got you out."

Mark smiled feebly. "Kind of hard to believe we lost."

"But we haven't," Ikawa replied.

"Sure as hell seems like it," Kraut said, his voice sad and distant. "We're all gonna die in about another ten minutes."

Ikawa looked up at Kraut and the others.

"Yet it's worth it in the end. We all should have died back in China, when we were enemies. Instead we came here, and found our power, our loves, our adventures—and far more, we learned that we are brothers. Shigeru and Walker, who once hated each other, would now lay down their lives for the other."

Shigeru and Walker looked at each other nervously.

"Ah hell, Captain, the big lug needs someone to look out for him, that's all."

The men laughed.

"So we have found that. We are all fated to die some day. Yet as a samurai, as a warrior of Allic, I find this a fine moment to choose that death. For we will die saving a world that is precious to us."

He paused, and saw Leti coming to the edge of the group.

"And we die together as friends."

"It's time, my love." Her thought whispered through his mind.

"I cannot tell you how much I love you," Ikawa thought in reply. "You are my joy beyond words, beyond thoughts."

"On the other side of the sea we will meet again. I will wait for you there."

The two looked at each other in silence.

"It's time," she whispered, this time out loud.

The warriors looked shyly at each other, exchanging hand-clasps.

Ikawa looked down at Mark again. "Good-bye, my brother. If we should succeed, just remember . . . " He found he could no longer say the words.

"But I'm going with you." Mark forced a smile.

"Captain, that's kind of crazy," Walker announced. "You're busted to hell."

"I'm going with you," Mark insisted. Weakly, he tried to struggle to his feet, then looked imploringly at Ikawa, who gazed at him with a sad smile of understanding.

"Shigeru, give him a hand."

The wrestler strode forward and gently lifted Mark onto his feet. Mark looked back at Kochanski and Smithie, who were still unconscious.

"Let's get going." Mark's voice was cold and even.

The group turned away and followed Leti back to where a team of sorcerers had formed around the Heart.

From out of the crowd, Giorgini pushed his way through and came to stand before Mark.

"Mind if I fight alongside you?"

Mark looked over at Boreas, who nodded.

"Of course," Mark said, and a broad grin crept across Giorgini's features.

"At least Imada will be saved his life of humiliation," Shigeru said darkly. The wrestler had been stunned to hear of his friend's betrayal and openly wept at the news. His mood was now grim.

"Yeah, I can't believe it," Walker sighed. A quizzical look crossed his face, and he reached into his tunic and pulled out a slip of paper.

"Funny—just before we lifted to attack I saw him scribbling something, and then he gave this to me. Looks like Japanese or something."

Walker held out the paper. Saito took it and unfolded it.

"She destroyed my life, though I am still living," Saito read. "Now I shall finish it all for both of us. Good-bye, my friends."

"What is he up to?" Kraut asked, looking at Ikawa.

"He was a boy with honor," Ikawa said evenly. "Perhaps he thought he could still do something. I think our friend was not a traitor, but just someone who could no longer see the world clearly," and then he could say no more.

"Say, anybody got a cigarette?" Walker ventured, breaking the silence.

"Yeah, I remember that," Kraut laughed. "Here we're getting our butts blasted off during the siege of Landra and you're pulling out cigarettes. Shit, I could go for one."

The group chuckled, trying to control their nervousness.

Leti smiled at the offworlders.

"I'll be with the Heart," she said evenly. "Boreas, can you fly?"

The demigod nodded, but all could see that his strength was gone. The blow he had suffered would have killed any normal human, or even a sorcerer.

"We'll stay low," Leti told her command. "They must have a picket screen out ahead. We punch through, and move as fast as we can. I want to try and get this straight over the palace, but if that is impossible, at least to the base of the city wall. As I said before, if there's time I'll give a minute's warning. Then you are free to escape, but if I fear we are being overwhelmed I will strike this," and reaching into a pouch by her waist she pulled out a red crystal, "against the Heart without warning.

"Do you all understand?"

No one replied.

"Then let's move!"

The sorcerers surrounding the Heart lifted into the air, holding on to the rope netting which encased their burden. Ikawa swung in by Leti's side as she rose a scant dozen feet into the air and then started forward.

Leti looked over at him.

"Do you remember our first night together?" her thoughts whispered through his mind.

He smiled.

"Then let us think of those things once again."

The group pressed in toward the city.

From a wooded grove half a mile forward, six sorcerers rose and started back toward the city.

"They're on to us," Ikawa shouted. "Keep our formation close!"

As they streaked low over a village, a quick flurry of bolts shot up from sorcerers on the ground. Ignoring the strikes, the attack force pushed in.

"Those lousy bastards," Walker shouted.

Looking over his shoulder, Ikawa saw that a sizeable fraction of the group had turned away to flee in the opposite direction.

"Ignore them!" Ikawa shouted. "Their lives will be far worse than whatever we shall face."

Skimming low against light opposition, Ikawa dodged down between a row of trees, sending a flock of golden birds in every direction with his passage. It was a glorious moment, that now filled his entire world. He had felt this before, this certainty that he was about to die, and with the coming of that moment, never had he felt so alive, so completely bonded to his world and the magnificent splendor of it.

The picket line of sorcerers kept falling back, trading long-range shots with the advancing group. The city was now less than two miles ahead. Just another couple of minutes was all that they would need. Ikawa felt his heart soaring. Perhaps they could break all the way through, and his comrades could still escape while he and Leti finished what had to be done.

"Here they come!" Shigeru snarled.

Looking forward, Ikawa was stunned. A cloud of demons and sorcerers rose above the wall to greet them.

Staggered by the intensity of the power now revealed, Patrice felt as if she had torn open the entire world to his presence. Surging and coiling, Gorgon pushed against the last flimsy barrier.

It exploded into a wall of fire.

The temple floor swayed beneath her feet, the arched buttresses overhead cracking.

Gorgon stepped through into the world of Haven.

He was the essence of fire, the creator of torment, his flaming limbs dripping with oily smoke, his fangs oozing a green, sulphurous glow, his eyes like flaming diamonds.

He leaned back and laughed, the booming of his voice counterpointed by the shrieking calls of his minions, who groveled before him in a terrible ecstasy of lust.

And in that instant she knew.

He lowered his head and looked at her with sardonic bemusement. "Does my form still please you?" he whispered.

She said nothing, standing proud, alone, her mind screaming to her that all the dreams, all the desires had, after all, been only an illusion.

"Come to me," he snarled. "I wish to take you here, now. My servants can watch, for I have promised them this sport."

His mouth curled in a dark leer, flames running down its sides. A fiery hand reached out to grab her.

"We were to rule together as equals," Patrice snapped, backing away. "There's still a battle to be fought outside these walls."

Gorgon laughed, and looked over at his servants.

"Go out and finish them," he snarled. "I'll be along shortly."

The demons poured out of the room, shouting triumphantly, eager for battle.

Gorgon looked back at Patrice. "No one is my equal," he boomed. "Be my servant and submit to all my wishes now—or die. And if you die, I will enslave your soul in torment."

She raised her shield and leveled a bolt of flame into his face.

It seemed to stun him; he drew back. She fired again and the terror started to rise in her as she continued to pour out her strength, screaming in rage at him.

Ever so slowly, he raised his hand and pointed it at her.

A single shot took her off her feet, slamming her against the wall, her gown scorched, her shield gone.

"You are mine—Haven is mine—it is *all mine*," Gorgon laughed, rising over her.

*   *   *

"For God's sake, keep moving!" Walker roared, his shield glowing white hot. "We've got to keep moving!"

Crouching low on the ground, Ikawa slammed a burst into a demon hovering above the group. The shot seemed to have little effect as the demon, roaring his defiance, threw a bolt straight at Ikawa.

Walker turned with a wild scream and lifted back into the air. As he reached out, his hand seemed to touch the demon. There was an explosive flash and the creature plummeted into the circle of sorcerers surrounding the Heart.

"Up, get up!" Leti screamed.

The beleaguered group rose and started forward. The sky above them was dark with the enemy. But the wall was still a half mile off, and to Ikawa it seemed a nightmarish eternity away.

Shigeru looked around wildly, unable to fight with Mark in his arms, ignoring Mark's commands to put him down.

A stunning blow hit Ikawa from behind, and he fell to earth. He could feel the icy-hot talons tearing into his flesh.

"Captain!"

Kicking and clawing, Ikawa rolled away and got to his knees, then slammed a bolt into the demon's face. The creature's head disappeared. Frantically, Ikawa looked around. The group had pushed another hundred yards ahead. Saito was above him, shouting, "Come on, Captain!"

Ikawa flew back into the air. Cutting and slashing with their bolts, the two pushed forward. Smoldering bodies littered the ground in a bloody trail, and wounded sorcerers crawled away from the inferno of combat. Horrified, Ikawa saw one of Storm's retainers struggling on the ground, his legs gone. A demon alighted beside him and with a slash of razor-sharp talons decapitated the man. Holding the head aloft, the demon soared into the air, roaring with delight. In their killing frenzy, the demons had lost all control and were firing without care, striking enemies and allies alike.

The warriors cut their way back into the decimated group.

"Again!" Leti screamed.

They surged upward and forward, but a virtual wall of demons opposed them. The formation started to disintegrate into a confused melee of individual combats. Nearly half the sorcerers carrying the Heart were down, unable to effectively defend themselves. A knot of demons cut straight through the party, and suddenly the Heart tumbled out of the net and crashed to the ground.

Leti alighted beside it and looked around wildly.

"Almost there," she screamed. "Just a bit further!"

Ikawa landed beside her, and Boreas fought his way through to join them. Wildly, Ikawa looked around. Shigeru, still carrying Mark, and his escort—Saito and Walker—landed to join them. From over the wall Ikawa saw the sky darken further as several hundred more demons seemed to explode outward.

"More coming!" he cried.

"It's as far as we're getting!" Boreas shouted.

But the wall was still several hundred yards away, and the palace a quarter mile beyond it.

"I only hope we're close enough!" Leti reached into the pouch and held the red crystal high.

Despairing, Ikawa knew that it was not close enough. All they could hope for was to take as many with them as possible, and perhaps weaken Gorgon for Jartan, if he should ever return.

"Everyone clear out of here!" she screamed.

A demon exploded into the middle of the group, slamming Leti with a bolt that sent her staggering, so that she dropped the red crystal.

With a wild scream, Ikawa dove, scrambling for the gem. The demon set up a wild undulating roar and his comrades, hearing his warning, swarmed in.

Ikawa snatched the red crystal from the ground. Before him a demon rose up. The demon staggered and fell, the back of his head gone. Through the confusion Ikawa saw Mark, his broken arm up and his battle crystal glowing hot, Shigeru on the ground by his side.

"For God's sake, do it!" Mark screamed.

For an instant Ikawa saw Leti looking up at him, her eyes wide with pain and grief. Then he staggered forward to the Heart.

They had ignored him. Imada watched the struggle between his deceiver and the one who had deceived her in turn, and though he felt that it should fill his heart with joy, he was left instead with an infinite sadness. He had wanted to believe better of Haven, that one could love with innocence and truthfulness and that somehow it would be returned.

If that was possible, he would never know it.

A detached smile crossed his lips as he reached into his tunic and pulled the object out. With his thumb he pushed back a section of the clay to reveal the sharp glimmer of red underneath.

He walked forward into the circle of flame. With his shield down the fire leaped to his body, his hair curling, his flesh screaming in protest as it started to smoke and peel away. It was curious, but he felt no pain.

He came up to the large portal crystal, which was still glowing brightly, and felt as if he was looking straight into the heart of the sun.

"Patrice! Gorgon!"

Locked in their loathsome struggle, the two paused and looked back at him, even as the fire swirled about his body.

He held the great red crystal up high.

"No!" Gorgon screamed.

Even as his eyes burned away, he could see her face, the one who had destroyed his life. It was strange, he realized; there was no rage, no horror. In Patrice's tormented eyes he saw only relief.

Imada brought Jartan's great red crystal down, striking it hard against the crystal of Horat.

There was no pain, just a final flash of thought, the sense that the real Vena, the one that must have truly existed and been killed, was waiting for him after all. And then there was silence, and peace.

An explosion filled the sky, first flashing white-hot, changing in an instant to a boiling black cloud that raced straight up to the heavens. The sun seemed to be blotted from the sky. Stunned, Ikawa looked up. The palace had disappeared, and for a wild moment he thought he had actually hit the Heart and he was seeing the results from beyond the realm of the living. And then the shock wave hit him, slamming him backward to the ground.

It felt as if the earth was being torn asunder. The piercing shrieks of the demons counterpointed the explosion. A swirling maelstrom seemed to fill the entire world.

"He's come through!" Saito cried. "The Heart—destroy the Heart."

Ikawa tried to regain his feet.

"Wait," Leti cried, and her voice was filled with hope. "Look, look what's happening!"

The demons that had swarmed over the group twisted and writhed in agony. As if suddenly weightless, they were pulled back into the conflagration. The sky was filled with their forms, their agonized cries audible even above the roaring inferno.

The demons burst into flames as they were pulled inexorably into the storm. The sky was awash with their fire as they tumbled end over end into the heart of the storm, trailing plumes of oily smoke.

"The portal's gone!" Boreas cried. "The bastards are finished!"

Ikawa let the red crystal fall, and walked over to stand beside Leti.

Stunned, he watched as the maelstrom swirled and seemed to fall in upon itself. Suddenly there was only silence, though black smoke seemed to fill the very heavens.

"We've won," Leti sighed. "Gorgon has been destroyed, and the portal is closed."

"How in the name of all the gods?" Boreas whispered.

"It was Imada," Walker whispered.

A thin smile crossed Ikawa's features. He looked over at Shigeru and Saito, their sad smiles matching his.

"A good death," Shigeru sighed. "Good-bye, my little friend."

"Perhaps the real Vena waits for him on the other side," Leti said softly, slipping her hand around Ikawa's waist.

Her gaze held his for a moment, and for the first time since their swim in the lake long ago, Ikawa felt as if his old lover was truly back again.

"We better get into the city," Leti finally announced.

"I think the fight's over," she continued, raising her voice, "but a lot of people in there are going to need help." Patrice's surviving sorcerers, who had been staring at the ruined city in stunned disbelief, looked over at Leti. A sorcerer stepped forward and tore the offensive crystals from her right wrist, dropping them by Leti's feet.

"She betrayed us, too. We had no idea, even to the end, what this was truly about."

"She betrayed all of us," Leti told her.

"My family's back there," the sorcerer said, fighting to control her emotions.

"I'll take your parole later," Leti said soothingly, touching the woman on the shoulder. "Go save them. Pass the word that the fighting is over. We'll come in shortly to help with the injured."

The sorcerer bowed low, lifted into the air, and streaked toward the city. The other sorcerers came up before Leti, so that within a moment there was a pile of offensive crystals at her feet.

"Boreas, will you stay with the Heart? I'll take anyone who's still fit and go into the city."

"Gladly. I've had enough for one day," Boreas said, his voice full of exhaustion and infinite sadness.

"Say, what in hell is that?" Kraut called, pointing toward a lone figure flying naked above the city.

"It's him. I'll be damned, it's him!" Shigeru cried, his voice near breaking with delight.

For a demigod whom Ikawa thought was cold and devoid of all emotions, Boreas suddenly appeared as if he had returned to life. For the first time since meeting Boreas, Ikawa saw a grin cross his features.

"Tulana!"

The prince swung in and alighted. He was covered from head to foot with blood and a slimy coating of gore, his great mane of hair and flowing beard were streaked white, and matted to his body.

Boreas rushed forward and the two giants roared with delight, slapping each other on the back, tears streaming down their faces.

"By the hairy asses of all the gods," Tulana bellowed, pointing back to the inferno raging in the city, "just what the hell did you bastards do?"

"Never mind that," Shigeru cried, coming up to give Tulana a slap that sent the prince staggering. "We saw you get swallowed. How did you ever come back?"

"I gave that Cresus the worst bellyache of its life, I did." Throwing his head back, he howled with laughter.

Ikawa grinned, watching the exuberant exchange. For a second, Tulana caught his gaze, and in that moment Ikawa could sense that beneath the bravado, the terror of what he had been through had left the prince shaken. Then, grinning, Tulana looked away.

"Long I fell into the darkness. In the buffeting I lost my defensive crystals," he said, "and then I knew I was in the pit of his stomach. And by my hairy jewels, the stench was worse than the vomit of my grandfather here. I felt the burning, and I thought I was cooked.

"And then I thought, not me, not Tulana coming out as nothing but bones from that big beast's fat ass. So I pointed and started to cut with my crystal. And by Jartan's teeth, you should have felt that thing kick and squirm. Never did he have a meal like me!

"So I'd cut with the crystal, and then slash with my dagger, and then cut and slash, cut and slash. I thought I'd drown in his blood in that darkness. And all the time his stomach juices are burning my clothes off, so that I finally tore off the shreds."

"And then what happened?" Shigeru asked, drawing back slightly from the stench which hung around his friend.

"Well, I'm here, aren't I?" Tulana yelled. "And somewhere out there is a Cresus with a hole in his side, off to tell old Naga he better stand clear of me from now on. Hell, I'm not going to breach that old bastard next time I see him, I'm going to let him swallow me whole!"

Boreas roared with delight again and hugged his grandson in a bearlike embrace.

Mark got slowly to his feet and went to Ikawa to mutter, "He's just amazing."

Ikawa, smiling, looked at Mark. And in the clarity of that moment, he knew that if a gateway to Earth could ever be opened, the men would cross back through as friends, and remain that way, no matter what madness their old world was still creating.

"So we won!" Tulana shouted happily. "I could sure use a drink!"

"I think we all could," Ikawa laughed. Tulana's words had certainly summed it all up. They were alive, and their precious world of Haven would survive.

With his left hand, Mark fumbled in his tunic and pulled out a silver flask.

"Allic's," he said. "He left it behind the night he left. I've been keeping it for him."

Clumsily Mark uncorked it, and offered the first drink to Ikawa. Then they passed it on to their circle of comrades, who stood laughing with joy and exhausted relief.

"We have survived again," Ikawa whispered. Looking over at Leti, he smiled.

Chapter 18

"So there was Tulana, as naked as the day he was born, and he actually sneaked up on Leti and hugged her. I thought she was going to lose her last meal." Mark laughed, wiping the tears from his eyes.

"And you should have seen Ikawa's face," Kraut interjected. "It looked like he was going to kill him."

Ikawa forced a smile and shook his head as he looked over at the drawn features of his old friend and lord.

Allic smiled to show that he was interested in the conversation, but his exhaustion was evident.

Jartan and the attack contingent had returned that morning. The reunion had been a painful one as both sides, now fully aware of what had happened, eagerly sought the faces of loved ones, and in more than one case had retreated to a private room to hide their grief at the terrible price that had been paid.

Minar had lost a beloved son. Chosen had left as silently and mysteriously as he had arrived, his only living granddaughter gone. Several of Jartan's grandchildren were dead as well, and many of the party had suffered some injury, either physically or worse yet, to their inner senses from the horrors they had fought.

Whether or not Gorgon had survived the destruction of the portal was not known. Jartan's attack had reached to the final gate into the nightmare world which was Gorgon's home, and had pressed no further—for that was a place no one of Haven could endure. They had started back, leaving a wake of destruction behind them, laying down barriers and traps, sealing Gorgon off.

The rescue of Allic had been a near thing as well. The relief force, led by Storm, had arrived to find Allic and eight survivors cornered in a cave and fighting off repeated attacks. It would take time, Ikawa realized, for Allic to heal—not just physically, but also from the nightmare of what he had endured.

"The druid and the portal?" Allic asked. "What happened?"

The group looked over at Kochanski, who stood in the corner with Sara beside him holding a possessive arm around his waist.

"It won't work. I'm trying to create a replica from a hazy memory of seeing Stonehenge years back while in England, but the druid's version is a model of how it appeared two thousand years ago. I guess I just never realized how precise the reproduction would have to be here on Haven. Besides, the druid told me he tried countless times to go back, always without success."

"So there's no going back, then?" Storm asked.

Kochanski shook his head, and a smile that almost looked like relief crossed his features.

"I guess not."

"That's too bad," Storm replied, and Mark chuckled at the obvious lie.

Ikawa looked around the group. He could sense the tension leaving most of them, the burden of the decision having been lifted. Only two of his men, and Smithie, looked crestfallen, though he could only hope that with time they would come to accept their new world.

He bid a silent farewell to his parents and the world he had left. He would always regret that they could never know that he was safe, that his world had not ended in an unnamed skirmish in China, but in fact had barely begun.

"I think it's time you got some sleep, Allic," Storm said affectionately, kissing her brother on the forehead.

He looked at the circle of friends around him and nodded.

"You've got the best of worlds right here," he whispered. "Believe me, I know."

Ikawa nodded and came up to take Leti's hand.

"Of course, Mark and Ikawa need their sleep now as well," Allic said, a mischievous grin lighting his face.

"You've got to be kidding," Storm laughed. Taking Mark's hand, she left the room, the rest of the group following.

"Come on, Kochanski, let's go for a swim. There's a beautiful spot—a secret place only I know about," Sara said as they stepped into the hallway.

"Are you crazy? The last thing I want to see is water," Kochanski replied, looking nervously at his friends, who filed past him. "I was thinking of going with the guys for a drink."

"Well, I'll come along then," she announced.

Going down the hallway, they passed through Jartan's audience chamber, again aswarm with activity as the god set about bringing order back to his realm.

Kochanski looked over at the column of light as he passed through.

"Sorry about the portal, Kochanski," the god whispered in his mind.

"Actually, I'm glad it turned out the way it did," Kochanski thought in reply. "We all thank you, though, for making the offer to us."

"You deserved it. But I must say I'm glad you'll be staying. Once things settle down we'll have a talk."

"With pleasure, my lord."

"Take care of that granddaughter of mine. Give her a couple of more years and you might find her a wonderful lady to be with. And for all our sakes, don't get her angry, or we'll never hear the end of it."

As Jartan's thoughts pulled away, Kochanski felt as if he heard booming laughter.

"Did he say something?"

"Nothing, kid."

"I'm not a kid," Sara replied, pressing close to him. "I'm damn near eighteen."

"In my book you are, at least for the next year or so. After that, we'll talk."

"You promise?" She looked up at him, beaming.

"Sure." He couldn't help feeling a growing warmth for her, even though she did drive him crazy.

Leaving the chamber, they turned down a hallway that led past the workshops. A door swung open, and Kochanski felt Sara's grip tighten.

"Hi, Kochanski." Deidre, her eyes warm and seductive, looked straight into his. "Going any place special?"

"Well, I was going to join my friends for a drink to celebrate," Kochanski replied, unable to drop his gaze.

"We were planning to go there *alone*," Sara interrupted, her voice dripping with venom.

"Oh, I'd love to join you, though," Deidre replied.

She looked back through the doorway.

"Grandfather, I'll be back later," she called, and closed the door behind her.

She came up on Kochanski's other side even as Sara pulled him along.

"It's Sara, isn't it?" Deidre said sweetly. "Tell me, are you still enjoying school?"

Kochanski gulped, wondering if, after all that had happened, he'd live to see the end of the day.

The druid looked up and saw the door closing.

Damn girl. She'd kept him out of a good fight, hovering over him and not giving him a moment of peace. In addition, the Sorcerers Guild was already putting heavy pressure on him to tell them the secret of how he'd extended his lifespan. After all, he *was* over two thousand years old, and a sorcerer's life expectancy was only a thousand years, or at most, twelve hundred.

Maybe he would share the secret formulas—maybe not. He did know that none of their bribes had piqued his interest yet. Oh, well, he had lots of time.

Still, he *had* been under a lot of pressure lately. Maybe he could slip away for a while. There were a number of interesting young ladies about, and it would do his spirits good to meet some of them.

He looked back at the model on the table.

All wrong, all of it wrong. And what was that fool doing by knocking down the lintels and leaving them scattered about? What conjuring could he ever hope to do with it?

The druid lowered his staff to knock the model apart, and the piece of amber which had come with him from the old world—now shaped as his most sacred crystal—started to glow.

Startled, he hesitated.

There was a tiny snap of light in the middle of the model and he drew closer, holding his staff above it and gazing in.

People! There were people on the other side! And another Stonehenge!

He could never allow this to happen. These men who had come to him might be all right, but Caesar—dead or not—had sworn to hunt him forever. He still considered himself fortunate that Kochanski had believed him when he'd said he'd never been able to find Earth. The fool!

"I'm still alive, you bastard! You'll never get me!" the druid roared.

The images on the other side shifted, faces looking about in fear. He laughed darkly, screaming a cursing incantation, and brought down the staff to smash the model into a thousand broken splinters.

No, they'll never get me, the druid laughed to himself, panting from the excitement.

He went to the door and started to open it, then looked back at the fragments. With a wave of his hand they reassembled, but the pattern was different, though already he wasn't sure how.

Ah, well, other things to worry about, such as the ladies. He quickly combed his hand through his long flowing beard, fluffing it out.

He waved the door open, stepped into the hallway, and looked back once more at the model.

Already he wasn't quite sure what had happened.

Must have been that wonderful brandy I snuck earlier.

Now, brandy and ladies *together*, he thought gaily. Humming a tune from the old fertility rites, he closed the door behind him.

Epilogue

Sarnak cleared his throat, and the argument that had been raging among his advisors instantly ceased.

"Let us summarize what we have learned. Gorgon was presumably killed by the blast. Correct?"

"There is a ten percent probability that he managed to leap back through the portal as it blew. Therefore, there is a very slim possibility he still lives. However, his armies are decimated, and Jartan and his allied gods left Gorgon's realm in a shambles. So, as a player, he is off the board."

"And Patrice?"

"More difficult to determine, sire. If she had an escape hole with powered pentagrams as we have set up here, she could easily have fled relatively intact. But she is an outlaw without a power base, since Jartan has already assimilated her realm. Her sole strength, assuming she lives, would be that she is in possession of the Crystals of Fire."

"Which would give her tremendous individual power, but nothing else," interjected another advisor.

"Hmm," Sarnak mused. "Perhaps we can use this. Ralnath, set up a team to surreptitiously investigate all the outer worlds she might have ported to in an emergency. I'll expect my first report in a ten-day.

"Anything else for now?" he continued, glancing down the conference table. "All right, you are dismissed until tomorrow."

As the advisors stood and mingled, Ralnath followed his master into his inner office.

"Sire, I have news that I knew you would not want mentioned at the staff meeting. The information reached me as the meeting was about to begin." He paused nervously, trying to gauge Sarnak's mood. "It is an analysis of the potential danger to you that our sensitives and detection team have been picking up."

Sarnak's face froze slightly, and though his voice remained calm, his eyes went flat and lifeless. Ralnath had seen this reaction before, and trembled inwardly.

"Well?"

"Not good, sire. We've determined that Boreas has made a breakthrough in farseeking." He paused for a reaction or comment, then continued hurriedly.

"Apparently the offworlder Giorgini came up with a new method of directional finding. He has set up sites across the world with sensitives and farseekers. They cannot locate you by themselves, but over a period of time they will be able to pick up your aura in a general area and be able to triangulate these findings to center your location."

Sarnak turned away, to seemingly study the map on the wall. "I presume destroying those stations would be useless."

"Correct, sire. It would merely alert them as to their effectiveness."

There was a period of silence and Ralnath wisely kept his mouth shut, though he watched Sarnak's aura begin to brighten as the demigod fought for control.

"How much time?"

"They calculate three to six months, sire."

Again there was a moment of silence; then Sarnak said briskly and casually, "I wish to see the report in its entirety before we come to any hasty conclusions. If it is correct, then we have to set up alternate plans of action. That is all for now, Ralnath. You may leave me."

Ralnath was grateful to be dismissed. His master was never so deadly as when he reacted in so detached and perfunctory a manner.

When he was alone, Sarnak's self-discipline began to deteriorate rapidly.

Boreas will find me, he thought desperately. *That creature of ice and hate won't just kill me*—he shivered—*I'll be tortured for eons. If he can find me here, shielded as thoroughly as I am, then he will be able to track me down wherever I run, be it this world or another.*

In desperation he analyzed his options. There was only one solution he could think of.

Now I am truly accursed, for I will have to awaken the Old Gods. Only they will have the power to save me from Boreas.

WILLIAM R. FORSTCHEN was raised in New Jersey but has spent most of his life in Maine, having worked for more than a decade as a history teacher, educational consultant on creative writing, and a living history reenactor of the Civil War period. Bill is now a graduate student in military history at Purdue University in Indiana. His interests include working for the peaceful exploration of space, ice-boating, scuba diving, flying, and pinball machines. He is the author of the Ice Prophet trilogy, the Gamester Wars series, and the Lost Regiment series.

GREG MORRISON has made his home in Pennsylvania since 1961, and lives with his wife, Patti, and daughter Kristin in the Harrisburg area. He attended Penn State, then joined the army as a deep-space telemetry analyst, serving in Ethiopia and Turkey. Currently he is owner of Technical Search, an executive recruiting firm specializing in the fields of data processing, engineering, and finance. In collaboration with William R. Forstchen, he has written *The Crystal Warriors* and *The Crystal Sorcerers*, which you are holding.

Magic...Mystery...Revelations
Welcome to
THE FANTASTICAL
WORLD OF AMBER!

ROGER ZELAZNY'S
VISUAL GUIDE to
CASTLE
AMBER

by Roger Zelazny and Neil Randall

75566-1/$8.95 US/$10.95 Can

AN AVON TRADE PAPERBACK

Tour Castle Amber—
through vivid illustrations, detailed floor plans,
cutaway drawings, and page after page
of never-before-revealed information!

ARTHUR C. CLARKE'S VENUS PRIME

by Paul Preuss

VOLUME 1: BREAKING STRAIN 75344-8/$3.95 US/$4.95 CAN
Her code name is Sparta. Her beauty veils a mysterious past and abilities of superhuman dimension, the product of advanced biotechnology.

VOLUME 2: MAELSTROM 75345-6/$3.95 US/$4.95 CAN
When a team of scientists is trapped in the gaseous inferno of Venus, Sparta must risk her life to save them.

VOLUME 3: HIDE AND SEEK 75346-4/$3.95 US/$4.95 CAN
When the theft of an alien artifact, evidence of extraterrestrial life, leads to two murders, Sparta must risk her life and identity to solve the case.

VOLUME 4: THE MEDUSA ENCOUNTER
75348-0/$3.95 US/$4.95 CAN
Sparta's recovery from her last mission is interrupted as she sets out on an interplanetary investigation of her host, the Space Board.

VOLUME 5: THE DIAMOND MOON
75349-9/$3.95 US/$4.95 CAN
Sparta's mission is to monitor the exploration of Jupiter's moon, Amalthea, by the renowned Professor J.Q.R. Forester.

Each volume features a special technical infopak, including blueprints of the structures of *Venus Prime*